The Shark Mutiny

PATRICK ROBINSON is the author of four previous international bestselling novels: *Nimitz Class*, *Kilo Class*, *HMS Unseen* and *USS Seawolf*. He is also the author of several non-fiction bestsellers including *True Blue* (with Dan Topolski) and *Born to Win*. He is the co-author with Admiral Sir Sandy Woodwood of *One Hundred Days*. He can be reached through his web-site at *www.patrickrobinson.com*.

Praise for Patrick Robinson

Nimitz Class
'A stunner that irresistibly hurtles the readers to the exciting climax'   Clive Cussler

'An absolutely marvellous thriller, one of the best things of its kind I have read in years'   Jack Higgins

Kilo Class
'*Kilo Class* confirms the author's reputation as Britain's answer to Tom Clancy'   Sarah Broadhurst, *Bookseller*

'Gripping . . . a sure hit'   *Publishers Weekly*

HMS Unseen
'Brilliant . . . a dazzling, page-turning yarn . . . impossible to put down'
Carlo D'Este, author of *Patton: A Genius for War*

Also by Patrick Robinson

Classic Lines
Decades of Champions
The Golden Post
Born to Win
True Blue
One Hundred Days
Horsetrader

Nimitz Class
Kilo Class
HMS Unseen
USS Seawolf

THE SHARK
MUTINY

Patrick Robinson

ARROW

Published by Arrow Books in 2002

1 3 5 7 9 10 8 6 4 2

Copyright © Patrick Robinson 2001

First published in the United Kingdom in 2001 by Century

Arrow Books
The Random House Group Limited
20 Vauxhall Bridge Road, London SW1V 2SA

Random House Australia (Pty) Limited
20 Alfred Street, Milsons Point, Sydney,
New South Wales 2061, Australia

Random House New Zealand Limited
18 Poland Road, Glenfield
Auckland 10, New Zealand

Random House (Pty) Limited
Endulini, 5a Jubilee Road, Parktown 2193, South Africa

The Random House Group Limited Reg. No. 954009

www.randomhouse.co.uk

A CIP catalogue record for this book is available from the British Library

Papers used by Random House are natural, recyclable products made from
wood grown in sustainable forests. The manufacturing processes conform to
the environmental regulations of the country of origin

ISBN 0 09 940527 X

Typeset by SX Composing DTP, Rayleigh, Essex
Printed and bound in Germany by
Elsnerdruck, Berlin

This book is respectfully dedicated to everyone who opposes the reduction of US Naval budgets, especially those politicians willing to reverse the process.

Acknowledgements

As usual I have a list of serving officers who have no desire whatever to be formally acknowledged as my advisers. The subject is always too secretive, too classified in its nature, and my sources too senior for identification.

Do I want to be named in one of YOUR books? Are you kidding! And yet they help me every year, ensuring that I am able to tell my story, handing me advice and detail, which they believe will give the public a greater appreciation of the armed heroes of the United States military.

Mostly my land attacks are planned with the help of former Special Forces officers. My insights into the diabolically secretive Intelligence world of Fort Meade are provided by a couple of former spies who seek only to highlight the sheer professionalism of the place.

However, at sea, my principal adviser, as always, is Admiral Sir John 'Sandy' Woodward, the Task Force Commander of the Royal Navy fleet which won the Battle for the Falkland Islands in 1982.

On, and under, the surface, Admiral Sandy plots and plans with me to help bring readers right into the control room of the submarine. Without him, I could not bring reality to the subject of underwater warfare.

I did not trouble him with the final details of the court martial, but rather relied on legal sources in the US Navy, who again did not wish to be named.

They joined a whole range of new advisers who wished to protect their anonymity: the oil tanker captains who expressed their opinions on their highly combustible cargo; the oil company executives who tried to guess what they would have done in the face of crisis; the Aeroflot exec who told me all about the Andropov, not knowing the purpose for which it was being used!

One of my rare identifiable sources is the excellent geopolitical writer, traveller and scholar Charles Stewart Goodwin of Cape Cod who provided research on the ancient Chinese fleets and the contents of the National Palace Museum in Taipei. He knows how grateful I am. His own writings on global politics provide for me an unfailing guide.

For insights and expertise on the subjects of reincarnation and post-traumatic stress, I have to thank Dr Barbara Lane of Virginia, whose own book, *Echoes from the Battlefield: First-Person Accounts of Civil War Past Lives*, is probably the best of its kind. Dr Lane's wide knowledge of these two subjects, plus a certain sure-footedness in planetary matters, provided research of the highest order. In matters of battle stress, her own views dovetailed almost precisely with those of Admiral Woodward.

I also thank my friend Chris Choi Man Tat, whose suave and courteous manner running Kite's, Dublin's best Chinese restaurant, quite conceals the fact that he was once bosun on a gigantic crude-oil tanker plying between the Gulf and the Far East. His insights on the great ships were constantly helpful.

Finally I thank my friend Olivia Oakes who thought she was coming for a quiet weekend with my family, and ended up reading this manuscript for almost 15 hours, checking spelling and punctuation. Any errors in this regard I intend, unfairly, to blame on her.

The Shark Mutiny is a work of fiction. Every character in it is a product of my imagination only, though there may be certain College baseball players who recognize their names but not their lives, nor any other connection with reality.

– Patrick Robinson

Cast of Principal Characters

Senior Command

The President of the United States (Commander-in-Chief US Armed Forces)

Vice-Admiral Arnold Morgan (National Security Adviser)

Robert MacPherson (Defense Secretary)

Harcourt Travis (Secretary of State)

General Tim Scannell (Chairman of the Joint Chiefs)

Jack Smith (Energy Secretary)

US Navy Senior Command

Admiral Alan Dickson (Chief of Naval Operations)

Admiral Dick Greening (Commander-in-Chief Pacific Fleet CINCPACFLT)

Rear-Admiral Freddie Curran (Commander Submarines Pacific Fleet COMSUBPAC)

Rear-Admiral John Bergstrom (Commander Special War Command SPECWARCOM)

USS *Shark*

Commander Donald K. Reid (Commanding Officer)

Lt. Commander Dan Headley (Executive Officer)

Lt. Commander Jack Cressend (Combat Systems Officer)

Lt. Commander Josh Gandy (Sonar Officer)

Master Chief Petty Officer Drew Fisher (Chief of Boat)

Lt. Shawn Pearson (Navigation Officer)

Lt. Matt Singer (Officer of the Deck)

Lt. Dave Mills (ASDV helmsman)

Lt. Matt Longo (ASDV navigator)

USS *John F. Kennedy*
Admiral Daylan Holt (Group Commander)
US Navy SEALs
Commander Rick Hunter (Team Leader, Assault Team Two)
Commander Russell 'Rusty' Bennett (Overall Commander, Assault Team One)
Lt. Commander Ray Schaeffer (Team Leader, Assault Team One)
Lt. Dan Conway (2 I/C Assault Team One)
Lt. John Nathan (High Explosive Chief, Assault Team One)
Chief Petty Officer Rob Cafiero (Base Camp Chief, Assault Team One)
Petty Officer Ryan Combs (Machine Gunner, Assault Team One)
Combat SEAL Charlie Mitchell (Electrics, Assault Team One)
Lt. Dallas MacPherson (2 I/C and Explosives Chief, Assault Team Two)
Lt. Bobby Allensworth (Personal Bodyguard to Commander Hunter)
Chief Petty Officer Mike Hook (Explosives Assistant to Lt. MacPherson)
Petty Officer Catfish Jones (Combat assistant to Lt. Allensworth)
SEAL Riff 'Rattlesnake' Davies (Machine Gunner, Assault Team Two)
SEAL Buster Townsend (Assault Team Two)

National Security Agency, Fort Meade
Admiral David Borden (Acting Director)
Lt. Jimmy Ramshawe (Security Ops Officer)

The Court Martial
President: Captain Cale 'Boomer' Dunning
Judge Advocate General: Captain Sam Scott

Judge Advocate/Observer: Captain Art Brennan
Trial Counsellor: Lt. Commander David 'Locker' Jones
Defense Counsellor: Lt. Commander Al Surprenant

Chinese High Command
Admiral Zhang Yushu (Senior Vice Chairman Peoples'
    Liberation Army/Navy Council)
Admiral Zu Jicai (Commander-in-Chief Navy)

Civilian Oil Tanker Masters
Commodore Don McGhee (*Global Bronco*)
Captain Tex Packard (*Galveston Star*)

Fiancées
Kathy O'Brien (Admiral Morgan)
Jane Peacock (Lt. Ramshawe)

Prologue

Summer 1987.
Hunter Valley Farms
Lexington, Kentucky.
It was pretty damn hot for baseball. Only a light breeze ruffled the sweltering Blue Grass paddocks in this big thoroughbred breeding farm along the old Iron-Works Pike, out near the village of Paris.

Young Dan Headley couldn't hit Rick Hunter's fastball to save his life. 'Easy, Ricky. Take something off it, I can't hit that.' But again and again the baseball came screaming in, low and away, and slammed into the base of the red barn wall behind the hitter.

The giant sixteen-year-old pitcher kept howling with laughter as his best buddy swung and missed yet again. 'You gotta concentrate, Danny.'

'On what?'

'The baseball, stupid.'

'How can I, when I can't even see it? Nobody could see it.'

'Pete Rose coulda seen it,' said Rick solemnly, referring to the former Cincinnati Reds legend.

'Pete Rose coulda seen a howitzer shell.'

'Okay, one more?'

'Nah. I'm all done. Let's go back and get some lemonade. I'm sweating like a bull.'

Rick Hunter pulled off his glove, stuck the ball into the pocket of his jeans and tied the sleeves of his warm-up

1

jacket around his waist. He jumped over the post-and-rail fence into a wide paddock containing a half-dozen mares and foals. Dan Headley followed him, swinging the Louisville Slugger bat, looking over at the foals, at the Kentucky-bred baby racehorses, the best of whom might one day hear the thunder of the crowds at Belmont Park, Royal Ascot, Saratoga and Longchamp. Perhaps even Churchill Downs.

'Still beats the hell outta me why you don't just stay here and get rich,' said Dan. 'Raisin' the ye'rlings, sellin' 'em for fortunes, just like yer daddy. Jeez, Rick. You got it all made for you, right here.'

'Danny, we been havin' this particular conversation for the biggest part of three years and my answer ain't varied none. I just ain't interested. 'Sides, in my judgement, this bull market for thoroughbreds ain't here for ever.'

'Well, it's been here for more'n ten years. Ain't showing no sign of flagging.'

'It'll collapse, ole buddy. Bull markets always do in the end and right then there's gonna be a whole lot of penniless ole hardboots around here, guys who thought their good luck was some kinda birthright.'

'Yeah, but that ain't why you plan to leave. You're leavin' because it bores you, even with all that money swilling around. But why the hell you want to be an officer in the US Navy instead of riding around here like some goddamned czar – master of the Hunter Valley, right here in the thoroughbred breeding capital of the world – well, like I said. Sure beats the hell outta me.'

'Well, you're planning to leave with me, right?'

'Sure I am, Ricky. But, Christ, my daddy's just the stud groom here. Your ole man owns the whole place. And you don't even have any brothers and sisters. It's all gonna be yours. All 2000 acres of it and all them goddamned blue-chip brood mares.'

'Come on, Danny. You understand the horse-breeding business better'n I do. You could make a real go of it yourself if you wanted. Your daddy's got a coupla mares of his own. Everyone has to start somewhere.'

'Ricky, I couldn't save enough money for a place like this in a thousand years. I'd just end up another stud groom. Anyone could see why I'd rather be Captain Dan Headley, commanding officer of a US Navy battle cruiser than Danny Headley, stallion man at the Hunter Valley.'

'Raisin' horses bores you too, don't it?' said Rick, grinning, in the sure knowledge that he had a soulmate.

'Some. But I just don't have the advantages.'

'Wouldn't change nothin' in my opinion. You just want adventure, I guess, like me. Fast horses take too long to raise. We just ain't got the time, right?'

Dan grinned. He was much shorter than the towering Rick Hunter and he had to walk about half a stride faster to lay up with his lifelong friend. They moved steadily across the magnificent grassland, walking on a slight uphill gradient, watching the foals edging towards them, eager, curious, the mares moving at a much slower pace behind.

'Who's that chestnut filly by?'

'Which one, Danny? The one in front with the white star?'

'Yeah. She's gonna have a backside like a barmaid when she grows up.'

'Guess she could have a motor. She's by Secretariat, out of a halfway decent daughter of Nashua.'

'That's real local, right. Nashua's next door and the Big Horse is just up the road.' Kentucky horsemen always referred to the 1973 Triple Crown winner as the Big Horse, despite his unspectacular performance in the stud.

'Dad owns the mare, swears to God Secretariat's gonna be a great sire of brood mares. We'll be keeping that filly for sure.'

'How about that little bay colt over there, the one who keeps pushing the others around?'

'He's by Northern Dancer. Typical, kinda boisterous and small. He'll go to the sales, probably end up in Ireland with Mr O'Brien. Unless the Arabs outbid everyone. Then he'll end up in Newmarket, which ain't quite so good.'

'Guess the dark gray is by the Rajah, right?'

'That's him. He's by our own Red Rajah. Bart Hunter's pride and joy. That stallion is one mean sonofabitch. But my daddy loves him and your daddy copes with him. Bobby Headley, best stallion man in the Blue Grass. That's my old man's verdict.'

'Well, I been around the Rajah for five years and I ain't seen nothin' mean about him.'

'I have. Trust me. He just don't like strangers, Dan. But he acts like an old dog when your daddy's with him.'

They walked on to the fence, climbed it and came around into the main yard, walked right into Bobby Headley, hurrying down to the feed house. He was a slim, hard-eyed Kentucky horseman of medium height, not so instantly handsome as his dark-haired sixteen-year-old son, and he had a deep, resonant voice, which seemed out of place in a man so lacking in bulk. 'Hey, boys, how you doin'?' he said, looking at the baseball bat. 'Still gettin' that fast ball past 'im, eh, Ricky?'

'Yes, sir. But it ain't easy. Lose your concentration and that Danny can really hurt you.'

Bobby Headley chuckled. 'Hey, Dan, do me a favor, willya? Run along to Rajah's box and pick up my brushes. I left 'em right inside the door.'

'Sure. Rick, will I see you back at the house?'

'In five, right?'

Dan Headley jogged along to the three big stallion boxes at the far end of the yard, unclipped the lock on the eight-year-old Red Rajah's door and slipped inside, muttering softly, 'Hey, Rajah, ole boy, how you bin? They still treatin' you good?'

The big stallion, just a tad under seventeen hands and almost milk-white now with the advancing years, did not have a head collar on and he was not tethered on a long shank to the sturdy iron ring on the wall. This was a bit unusual for a stallion of his hot-blooded breeding. The massive ex-California stakes winner was a grandson of the fiery Red God, out of a fast daughter of the notorious English sire, Supreme Sovereign. To a professional horseman this was an example of breeding made in hell, a recipe for a truly dangerous stallion. Supreme Sovereign was so unpredictable, so lethal to any human being that they kept a high-powered fire hydrant in his box in case of an emergency. Red Rajah himself had several times attacked people, but he'd been a high-class miler in his time, a good, tough battler in a finish, and he was a highly commercial sire, standing for $40,000. In the last couple of years Bobby Headley seemed to have him under control.

The Rajah gazed at young Dan Headley moving softly behind him. He betrayed no anger, but those who knew him would have noticed his ears set slightly back and his eyes flicking first forward, then back; far back, looking at Dan without moving his head.

The boy bent down to pick up the brushes and, as he straightened up, the stallion moved imperceptively. Dan, sensing a shift in the horse's mood, reacted like the lifelong horseman he was, lifted up his right arm like a traffic cop and murmured, 'Whoa there, Rajah, good boy, easy, ole buddy.'

Right then Red Rajah attacked, quite suddenly, with not a semblance of warning. He whipped his head round and slammed his teeth over Danny's biceps, biting like a crocodile, right through the muscle and splintering the big

5

bone in the upper arm, and he didn't let go. He dragged the boy down, pulling him on to the straw, preparing for the killer stallion's favorite trick, to kneel on his prey, like a camel or an elephant, crushing the ribcage. The thoroughbred breeding industry is apt to keep this kind of savagery very quiet.

Dan Headley screamed with pain and terror, and his scream echoed into the yard. Rick Hunter was on his way down the walkway towards the main house when he heard it. No one else did and a thousand dreads about the true nature of the grandson of Red God flew through his mind.

Back in the barn, Danny screamed again. He was facing death. He knew that and he kicked out at the stallion, but it was like kicking a pick-up truck.

Rick Hunter was by now pounding across the grass quadrangle towards the boxes. He heard his friend's second scream and flew over the ground straight to the first box where Red Rajah lived. When he got there he searched instantly for a weapon and saw the trusty Louisville Slugger against the wall. Grabbing it with his right hand, he whipped open the door and faced with horror the scene before him: Danny, blood pouring from his smashed right arm, trying to protect himself against the onslaught of the stallion glowering over him, preparing to kneel. Rick never hesitated, wound back the bat and slammed it into Red Rajah's ribs with a blow that would surely have killed a man. It did not, however, kill Red Rajah. The great white horse swung his head round, as if deciding which of the two boys to attack first. So Ricky hit him again, with all his force, crashing the bat into the ribs of the stallion, simultaneously yelling, 'Get out, Danny! For Christ's sake get out. Shut the door but don't lock it.'

Dan Headley, half in shock, maddened by the pain, rolled and crawled out of the box. Still flat on the ground, he kicked the door shut and sixteen-year-old Rick Hunter turned to face the raging killer horse again. By now he was in the corner fifteen feet from the door, watching the Rajah backing off a stride or two. Rick held the bat in both hands, not daring to swing in case he missed the head and the horse came at his throat, or, much more likely, his testicles. In a split second he got his answer. Red Rajah came at his face, mouth open. Rick shoved the bat straight out in front of him, still holding the handle with both hands, and the Rajah's teeth smashed down on to it, splintering it like matchwood.

Outside, Dan Headley had passed out with the pain.

Now Rick was on his own. Again the Rajah moved away a stride, his ears flat back, his wicked white-rimmed eye still flicking back and forth. Rick's mind raced back to a conversation he had once with an old local hardboot, who had told him *there's only one way I know to stop a stallion who's bent on killing you*. Rick Hunter dropped down on to all fours, knowing that if this ploy failed he might be as dead as Danny would have been if he hadn't arrived in time.

Rick flattened himself into the pose of the horse's most ancient and feared enemy, the lion. He tried to assume the crouched, threatening stance of a big cat preparing to pounce, trying to reawaken thousands of years of unconscious phobia in the psyche of the horse. He burrowed his boot into the straw, made a scratching noise on the concrete beneath, snarled deeply under his breath, staring hard into the horse's eyes. Then he moved his head forward, let out a roar and then another, crawling one step nearer.

Red Rajah stopped dead. He moved a half-step backwards, a slight tremor in both shoulder muscles. He backed up some more, dipping his head as if to protect his throat. It was an instinct, not a reaction.

Rick roared like a lion again, all the while trying to get the warm-up jacket from around his waist. The fight seemed to have gone right out of the Rajah, who was now standing stock still. He was not prepared when the 6ft 4in heir to Hunter Valley jumped up and dived at his head, ramming the jacket hard down over his eyes and face. Red Rajah was in the pitch dark now and no horse likes to move when he's unable to see anything. He just stood there, stock still, trembling, blind, with the jacket over his head. Rick carefully edged towards the door, eased it quietly open and made his escape, slamming the lock shut as he went.

Outside, Dan was conscious again. Rick hit the alarm bell and sat with his buddy until help arrived minutes later.

He, and both of their fathers, remained with Dan all night in Lexington Hospital, while two surgeons meticulously restitched the muscle, reset and pinned the shattered right arm.

In the morning, when Dan was in the recovery room, the patient finally came to, slowly focusing on the young lion from Hunter Valley. He shook his head in silent admiration of his friend's courage, grinned and said, 'Jesus, Ricky. You just saved my life. I told you we'd be better off in a warship.'

'You're right there, ole buddy,' said Rick. 'Screw this racehorse crap. You can get killed out here. I'd rather be under fire. You think Annapolis is ready for us?'

One

January 23, 2007.
The White House, Washington DC.
Admiral Arnold Morgan was alone in his office contemplating the two major issues in his life at this particular lunchtime. The first was his decision to stay on as the National Security Adviser to the President for one more year, against all his better judgement. The second was a Wagnerian-sized roast beef sandwich, fortified with heavy mayonnaise and mustard into a feast he would never have dared to order had his secretary and wife-to-be, the gorgeous Kathy O'Brien, been anywhere near the precincts of 1400 Pennsylvania Avenue. Happily she was out until 4 p.m.

The Admiral grinned cheerfully, circling his desk like a mountain lion poised to pounce upon his prey. He saw it as a richly deserved gastronomic reward for having succumbed to weeks of being badgered, harassed, coaxed and ultimately persuaded to remain in this office by some of the most powerful figures in American politics and the military.

His decision to hang in there had been wrung out of him, after nine weeks of soul-searching. The decision to hit a roast beef sandwich *el grando*, before Ms O'Brien came sashaying back into the office, had been made with much less anguish: nine weeks' less. The Admiral, sixty-one years old now, was still, miraculously, in robust health and not more than eight pounds heavier than he had been

9

as a nuclear submarine commander twenty-seven years previously. Immaculately tailored, wearing a maroon and gold Hermès tie Kathy had given him for Christmas, he tucked a large white linen napkin into his shirt collar and bit luxuriously into his sandwich. Through the window he could see it was snowing like hell. The President was, shrewdly, visiting southern California, where the temperature was a sunlit seventy-eight degrees and here, in the West Wing of the White House, there was absolutely nothing happening of any interest whatsoever to the most feared and respected military strategist on planet earth.

'I still have no idea what the hell I'm doing here,' he muttered to himself. 'The goddamned world's gone quiet, temporarily, and I'm sitting here like a goddamned lapdog waiting for our esteemed but flaky leader to drag himself out of some fucking Beverly Hills swimming pool.' *Flaky. A complete flake.* The words had been used about the President, over and over at that final meeting at the home of Admiral Scott Dunsmore, the wise and deceptively wealthy former Chairman of the Joint Chiefs. Arnold Morgan could not understand what the fuss was about. Plenty of other NSAs had resigned, but apparently he was not permitted that basic human right.

Christ, everyone had been there and no one had even informed him. He'd walked, stone-cold, into a room containing not only General Scannell, Chairman of the Joint Chiefs, but *two* former chairmen, plus the Chief of Naval Operations and the Commandant of the United States Marines. The Defense Secretary was there, two senior members of the Senate Committee on Armed Services, including the vastly experienced Senator Ted Kennedy, whose unwavering patriotism and endless concern for his country had always made him a natural leader among such men. Altogether there were four current members of the National Security Council in attendance. Their joint mission was simple: to persuade Admiral Morgan to withdraw his resignation and to remain in office until the Republican President's second term was over. A few weeks previously, at the conclusion of a particularly dangerous and covert naval operation in China, the President had demonstrated such shocking self-interest and lack of judgement, that he could no longer be trusted to act in the strict interests of the USA.

The world was presently a volatile place and no one needed to remind Admiral Morgan of that. But the man in the Oval Office was prone to appoint 'Yes Men' to influential positions and now, in the final two years of his presidency, he tended to think only of himself and his image and popularity. Without Admiral Morgan's granite wall of reality and judgement in the crucible of inter-national military affairs, the men in Admiral Dunsmore's house that day were greatly concerned that a terrible and costly mistake might occur.

Looking back, Arnold Morgan could not remember precisely who had put into words the hitherto unspoken observation that the President was a 'goddamned flake, and getting worse'. But he remembered a lot of nodding and no laughter. He also remembered their host, Admiral Dunsmore, turning to his old friend the Senator from Massachusetts and saying, 'The trouble is he's interested in military matters and we cannot trust him. Talk to Arnold, Teddy. You'll say it better than anyone else.' He had, too. At the conclusion of a short but moving few words from the silver-tongued sage of Hyannisport, Admiral Morgan had nodded and said curtly, 'My resignation is withdrawn.'

Now he was 'back at the factory', ruminating on the general calm that had existed in the world's known trouble spots for the past month. The Middle East was for the moment serene. Terrorists in general seemed still to be on their Christmas break. India and Pakistan had temporarily

11

ceased to threaten each other, and China, the Big Tiger, had been very quiet since last fall. Indeed, according to the satellite photographs they were not even conducting fleet exercises near Taiwan, which made a change. As for their new ISBM submarine, *Xia III*, there was no sign of it leaving its jetty in Shanghai.

The only halfway interesting piece of Intelligence to come Admiral Morgan's way since Christmas was a report put together by the CIA's Russian desk. According to one of their field operators in Moscow, the Rosvoorouzhenie factory on the outskirts of the city was suddenly making large quantities of moored mines. This was regarded as unusual since Rosvoorouzhenie's known expertise was in the production of seabed mines, the MDM series, particularly the lethal one-and-three-quarter-ton ship-killing MDM-6, which can be laid through the torpedo tubes of a submarine. Rosvoorouzhenie was now, apparently, making a lot of updated, custom-made PLT-3 mines, moored one-tonners, which can be laid either through torpedo tubes or from surface ships. The CIA man had no information where the mines were going, if anywhere, but their man had been certain this was a very unusual development. Most Russian-made mines these days were strictly for export.

Admiral Morgan growled to himself, *now who the hell wants a damn large shipment of moored PLT-3s, eh?* He would have growled it out loud, but for the fact that his mouth was full of roast beef and mayonnaise. As it was, he chewed and pondered silently. But on reflection he did not much like it. *If the goddamned penniless Russians are building several hundred expensive mines, someone has ordered 'em. And if someone's ordered 'em, they plan to lay 'em, right? Otherwise they wouldn't have ordered 'em. Where? That's what we wanna know. Who's planning a nice little surprise minefield?*

He finished his sandwich, sipped his coffee and

frowned. When Kathy came back he'd have her call Langley and make sure he was kept up to speed on Russian mine production. And if the overheads picked up any large mine shipments leaving any Russian seaports, he wanted to know about that. Immediately. *Just don't want some fucking despot in a turban getting overly ambitious, right?* The Admiral glared at the portrait of General MacArthur which hung in his office. *Gotta watch 'em, Douglas. Right? Watch 'em, at all times.*

0900 (local) January 23, 2007.
Renmin Dahuitang, The Great Hall of the People
Tiananmen Square, Beijing.
The largest government building in the world, home of the National People's Congress, was locked, barred and bolted this Tuesday morning. All 561,800 square feet of it. Business was cancelled, the public was banned and there were more armed military guards patrolling the snow-covered western side of the square than anyone had seen since the 1989 massacre of the students.

Inside, there were more guards, patrolling the endless corridors. Sixteen of them stood motionless, with shouldered arms, in a square surrounding the only elevator which travels down to the brightly lit Meridian Gate, the spectacular entrance once reserved for the Emperor alone. Tiananmen Square itself was under an immense blanket of white. The total absence of thousands of government workers gave the heart of Beijing a look of abandonment. It was windswept, quiet, deserted, like a great stadium after the games were over.

Inside the ops room there was an atmosphere of high tension. Standing at the far end of the room, next to a ten-foot-wide illuminated computer screen, was the formidable figure of Admiral Zhang Yushu, recently resigned from his position as Commander-in-Chief of the People's

Liberation Army/Navy and now installed, by the Paramount Ruler himself, as the senior of the four vice-chairmen of the all-powerful PLAN Council. Eight weeks previously Admiral Zhang had leapfrogged clean over the other three highly experienced members and now occupied a position of such authority that he answered only to the State President, the General Secretary of the Communist Party and the Chairman of the Military Affairs Commission – and that was all the same person. The Paramount Ruler had once occupied these three highest offices of State and there were those who thought it was just a matter of time before Admiral Zhang himself rose to such eminence. The Paramount Ruler would hear no word against him.

Now the Admiral addressed his audience for the first time, speaking carefully, welcoming them all to the most secretive meeting ever assembled in the forty-eight-year history of the Great Hall – a gathering so clandestine they'd shut down the entire government for the day to avoid eavesdroppers.

Admiral Zhang's three elderly colleagues on the Military Council, all ex-Army commanders, were in attendance. The new Commander-in-Chief of the Navy, Admiral Zu Jicai, was there, seated next to Admiral Yibo Yunsheng, the new Commander of China's massive northern fleet. The Navy's powerful Political Commisar, Vice-Admiral Yang Zhenying, had arrived the previous night from Shanghai in company with the Chief of the Naval Staff, Vice-Admiral Sang Ye. The most influential of the Chinese Navy's deputy commanders-in-chief, Admiral Zhi-Heng Tan, was seated next to Zhang himself at the head of the broad mahogany table. Behind them was a single four-feet-high framed print of Mao Zedong, the great revolutionary whose only wish was for a supreme China to stand alone against the imperial West. The print

14

was a replica of the giant portrait of Mao which gazes with chilling indifference across the square from the Tiananmen Gate. Today, it served to remind the Chinese High Command in this brightly lit room precisely who they really were.

The other three men in the room were Iranian: the most senior a black-robed, bearded ayatollah, whose name was not announced. The two naval officers accompanying the holy man were Rear-Admiral Hossein Shafii, Head of Tactical Headquarters, Bandar Abbas and Rear-Admiral Mohammed Badr, the Iranian Navy's Commander-in-Chief Submarines.

Admiral Zhang, who stood six feet tall, was by far the biggest and the most heavily built of the Chinese. But he spoke softly, in an uncharacteristic purr, a smile of friendship upon his wide impassive face. The language was English, which all three Iranians spoke fluently. The words were translated back into Chinese by Vice-Admiral Yang who had, in his youth, studied for four years at UCLA.

'Gentlemen,' said Admiral Zhang Yushu. 'As you are all well aware, the new Sino-Iranian pipeline from the great oilfields of Kazakhstan will come on stream within a few weeks. Thousands of barrels will flow daily out of Russia, right across your great country, south to the new Chinese refinery on the shores of the Hormuz Strait. 'This, gentlemen, should herald a new dawn for all of us, a dawn of vast profits for Iran and, thank God, an end to China's endless reliance on the West in the matter of fuel oil. The alliance of the past ten years between our two superb nations was indeed made in heaven.'

Admiral Zhang paused and opened his arms wide. He walked round to the right side of the huge table and stood beaming at the men from the desert. The Ayatollah himself stood first and took both of the Admiral's hands in his own, wishing everyone the everlasting peace of Allah.

15

Then the two Admirals from Bandar Abbas stood up and embraced the legendary Chinese Navy Commander.

Zhang walked back to his position at the head of the table and glanced briefly at his notes. He allowed a flicker of a frown to cross his face, but then he smiled again and continued, 'I have no need to remind anyone of the enormous cost of building this 1000-mile pipeline and the construction of the refinery. It ran, of course, into billions of US dollars. However, as of this moment, there is but one dark cloud on our horizon and that is the extra-ordinarily low cost of a barrel of oil on the world market. Last night it was down to $13 and falling towards a ten-year low. The Arab nations cannot be controlled because of their reliance on American protection and commerce. Which leaves us to sell at a half, or even a third, of our oil's true value. Now, Iran is earning twenty per cent of every barrel to reach the new refinery and at present that's under three dollars. It will thus cost your country millions and millions in unearned revenue every month. Gentlemen, I ask you. What is the solution? I must remind you this is a *plot*, a diabolical Western PLOT to devalue our great economies, to allow them to dominate us, as they have always tried to do.'

Admiral Zhang's voice had risen during this delivery, but now it fell very softly again to the calm, gentle tones of his welcome. 'We have the solution, my friends. It is a solution we have discussed before and I believe it is one that will find much favor with both our governments.'

The Ayatollah seemed genuinely perplexed and looked up quizzically.

Admiral Zhang smiled back and, without further ceremony said flatly, 'I am proposing we lay a minefield deep in the historic national waters of the Islamic State of Iran. Right across the Strait of Hormuz.'

Admiral Badr looked up sharply and said immediately,

'My friend Yushu, you have become a tried and trusted confidant of my nation. But I feel I must remind you that we have considered many times a blockade of the Strait of Hormuz. We have been frustrated for the same three reasons every time: one, the far side of the Strait belongs to Oman, a country which is totally influenced by the American puppets in London. Two, we could never lay down a minefield quickly enough without being seen by the American satellites, which would surely bring down upon us the wrath of the Pentagon. Three, well, ultimately the Americans would clear it and paint us as lawless outcasts, enemies to the peaceful trading nations of the world. No good could come of it, not from our point of view.'

Admiral Zhang nodded and asked for the forbearance of the meeting. 'Mohammed,' he said. 'All your reasons are correct. But now times have changed. The stakes are much higher. You and I have different oil both to sell and to use. We also have an unbreakable joint interest, our own oil routes from the Strait to the Far East. You, Mohammed, have the entire backing of the People's Liberation Army/ Navy. Together we could most certainly lay down a minefield, using both submarines and surface ships, and we could achieve it so swiftly that no one would have the slightest idea who had done what.'

'But they would find out, surely?'

'They would not find out. Though they might guess. But they would not be in time. Because one day a big Western tanker is going to hit one of the mines and blow up, and for the next year oil prices will go through the roof, except for ours. Which will, of course, cost us just the same – almost nothing. But that which we sell will be worth a fortune, while the world's tankers back up on both sides of the minefield, all of them afraid to go through. For a while we'll very nearly own the world market for fuel oil.'

Admiral Badr smiled and shook his head. 'It's a bold plan, Yushu. I'll give you that. I suppose it just might work. But my country and my Navy have been on the wrong end of the fury of the Pentagon before. It is not a place we want to go again.'

'So has mine, Mohammed. But they are not invincible and in the end they are a godless society interested only in money. They will raise heaven and hell to free up the tanker routes to the Gulf, but I think they will see it as a business problem, not cause for armed conflict. Besides, they will not want an all-out shooting war in the Gulf because that will just compound the oil problems and send prices even higher, and the sacred New York Stock Exchange even lower.'

'But Yushu, if they suspect China is behind it they may become very angry indeed.'

'True, Mohammed. True. But not sufficiently angry to want a war with us. That would send their precious Stock Market into freefall. No, my friends, the Americans will clear the minefield, open up the tanker routes again and send in heavy US naval muscle to make sure they stay cleared. By then we will have made vast sums of money, China and Iran, and, hopefully, many new friends and customers, who will perhaps prefer to do business with us in future. One little minefield, Mohammed, twenty miles wide, and we open a gateway to a glittering future together.'

Same day.
Headquarters, National Security Agency
Fort Meade, Maryland.
Lieutenant Jimmy Ramshawe downloaded his computer screen for the umpteenth time that afternoon. As SOO (Security Ops Officer), his tasks included designating printouts to selected officers all over the ultra-secret

labyrinth of the US Military Intelligence complex; a place so highly classified that the walls had built-in copper shields to prevent any electronic eavesdropping.

The Lieutenant had been routinely bored by the entire procedure since lunchtime, sifting through screeds of messages, reports and signals from United States surveillance networks all over the world. But these two latest documents just in from the CIA's Russian desk caught and held his attention:

Unusual activity in Rozvoorouzhenie mine production factory outside central Moscow. Three heavy transit military vehicles sighted leaving the plant, fully laden. Sighted again at Sheremetyevo II Airport, Moscow, two hours later. Then again leaving the airport 1400 EST, empty. Destination unknown.

From the same source another signal came in ninety-four minutes later at 1534 EST. Langley had so far offered no comment. Just the bald fact:

Russian Antonov 124 took off Moscow 2300, believed heading due east. Aircrew only, plus heavy cargo. AN-124 took 3000 metres to lift-off. CIA field officer traces no flight plan. Inquiries continue.

To Jimmy Ramshawe this was food and drink – a complex, slightly sinister problem which wanted studying, if not solving. He knew the gigantic Antonov freighter – known as the *Ruslan* after a mythological Russian giant – could carry a colossal 120 tons of freight 35,000 feet above the earth's surface. He had a good imagination and did not need to utilize much of it before he could visualize 120 big sea mines hurtling through the stratosphere at 550 knots, bound for some distant ocean where they could be primed to inconvenience US Navy fleets.

At the age of twenty-eight, Jimmy had been selected by the Navy to serve in the Intelligence Service. A tall dark-haired young officer, he possessed an acutely analytical mind. He was a lateral thinker, an observer of convolutions, complications and intricacies. As a commanding officer he would have developed into a living nightmare. No team in any warship would ever have provided him with *quite* sufficient data to make a major decision. But he had a superb intelligence, the highest IQ in his class at Annapolis and his superiors spotted him a long way out. Lieutenant Ramshawe was born for Intelligence work at the highest level and, while his young fellow officers went forward, following their stars as future commanding officers of surface or sub-surface warships, the lanky athletic Jimmy was sent into the electronic hothouse of America's most sensitive, heavily guarded Intelligence agency where, to quote the admissions admiral, 'there would be ample outlet for his outstanding talents'.

He was an unusual member of Fort Meade's staff for the simple reason that he looked and sounded like an Australian. The son of a Sydney diplomat, he had been born in Washington DC while his father served a five-year tour of duty as Military Attaché at the grandiose Australian embassy on Massachusetts Avenue. They'd returned to New South Wales for just two years before Admiral Ramshawe accepted a position on the Board of the Australian airline, Qantas, working permanently in New York.

Young Jimmy, with his US passport, went to school in Connecticut, starred for three years as a baseball pitcher who sounded as if he should have been playing cricket and followed his father into a career in dark blue – American dark blue, that is. He'd been in the US Navy now for ten years, but a couple of weeks earlier he had still brought a smile to the lugubrious face of the NSA's Director,

Admiral George Morris, by announcing, 'G' day, sir. I picked up that stuff you wanted. Gimme two hours and she'll be right.'

Ramshawe was always going to *sound* like Banjo Patterson and other members of Australian folklore, but he was American through and through, and Admiral Morris valued him highly, as highly as he valued his long-time friendship with Ramshawe senior, the retired Aussie diplomat/admiral. The trouble was that Admiral Morris had just been admitted to the Bethesda Naval Hospital with suspected lung cancer and the deputy director, Rear-Admiral David Borden, was a more remote, formal figure, who was not instantly available to young Lieutenant Ramshawe's observations. That might prove difficult for both of them – the Acting Director because he might miss something, Jimmy because he might not be listened to.

He stared at the two signals in front of him and attacked the problem as he always did: going instantly for the obvious worst-case scenario. That is, *some foreign nutcase has just bought several hundred sea mines from the bloody Russians with a view to laying the bastards somewhere they want to keep private.* Lieutenant Ramshawe frowned. It seemed unlikely that the Russians were using the mines themselves. They had nowhere to mine and these days they rarely manufactured naval hardware unless it was for export. *So who the hell did they make 'em for?* Jimmy Ramshawe ran the checks swiftly through his mind. *One of those crazy bastards in the Gulf? Gaddafi? The ayatollahs? The Iraqis? No reason really for any of them, but the Iranians had threatened a minefield more than once. But then the AN-124 would have been running south, not east. Or else the mines would have been transported by road. China? No. They'd make their own . . . I think. North Korea? Maybe. But they make their own.*

Lieutenant Ramshawe deemed the puzzle worthy of careful consideration. He gathered up the two signals, muttering to himself, *I don't think we better fuck this up, because if ships start blowing up, somewhere in the Far East or wherever, we're likely to get the blame. 'Specially if an American ship was lost. Bloody oath there'd be trouble then.* He stood up from his screen, pushed his floppy dark hair off his forehead and walked resolutely out of the ops area down to the Director's office.

He was still reading the signals when he arrived in the hallowed area once occupied by Arnold Morgan himself and he walked through absent-mindedly, still reading, tapped on the door, pushed it open and walked in, as he always did. 'G'day, Admiral,' he said. 'Coupla things here I think we want to take a sharp look at.'

David Borden looked up, an expression of surprise on his face. 'Lieutenant,' he said. 'I wonder if you could bring yourself to give me the elementary courtesy of knocking before you enter my office?'

'Sir? I thought I just did.'

'And then perhaps *waiting* to be invited in?'

'Sir? This isn't a bloody social call. I have urgent stuff in my hand which I think you should know about right away.'

'Lieutenant Ramshawe, there are certain matters of etiquette still observed here in the US Navy, though I imagine they have long been dispensed with in your own country.'

'Sir, this is my country.'

'Of course. But your accent sounds like no other US officer I ever met.'

'Well, I can't help that. But since we're wasting time and I don't want to get off on the wrong foot now you're in the big chair, I'll get back outside and we'll start over, right?' Before Admiral Borden could answer, Jimmy Ramshawe had walked out and closed the door behind him.

Then he knocked on it and the Director, feeling slightly absurd, called, 'Come in, Lieutenant.'

'Christ, I'm glad we got that over with,' said Jimmy, turning on his Aussie-philosophical, lopsided grin. 'Anyway, g'day, Admiral, got something here I think we should take a look at.'

He handed over the two signals and David Borden glanced down at them. 'I don't see anything urgent here,' he said. 'First of all we do not even know the mines were on board the Russian aircraft. If they were, we don't have the slightest idea where they might be going and, wherever that might be, it's going to take a long time for anyone to unload them, transport them and then start laying them in the ocean. At which point our satellites will pick them up. I shouldn't waste any more time on it if I were you.'

'Now, hold hard, sir. We got possibly several hundred brand-new sea mines almost certainly packed into the hold of the biggest freight aircraft on earth, now heading due east towards China, maybe India, maybe Pakistan, Korea, Indonesia? Brand-new mines specifically ordered and manufactured. And you don't think we want to trace the bloody jokers who own them right away?'

'No, Lieutenant. I think we'll find out in good time without wasting any of our valuable resources and, in particular, your energies.'

'Well, I suppose if you say so, sir. But that's a lot of high explosive and, well, I mean some bugger wants it for something pretty definite. I think Admiral Morris would want it investigated, maybe alert the Big Man in the White House.'

'Lieutenant, Admiral Morris is no longer in command of this Agency and from now on I trust you'll respect my judgement. Forget the mines. They'll come to the surface in good time.'

'Just hope they don't bring a pile of bloody wreckage with 'em, that's all.' Lieutenant Ramshawe nodded curtly, turned on his heel and left, muttering to himself an old Australian phrase, 'Right mongrel bastard he's turned out to be.'

Evening. Same Day.
Ops Room, Great Hall of the People.
The big computer screen had been switched off now. The Iranian delegation was heading north-east out along Jichang Lu towards Beijing International Airport and Admiral Zhang was talking with Zu Jicai. Everyone else had gone. The two great friends and naval colleagues sat alone, sipping tea, which Yushu had coerced a guard to produce, in the absence of any staff whatsoever in the Great Hall. It tasted, he thought, like a leftover thermos from Mao's Long March of 1935.

'I am still slightly mystified, Yushu. Do you really think there is enough advantage in this for us to become involved in a worldwide oil catastrophe?'

'Ah, Jicai. You are ever the tactician, ever the strategist. Always the battle commander. You see things very clearly, the immediate crunch, the immediate aftermath.'

'Well, don't you?'

'I used to, when I was C-in-C of the Navy. But I must be political now and I have changed my perspectives. I am trying to look at a wider picture.'

'I think, my Yushu, you will face a very wide picture indeed if an American tanker should collide with one of those Russian mines in the Strait of Hormuz.'

Admiral Zhang smiled, sipped his tea, grimaced and said softly, 'Do you think they accepted my plan? Do you think Hossein will call back with the agreement of his government?'

'I am quite sure they accepted it. You can be very

24

persuasive towards people who want to be convinced.'

'That's part of my strategy, Jicai. I know that deep in the soul of every Iranian military officer there beats the heart of a revolutionary. Oh yes, they would like to make colossal sums of money from a world oil crisis. But what they really want is to strike a violently disruptive blow against the Great Satan, particularly one with the potential to cause widespread chaos in the everyday lives of ordinary Americans.'

'I am afraid you read them accurately, Yushu, and that your plan will take place. The minefield will be laid. But I am very afraid of the consequences. The Americans are likely to turn up in the Gulf with guns blazing, possibly against our own warships, and we are not really a match for them.'

'There you go again, my good Jicai, the immediate crunch, the immediate aftermath. Soon I will ask you to raise your sights. But not quite yet. Not until we are given an affirmative answer by the Iranians. Then all will be revealed to you.'

'I look forward to that immensely, Yushu, but we have been in this room for almost twelve hours now. I think we should go and find some dinner together.'

The two men traveled up in the elevator to the central floor of the Great Hall and an eight-man military escort took them to the main doors, beyond which lay dark, freezing Tiananmen Square. A long black Mercedes, its engine running, awaited them and the guard escort remained in formation until its tires had creaked out across the fresh uncluttered snow, bearing its two high commanders north along the west side of the square, towards the Forbidden City, the old guardian of the Dragon Throne, and still, in the eyes of most Westerners, the symbol of the might of Communist China.

The great portrait of the unforgotten Mao Zedong,

staring out, somehow shy and cold, may not have formed a secret smile through the failing snow as the admirals' Mercedes swept past Tiananmen Gate, but it should have. Mao, above all other men, would have loved Zhang Yushu's as yet unspoken plan.

2100 (local) Same day.
NSA
Fort Meade, Maryland.
Admiral Borden had gone home. A new shift of US surveillance operators was working through the night. Only one member of the day staff was still on duty: Lieutenant Jimmy Ramshawe was in his office, still working, behind closed doors, poring over maps of Asia, pulling up charts on his computer, trying to ascertain where the giant Antonov-124, with its lethal cargo of ship-killing high explosive, could be headed and where, more importantly, it would have to refuel. *Those four big D-18Ts have gotta guzzle up more than ten tons of fuel per hour – which gives it a range of 2600 miles maximum. The bastard's gotta stop somewhere. And it's gotta stop soon.*

Jimmy's thoughts were clear and accurate. He thought the aircraft would have to land around five hours after take-off. Twice he checked with the CIA's Russian desk at Langley, but there was nothing new. Three times he checked with MENA, Fort Meade's Middle East North Africa desk, and they knew nothing either. Lieutenant Ramshawe, however, had a stubborn streak the size of Queensland and he had resolved to sit right here until someone told him precisely where the world's biggest cargo aircraft had landed.

The hour 2200 came and went. Then 2230 and right after that the phone rang, secure line from Langley. No one was telling him where it had landed, but the news was definite. The Antonov had just taken off from a guarded airfield outside the remote central Kazakhstan city of Zhezkazgan. The interesting part was the name of the airfield, Baykonur — top-secret home base of the Russian space program. The CIA had always had a man in there.

'Very nice and quiet, old mate,' muttered Jimmy Ramshawe thoughtfully to the air traffic controller 7000 miles away in central Asia. 'Very nice indeed.' Then he pulled up his computer maps again and tried once more to assess the destination of the 120 sea mines. He checked the routes south-east to India and gazed at the great high-peaked mass of the Himalayas, but in the end there was only one conclusion. The mines were on their way to China. 'And since the bastards only work underwater,' he murmured, 'a mighty intellect like mine would conclude they might be going all the way to the ocean, possibly Shanghai, or maybe one of the Chinese naval bases in the south.'

Either way, he decided, the Antonov would certainly have to be refueled again. But that would probably happen in a remote Chinese military base in the western part of the country. *In which case I'm going home to bed*, he thought. *But twelve hours from now, a little before midday tomorrow here, I'm looking for a report that it's landed on the shores of the China Seas — probably near a naval base. Still, there's no point getting excited since the new bloke I work for wouldn't give a kangaroo's bollocks for my opinions.* He walked, somewhat disconsolately, through the huge main room, the dimly lit National Security Operations Center (NSOC), heading home. Thus Lieutenant Jimmy Ramshawe, like his boss, was sound asleep when the Antonov touched down to refuel in north-west China's remote and forbidden airstrip — the one on the edge of the pitiless Takla Makan Desert, at Lop Nor, home of China's nuclear weapons research and testing facility.

The Takla Makan is China's largest desert, 1200 miles

long, uninhabited for vast areas. Its name means 'the desert one enters, but never leaves'. The Antonov, being Russian, completely ignored that and, one hour after landing, took off again with full tanks, heading south-east for another 1700 miles to the headquarters of Admiral Zu's southern fleet.

Seven weeks later, March 13, 2007.
Southern Fleet Headquarters
Zhanjiang, Province of Guangdong.
The dock lights along the jetties did their best to illuminate the gloomy late evening. But rain from the west swept across the sprawling naval base under low cloud and cold drifting mist. Out on Jetty Five a black Navy staff car, its engine running, headlights on, windshield wipers fighting the downpour, was parked in the shadows. Its two occupants, Admirals Zhang and Zu, were watching the departure of, probably, the first Chinese Blue Water Fleet to leave these shores for a foreign mission beyond home waters, since the treasure-ship voyages of the eunuch Admiral Zheng He in the first half of the fifteenth century.

Back then, the seven epic voyages of Admiral Zheng, across the Indian Ocean, to the Persian Gulf and the coast of Africa, were acclaimed as the highest achievements of the greatest navy the world had ever seen. And it was a great navy. At its zenith there were 3500 ships, 2700 of them warships, based in a network of major navy bases and dockyards along China's eastern coast. Admiral Zheng took over 100 ships and almost 30,000 men to the east coast of Africa, to Kenya, to Arabia, way up into the Red Sea, right into the Gulf, through the Strait of Hormuz, anchoring and trading their silks and porcelain for advanced Arab medicines and the Egyptians' preservative, myrrh. Pearls, gold and jade were taken on board from Siam en route home. Admiral Zheng's own flagship was a massive 400-foot-long nine-master, almost five times the size of Christopher Columbus's *Santa Maria* sixty years later. The Chinese Navy's greatest explorer beat Vasco Da Gama to the coast of East Africa by eighty years and it was just as well they did not arrive at the same time because the massive warships of Admiral Zheng would surely have obliterated the 'tiny' eighty-five-foot-long Portuguese caravels that struggled around the Cape of Good Hope.

Whatever possessed the Ming Dynasty Emperor wilfully to eliminate his mighty fleet a few years later can only be guessed at: China's endless suspicion of foreigners, all foreigners? Its view of itself and its ancient feelings of superiority? Perhaps its own melancholic sense of isolation? It is possible that the death of the immortal Admiral Zheng He, halfway across the Indian Ocean during the final homeward voyage in 1433, may have left a gap in the high command of the Chinese Navy which was just too large to fill. But perhaps the ultimate truth of the amazing decision to ban entirely overseas naval adventures may be found in the words of the young Ming Emperor Zhu Zhanji who presided over many of Zheng's momentous journeys. 'I do not', he once said, 'care for foreign things.'

He was not, of course, referring to sweet crude oil from the vast fields of Kazakhstan.

Now, fast-forward in the long winter of 2007, Admiral Zhang Yushu could not afford to ignore foreign things and he was about to reverse almost 580 years of Chinese naval policy: policy from which that huge nation had not departed. Not until World War I were the giant battle fleets of the Ming emperors matched either in size or relative firepower by any of the world's great powers.

Zhang Yushu stared through the windshield of the Navy car, watching them cast off the lines of the 1700-ton guided-missile frigate *Shantou*, a warship which would have been dwarfed by Zheng He's *Pure Harmony*. 'She's going, Jicai, and it's an historic moment in the long records of our sea power. Just think of it, that little Jianghu Type 053 frigate is steaming off in the wake of our ancestors of 500 years ago. The same old sea lanes, from the most glorious days of our history, just like the Silk Road. They're going back as the main power in the Persian Gulf, in a sense to conquer the trading world all over again.'

'I'm not sure the Americans would be appreciative of your phrasing, Yushu. They think they have rights to the Gulf and its waters any time they see fit.'

'Ah, yes. So they might. But remember, we were there as welcome guests and trading partners with the Arabs half a millennium ago and longer. Remember too, in recent years Chinese porcelain from the Ming dynasty has been discovered along the shores of Hormuz. We have long historic roots in that area *and* the Persians want us back to help them in the struggle against the West. Oh yes, Jicai. We belong in those ancient waters of our forefathers.'

'And we're taking a lot of high explosive to prove it, eh, Yushu?'

Shantou eased out into the main channel, the driving rain gleaming on her big surface-to-surface guided-missile launchers. Her six twin 37mm gunhouses stood stark against the shore lights. Her five-tubed fixed anti-submarine mortar launchers could still be seen through the rain squalls. What could not be seen, however, were the principal weapons of her forthcoming voyage, the sixty Russian-made sea mines, secluded under heavy tarpaulin from the prying eye of the American satellite which had passed overhead two hours previously.

Out on the pitch-black horizon, there waited *Shantou*'s two Shanghai-built sister ships, *Kangding* and *Zigong*. They were in company with the first of China's new $400-million Russian destroyers, the 8000-ton, 500-foot-long Sovremenny Class *Hangzhou*, with its supersonic guided missile, the Raduga SS-N-22 Sunburn. But the *Hangzhou* was not there to engage in surface-to-surface warfare. Her mission was strictly clandestine. She would lead her three frigates on the 6000-mile journey to Hormuz, essentially to carry forty more mines, but also because in the event of a confrontation she was best equipped to fight the little fleet out of trouble – though she would be no match for a determined US commanding officer in a big cruiser.

Their voyage would take them down the South China Sea, up through the Malacca Strait into the Bay of Bengal, where they would immediately rendezvous with the 37,000-ton Chinese tanker *Nancang*, operating out of their new naval base on Haing Gyi Island, at the mouth of Burma's Bassein river, across the wide, flat rice-growing delta west of Rangoon.

Haing Gyi Island had caused many a sleepless night for the American President's National Security Adviser Admiral Morgan, who was suspicious of Chinese motives at the best of times. The creation of a big Chinese fueling base and naval dockyard in Burmese national home waters sent a shiver right through him. Particularly since the Chinese had constructed a railroad from Kunming, the 2000-year-old capital of Yunnan Province, straight across the Burmese border to the railhead city of Lashio, from where heavy military hardware could easily join the rest of the $1.4 billions' worth of weaponry China had already shipped into Burma.

Back on the rainswept dock at Zhangjiang, Admiral Zhang pulled his greatcoat around him and stepped out to watch the *Shantou* heading out towards the black shape of the harbor wall and beyond to the South China Sea. 'Don't you get a thrill from this, Jicai? Just seeing our great modern Blue Water Navy moving into action on this dark night, bound for a major foreign adventure, the first for more than 500 years?'

'I suppose so, Yushu. I'll let you know more when we discover how seriously infuriated the Americans are by the exercise.'

But even the wise and experienced Jicai looked quizzical at the non sequitur which served as a reply from his lifelong friend. 'A mere diversion, my Jicai. The merest diversion.'

1200 (local) March 13.
The White House, Washington DC.
'Now where the hell are they going?' demanded Admiral Morgan, staring at the grainy, poor-quality satellite photographs taken through the rain clouds above the Chinese coast. 'Looks like three frigates and a Sovremenny destroyer, going south. What the hell for and how far? And who the hell's going to refuel 'em? Answer that.'

'I'm afraid I'm not really qualified to do that,' said Kathy O'Brien sweetly.

'Well you ought to be. Ought to be general knowledge for anyone in Washington.'

'Oh, I hadn't realized.'

'How far do you think they're going, then?'

'How could I possibly know?'

'I know you don't know. I'm just asking for guidance. Is that too much? What I'm interested in is whether they are going on a long voyage, maybe to visit their friends in Iran, and if they are, those frigates are gonna get refueled from that damned new base of theirs on that frigging Burmese island.'

'Which Burmese island?'

'Haing Gyi Island, their first serious naval base of operations outside of China – *ever*,' the Admiral thundered. 'Right now we're returning to the goddamned fifteenth century when their fleets dominated the Indian Ocean and the Persian Gulf. And another thing,' he yelled. 'What the hell happened to all those sea mines from Russia, the ones we saw getting unloaded at Zhanjiang? Where the hell are they and why isn't anyone keeping me up to speed on this? Where the hell's George Morris?'

'As you well know, my darling, he has cancer of his right lung.'

'Serves him right for smoking so much,' grunted the Admiral, puffing away on his cigar. 'Where is he right now?'

'He's undergoing intensive chemotherapy, as you also well know. Since that awful treatment has been making him extremely ill, I imagine he's asleep.'

'Well, have someone wake him up.'

'Honey, please.' The best-looking redhead in Washington sighed.

Two weeks later, March 27.
Fort Meade, Maryland.
Lieutenant Ramshawe was sifting methodically through a pile of satellite photographs. He had singled out a dozen shots and he was trying to fit them together into a montage, trying to see if the three submarines were actually forming some kind of a small convoy out there in the Arabian Sea. He had a couple of VLCCs (giant tankers, very large crude carriers) in focus to help him and the conclusion he reached was the submarines were all together, moving on the calm blue surface about a mile apart, heading north. More important, they were Russian Kilo Class boats, the deadly little diesel–electric attack submarine, currently being exported by the old Soviet Navy to anyone with a big enough checkbook to buy, especially the Chinese, the Indians and the Iranians.

Lieutenant Ramshawe was in the process of identifying the nationality of these particular ships and was more or less certain that he had located all three of Iran's Kilos, one in Bandar Abbas, two in their submarine base at Chah Bahar, outside the Gulf on the north shore of the Gulf of Oman. So far as he could tell, the Indians had no submarines at sea, which meant almost certainly that the three Kilos were Chinese and they were headed directly to Chah Bahar. This was mildly unusual but not earth-shattering. Chinese warships were no longer rare in the Indian Ocean and the Arabian Sea. They were occasional visitors to the Gulf of Hormuz and just today there were new satellite pictures of a four-ship Chinese flotilla, including their big Sovremenny destroyer, heading across the Bay of Bengal towards the southern headland of the Indian continent. *Wouldn't be that surprised if the whole bloody lot of 'em were going up to Hormuz*, pondered Jimmy. *What with that new refinery and Christ knows what else up there.*

Lieutenant Ramshawe was thoughtful. The four surface ships had been steaming very publicly all the way from the South China Sea. 'No worries,' he muttered. But the Kilos had been much more secretive. No one had spotted them since they had left their base, because they'd mostly been deep, only snorkelling for short periods. But here they were now, large as life, making their way up to their close friends on the southernmost Iranian coast.

'That's seven Chinese vessels, possibly going in the same bloody direction to the same bloody place,' murmured the Lieutenant, reaching for the latest edition of *Jane's Fighting Ships*, the bible of the world's navies. *Now let me have a look here, right. Jianghu frigates. They can hold sixty sea mines apiece and that destroyer has rails for forty more. Now, how about the Kilos? What's it say here? They can carry twenty-four torpedoes or twenty-four mines, not both. So if those little bastards were carrying mines, that'd be seventy-two, plus the 220 in the surface ships. That's close to 300. My oath, you could cause a lot of trouble with that little lot.*

The Lieutenant knew he was just trying to connect two separate mysteries. The first, *what the bloody hell happened to all those sea mines which ended up in Zhanjiang?* Second, *what the hell are all these bloody Chinese warships doing in the Indian and Arabian seas?* He had, of course, not the slightest shred of evidence that there was one single solitary mine on board any of the ships. Certainly nothing that showed on the satellite photos, except for the big covers. But still he considered it his duty to alert his immediate superior, Admiral Borden, as to the possibility, even if it did mean rejection. So he drafted a short memorandum and sent it in.

Fifteen minutes later he was summoned to the Acting Director's office, knocked firmly on the door and waited to be instructed to enter.

'Lieutenant, I appreciate your diligence in these matters, but I heard earlier this morning from Langley that the Iranians are staging some kind of a forty-eight hour military hooley with the Chinese Navy down there in Bandar Abbas. Bands, parades, red-carpets, dinners, speeches, television, the whole nine yards. Apparently the surface ships are scheduled to arrive there next Monday. So I'm very afraid your theory of a large traveling minefield is out. Thank you for your efforts, though, but do remember, I did warn you to forget about it. If someone's laying a minefield, we'll see them . . . all in good time. That's all.'

'Sir,' said Lieutenant Ramshawe, making his exit, muttering, 'Supercilious prick. Serve him right if the bloody hooley was just a cover-up and the entire US tanker fleet was blown up.'

2015 *Tuesday, April 3.*
Navy Base, Bandar Abbas.
The festivities were over for the evening. The last of the

Iranian public were driving home out of the dockyard and the great arc lights which had floodlit the magnificent parade were finally switched off. The huge fluttering national standards of the Islamic State of Iran and the People's Republic of China had been lowered. A sixty-strong Guard of Honor from the People's Liberation Army, resplendent in their olive-green dress uniforms and hard flat-top caps with the wide red band, were retiring back to their quarters in the *Hangzhou*. The lines of electric bulbs which had floodlit the masts and upper works of both nations' warships were methodically being extinguished. But as yet no air of calm had settled over the fleet. They were running down the flags, but turbines were humming, senior officers were on the bridge, lines were being cast off. It was a curious time to arrange a night exercise after such an exhausting day of preparation and celebration. But that, ostensibly, was precisely what was happening.

The three Chinese frigates were already moving, slowly, line-astern, led by *Shantou*, out through the naval basin into the main channel, now dredged to a low-tide depth of thirty-three feet. Thirty minutes later China's 6000-ton Sovremenny class destroyer, the largest ship ever to enter this harbor, was escorted out by two ninety-foot harbour tugs, the *Arvand* and the *Hangam*. Astern of the destroyer a 900-ton twin-shafted Iranian Navy corvette, the *Bayandor*, almost forty years old, originally built in Texas, followed, still flying the green, white and red national flag despite the late hour of the evening. Her sister ship, *Naghdi*, also armed with modern Bofors and Oerlikon guns, awaited the flotilla one mile south-east of the harbor, ready to guide them round the long shallow outer reaches of the shelving Bostanu east bank.

Their sixty-five-mile journey would take them past the great sand-swept island of Qeshm and on into the deeper waters of the Hormuz Strait. Forty miles further on, east of

36

the jutting Omani headland of Ra's Qabr al Hindi, they would make their rendezvous, at 26.19N 56.40E. Admiral Mohammed Badr himself was on the bridge of the *Hangzhou*, accompanying the Chinese Commanding Officer, Weidong Gao, who like all Chinese Navy COs was a three-star Colonel. Under clear skies they pushed on south-east through light swells and a warm twenty-knot breeze out of the west. Finally at 56.40E Colonel Weidong ordered a course change to one-eight-zero, and running over sandy depths of around 300 feet they headed due south for the final six miles. Gradually the little flotilla reduced speed until the sonar room of the big destroyer picked up the unmissable signal of the Chinese Kilos, patrolling silently at periscope depth in the pitch-dark waters off the jagged coast of Oman.

The plan had been fine-honed several weeks before. The Kilos would take the southerly six miles of the designated area where the water was now 360 feet deep. Each of the three submarines would make a course of zero-nine-eight, starting from the deep trough off Ra's Qabr al Hindi. They would thus move easterly a half-mile apart, launching out of their torpedo tubes a one-ton Russian-made PLT-3 contact sea mine every 500 yards – the ones made at the Rosvoorouzhenie factory in Moscow: the same ones which had so vexed young Jimmy Ramshawe on their top-secret journey all the way across Asia to the South China Sea.

At the conclusion of these three death-trapped parallel lines, six miles long, the minefield would make a ten-degree swing north, and then run for twenty-four miles dead straight, all the way across the Strait of Hormuz to the inshore waters of the Iranian coastline, at a point twenty-nine miles due south of the new Sino-Iranian refinery outside the little town of Kuhestak.

And right now the three Chinese mine-laying frigates

were moving into position. *Shantou, Kangding* and *Zigong*, a half-mile apart, heading east-nor'east, slowly in the darkness, the soft thrum of their big diesel engines interrupted only by the splash, every 500 yards, as they sowed their treacherous seed in a barrier across the world's most important oil sea lanes. The sixty mines on board each frigate would string out for seventeen miles. The final coastal area would be handled by the destroyer and they would designate a sizeable three-mile gap through which Chinese and Iranian tankers could pass, principally because they would be the only tankers informed of the position of the safe passage.

Meanwhile the newly laid mines sat at the bottom of the ocean secure on their anchors, awaiting the moment they would be activated electronically, released on their wires to rise up towards the surface and then hang there in the water, twelve feet below the waves, until an unsuspecting tankerman came barreling along and slammed it out of the way, obliterating his ship in the process.

It was a two-and-a-half-hour journey back to Bandar Abbas and the surface convoy set off at 0400, leaving the Kilos to make their own way back to Chah Bahar, running at PD. There was time to spare because the big US satellite did not pass overhead until 0800.

The frigates and their 6000-ton bodyguard docked in Bandar Abbas at 0630, when the next stage of Admiral Zhang's plan went into operation. The *Hangzhou* was immediately reloaded with forty PLT-3 contact mines, plainly visible, as her original cargo had been the previous evening. When 'Big Bird' took her photographs a few minutes after 0800, the fully laden Chinese destroyer would look precisely the same as she had on the last daylight satellite pass, just before the grand parade yesterday evening. The signal back to Zhangjiang was as agreed, in the event of a successful mission: DRAGONFLY.

1130 (local) Tuesday, April 3.
Fort Meade, Maryland.

There is an irritating eight-and-a-half-hour time difference between the east coast of America and Iran. This is
caused by a time zone which runs bang through the
middle of the country near Tehran. Instead of one half of
the nation being four hours in front of GMT and the other
half only three, they compromised and put the whole place
three and a half hours ahead of London, which is, of
course, five in front of New York. Thus satellite pictures
taken at 1930 (Iran) were shot at 1100 (Fort Meade) on the
same day. And this particular set of pictures of Bandar
Abbas Dockyard landed on Lieutenant Ramshawe's desk
just as he arrived a half-hour early for work.

Before him, in sharp focus, was the major event
Admiral Borden had mentioned. Jimmy could see civilian
cars parked in the dockyard with the joint Sino-Iranian
fleet lit up brightly in the gathering darkness for the public
to view. He guessed he would receive new pictures,
intermittently, throughout the day, showing more or less
what was happening in Iran's navy headquarters. Still
allowing the issue of the Russian mines to burn away at the
back of his brain, Lieutenant Ramshawe searched the
decks of the Chinese frigates under a powerful glass to see
if there was a sign of them. But there was none. Not so the
destroyer. All forty of the mines she carried could now be
seen on her rails, though they had plainly been covered
during her journey from China.

A new set of pictures arrived mid-afternoon, which
actually caught the little fleet on the move. It was very
dark in the Gulf now and the photographs were not of the
same quality. But this hardly mattered. What did matter
was the sight of three Chinese frigates, one destroyer and
two Iranian corvettes heading off on a mission in the
middle of the night. For all he knew they were off to attack

Iraq or Oman, 'or some other godforsaken place', and Jimmy Ramshawe hit the button to the Director's office, from where he was given his usual short shrift.

'I wouldn't worry about it, Lieutenant, if I were you. They're probably going to conduct a night exercise together. Not unusual at one of these international junkets between two navies.'

'Yes, sir. But I can see a full load of mines on the destroyer.'

'I expect they'll still be there in the morning, Lieutenant. That's all.'

Jimmy Ramshawe put the phone down slowly. The same question he had asked himself a thousand times popped into his mind: *Why had the Chinese plainly ordered an extremely expensive consignment of specialist contact mines from Russia if they weren't planning to lay out a bloody minefield somewhere?* He also considered it a slice of blind luck that the Andropov freighter had been spotted taking off from Moscow and then again at secretive Baykonur. No one ever traced its second refueling stop and in Lieutenant Ramshawe's opinion it was entirely possible there had been a second trans-Asian flight of the giant aircraft. That would have brought the total mines carried to 240, sufficient to fill all four surface ships with their combined quota of 220. He had not given the three Kilos much thought since they had not been seen for a few days. But he could not get those mines out of his mind.

It was all very well Admiral Boredom saying it was best to forget the whole thing until something more definite emerged, but, streuth! What if those crazy bastards were out there right now planting a minefield in the middle of the Strait? What then? Lieutenant Ramshawe wandered off in search of a cup of coffee, reasoning to himself that if the satellite pass was made at 0800 over Bandar Abbas, which he knew for certain, then he might see some good pictures of the ships back in harbor some time after midnight Fort Meade time. Anyway, he was going nowhere until he had seen those pictures. And he knew this was a state of affairs guaranteed not to thrill his girlfriend, the dark-haired Jane Peacock, daughter of the Australian ambassador to Washington. The Peacocks and the Ramshawes were lifelong friends, and it was widely assumed that Jimmy and Jane would ultimately marry.

Right now he looked forward to telephoning Jane even less than he dreaded calling his boss. *The pair of them could probably run a contest to see who could give me the hardest bloody time.*

He was right too. 'Jimmy, for crying out loud, why this sudden interest in an Arab Navy?'

'They're not Arabs,' he corrected her. 'They're Persian. That's different.'

'*I don't care if they're bloody martians,*' she yelled. 'We were supposed to have supper with Julie in Georgetown and you're hopeless. I'm not going by myself.'

'Janie, listen, I believe this is really important. Like maybe a life-and-death matter.'

'Well, there must be more important people than you to deal with it?'

'There isn't anyone more important than me who even believes it, never mind wants to deal with it.'

'Well, leave it alone, then, until someone instructs you to do something.'

'I can't, Janie. I have to stay. But I'll pick you up early tomorrow and we'll have breakfast before you go to your class – I'm free till 11.30, same time you have to be in Georgetown.'

'Okay,' she grumbled. 'Nine at the embassy, but you're still a bloody nightmare. Even your own mother thinks that.'

Jimmy chuckled. He adored his beautiful, clever fiancée

and he hated letting her down. But in his own mind he alone stood between world order and possible world chaos. *Well, something like that. I just don't trust the bastards. That's all.*

The night passed slowly and he spent the hours before midnight reading a book about international terrorism, a fundamentally depressing read, citing samples of inordinate stupidity by the Intelligence Services of various Western governments. *Jesus, a whole lot of this crap could have been avoided if people were just that little bit sharper. Even at the business end of the Intelligence game there are still people more intent on protecting their own jobs rather than concentrating on getting it right at all costs.* Jimmy Ramshawe was still young enough to own those ideals. Just. But he would not want to work too long for a conservative cynic like David Borden, whose pension beckoned and who preferred to pass the buck rather than start a high-profile scare over nothing.

Midnight came and went. It was a half-hour since the morning satellite shots had been taken again, high above the harbor of Bandar Abbas. Nothing arrived until 0040, and the young Lieutenant shuffled the new photos from the National Reconnaissance Office, searching for a shot of the Chinese destroyer. And here it was: fully laden with its mines, just as it had been before the midnight naval exercises in the Gulf. The frigates too were back on their Iranian jetties, the tarpaulins which covered their cargo still in place. There were also the standard daily shots of Chah Bahar and they showed empty spaces where the three Chinese Kilos had been last Saturday night. 'Christ knows where they are,' muttered Jimmy.

He picked up his jacket and made his way out of the office, walking through the main doors of the building and across to the dimly lit parking lot where two Marine guards saluted him. He climbed into the driver's seat and drove to the main gates, showed his pass to the duty guards and gunned his ten-year-old black Jaguar out to the exit road and on down to the Washington-Baltimore Parkway. It was a fast ride at this time of night and he let the speedometer hover around 75 as he cruised down to the Beltway for the ten-mile run to exit 33, Connecticut Avenue, which would take him straight into the center of the capital. He made a right at Dupont Circle, skirted the campus of George Washington University and ran on down to the Watergate complex where his parents had owned an apartment for the better part of thirty years. Naturally they rarely, if ever, used it, since they lived mostly in New York. Which was excellent news for Jimmy who thus had a millionaire's residence for free.

He drove into his underground parking space and turned off the engine. It was nearly 2 a.m. and he was almost too tired to get out of the car. But he still wished Jane could have been there waiting for him. He thought again of how much easier life had been when Admiral George Morris had been in charge at the NSA.

The thing about George was he was damned confident and he had the ear of the Big Man in the White House. No one was closer to Arnold Morgan than George and the two of them always consulted. Admiral Morris was thus a fabulous guy to work for. He always listened. He invariably weighed up all the eventualities and all the possibilities, never tried to second-guess his staff. He worked on the theory that if one of his chosen men thought something should be investigated then that was probably correct. Not like this bloody Boredom character.

Jimmy sat there in the driver's seat for a moment, pondering his dreary task tomorrow when he had to talk to Admiral Borden and admit the Chinese destroyer was still fully laden with her sea mines, as she had been the previous night. He could hear the world-weary old bastard right now: *Well, Lieutenant, what a great surprise that must be to you, but don't say I didn't warn you.*

'Just as long as he doesn't tempt me to tell him another unlikely truth,' muttered Jimmy to himself. 'That the bloody morning mines might be different from those we saw last night. He'll say that's bollocks, probably paranoid bollocks. But it isn't. Because that's what I'd do myself if I wanted to lay a minefield in the Strait of Hormuz.' He climbed out of the car and locked it. Wandering over to the elevator, he was still muttering, 'Replace the mines on deck before the 0800 satellite pass, right? Put the stupid Americans off the trail.'

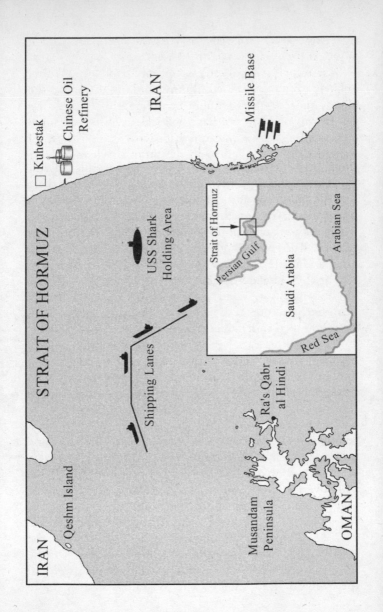

Two

On Saturday morning, April 7, at first light, the Chinese warships sailed, apparently for home. At least two of them did, the *Hangzhou* and the *Shantou*. The other two stayed where they were on the jetties in Bandar Abbas harbor. Three hours later, shortly before 0950 (local), the three Chinese Kilos pushed out of Chah Bahar into the Hormuz Strait and made their way south towards the Arabian Sea.

The US satellites picked up the entire scenario on bright, sunlit waters and, back in Fort Meade, Lieutenant Ramshawe wrote a short memorandum to the NSA's Acting Director, detailing the ship movements.

Two days later a report came in from the Middle Eastern desk at Langley that Iran was moving heavy Sunburn missiles, plus launchers, plus anti-aircraft artillery, to a point along their south-eastern coast on the Gulf of Oman. Langley's man did not know precisely where the hardware was headed, but Fort Meade made a slight adjustment in the satellite's photographic direction and from way up in the stratosphere the massive US camera snapped off two shots of the big Sunburns being maneuvered into position facing out to sea, twenty-nine miles south of the coastal town of Kuhestak.

Lieutenant Ramshawe marked up his wide chart, 26.23N 57.05E. He automatically glanced across to see the nearest point of land, but there really was nothing. If the missiles were fired westerly at ninety degrees to the coast, they would head straight out to sea. A slightly more southerly course would aim them at the northern headland of the Iranians' friends, the Omanis. That headland, the outermost point of the barren Musandam peninsula, scarcely had a town or a village on it. The only name marked on Jimmy Ramshawe's chart, way out on the jutting eastern coast, was Ra's Qabr al Hindi. 'Christ,' he muttered. 'What kind of a bloody name's that? Imagine coming from there and traveling to the States: *Er, place of residence, sir? Ra's Qabr al Hindi.* Jeez, they'd probably lock you up on principle!'

In any event, the Lieutenant drafted a report confirming they now had a firm position for the Iranian missiles. Then he returned to his consistent preoccupation, the two remaining Chinese warships in Bandar Abbas, the *Kangding* and the *Zigong*. The photographs which had just arrived showed both ships now flying Iran's national flag. Jimmy Ramshawe stared at them for a long time. *What if they had laid a secret minefield somewhere out there last week? What if the two frigates had been left behind in readiness to go out and activate the mines?* He knew that such a theory would be ridiculed by Admiral Borden, who had, of course, ridiculed his every thought about the mines and, thus far, had been proved right. Nonetheless, Lieutenant Ramshawe elected to go and see his leader and present his worst fears.

The veteran Admiral smiled, with a jaded, indulgent air. 'James,' he said. 'May I call you James?'

'Jimmy, sir, actually. No one's ever called me James. I'd think you were talking to someone else.'

The Admiral blinked at the Australian's forthrightness, which always caught him off-guard. 'Right, Jimmy. Now listen to me. Do you know why the two frigates are now flying the flag of Iran?'

'Not really, sir. But it could be some kind of a Chinese cover-up, while they're getting ready either to lay mines or activate them.'

'No, Jimmy,' said Borden with heavy emphasis. 'That is not the reason. They are flying the Iranian flag because Iran has just bought the two Chinese frigates. That was the objective of the big dockyard junket. It was a Chinese sales tour. You don't think they'd come all that way for nothing, do you? Not the Chinese. They like money a lot more than they like anything else. It was a goodwill sales visit. No doubt in my mind. They conducted a fleet exercise together, exchanged information and at the conclusion of the festivities Iran agreed to purchase the two ships. The first two guided-missile frigates they've ever owned.'

'Well, sir, if that's your opinion, I'll have to agree.'

'Do you have a different opinion?'

'Well, sir. I have been wondering about the mines and I'm still not sure the Chinese haven't made some kind of a devious move with a view to laying them.'

'Ah, that's your prerogative as an Intelligence officer, Jimmy. But it's been your prerogative for weeks, months, and nothing has happened, as I told you it wouldn't.'

'Righto, boss. I'll buy that. Maybe they did just want to store up some Russian mines for some future mission. Anyway, if you're right, they just paid for them with the frigate money. Good on 'em, right?'

The Admiral smiled. 'You're learning, Jimmy. In this business it's very easy to spend your life chasing your tail, seeing spooks, plots and schemes around every corner. Just stay focused and keep a weather eye out for the really big stuff, when you've got genuine evidence. That's all.'

The young Lieutenant left, returning to his office and gazing once more at his wide marked chart of the Strait of Hormuz. He stared at it for several minutes and muttered to himself, 'I just wonder what's sitting down there on the seabed, right offshore of those new missile placements.'

Two weeks later, April 24.
China's Southern Fleet HQ, Zhanjiang.
Admiral Zu Jicai, now C-in-C of the entire Navy, was back in his old office and he opened up the secure line to Beijing, waiting quietly for Zhang Yushu to come to the phone. When the great man finally spoke down the line from the Chinese capital, the conversation was unusually brief for two such old friends. 'Nothing on any foreign networks re DRAGONFLY.'

'No suspicion anywhere?'

'None. Shall I activate the field in the next two days?'

'Affirmative.'

'Goodbye, sir.'

'Goodbye, Jicai.'

Three days later, April 27.
The Strait of Hormuz.
Hardly a ripple disturbed the flat blue calm of the southern waters of the Strait. It was one of those sultry Arabian mornings, in which the livid heat of the desert sun makes life on land almost unbearable and life on board any ship not a whole lot better.

Six miles north-east of the Musandam peninsula the waters were almost oily to look at, as the tide began to turn inwards from the Arabian Sea. There was no ocean swell, no little eddying cat's paws on the surface, no movement in the hot, still air. But ripples were on the way. Giant ripples, from the big white bow wave of the 80,000-ton black-hulled gas carrier, *Global Bronco*, making a stately eighteen knots, south-easterly through the water. The 900-foot carrier was laden down with 135,000 cubic meters of liquified natural gas, frozen to *minus* 160 degrees centigrade. In more comprehensive stats, that's 3,645,000 cubic feet, or a 100-foot-high building, 200 feet long by 200 feet wide. Which is a lot of frozen gas and it forms, by general consensus, the most potentially lethal cargo on all the world's oceans.

Unlike crude oil, which does not instantly combust, liquid natural gas is hugely volatile, compressed, as it is, 600 times from normal gas. Tanker corporations are near paranoid about safety regulations for its transportation around the world. Layer upon layer of fail-safe back-up systems are built into every LNG carrier. They are not the biggest tankers on the ocean, but then neither is the nuclear-headed torpedo the biggest bomb. In any event, the worldwide industry of transporting liquid gas has never once suffered a fire, never mind an explosion.

Up on the bridge, almost 100 feet above the water, the obsessively careful Commodore Don McGhee stared out over the four gigantic bronze-colored holding domes, which each rose sixty feet above the scarlet-painted deck. The bow of the *Global Bronco* was nearly 300 yards in front of him and the veteran Master from the south-east Texas gulf port of Houston had a view straight down the massive gantry, which ran as a steel catwalk clean across the top of each dome, all the way down to the foredeck.

Right now the ship was making its way well outside the Omani inshore traffic zone, with the local Navy's firing practice area ten miles astern. Ahead of them was the narrowest part of the Hormuz Strait and in this clear weather they would see plainly the Omani headlands of Jazirat Musandam and, two miles further south, Ra's Qabr al Hindi. They were too far away to catch a glimpse on the horizon of the glowering shores of Iran on the eastern side of the crescent-shaped thirty-mile-wide seaway.

Commodore McGhee was in conference with Chief Engineer Andre Waugh. And up ahead of them they could still see a gigantic Liberian-registered British tanker, a 300,000-ton VLCC bound for the North Atlantic. They had been catching her slowly all the way down from the new gas-loading terminal off Qatar, right around the Emirates peninsula, past Abu Dhabi and Dubai, and now they were less than fifty miles from the open waters of the Arabian Sea. All tanker captains were glad to get out of the Gulf and McGhee was no exception. There was always a menace about patrolling Iranian warships, a menace compounded in the past few months by yet another Iranian militant threat to lay a minefield directly off its coast at the choke point of the entrance.

Both tanker officers knew there had been for several weeks a worldwide unease about China's warships currently parked in the Ayatollah's navy base at Bandar Abbas. They knew also of the tensions caused by the opening of the brand-new Sino-Iranian refinery at the end of the Chinese-built pipeline, which ran 1000 miles out of the Kazakhstan oil fields, across Turkmenistan and clean through the sweltering Iranian desert to the coast. Everyone in the Western oil business knew this pipeline gave China something close to a 'lock' on the second-largest easy-access oil deposits on earth.

One more threat by Iran's increasingly noisy anti-West politicians to bottle up the entrance to the Gulf would probably send the Pentagon into a collective dance of death. It was all politics, threat and counter threat, but to men like Commodore McGhee, masters of the big crude-oil and gas carriers working the north end of the Arabian Sea those politics had an edge of grim reality. 'This darned place always gives me the creeps,' he said. 'I'll just be glad to make the open ocean.'

'I know what you mean,' replied Chief Andre Waugh. 'So do the British by the look of it. That's a Royal Navy helicopter up ahead, checking that big tanker out of the area. Right now they're checking every British ship in and out of the Gulf. Guess they don't like the political situation, right?'

No ships in the entire history of navigation have been more political than the big tankers, upon whose safe passage half the world depends in order to keep moving. The fate and prosperity of nations literally hangs in the balance as these great leviathans carry the principal source of world energy from where it is to where it is needed.

Commodore McGhee, a tankerman for thirty years, had never once entered Iranian waters, always keeping well over on the Omani side. Back home in Texas, in the Houston control room, on the thirty-second floor of the Travis Street headquarters of Texas Global Ships Inc., Robert J. Heseltine III, the President, had issued specific instructions: stay well clear of the ayatollahs and their navy. Don McGhee did not need reminding.

Texas Global ran six ships, but *Global Bronco* was the only LNG carrier. Heseltine was right proud of his Texan roots and he had named the other five ships *Global Star*, *Global Rose*, *Global Brand*, *Global Steer* and *Global Range*. They were all 300,000-ton VLCCs, which normally plied between the Gulf of Iran, southern Africa, the north-east tanker ports of the USA and Europe. *Bronco* usually worked in the east, steaming between the gas-rich Gulf ports of Qatar and Abu Dhabi, and Tokyo Bay, where Japanese Electric unloads millions of cubic meters of natural gas every week. This particular voyage, however, was shorter, just as far as the southern Taiwan port of Yungan. The massive liquid gas cargo would be used almost exclusively for electric power generation.

Robert J. Heseltine III had not laid eyes on one of his ships for three years and probably wouldn't for another three years. Giant tankers cost $100,000 a day to operate and they have to keep working, roaming the world picking up cargo and unloading it. There never was a reason for any of the ships to return to home base in Texas, and both crew and supplies were ferried out to them by commercial airlines, then by helicopter, while the great energy ships kept right on moving, thousands of miles from home. No merchantman since the days of sail – indeed, since the clipper ships – had ever undertaken such vast and endless transworld journeys.

Commodore McGhee was now traveling a couple of knots faster than the VLCC up ahead and he positioned himself accordingly, preparing to run past, a half-mile off the tanker's port beam, a couple of hours from now. The sun beat down on the scarlet deck as the *Global Bronco* crossed the 26.20-degree line of latitude right on 56.38N. They were eight miles off Ra's Qabr al Hindi and the Captain could just make out the headland through his glasses. He ordered a steward to bring him up a cup of coffee and a ham-and-cheese sandwich, and the 80,000-tonner ran on due south for another mile.

It was 12.10 p.m. precisely, in glaring sunshine on a still calm sea, when the *Global Bronco* nudged into Admiral Zhang Yushu's Russian PLT-3 contact mine. The one-ton steel container of compressed high explosive, riding high on its anchor line, detonated with savage force. The massive forward inertia of the ship carried her on for just a few yards before the echoing underwater blast blew a huge hole in her hull, starboard side of the keel, right behind the bow. All the for'ard plates along the starboard side buckled back with a tearing of metal, showering a hailstorm of sparks inside the hull. The for'ard liquid gas tank, reinforced aluminium, held, then ruptured and nearly 20,000 tons of one of the world's most volatile liquid gases, its content bolstered by both methane and propane, began to flood out of its refrigerated environment. It hit an atmosphere almost 200 degrees centigrade warmer and it flashed instantly into vaporized gas, exploding with a deafening WHOOSH!

The destruction to the entire front section of the ship

was staggering. The sheer volume of LNG contained in the vast holding tanks of the *Global Bronco* caused a monumental blast and the blast from Tank Four somehow smashed a hole in Tank Three, and seconds later the 20,000 tons of liquid fuel in there also blew. The great ship shuddered. Flames leapt a hundred feet into the sky. Against all odds, Tanks Two and One held. But thousands of tons of fuel from the for'ard tanks poured through the fractured hull plates on the smashed starboard side of the ship below the waterline and into the waters of the Hormuz Strait, rising rapidly to the surface.

Commodore McGhee and his Chief Engineer were still on the bridge, almost in shock at what they had seen erupt 250 yards in front of them. Heat from the for'ard inferno was already melting the metal. They could see the white-hot bow end of the high gantry sagging like strips of putty. But the still powerful forward motion of the *Bronco* was allowing her to leave a wide, unexploded slip-stream lake of liquid gas in the water, which was evaporating at a diabolical rate, rising up off it.

Don McGhee realized the danger. The gas, decompressed and now in contact with the atmosphere, would evaporate over a relatively short period of time. But the danger of ignition was paramount. Miraculously, the great diesel engines were still running and the Captain ordered 'ALL STOP!'. The bow of the ship was now dipping deep and the fires were reducing. The glowing-hot foredeck sent clouds of steam into the air as the waters of the Strait washed over. But the gas continued to gush into the ocean, twenty feet below the surface. Don McGhee did not think his strongly compartmentalized ship would go down and he did think the fires would reduce as the bow went lower. It was the unseen gas cloud he knew was rising rapidly up off the surface which worried him. Both he and Andre Waugh could smell it, light and carbonized on the air.

Members of the crew were racing towards the bridge, terrified, uncertain what to do. Astonishingly, no one had been for'ard at the time the ship hit and no one was hurt. The problem was how to get off. There was no chance of jumping over the side into the toxic lake of liquid gas and Commodore McGhee knew it would be lethal for a helicopter to try to reach them, since a tiny spark from the engine could ignite the gas cloud into a mountainous pillar of fire, which would climb thousands of feet into the air, the heat almost certainly vaporizing the ship and the final two 20,000-ton tanks of liquid gas.

The roar of the for'ard fire way down the deck was like a fifty-foot-high gas cooker blasting out blue flame, too loud, too intimidating to allow any question of trying to control it. Commodore McGhee ordered: 'ABANDON SHIP! MAN THE LIFEBOATS PORT SIDE.' The crew charged off the bridge. The radio operator shouted, 'I'll transmit a "MAYDAY" before we go.' The rest of them made for the three big orange Zodiacs moored on their davits along the deck rails.

Then Commodore McGhee saw it – the Royal Navy's helicopter clattering towards them, low over the surface, totally unaware of the gas cloud rising up along the *Bronco*'s aft starboard side and stern. The tanker's Master ordered his radio operator to open up the VHF on 16 and stop the chopper's advance at all costs. Then he opened the door to the viewing catwalk, a white walkway jutting over the main deck. He raced out on to it, jumping up and down, waving his arms, yelling to the pilot at the top of his lungs in futile desperation: 'STOP. FOR GOD'S SAKE STOP. PLEASE STOP. TURN AROUND!'

Inside the helicopter both the pilot and his navigator saw the Captain's frenzied signal. The navigator just had time to say, 'Take a turn to the left here. This guy's waving us off. I'll try the radio.' But it was too late. The Royal

Navy's Sea King Mk 4, making just over sixty knots, flew bang into the middle of the rising gas cloud, which ignited like a nuclear bomb, causing a gigantic blowtorch to rear up off the surface of the water, roaring a black, scarlet and blue tower of fire 5000 feet into the air.

The Navy helicopter was incinerated instantly. The *Global Bronco* and her crew perished in a split second, when the entire after end of the ship was enveloped by the searing near 2000-degree-centigrade petrochemical blaze. Two minutes later there was just a blistered, white-hot steel and aluminium hulk sizzling in the water, where once the mighty tanker had been. The flames on board were dying. There was *nothing* left to burn, not even a coat of paint or an electric wire.

By some fluke of science and nature, Tank Two had held, but the aluminium of Tank One had melted and 20,000 more tons of liquid gas exploded in another deafening fireball. The gas in the bottom third of the tank just poured into the water, feeding the gas inferno, fueling the 200-yard-wide column of raging fire, which fought its way higher and higher as the liquid fuel flashed off into the atmosphere. Furiously hot, now, sucking in oxygen and nitrogen like a tornado, it rose up thousands of feet into the clear skies. It was as if Satan himself was attempting to communicate with God.

0800 Friday, April 27.
Office of Admiral Arnold Morgan
The White House, Washington DC.
Arnold Morgan was watching CNN news with rapt concentration. The destruction of a big US-owned tanker, with no survivors, deep in the Gulf of Hormuz was the lead item. Despite being six miles from Oman and at least forty from Bandar Abbas, the *Global Bronco* had very quickly become public property. Right now CNN was

showing graphic pictures of the burning hulk and its accompanying column of fire. The reporter was mentioning the overall problem, that Tank Two might suddenly blow and for that reason no one was taking the risk of going closer. Because the ship was well over on the Omani side of the Strait, news-gathering operations were being conducted with a friendly nation, and most broadcasters and media organizations had offices and satellite facilities in nearby Dubai. Two clattering helicopters were already prowling the shore, trying to take pictures, but unable to fly in close.

The Omani Navy had two 1450-ton guided-missile corvettes circling the area, warning ships off, and CNN had close-up pictures of these two British-built body-guards. There were also two Chinese-built guided-missile frigates, flying the flag of Iran, within ten miles of the disaster. The dimensions of the story outshone the limited coverage possible at this time. The twenty-four hour news station was already off-line, reporting, wrongly, that the *Global Bronco* was still burning. It wasn't the tanker on fire. It was the released gas in the water. They interviewed a Royal Navy lieutenant commander serving with a patrol out of Dubai, who speculated that it might be necessary to bang a torpedo right into the hull, starboard of Tank Two, in order to blow up the remaining liquid gas. Either that or shell the giant on-deck holding dome. 'It cannot', he said, 'just be left out there, ultimately to sink and take its 20,000-ton cargo with it.'

Arnold Morgan sipped his black coffee and listened, nodding slowly and pondering. 'Now who the hell are Texas Global Ships and what do they have to say for themselves? Come on, guys, get some reporters on this. Gimme the only information worth having. What do the owners think of the destruction of their ship? Accident? I suppose so. But if so, how? I don't think there's ever been a major explosion and fire on one of those gas ships, except for one in Tokyo Bay nearly twenty years ago.'

He switched off the channel and walked over to his desk. 'I wish I knew a little more about gas carriers,' he said. 'They must have the best possible safety systems, hm? I suppose there's no chance the goddamned towelheads whacked it with a torpedo, or the Iranians planted a minefield out in the exit lanes from the Gulf? No. I guess not. There seems to be no suggestion of that. Still, I'd better get Fort Meade on to it. I'd just like to know a little more about the *Global Bronco*. KATHY!' he yelled, scorning as ever the delicate little green telephone on his desk, which would have connected him to anyone in the world, including the lady right outside the door, the spectacular redhead Kathy O'Brien who for three years had refused to marry him until he retired.

The wide wooden door opened and she came in, shaking her head, saying she understood he would rather have a ship's tannoy system so he could bellow at everyone at the same time, but this was the twenty-first century and normal telephones were becoming quite acceptable, and would he ever consider using one?

'Could I have some more coffee?' he asked, smiling. 'Then I've got a little task for you.'

'I'm not here to do little tasks,' she replied. 'Don't you have any big ones?'

The Big Man chuckled, all five feet eight and a half inches of him. He ignored her request and asked if she had been watching the news.

'No, but I heard on the radio about the tanker which just blew up in the Gulf. Soon as they mentioned it I guessed it would be right up there on the priority list.'

'Well, Kathy, it's a volatile area and we always have to guard against lunatic action by the locals. Anyway, the ship was owned by an outfit called Texas Global Ships. I

58

want you to locate them and get their president on the line.'

'You have an address?'

'No. But try "information" in the Houston Galveston area. It's bound to be down there in the gulf oil ports. You'll find it.'

Five minutes later she returned to tell the Admiral that she'd found it, but had spoken only to a security guard since the place was not yet open.

'What's the name of the president?'

'Robert J. Heseltine III.'

'Call the guard back and tell him to have the boss call the White House right away. Give him the main switchboard number and have him put through here immediately.'

Kathy retreated, full of optimism. She knew the galvanizing effect a call from the White House can have on any American and she was right about the guard.

'Yes, ma'am,' he said. 'Right away.'

Three minutes and fifteen seconds later she answered her phone and a deep Texan voice said, 'Morning. This is Bob Heseltine.'

She switched him through to the Admiral who commiserated briefly about the ship and then asked him, 'Bob, do you have any reason to think the *Global Bronco* might have run into some form of naval hardware down there . . . a mine or a torpedo or something?'

'Well, every tankerman worries about the Strait, but it's always been safe on the Omani side. We didn't hardly get a warning from the ship. Apparently, according to the Royal Navy our operator just had time to call "MAYDAY" twice, before the line went dead.'

'So whatever happened, happened pretty damned quickly,' replied the Admiral.

'Yes, sir. I do believe so.'

'Any idea what might have caused the explosion?'

'Not really, Admiral. We do have some kind of an eyewitness report from a Liberian-registered crude-oil tanker about two miles ahead of the *Bronco*. Just said the for'ard holding dome definitely blew first. Then they saw the one next to it go up as well.'

'I guess that would confirm the possibility of a mine. All ships hit them bow first. A torpedo would have been much more likely to come in amidships.'

'Yes, sir. But I really don't think we ran into a mine-field. On the other hand it's hard for me to think of one reason why the almost brand-new gas-holding tank way up for'ard, 200 yards away from hot machinery, or even people, should suddenly have ruptured and exploded.'

'That's really my main question, Bob. How could it have ruptured, then blown up?'

'No reason I can think of, sir. 'Cept sabotage. But I can't imagine anyone wanting to blow up the ship they were in. Suicide sabotage's pretty rare.'

Arnold Morgan persisted. 'What causes natural gas to ignite?'

'Well, it's gotta be a flame or a spark of some kind. It's the gas, flashing off from the liquid that burns. Beats the hell out of me how that gas started to leak and what blew it.'

'Well, keep your ear to the ground, willya, Bob? Anything shakes loose, lemme know right away. Just call the number here and they'll find me.'

'Glad to, sir. Nice talking to you.' The last words were somewhat lost because the Admiral had already rung off. Bob Heseltine was not yet aware of the National Security Adviser's habit of never saying goodbye to anyone, just banging down the phone. He even did it to the President. These days, especially to the President.

'KATHY!' he yelled. 'Get Fort Meade on the line.'

Admiral David Borden jumped to it, front and center,

as he prepared to take his first call from the Big Man. 'Admiral?'

'Morning, David. Got that job under tight control?'

'Trying to, sir.'

'Good. Start off by telling me all you know about that tanker just went sky-high in Hormuz.'

'Well, sir. I only just received a preliminary report.'

'You did? Well, it's 0845 now and the tanker blew right after 0330. What are you using for comms, satellites or pigeons?'

Admiral Borden gulped. 'Sir, I only just got out here.'

'You mean you're not only operating some kind of dark ages communication system, you're also late for work.'

It was a while since anyone had addressed David Borden in quite such a manner, but he knew Arnold Morgan's fearsome reputation. He knew also that his bite was a lot worse than his bark. And this conversation was headed south, in a significant way. 'Sir, will you give me a half-hour to get right on this?'

'Yes. But please remember the following. Any time there's an explosion as big as this one in the middle of the Strait of Hormuz, or indeed anywhere near the Strait of Hormuz, you better get on it real quick. Right here we have a major incident involving a US freighter being destroyed forty miles from Bandar Abbas. We got goddamned Iranian missile ships circling her. We may have a fucking minefield out there. Admiral Borden, I don't actually give a flying fuck what you've been doing. I don't care if you have to turn up in your office in a goddamned nightshirt and jockstrap at 3 a.m. But when something goes off bang anywhere near the ayatollahs I want Fort Meade on it like a starving wolf chasing a pork chop. Do you hear me, Admiral?'

'Absolutely, sir.'

'Then get your ass in gear, sailor, and get your best men

moving. Don't bother chasing the shipowner. I dealt with him while you were still eating your fucking cornflakes.' *Crash*. Down phone.

Admiral Borden was visibly shaken, as many an occupant of Fort Meade had been before him. He actually debated putting in a written complaint to the President about the 'unforgivably disrespectful' manner in which he had been treated by the National Security Adviser. He went as far as to call his old friend in the White House, Harcourt Travis, the Secretary of State, who laughed and told him, 'That would be, I'm afraid, a suicide note. Arnold Morgan would probably have both you and the President out of here in an hour. Arnie's the Big Man on Campus right now. Don't even think of taking him on.'

Admiral Borden retreated, but in his mind he was planning to play this whole incident way down, which he believed would exact him a quiet, dignified revenge: that of military intellect over a blow-hard. As plans went, that one was dead moderate. If David Borden did but know it, career-threatening moderate.

At that moment there was a knock on the Director's door. He called to enter and was not especially pleased to see the frowning face of Lieutenant Ramshawe. 'Morning, sir. I got in here soon as I could when I heard about the tanker, but it didn't get on the news till 0500 so I guess I was a bit late. Anyhow, my conclusions are that we really do need to examine the possibility of a Chinese-backed Iranian minefield right out there in the Strait.'

'But I believe the tanker exploded off the coast of Oman, miles and miles from Iranian waters?'

'I know that, sir. But there's still got to be a suspicion. We know the Chinese ordered a ton of mines from Moscow and we know they could easily have brought them to Iran. We also know they were groping about in the Strait with four warships and possibly three submarines, all mine layers, at least one night and possibly more. We simply cannot dismiss the issue.'

'The Omanis appear to have done so. There's not a word from them to cast any suspicion on the Iranians whatsoever.'

'That's because they don't know their ass from their elbow.'

'Very possibly. Nonetheless, in the absence of one shred of proof, one floating mine, one whisper of skulduggery from any of our people in Beijing or Tehran . . . Jimmy, I cannot instigate anything without being in possession of at least some evidence.'

'But I have some evidence. First of all the bloody mines, maybe several hundred, were delivered under top-secret circumstances and have essentially disappeared. Then we had a fairly large flotilla of ships sail from Chinese bases direct to Iran. Then we have these night exercises, during which they could easily have laid a minefield out there in the Strait. Then we have a very strange situation. You know, and I know, you can lay a minefield and not activate it electronically till you're good and ready. Now, the Chinks bugger off towards the Bay of Bengal, leaving behind two mine layers, the frigates *Kangding* and *Zigong*, and what are the first ships to be seen after the bang? Those two frigates, out there in the Strait, flying the Iranian flag. In my view they were out there activating just *some* of the mines. But here's what's really important: remember a couple of weeks ago we picked up pictures of the Iranian missiles being established way down the coast, twenty-nine miles south of Kuhestak? Well, I marked the point hard on my big chart of Hormuz. The *Global Bronco* went up in a near dead-straight line from there, about twenty-four miles west-sou'west.'

'Jimmy, you can make a dead-straight line from any one point to any other. You need three to show evidence of a straight line.'

'Well, sir, at least the proximity of the missiles must be significant.'

'Not necessarily so, Jimmy. I am afraid that all the "evidence" is very circumstantial. By which I mean we know nothing. The mines China ordered may well still be in Zhanjiang. Their trip to Iran may easily have been to sell the two frigates. *Global Bronco* was carrying 80,000 tons of the world's most volatile petrochemical. Anything could have set it off. I would be sympathetic if you could locate for me one indisputable fact. Leave it for now, Jimmy. Until we get hard evidence."

The Lieutenant stood up and looked Admiral Borden square in the eye. 'I just have a damned weird feeling that when the next evidence turns up we're not gonna love it.'

Admiral Borden shook his head and called back Arnold Morgan. 'Sir,' he said. 'I do not have one single piece of intelligence that points to anything but a bad accident in that tanker which caused it to explode.'

'I do not doubt that, Admiral. The issue is whether you should be raising heaven and hell to find some.'

'Sir, sometimes there is simply nothing to find.'

'The fact that you can't find it does not mean it doesn't exist.' Arnold Morgan was beginning to dislike the Acting Director at Fort Meade and that was bad news for the Acting Director. But Admiral Morgan was receiving a distinct impression that David Borden did not *want* to find anything. 'If I were you, David, I should be damned careful about taking a negative view, because if you delay us, put us behind the eightball, I shall be forced to *have your ass, right*?' Click. Down phone. '*KATHY!*'

The door opened once again and Ms O'Brien entered, smiling sweetly. Too sweetly.

'Kathy, upon whom the sun rises and sets for me, I wanna let you into a deep and, thus far, unspoken secret.

64

Right here I suspect I'm dealing with a total asshole in the chair of the good George Morris at the NSA.'

'Oh, how very depressing.'

'Possibly more than you know. Book us a table at the restaurant in Georgetown tonight, will you? Between you and Monsieur Pierre, and my old friend Billy Beychevelle, perhaps you can raise my spirits.'

'Why, sir,' she replied, putting on a southern accent even more firmly than her own far-lost Alabama drawl. 'Ah sure would be deeply honored to bring y'all raaht back into the world of good cheer and fahn manners.'

Arnold watched her strut out, shook his head, smiling, and turned CNN back on.

Meanwhile, back at his desk in Fort Meade, Jimmy Ramshawe, surrounded by ocean charts, was glaring at the one which mapped the Bassein river on the Bengal Bay coast of Burma, or, as it is now known, Myanmar. 'Crazy bastards,' he muttered. 'Like changing the bloody name of Australia to Michelob.' He picked up the telephone and called the embassy, trying to catch Jane before she left for Georgetown. He just made it. 'Just a quick question,' he said. 'Can I meet you at home tonight instead of in the bar?'

'You mean my home?'

'Right.'

'Okay. What time?'

'Six. I got a little project you might want to help me with.'

'No worries. I'll be waiting.'

The day passed without further drama, or knowledge as to what happened to the *Global Bronco*. The great tower of fire alongside the ship raged on into the heavens until the evaporating gas had burned off and when it finally died it left the starboard side of the *Bronco* shimmering white-hot. The huge tanker was wallowing in the water, bow down, the waves now washing right up to the still intact Tank Two, which sat, full of liquid gas, poised between the devil of the melting aft quarter of the ship and the ripped-metal destruction in the deep blue sea up for'ard.

CNN, and the rest of the media, could elaborate no further. Bob Heseltine had called Admiral Morgan to inform him that Texas Global was sending its own investigators immediately to Dubai. He also mentioned he had been in conference with his technical advisers all day and no one could come up with one single reason how the for'ard tank could possibly have exploded, short of being blown apart by a mine or a torpedo.

When Arnold replaced the receiver, he was so thoughtful, so concerned that he had actually found time to say goodbye to the helpful Texan on the wire from Travis Street, Houston.

Lieutenant Ramshawe spent the day studying satellite photographs and charts of the Strait. He also talked to the CIA's Middle East desk, searching for any clue as to whether Iran might have decided to lock the rest of the world out of the almost-landlocked sea they regarded, historically, as their own.

Satellite photographs showed the two Chinese warships, *Hangzhou* and *Shantou*, now moored alongside, in China's new Burmese naval dockyard on Haing Gyi Island, which sits north of a wide six-mile shoal, surrounded almost entirely by sea marshes but with a short easterly coastline facing a surprisingly deep trench with varying low-water depths of well over forty feet. In a massive building program in recent years China had converted a stretch of this two-mile coastline into a concrete haven for its warships far from home. The island was strategically perfect, on the eastern coast of the Bay of Bengal, at the mouth of the twelve-mile-wide estuary of the Bassein river. It was equipped with long jetties and standard shipyard equipment, cranes, loading facilities, refueling pumps, sixteen big concrete holding tanks and sprawling lines of ships' stores. It was the first fully equipped overseas naval base China had possessed for over 500 years, 7500 sea miles from Shanghai.

Jimmy Ramshawe did not like it. The two Chinese warships, even in a long-range satellite photograph, looked a lot too comfortable on the Burmese jetties, just around the coast from a foreign ocean. 'Like someone parking a couple of Iraqi frigates outside the Opera House by Sydney Harbor Bridge,' he muttered. 'Seriously out of place. I just wish I bloody knew what the Orientals were at – maybe I'll get my last name changed to Rickshawe and get in there as a spy and find out.'

Tickled by his own groan-inspiring humor, the Lieutenant made out a brief report, detailing the information that the Chinese frigate and destroyer were now refueling for the journey home. He made a note that the three Kilos were not in residence in Burma and assumed they had taken a more southerly route to avoid the Malacca Strait, through which they would have been forced to travel on the surface. 'It looks rather as if they do not wish to be seen,' he wrote, 'for reasons unspecified.' For good measure he added the words 'as yet'.

He then returned to his big chart of the Hormuz Strait, published by the US Navy and likely to be extremely accurate. He took a long ruler and drew a line from the new Iranian missile position at 26.23N 57.05E. The line was precisely fourteen inches long. The chart's scale was 1 inch: 125,000. So he divided 125,000 by 36 to give him yards, then that number by 1760 to give him miles. The calculator told him that on this chart one inch equalled

1.97 miles. Which meant the tanker had exploded in 360 feet of water, 27.58 miles from the missiles, right along his straight line at 26.18N 56.38E.

He noted that from the point of the explosion the water stayed very deep west towards the Omani coast. Heading east it began to shelve up steadily all the way back along his line, growing a regular thirty or forty feet shallower every few miles. Absent-mindedly he muttered to himself, 'If there really is a minefield out there, I'd say they used Kilos to lay 'em in the deep water over on the Omani side and the surface ships where it gets shallower. I wonder . . .'

His shift ended officially at 1600, but he'd been in the office since before 0600 and he was still there at 1700, wrestling with his decision. It was a drastic step, he knew, and might very easily cost him his career. But he was going for it. Jimmy Ramshawe folded up his chart and took it with him when he left his desk. A minute later he was aiming the Jaguar towards the highway which would take him to the Australian embassy on Massachusetts Avenue. The traffic was 'the usual bloody awful' and he drove in through the gates just before 6 p.m. Jane Peacock and her mother were chatting in the parking lot and they killed a few minutes discussing the spectacular spring weather, blossom and associated flora, before Jane and Jimmy headed back into the embassy to the ambassador's private quarters.

She ordered tea, then sat down next to him on a large sofa and told him to spill the beans. 'Come on, Jimmy, what's happening?'

'Well, it's like this. I am planning to speak to the President's National Security Adviser, Admiral Arnold Morgan.'

'You don't have to tell me his bloody name, sweetness. Everyone knows his name.'

'Yeah, but everyone isn't about to call him on his private line.'

'You have that number?'

'No, actually, I don't.'

'Well, how're you going to get it?'

'You're going to get it for me.'

'*ME*?'

'Right. The thing is this, I'm going over the head of all my superiors, including the Acting Director. If anyone finds out, I'm probably dead in the Navy.'

'Wow! What would you do?'

'Well, I was thinking of changing my name to Rickshawe and becoming a Chinese spy.' Jane laughed, which pleased him. He'd thought it was a good joke earlier, but there was nothing like testing it on a live audience.

'Jimmy, can I ask you why you are doing this and how you expect me to find a number which is probably private to the President of the United States.'

'No, it's not that private. The switchboard here could get it on behalf of the ambassador. At least, they'd get patched through by the main White House operator.'

'You want me to use Dad's name?'

'No. I'll talk. But I want to make the call from here and then verify it by having them call back on your dad's private line, which will be on record at the White House. They have a direct line to all major Washington ambassadors. That way I'll get patched through to the Admiral.'

'Well, I suppose so. Doesn't seem much harm and if there is, the only one in trouble is going to be you. You better have something pretty important to say; that bloody Admiral's supposed to be a tiger.'

'Yeah, I know. My dad knew him a bit when he was in the Navy.'

'Anyway, you picked a good night. Both my parents are going out.'

'I know that too. You told me. Dinner at the British embassy, right?'

'Yup. They'll both be gone by seven o'clock.'

'That's good. I want to call around eight. Because that way I'll know he's settled wherever he's going to be. Hopefully at home. I don't want to have to go through this rigmarole twice, or even three times. And that's what'll happen if I make the call while he's in transit somewhere.'

'Can I know what you want him for?'

'Not really. But since I can't make the call without you, certainly not from my office, I have to tell you. Janie, I think the Chinese and the Iranians between 'em have put some kind of a minefield across the Strait of Hormuz. That tanker that blew up this morning: no accident. And I think there might bloody easily be more.'

'Jesus. I read about that. But why doesn't Fort Meade get on to it?'

'Because Admiral Borden, the Acting Director, doesn't believe it. Doesn't want to do anything until he has some proof.'

'Well, why do you think Admiral Morgan will be any more interested than Admiral Borden?'

'I don't have a reason. Just a gut feeling, that's all.'

'Pretty expensive gut feeling, if you're wrong and he goes to Borden and tells him he's got some kind of a nutter on his staff.'

'Yeah. I know. What a ripper. But I don't think he will.'

'Anyway let's go and watch the news in Dad's study, see if they've blown any more ships. Then you can get started on blowing your entire career. Want some more tea?'

The ninety minutes passed quickly, Ambassador John Peacock came in for a brief chat, then went off to meet his wife. At eight o'clock sharp Lieutenant Ramshawe went and sat behind the big desk in the study, picked up the blue

70

phone and dialed the main number of the White House. His Aussie accent undiminished, he said, 'Good evening. I'm calling from the office of the Australian ambassador and he would like to speak immediately to Admiral Arnold Morgan. You probably want to verify this call so get back to me right away, would you?'

'Yes, sir, we'll check the private number for the Australian ambassador and come right back.'

Thirty seconds later the phone rang. 'Ambassador Peacock's office?'

'Correct.'

'Sir, I'm afraid the National Security Adviser is not in right now. If it's urgent we can locate him.'

'Please do.'

'Hold a moment . . .'

Three full minutes went by, mostly taken up by Le Bec Fin's maître d', Pierre, asking the White House to wait while he took and connected a telephone into the private booth occupied by Admiral Morgan and Kathy. He'd done this a few times before and he placed it right next to the bottle of 1995 Château Beychevelle, which was 'breathing' as yet untouched in the middle of the table.

Arnold Morgan thanked him and picked up the phone. 'Morgan. Speak.' His telephone manner never varied, but Kathy still giggled.

'Just a moment, sir. Connecting you to the Australian ambassador.'

'Sir, is that Admiral Morgan?'

'In person, Ambassador Peacock. I guess this is pretty important? I'm just sitting down to dinner.'

'Sir, this is not actually Ambassador Peacock. My name is Lieutenant Jimmy Ramshawe and I work in surveillance at Fort Meade. I'm calling you under what you might think are somewhat dishonest circumstances.'

Arnold Morgan's eyes opened wide in surprise. 'Fraud

phone call from an Aussie, right before a little dish of grilled prawns. Jesus, what's the place coming to?'

'But sir, it is important.'

'I guess it must be. You've gone to a lot of trouble to interrupt my goddamned dinner. What did you say your name was? Jimmy Ramshawe?'

'Yes, sir. Surveillance.'

'Okay, Jimmy. Shoot. And hurry. Wait a minute. (*Aside*) Kathy, tell Pierre to put the prawns on hold for five minutes and lemme have a glass of that Bordeaux, I have a feeling I'm gonna need it. Go, Jimmy.'

'I don't know, sir, how well up to date you are on the *Global Bronco* situation?'

'Well, I haven't spoken to the tanker's owner for at least four hours.'

'Sorry, sir. Anyway, I was the operator who tracked, or tried to track, all those sea mines China bought from Moscow three months ago.'

Arnold Morgan's antennae flew up like lightning rods. But he stayed calm. 'Aha.'

'Well, sir, they transported them under terrific secrecy, then we had that little convoy of surface ships, three frigates and a Sovremenny destroyer, making a special journey all the way from the South China Sea to Iran. Then I picked up three Chinese Kilo Class submarines making their way north up the Arabian Sea. They ended up in Chah Bahar. All seven of the ships, as you know, have mine-laying capacity. Then we had night exercises with the Iranians. We picked up very little, but they were out there all night off the Omani coast. Then we picked up a missile movement, Sunburn S-As on the south-east coast, and suddenly, a couple of weeks later, a damn great tanker explodes, twenty-seven miles in a straight line from those missile launchers. What's the first thing we see next? Two of those Chinese frigates, now flying the Iranian flag, just five miles from the explosion, forty miles from their jetties in Bandar Abbas.'

Admiral Morgan was listening.

'Sir, I think they may have been out there activating the mines and it is my opinion that there could be a serious minefield out there, maybe running from the Omani coast, place called Ra's Qabr al Hindi, right across to Iran. I think we ought to find out.'

'Jimmy, I assume you have reported all this to Admiral Borden?'

'Of course, sir. But he doesn't want to know. Keeps asking for evidence. Well, I don't have any bloody evidence, but I've got enough clues to warrant a damned careful look.'

Arnold Morgan thought carefully. Then he said, 'I suppose you've considered the consequences of a phone call like this. Bypassing the regular channels of command?'

'Yes, sir.'

'But you decided to take the risk anyway?'

'Yes, sir.'

'Now, I'm going to be very formal with you. Lieutenant Ramshawe, it is entirely out of order for you to have taken this action. You must return to Fort Meade and place the entire matter with Admiral Borden. It is essential you use our regular channels of information. Neither the Navy nor the Intelligence Services can afford this kind of undisciplined and unorthodox method of operation. Kindly see that it does not happen again.' At which point he put down the phone. 'Kathy,' he said. 'That was rather an interesting phone call. It confirmed what I have unfortunately suspected: that the man sitting in George Morris's chair is a total asshole.'

Back in the Australian embassy Jimmy Ramshawe was perplexed. 'He listened carefully to all I had to say,' he told Jane. 'Then he gave me a right choking off for not going through Admiral Borden. Jesus, I was only calling him because I *could not* go through Admiral Borden.'

'Well, I'm sure he understood that,' said Jane. 'Even I understood that and I only heard one half of the conversation.'

'Right. But it still puts me in a no-win situation. If Admiral Morgan believed me, he'll probably call and report me to the Director, and use the information to give him a right bollocking. If he didn't believe me, he'll probably call anyway and recommend I be removed from any position of trust. The ole bastard never even gave me a chance to ask him to keep it confidential.'

'Jimmy, Arnold Morgan did not get where he is by being stupid. I'm sure he plugged right into the situation and will very likely be grateful for the call, may even act on it. He'll appreciate what you did and I don't think he'll betray you.'

'Christ, I hope you're right. Come on, let's get out of here.'

Jimmy and Jane did not dine as well as Arnold Morgan and Kathy, nor in such opulent surroundings as Le Bec Fin. But they were not far away in a bar in Georgetown, eating a couple of cheeseburgers and drinking Budweiser instead of grilled prawns, veal marsala and Château Beychevelle. The Lieutenant was on duty at 0600, so he dropped Jane off home some time before midnight and headed back to the Watergate, a distance of less than two miles. Inside the apartment he kicked off his shoes, put the kettle on, checked his messages (none) and switched on the television, CNN automatically, muttering to himself, 'Just better make sure no one's declared war.'

No one had. The news, he thought, was unfathomably dreary, lightweight: health care, second-rate pop star getting divorced, famine in Africa. All-Star third baseman dying of drugs. *Blah-blah-blah*, grumbled Jimmy to himself.

These guys ought to be called the Four Newsmen of the Apocalypse, Conquest, Slaughter, Famine and Death. Especially Death, on his pale horse. That's all they bloody think about.

But then he stopped dead in his tracks as he headed back to the kitchen, half-listening to some other late report from the newscaster: '*Reports are coming in of a major oil spill in the Gulf of Iran. A giant crude-oil tanker is currently listing off the coast of Oman, with an apparently damaged bow section. According to Dubai shipping sources, oil is pouring out of her for'ard tanks.*'

'*Holy shit!*' The Lieutenant charged right back into the living room, but the item was over. They were back on the President's forthcoming visit to India. Jimmy picked up the phone, dialed Fort Meade, spoke immediately to Lieutenant Ray Carpenter. 'You got anything on a tanker leaking oil in the Gulf?'

'Come on, Jimmy, what do you think this is? Greenpeace? Nothing right now.' Despite himself, Lieutenant Ramshawe laughed. Then he called CNN news headquarters in Atlanta and asked if they had an accurate fix on where the tanker was. He announced himself as a director of Texas Gas Transport, told them he was afraid it might be one of his ships. In return he'd keep them posted if it was.

The CNN foreign desk was not much help but said he was more than welcome to call their man in Dubai, since it was already almost nine o'clock the following morning in the Middle East. He thanked them profusely, dialed the number in Dubai and spoke to the reporter David Alidai.

'Sorry, pal. I'm dealing with the Omani Navy's public affairs office. The only person in there's called Hassam, but he doesn't know much. I think he's been told to shut up until they assess the damage to the environment. But if you guys own the ship, he might be a bit more forthcoming. I'll give you his number. Good luck.'

Jimmy hit the dial buttons to Oman and was put through to the aforementioned Hassam. 'I'm sorry. I cannot tell you anything. We know very little ourselves.'

'Listen, Hassam, this may be our ship. We had a VLCC right in that area. I'm just asking for a position. Surely you can provide us with that. Please try, otherwise I'll have to speak to the Admiral.'

Jimmy had no idea what Admiral he was going to speak to, and Hassam could not have cared less and kept him waiting on the line for five minutes. Then he came back and said, 'Mr Haig, the damaged ship is positioned at latitude 26.19N 56.49E. She's in 250 feet of water.'

'Hassam, I'm grateful. But I don't think that's us. It's a bit too far south. Do you know if there are any other ships in the area?'

'Well, we have two Qahir corvettes out there trying to keep order. The Strait is very busy. All tankers are being brought to a halt right now. I believe there are two Iranian frigates out there also, but I can tell you no more.'

Jimmy rang off and sprinted out of the apartment, willing the elevator to take him instantly down to the parking lot. He unlocked the Jaguar and retrieved the chart he had left in the leather side pocket. He relocked and sprinted back to the elevator, which had not yet resumed its upward journey.

Inside the apartment he spread the chart on the dining table, scrabbled around for a ruler and measured. The stricken VLCC in the Hormuz Strait was only nine inches from the missile site, a fraction less than eighteen miles. It was six inches from the *Global Bronco*, just less than twelve miles. And it was pretty much on the line that joined the Iranian missile site and the spot where the *Bronco* had exploded yesterday. 'Jesus, Mary and Joseph,' breathed Jimmy. 'The bastards have mined the Strait and it's dollars to doughnuts the VLCC hit one of 'em with its bow.'

He reached into his pocket and found the scrap of paper with the White House phone number. He checked his watch and saw it was 12.45 a.m. 'Well, I didn't manage to get fired five hours ago, but I'm damn sure certain I'm going to pull it off now.' And he dialed the main switchboard of the White House. When they answered, he said, 'This is Lieutenant Ramshawe, Chief Surveillance Officer Middle and Far East, National Security Agency, Fort Meade. I need to speak to Admiral Arnold Morgan on a matter of extreme urgency. He *will* take the call. Please make it and then patch me through.'

For the second time that evening the White House interrupted the fearsome Security Chief. He and Kathy were home, sipping a glass of their favorite Sauternes, a sweet, silky 1995 dessert wine from the Gironde, before going to bed, when the phone rang. 'Sir, this is the White House main switchboard. We have a Lieutenant Jimmy Ramshawe on the line, who would like to be connected to you.'

Admiral Morgan raised his eyes heavenwards. But he took the call. 'Jimmy,' he rasped. 'This better be awfully important.'

'It is, sir. There's a second big tanker crippled in the Hormuz Strait. I just heard a flash on CNN. But I called Dubai, then the Omani Navy and I got a position on the ship. Its eighteen miles from the missile site I mentioned, and it's twelve miles from the *Global Bronco*. More important, it's on a *dead-straight line* linking the two ships and the missiles. The odds against that have gotta be a zillion to one. They've mined it, sir. Of that I am now very sure.'

Arnold Morgan hissed his breath inwards. His thoughts raged through his mind. 'Jimmy, where are you?'

'I'm in my apartment, sir. The Watergate.'

'You are? Hell, I used to know an Australian admiral who lived in there. You any relation?'

'My father, sir. Naval Attaché here a few years back.'

'Jesus. This is getting worse and worse. Your dad and I had a few times together. Lives in New York now, right? With Qantas?'

'That's him, sir.'

'Okay. Now listen. I want you to meet me in my office in the White House in twenty minutes. I'm leaving right now. I'll have an escort for you at the West Executive Avenue entrance. You know where that is?'

'Yes, sir.'

'And Jimmy, speak to no one. Not a sentence. Not a phone call. This is very important. Believe me.'

'Yes, sir.'

'Make sure you bring your working chart with you.'

'Yes, sir.'

Arnold Morgan stood up and walked to the top of the basement stairs in Kathy's large Chevy Chase home. He yelled instructions to his Secret Service detail, organizing Lieutenant Ramshawe's escort at the White House. He kissed Kathy good night, pulled on his coat, and headed outside where his car and two agents were waiting.

'Straight to the factory, sir?'

'You got it.'

It was almost 1 a.m. when the black White House staff car came barreling over the Taft Avenue Bridge, driving swiftly down Connecticut Avenue. It was raining and the City was quiet. They crossed DuPont Circle and made their way to 17th Street, swinging into West Executive Avenue from where they could see a Jaguar already being waved through to the West Wing.

Admiral Morgan met Lieutenant Ramshawe outside the door, while four duty agents attended to his visitor's pass and parked his car. The Admiral stuck out his hand, smiled and said, 'Hello, Lieutenant, Arnold Morgan.'

Jimmy Ramshawe had met a few major men in his life,

but this was different. The Admiral exuded power. He was all of seven inches shorter than Jimmy but his gaze was dead straight, his eyes bright blue and his grip strong. The Admiral's dark-grey suit had been tailored somewhere in heaven and his black lace-up shoes were gleaming. The perfectly knotted tie was that of the Naval Academy, Annapolis, a place and experience which Arnold Morgan had never forgotten and never would. He made Jimmy Ramshawe feel like a little boy.

In response to the Admiral's curt but warm greeting he just managed, 'Sir.' He'd used up all his daring and bravado for one night, making two unauthorized calls on the private line to the right-hand man of the President of the United States.

'Follow me,' said the Admiral to anyone who might be listening, which included the two Secret Service agents who were with him at all times, four White House agents and Jimmy. Line astern, they set off in the wake of the Admiral, who never walked; he kind of pounded along the carpet, chin out, shoulders back, dead upright. If a regular wall had suddenly appeared in front of him he would have crashed right through it, like a Disney cartoon, leaving just the outline of his silhouette. He conducted the business of the United States of America on very similar lines.

At the big wooden door to his office he came to a halt and his commands were sharp: 'Get me a competent secretary to sit in Ms O'Brien's chair right now. Tell someone to bring us coffee. You hungry, Jimmy?'

'Yes, sir.'

'Chicken sandwiches for the Lieutenant and make sure someone's attending to my phone exclusively at all times. Aside from that, my regular agents take up positions right here and have the hot line to the President on high alert. I may have to speak to him in a major hurry.'

Everyone nodded.

Admiral Morgan glared. Turning to one of his regular agents, he barked, 'No bullshit, right, Bobby?'

Bobby snapped to attention. 'No bullshit. Sir. No sir.' It was a well practiced routine and everyone laughed.

'Okay, gentlemen, that's it. Lieutenant, let's get to work. And tell 'em to hurry up with the coffee in case we both fall asleep.'

Inside the office, Jimmy spread his chart out on the Admiral's big desk. Arnold Morgan stared hard as the key spots were pointed out to him: the missiles, the *Global Bronco*, the stricken VLCC, currently pumping oil into the Strait. 'Okay, Lieutenant, first things first. I want to know what the master of that ship actually saw. I guess if they slammed into a mine . . . what was it, a contact PLT-3 from Russia?'

'That was what the Chinese ordered, sir. So I'm assuming that.'

'So'm I. Well, they make a pretty big bang in the water. The captain must have heard something.'

'I agree, sir. But the guy I spoke to in the Omani public affairs office was giving nothing away. It took me all my time to get him to tell me where the ship was.'

'Well, if that's the case, I may have to kick a little ass. Hard. Do we know the name or the nationality of the ship?'

'No, sir.'

'Okay. Well, the news guys will have that very soon. Meantime I'm gonna get the Royal Navy in London to do our work. The Brits are well in with the Omanis, have been for years. Just about every warship they own is British.' He picked up the telephone and ordered the new secretary, 'Get me Admiral Sir Richard Birley on the line in Northwood, England. The numbers are in my big blue book, top right-hand drawer. He'll be at home, right near the base. He's head of the Royal Navy's submarine service.'

Less than two minutes later the Admiral's old friend from London was on the line. The two men exchanged greetings and the English submarine chief instantly agreed to have someone call the Omanis to find out precisely what was going on, who owned the ship and what the captain had to say. 'I'll be back inside the hour, Arnie. By the way, can I ask why you're treating this so urgently?'

'Not right now, you can't.'

'Well, you always have to wonder in those waters, hm?'

'You always have to wonder. Talk to you later, Dick.'

The Admiral turned back to Jimmy Ramshawe and said quietly, 'Lieutenant, I want you to listen very carefully. Only two people in this country believe the Iranians and the Chinese may have put a minefield across the Strait. That's you and I. We may be wrong. But I think not. Your straight line on that chart is just too much of a coincidence and I would not be that shocked if another ship blew before we're much older. But this is what I want you to understand. If this turns out to be true, we're going to be sitting on a colossal world oil crisis. The Gulf will have to be shut down while we sweep and clear it, which is going to take weeks. Oil prices will go through the roof. The entire global economy could go berserk. Japan could come to a complete halt. A gallon of gas could go to six bucks right here in the US and what I'm trying to do right here is avoid a national panic if that is at all possible.'

'Yes, sir.'

The chicken sandwiches arrived, a large plateful. Jimmy Ramshawe attacked them and the Admiral had one himself while they waited for the English Admiral to call back.

He was on the line before 0200. 'Arnold, the ship is Greek, Liberian registered. Only two years old. It's huge, 300,000 tons deadweight. Loaded with Saudi crude. The captain and the crew are still on board. The ship is not

81

sinking but it's ten degrees bow down and it's currently belching 70,000 cubic meters of oil from its for'ard tank.'

'Any word from the captain?'

'Yes, he made a statement to the Omani coastguard. Says there was a massive explosion, for no reason, way up at the bow. It completely ruptured one of the five holding tanks.'

'Was she double-hulled, Dick?'

'Oh, yes. Very heavily built in the Daewoo Shipyard, South Korea. Compartmentalized, too, throughout the hull. She'd be just about unsinkable. I expect you know, but she's only twelve miles away from the *Global Bronco* which blew up yesterday.'

'Yeah. We do know that and right now I'd have to say that this, Sir Richard, ole buddy, is not good.'

'This, Admiral Arnie, old chap, is becoming deeply unattractive.'

Three

April 28.
The White House, Washington DC.
With Lieutenant Ramshawe on his way home, sworn to total silence, Admiral Morgan stood alone in his office at 0230. It was a situation not entirely unfamiliar to him, even on a Saturday morning. He yelled through the door for someone to bring him some fresh hot coffee and debated whether or not to call the President. 'Maybe not,' he muttered. 'It won't do any good. As soon as the President knows, everyone knows. I think we need a little more time before the crap really hits the fan.'

The first thing to do was to get a couple of mine-sweepers into the Strait and take a closer look. Jimmy Ramshawe was to spend the morning screening all satellite pictures to check whether any tankers were making a successful through passage. Arnold Morgan suspected that those big fuel oil carriers which did make it through would be either Chinese or Iranian, and their cargo would either be direct from the refinery just east of Bandar Abbas, or from the new Chinese refinery further down the coast. But Lieutenant Ramshawe would find that out. The problem was minesweepers, the little specialist warships which locate the mines by towing a sweep wire through the water until it hits and cuts the mine's cable. The USA had some extremely effective sonar-mine hunters in the Avenger Class, but they were mostly based along the Texas coast and made only thirteen knots. 'Damn things would take for ever to get there,' the Admiral grumbled.

He pondered the Brits, wondering about the Royal Navy's excellent Hunt Class minesweepers. But again, the same problem: *slow and half a world away from Hormuz*. No. He had to get someone much nearer, which meant, essentially, the Indians. *What the hell time was it in Bombay?* The question was rhetorical. Arnold Morgan knew more or less what time it was *everywhere*: right now in the great Indian city of Bombay it was somewhere around midday. He picked up the telephone and asked his night-duty secretary, whom he'd never even seen, to connect him immediately to the Indian embassy in Washington. When the duty officer answered the Admiral said simply, 'This is Arnold Morgan, National Security Adviser to the President of the United States. I'm in the White House. Take down the following phone number and have the naval attaché call me in the next four minutes. Thanks. And hurry up.' Click.

Three minutes and twenty-two seconds later the telephone rang on his private line. 'This is Vice-Admiral Prenjit Lal speaking. I believe you wanted me?'

'Hey, thanks for calling. I do appreciate it's the middle of the night, but my request is easy. I would like Admiral Kumar, your Chief of Naval Staff, to call the White House immediately and ask for me. I guess he's in Bombay?'

'Yes, Admiral. Today he is. I'll contact him right away.'

'Stress that it's extremely urgent, will you?'

'The hour of the night tells me of the urgency, Admiral. I'll do it personally and immediately.'

It took eight minutes. Admiral Kumar came on the line, insisting that he would be honored to provide any assistance he could to India's very great friends in the White House.

Arnold Morgan, however, knew this was only half true. What the mannered and apparently pliable Indian officer had not said was, 'Just so long as it will not damage our relations with our neighbors or allies, and so long as the US would assist with whatever the cost might be.' Unspoken hurdles. Admiral Morgan elected to lay out the facts as swiftly and brutally as he could. He pulled no punches and he went very carefully over the iron-clad fact of Jimmy Ramshawe's straight line. He ended his little speech by saying: 'I'm afraid all the world's oil consumers are in this together. But yours is the nation with the most easily accessible minesweepers. Admiral Kumar, you will have the full backing of the USA. I'll have two destroyers there to meet you and you may assume all costs will be met by the big oil consumers, the US, the UK, Japan, France, Germany, everyone. I'm sure you can appreciate the urgency. We simply cannot just sit here and wait for another tanker to blow up. We have to get in there, check it out and, if necessary, sweep a safe channel and your Pondicherry Class minesweepers are the nearest.'

'Admiral Morgan,' replied the Indian Navy Chief, 'I am indeed grateful for your call and your trust. If the Iranian Gulf were closed for even three weeks, my country would be in the most terrible trouble. Aside from the regular petrol supplies, almost all our propane gas for cooking comes from there. My country could come to a complete halt. Obviously we had noted the two tanker accidents. But no one had any idea it might be a concerted plot by the Iranians and the damnable Chinese. You may assume we will sail six of the Pondicherrys in the next twenty-four hours. You think we should take a tanker?'

'Yes, I do. And escorts. Admiral Kumar, we do not yet know precisely what we are dealing with here. But I can assure you of massive US protection once your ships arrive at the Strait. One squeak out of the Chinese or the Iranians and we'll put 'em on the bottom of the ocean. That's a promise.'

'Excellent, Admiral. My attaché in Washington will be in contact in a few hours to give you times of sailing, an ETA and further details of our escort. It's 1000 miles to the Strait from Bombay, but the Pondicherrys make sixteen knots. We'll aim to sail at first light tomorrow morning, which should put us in the Strait before dark on Tuesday.'

'Thank you, Admiral Kumar. We look forward to working with you. I just wish the circumstances were less serious. Arnold Morgan replaced the telephone, checked his watch at 0320 and opened up his private line to the Pentagon. He told the duty officer in the Navy Department to get the CNO on the line right away.

Sixty seconds later Admiral Alan Dickson, former Commander-in-Chief of the Atlantic Fleet, betrayed no sign that he had been called in the small hours of the morning. The new Chief of Naval Operations said crisply, 'Morning, sir. Sorry if I kept you waiting.'

'Not a bit, Alan. But what I have to say is rather long and complicated. Can you come to the White House right away? Where are you, in the Yard?'

'Yes, sir. Give me thirty.'

'See you then. West Executive Avenue entrance.'

The minutes ticked by slowly for the National Security Adviser. He debated the rather appealing possibility of waking 'that stuffed shirt Borden', but decided there was nothing to gain from such a malicious act. So he waited, sipped his coffee, thought of Kathy and waited.

At 0348 sharp Admiral Dickson was escorted into the office and, for the second time that night, to a second slightly incredulous Navy chief, Admiral Morgan went over the whole scenario in the Strait of Hormuz.

Alan Dickson, a veteran destroyer CO from the Gulf War, nodded gravely. 'I guess two sinkings in much the same place are beyond the bounds of likely coincidence, almost impossible we could be mistaken – I haven't heard the theory before. I suppose that's your day's work, eh?'

'Not so, Alan. One of the brighter sparks on George Morris's staff. I'd like to support it, though.'

'An interesting bit of deduction and to tell the truth, sir, the Pentagon had not yet received a position on the second tanker when I left the office.'

'No. Neither had anyone else. This young lieutenant bamboozled his way into the public affairs office of the Omani Navy and prised it out of them.'

'Good job! Love to hear it. Anyway, sir, what now?'

'Well, the Indian Navy is going to work with us sweeping the Strait. We obviously have to start a major mine clearance operation ASAP, I hope on Tuesday evening. They'll have a half-dozen of those Russian-built Pondicherrys working, with an escort of their own. But I want to get a couple of our destroyers in there and a CVBG as soon as we can.'

Admiral Dickson pulled out a personal notebook, which detailed all the five currently operational US carrier battle groups. The fifty-five ships which surrounded the huge carriers were just a little too much to commit to memory and the highly methodical Boston-born Alan Dickson never went anywhere without that little notebook. 'Okay, sir,' he said. 'We're pretty well placed. The *Constellation* Group's stationed up at the north end of the Gulf off Iraq. We got *John C. Stennis* with nine guided-missile ships and two nuclear boats exercising in the Arabian Sea, probably a day and a half from the Strait. *Harry S. Truman*'s battle ready at Diego Garcia. She's got a full complement of escorts, one cruiser, two destroyers, six frigates, two nuclear submarines, an LA and a Sturgeon, plus a complete Under Way Replenishment Group. *John F. Kennedy* has a full operational group just about ready to leave from Pearl at any time, certainly in the next three days. Back in San Diego the *Ronald Reagan*'s almost finished a major overhaul. Her Group can be ready inside two months, if we need it.'

'That's great, Alan. I guess we ought to have one right in the southern approaches to the Strait and one inside the Gulf, spread across the exit, with a lotta muscle concentrated south of Bandar Abbas. There's been a couple of pretty heavy Chinese destroyers prowling around there these past few weeks. Once the Indian minesweepers get in there we'll get the President to issue a private warning to the Iranians: any ship attempting any kind of interference will be sunk. By us. No bullshit. Right?'

'Right, sir. Meantime I'll order the *Constellation* Group to proceed south towards Bandar and the *Stennis* to close the Strait. We'll put the *Harry Truman* on twenty-four hours' battle notice to sail north from DG. It's getting pretty damned hot out there right now and it's hard to keep guys on station for more than a couple of months without sending 'em all crazy. If I order the *Kennedy* to leave Pearl in the next couple of days she can go straight to DG. That'll give us a four-group *roulement*, keeping two of them comfortably on station all the time. We can keep that up for a year if we have to.'

'Good. How's the *Kennedy* doing? Christ, Alan, she's damn near forty years old.'

'No problem, sir. She had that complete complex overhaul in 1995, made her just about brand new. There's nothing wrong with her. No, sir. Old number 67 is a little smaller than the Nimitz Class boats, but she still holds nearly 6000 tons of aviation fuel. Seen a lot of service. She's like her little brother, Senator Ted. Indestructible. And just as bloody-minded when she feels like it.'

Admiral Morgan chuckled. The language of the Navy. He still loved it. Still felt pride swell in his chest when the big US ships prepared to flex their muscles. He'd felt it during his first nuclear submarine command more than twenty years ago and the feeling had never diminished. Arnold Morgan's soul was essentially held together with dark blue cord and gold braid.

Monday morning, April 30.
Officers Mess, US Naval Base,
Diego Garcia, Indian Ocean.

Lieutenant-Commander Dan Headley was just one tour of duty short of promotion to Commander in the US Navy's Pacific Submarine Fleet. At thirty-five, he was very proud of that. Right now he was generally regarded as one of the best submarine executive officers in the entire Navy. Experienced, a lifelong submariner, weapons and sonar expert, he had just flown to Diego Garcia to take up the number two spot in the aging Sturgeon Class nuclear boat, USS *Shark*.

This was one of the Navy's underwater warhorses, probably on her last tour of duty, since she had been due to decommission in 2005. *Shark* was the newest of the Navy's four Sturgeon attack submarines and probably the best. The 5000-tonner could make thirty knots through the water dived, she carried twenty-three weapons, Harpoon and Tomahawk missiles, plus torpedoes. On her deck, forward of the sail, there were two twin dry-deck shelters designed for the transport of a deep-submergence rescue vehicle (DSRV) an Advanced Swimmer Delivery Vehicle (ADV), or a dry garage for three, even four, high-powered outboard inflatables. *Shark* was quiet, extensively fitted with acoustic tiles, with anechoic coatings. She had the capacity to fire nuclear-warhead weapons and she was capable of operating under the ice, though Dan Headley doubted that would be needed on her next journey.

He had been in the base for only three hours when word began to spread that there was something happening up in the Strait of Hormuz. Everyone knew the CVBGs of

USS *Constellation* and *John C. Stennis* were already in the area. The issue was how soon would the massive 100,000-ton Nimitz Class *Harry Truman* and her consorts head north to join them in the narrow waters which guard Arabia's landlocked sea of oil? No one knew that, but senior officers considered it more likely to be hours than days. It was 2600 miles up to Bandar Abbas and the *Truman* Group could steam at thirty knots, making 700 miles a day. If they cleared DG by first light tomorrow (Tuesday), they'd be in the area before dark on Friday afternoon.

Lieutenant-Commander Headley had a lot of people to meet in the next twenty-four hours and from each of them he had a minor secret to conceal. SUBPAC was not real happy with the veteran Commander Donald Reid, *Shark*'s commanding officer, and they had specifically appointed Dan Headley to assist him in every way possible. So far as Dan was concerned it was just a wink and a nudge, because no one would tell him what, if anything, was wrong with Commander Reid, only that he was, well, 'kinda eccentric'. No one actually said 'weird'. But he'd been in the submarine service a lot of years and according to observers had shown 'very occasional signs of stress'.

Dan Headley was looking forward to meeting the boss with rather mixed anticipation. But before he met anyone he had a letter to write, so he parked himself in a corner of the mess with a cup of coffee and, following the habit of a lifetime, addressed the envelope before he wrote the letter: Commander Rick Hunter, US Navy Pacific Command, Coronado, California 92118.

Dear Rick,

Just a short note to congratulate you on your promotion. Well deserved, I'm sure, even in that crazy outfit which employs you. All those years ago, when we set off together for Annapolis, I always thought we'd both end up commanding US warships – rather than just me (I hope!), while you roll around in the mud with a dagger between your teeth and a pocket full of explosive.

Anyway I'm here in Diego Garcia waiting to take up my new position as XO in USS *Shark*. My last, I'm told, before they make me up to Commander. Some time in the next twenty-four hours we're due to sail north, to guess where? Anyway, by the time you read this the Kentucky Derby will be over. Hey, what a blast if White Rajah wins it. I guess your dad will forever regret selling him as a yearling and my dad will forever keep reminding him that he told him not to! Still, victory would be sweet, since Bart still owns the dam and two full sisters. That would be a real lock on a major American classic family – make you guys even richer.

Funny, isn't it, to look back at that wicked old bastard Red Rajah and think he might be the grandsire of a Derby winner, rather than an automatic selection for a lead role in *Natural Born Killers*. Jeez, every time I think about him my arm hurts!

I have to go now, meet my new crew, hope to catch a glimpse of you, certainly at Christmas, if not before.

Best always and love to Bart
Danny.

He folded the letter and sealed the envelope. Then he walked out to the front desk and asked the security guard to mail it. It was only a short walk over to the submarine jetties where the *Shark* awaited him.

Same morning, Monday, April 30.
Southern Fleet HQ, Zhanjiang.
'Yushu, you are very disappointed. I can see that.'

'Well, Jicai, you would have thought the Western press would have been much more alert to the consequences of two shattered oil tankers within a few miles of each other in the middle of the Strait of Hormuz.'

'Yes, I agree. But the time difference made it awkward.'

'How?'

'Well, the *Washington Post* ran a piece on Saturday morning covering the big fire in the liquid gas tanker. So did several other American newspapers, but no pictures. I suppose the cameras were just too far away. But when the second tanker was damaged it was too late for their editions. And it was a much smaller story. Just an oil spill in the Gulf.'

'You've studied the media more than I, Jicai. Has anyone made a connection?'

'Only the Sunday edition of the *Dallas Morning News* in Texas. They have an interview with the owner of the *Global Bronco* and right underneath it they run a story about the oil spill. But they're not making a major point about the closeness of the two "accidents".'

'Then, my Jicai, we will quickly have to persuade them otherwise.'

'Oh, I don't think that will prove too much of a problem. We are extremely well organized.'

0900 (local) Same Monday morning.
Washington DC.

Arnold Morgan had just issued a severe roasting to the Acting Director of the National Security Agency and Admiral David Borden, frankly afraid now for his future, had gone straight to the office of Lieutenant Ramshawe, full of quasi-indignation that he had not been kept up to speed on the Hormuz investigation. Jimmy Ramshawe debated the possibility of telling his boss to knock before he barged in, but decided against it. Nonetheless, he detected the Acting Director had been on the wrong end of the Big Man's wrath and that was not a great place to be. 'It is essential you keep me up to date,' he told the Lieutenant. 'I am the person who must answer to Admiral Morgan and it is most inconvenient when he knows more than I do.'

Again Lieutenant Ramshawe exercised discretion, resisting the overpowering temptation to tell Borden that everyone knew more than he did. Instead, he said simply. 'Sir, I was under the impression that you wanted the whole subject ignored until there was hard evidence. That's what you told me.'

'Correct. But when the second tanker was damaged, surely you knew I must be informed of your investigation, the fact that the ships were so close.'

'Sir, I wrote up my report and handed it to your duty officer on Saturday morning. I came in especially.'

'Well, it did not reach me. Which put me at a tremendous disadvantage, because Arnold Morgan had worked it out precisely as you did.'

The Ramshawe discretion vanished. 'Sir, it is beyond my imagination that anyone could work it out any other way. The bloody towelheads and the Chinks have mined the bloody Strait. I've been telling you that for a month. We even know where the bastards got the mines. I've also been telling you *that* for weeks. And if you still want my advice, I'm also telling you there's more to come on this.'

Admiral Borden retreated, saying as he left, 'Just make sure I'm kept up to speed. It is essential that I'm on precisely the same knowledge level as Admiral Morgan.' David Borden shut the door noisily, missing Jimmy Ramshawe's, 'That'll be the bloody day.' More important, he had forgotten to ask what further developments there were, even though he could see the pile of satellite photographs on the young surveillance officer's desk.

Big mistake. Jimmy Ramshawe had pictures of four tankers – three Iranians, one Chinese – making passage out of the Gulf on the Iran side of Hormuz. They had all crossed the line of the minefield, exiting through an area less than three miles wide, four and a half miles offshore at the nearest point. 'That's it,' he murmured. 'They're still transporting Iranian crude and Chinese refined oil from Kazakhstan, right through that gap, while the rest of the world sits and waits for clearance from the Omanis to continue on. And they're not going to get it. The Strait is going to become a giant tanker park, while the ayatollahs and the Chinese get rich.' He picked up the secure telephone and dialed the main White House switchboard, from where he was put straight through to Admiral Morgan, as instructed. 'It's between 56.56 and 56.59E, sir,' he said. 'Four ships so far, three Iran, one China.'

'Thanks, Jimmy. Go tell your boss, while I tell mine.'

The afternoon newspapers came up and still no one was making any kind of speculation that something was drastically wrong in the Strait of Hormuz. Arnold Morgan paced his office, racking his brains, waiting for the inevitable. Jimmy Ramshawe stayed at his desk long after his shift was over, staring at the satellite photographs, occasionally talking to the CIA's Middle Eastern desk at Langley. But there was nothing. Just the shattering coincidence of two ships damaged in the same stretch of water in the Strait.

The President had listened to Admiral Morgan's suspicions with equanimity. The relationship between the two men was at a very low point. Eight months previously Arnold Morgan had threatened to quit and to take the President with him. Everyone knew he could have done so. The grotesque scandal and cover-up over the incident last year in the South China Sea was like a loaded revolver at the Chief Executive's head. John Clarke would sit out his final months in the Oval Office courtesy of his National Security Adviser. He was not a man to relish this. Thus he treated any warning from his supposed right-hand man with suspicion and a negative turn of mind. He had been receptive to the idea of moving heavy naval muscle up into the Strait, because he recognized the lethal consequences of being wrong. He stated curtly that such matters were what the Admiral was paid to do and to proceed as he thought fit.

Later he sent a memorandum to Admiral Morgan outlining the gist of their conversation and absolving himself of any blame whatsoever if this thing blew up in everyone's face, with the entire Navy on the move at huge expense, for nothing. Arnold Morgan screwed up the memo and tossed it, dismissing its contents as the ramblings of a disarranged mind, if not those of a 'total asshole'.

1900 (local) April 30.
The Strait of Hormuz.
The American-owned crude carrier *Galveston Star* was, without question, the biggest VLCC currently operating in the Gulf. She had a dead weight of 420,000 tons and her six cargo tanks were fully laden with 450,000 cubic meters of oil, loaded from the man-made steel island at Mina al Ahmadi off the Kuwaiti coast. She was bound for the Gulf of Mexico and making twenty knots, just about due east, through Hormuz. Her comms room had picked up the warning from the Omani Navy that temporary restrictions were in operation and that there was no clear seaway out to the Arabian Sea at this time. The restricted area ran in a line from Ra's Qabr al Hindi on the northern Omani coast right across to the Iranian shore more than thirty miles away at position 25.23N 57.05E. No explanation was offered, save for the fact that an LNG carrier had burned

out three days ago and a damaged VLCC was still leaking oil a dozen miles further east.

Captain Tex Packard was unimpressed. His massive ship took almost four miles to come to a halt traveling at this speed. He was late, after a pump problem at al Ahmadi where he had spent almost thirty-four hours loading, instead of the scheduled twenty-one. And it was hotter than hell. All he wanted to do was 'drive this baby the fuck out of this godawful place and get home to the Gulf coast of the USA', where, incidentally, it was also hotter than hell.

Captain Tex was not just a dyed-in-the-wool lifelong tankerman. He was a copper-bottomed purist, even among the men who drive these technological atrocities along the world's oceans. His ship was almost a quarter of a mile long and he knew every inch of her. He was a great blond-haired bull of a man from the Panhandle Plains of north-west Texas where, he constantly reminded his shipmates, a man could still make a living on the back of a horse, riding the vast cattle ranches. Why, his own family had been doing so for generations and he was the very first of the Packard cowboys to leave those wide-open spaces for a different kind of wilderness. At the age of forty-seven, Captain Tex still spoke fondly of the Panhandle City of Lubbock, where he had attended Texas Tech University in the home town of the legendary rocker Buddy Holly. In fact, Buddy had died the year before Tex was born, but the big sea Captain spoke of him as if they had been fast friends 'back home in Lubbock'.

There were still sweltering evenings in the Iranian Gulf when the distant cries of the mullahs summoning the faithful on the echoing loudspeakers above the mosques mingled, out on the calm water, with the unmistakable sounds of 'Peggy Sue', 'Maybe Baby' and 'Oh Boy!' drifting out from the bridge of the gigantic *Galveston Star*. First thing

Captain Tex did when he welcomed a new crew was to make sure they could join in the chorus of 'Peggy Sue' and to make equally certain the cook knew precisely how to make the fabled Texas dish of chicken-fried steak (CFS). He showed them how to pulverize the beef to within an inch of its life with a kitchen mallet, then hand-dip it in egg batter, double-dredged in seasoned flour, before dropping it into searing-hot oil in an iron skillet. 'That's CFS, boy,' he would rumble in his deep baritone drawl. 'Cook that raht and you'll get a place on the highest honor role in mah home state. Ain't but a few cooks can git it just raht and I want you to *join* that golden group, hear me?'

There was, however, nothing of the buffoon about Tex Packard. He was a superb navigator and supremely confident in his own unique ability to handle his city-sized vessel, probably the biggest ship there had ever been and just about indestructible, with her double hull and water-tight compartments. As he frequently reminded his crew, 'Fifty years ago the British and French landed an army at Suez with nothing else to do 'cept keep the crude-oil carriers moving.' He knew the history of the world of tankers, understood that normal life, for millions and millions of people, rested entirely on the free and unimpeded passage of these monster ships.

It was thus a surprise to no one when Captain Tex Packard told his chief engineer, his cargo officer and his chief officer that he had no intention of stopping for the goddamned Omani Navy, whatever their problem was. 'Christ, you could lose their entire country in west Texas. We'll keep steering zero-nine-zero and make our southerly turn when we're just out of Oman's national water, but not far enough into the Iranian side. Right then we're going straight through. Next stop the Texas Gulf coast and no more bullshit. Hold this easterly course,' he ordered, 'and maintain speed.'

The Chief Engineer, Jeb Duross from south Louisiana, said routinely, 'This course is gonna take us clear across the incoming tanker lanes; we'd better keep a good watch and a lot of radar.'

'According to the Omanis, most every ship's stopped, waiting for clearance,' replied the Captain. 'So I don't guess we're gonna get a whole lot of tonnage coming across our bows. Anyway we'll pick 'em up miles away. No problem.'

The *Galveston Star* plowed forward. Twenty knots was a good speed for a VLCC, but she was already late and at this time Captain Packard was prepared to sacrifice fuel for speed. His ship had a range of over 12,000 miles and up on the bridge, 100 feet above the surface of the water, Buddy Holly was about to rock the high command of the tanker down towards the Iranian end of Jimmy Ramshawe's straight line.

By now there were several 'paints' on the radar, showing tankers making some kind of a holding pattern inside the Gulf in the north-eastern national waters of Oman. The far side of the tanker lanes, incoming, seemed more or less deserted. There was a depth of 180 feet below the keel and, in clear seas on longitude 56.44E, Captain Packard made a south-easterly turn, selecting a course which would take him five miles north of the stricken Greek tanker, before he turned due south and went for the line.

Of course, only Admiral Morgan and Lieutenant Ramshawe were certain of the existence of the regular three-line minefield, the PLT-3 moored sea mines every 500 yards. The laying of mines in the dark is an inexact science, but in general terms this meant there was a mine in the path of any ship separated by a maximum distance of around 170 yards. It also meant that if a ship slid by the first one, missing it by, say, ten yards to starboard, the next one would come up 160 yards to port and the next two after that 340 yards to port and 170 to starboard. It was thus possible to miss them altogether, as many ships had. But it was still the maddest game of Russian roulette ever invented, especially for this particular tanker. The giant *Galveston Star* was seventy-five yards wide.

Three miles short of the first line, Captain Packard received a formal warning from one of the Omani Navy corvettes that it was dangerous to proceed. No one was yet admitting that there might be a minefield and the warning thus had no teeth so far as big Tex Packard was concerned. 'Screw 'em,' he confirmed. 'We're outta here.'

Up ahead the seas were clear. At least they were on the surface and the *Galveston Star* came barreling down the Strait in a freshly developed high wind off the Arabian desert, an early harbinger of the evolving south-west monsoon. This part of the Gulf was a wind convergence zone where, in the late spring, the north-easters out of the central Chinese desert, which prevail all winter, gave way to the south-westers from Africa. This year they were early, and strong, gusty breezes can catch the massive hull of a VLCC and cause a significant leeway.

The *Galveston Star* was thus sliding infinitesimally east as she stood fair down the Strait, plowing through the short surface waves, having completed her long gentle turn towards the south. In fact, she missed the first of Admiral Zhang's mines by at least 150 yards to starboard. But the good news on line one was almost certainly going to put her bows awfully close to the PLT-3 moored on line two. On she ran for another 600 yards, still drifting very slightly east, closing the gap between her own course and the murderous one-ton, steel-encased hunk of TNT, which bobbed on its wire mooring twelve feet below the surface. The massive bows of the *Galveston Star* actually missed it completely and the wash of the widening hull pushed the mine away on its wire. However, it swung back inwards, hard and fast, crashing into the port side of the hull, 300 feet from the point of the bow.

At four minutes past 8 p.m. it detonated with awesome force, blowing the plates apart, right through both layers of the hull, blasting a massive hole in Cargo Tank Four. And Buddy Holly was still singing as the onrushing crude oil blew up in a raging fireball above the ocean: '*Stars appear and shadows a-falling . . . you can hear my heart a-calling . . . Oh Boy!*'

Tex Packard could not believe his eyes. The 420,000-tonner shuddered in its death throes as her colossal weight began to tear the entire hull apart. It was the biggest shipwreck in history and it was only four miles from the Greek tanker which had been pouring oil since Saturday. The *Galveston Star* was wallowing bang on Jimmy Ramshawe's straight line, twelve miles off the coast of Iran. Captain Packard knew a career-blowing decision when he saw one and he'd just made it.

'What are you going to do, sir?' asked Jeb Duross, anxiety written all over his face.

'Probably buy a cattle ranch,' replied Big Tex thoughtfully.

'Actually, I meant right now.'

'Send out a "MAYDAY". Radio Oman and Dubai, see if we can salvage any of the cargo, which I doubt. At least not yet, till we can get a couple of big ships out here to start pumping. Meanwhile we just gotta watch the fires. Crude sometimes doesn't burn, but ours is doing just that and, once it gets started, it's likely to go on for a long time.'

'Looks like the fire's inside the ship and that might be real dangerous,' said Jeb.

'Sure might. She gets much hotter we'll have to abandon. Sure hate to leave her, but this stuff can really burn if it gets hot enough. I'm not planning to be the hero, least not the dead hero. Have the lifeboats ready, Jeb, and have someone turn off the music, willya. Just don't want Buddy singing in a death ship. 'Sides, I wanna get mah CDs home to Texas. Buddy wouldn't wanna be singing to no towelheads.'

'*All mah life I been a-waiting . . . tonight there'll be no hesitatin' . . . Oh Boy!*'

Midday (local).
Fort Meade, Maryland.
Lieutenant Ramshawe had his small office television turned on several minutes early for CNN's twelve o'clock bulletin and when he heard the lead item there was no longer any doubt in his or anyone else's mind.

> We are receiving reports that one of the biggest oil tankers in the world, the 420,000-ton *Galveston Star* out of the Texas Gulf port of Houston, is currently on fire and breaking up in the Strait of Hormuz at the entrance to the Persian Gulf.
>
> The cause of the accident is at present unknown but the Captain and his crew are believed to be preparing to abandon her. Fires are reported raging over 100 feet into the skies.
>
> This is the third major shipping accident in the Strait in the past four days, following the inferno of the liquid gas carrier *Global Bronco* of Houston on Friday and the explosion in the Greek crude carrier *Olympus 2004* on Saturday.

The newscaster ended the report by saying the US Navy would be issuing a statement later in the afternoon, but as yet there was no suggestion that any nation had elected to place sea mines in the Strait to endanger world oil shipping routes.

101

At that moment Jimmy's phone rang and he heard the gruff and distinctive tones of Admiral Morgan: 'Okay, Jimmy, I guess that does it. Go keep your boss up to speed, but keep me personally alerted to any information you get off the overheads.'

The phone went down before Lieutenant Ramshawe could even answer. Before he could gather his wits, his other phone went and Jane was on the line, telling him how clever he was and would he be able to have dinner tonight, with her and her parents, at the embassy.

'You seen the television?' he asked her.

'Darned right I did. I was watching it with my dad. He said immediately the Iranians had mined the area, just like they'd been threatening to do. I told him that was my considered opinion too, that I'd suspected something like that since the *Bronco* went up last Friday. He gave me a real old-fashioned look.'

'I should think he did. But he doesn't know about the phone call, does he, the one from his private line?'

'No. At least he hasn't said anything. Anyway, are you coming tonight? He's got some Aussie sailors coming, yachtsmen, Americas Cup guys. Might be fun.'

'Yup. I'll be there. 'Bout seven.'

1300 same day.
The Oval Office.
Admiral Morgan recounted the events in the Gulf swiftly and with no elaboration.

The President sat impassively and asked curtly, 'Your recommendations?'

'Sir, I have already ordered the *Constellation* CVBG south from the Iraqi coast and the *John C. Stennis* Group is closing the Strait immediately from the Arabian Sea. Our third group in the area, the *Harry S. Truman*, should clear Diego Garcia by tomorrow morning and head north. I've arranged for the Indian Navy to begin a hunt and sweep operation with their Pondicherrys as soon as they can get there. Right now they're on their way from Bombay, probably be in Hormuz waters by tomorrow morning our time. I had them leave on Sunday.'

'Do you think there could be full-scale hostilities, Admiral? I don't want to get drawn into an unpopular war with Iran. Dead American sailors don't play well politically.'

'Sir, this is probably the height of our national interest. Do you have any idea what might happen if the Gulf had to be closed off for a month?'

'I cannot say I have given it deep thought, Admiral. But I am much more concerned about sitting in this chair being universally blamed for death, destruction and burned Americans. Because that's what happens when you start flexing the muscles of big warships.'

'If we don't start flexing them, sir, the entire world oil supply could go right up the chute. And if the lights went out in the USA you'd get yourself a very special place in history. Especially if you had refused to act in the Persian Gulf in the face of hostility and threats from Iran and their buddies in Beijing.'

'As usual, Admiral, you have my best interests at heart.' There was an edge of sarcasm in the President's voice.

'Perhaps not, sir. But I always have the best interests of this nation at heart.'

'Then proceed as you think fit, Admiral. You always do anyway. Just let me know if I need to make a speech, will you? And perhaps Harcourt should make some kind of diplomatic overtures to the Chinese and the Iranians?'

'Two reasons not to, sir. One, it will alert the entire world to a crisis we may be able to strangle at birth. Two, they'll just deny everything anyway and probably be very amused at our concern. 'Specially if they've done it, which

I already know they have.' Arnold Morgan did not wait for a reply. He turned on his heel and left, muttering to himself, 'What a lightweight. What a goddamned lightweight. In five years he's gone from being a damned good president to a self-seeking wimp.'

By late afternoon every evening newspaper in the country was speculating on the possibility of a minefield in the Strait of Hormuz. The long-time threat of the ayatollahs was uppermost in the mind of every defense correspondent in every corner of the media. Television networks waited with scarcely contained excitement for the statement from the US Navy. But when it came it was stark and non-committal, precisely the way Arnold Morgan had instructed. The CNO had declined a press conference and issued his written statement, deliberately late, at 21.30, through the main wire services, carefully avoiding anything which would suggest panic to either the Chinese or the Iranians. It read:

The United States Navy has noted the three tanker incidents in the Strait of Hormuz during the last four days. In particular, we noted that two of them burned and one suffered an apparent explosion, which released large quantities of oil into the sea. In addition we noted that all three incidents occurred in a narrow seaway between the countries of Oman and Iran.

We have been in contact with our major allies in the area and have agreed to support them in their efforts to ascertain the causes of these incidents, and to discover whether there might be a link between them.

However, it is too early to draw any conclusions. We expect at least one of our aircraft carriers and her escorts to arrive on station in the Strait in the next twenty-four hours. Another US CVBG is currently steaming towards the Strait from the Arabian Sea.

In company with several other industrial nations, we are extremely concerned to insure the continued free passage of the world's fuel tankers through the Strait both into and out of the Gulf of Iran.

We have assured our allies of our continued assistance, should it become necessary to rectify any wrongdoing by any nation in these peaceful trading waters upon which so many countries depend.

It was signed 'Admiral Alan Dickson, Chief of United States Naval Operations'.

It was good, but not good enough. Four east-coast tabloid dailies were already setting headlines like: MINEFIELD TERROR IN THE GULF. TANKERS BLOWN UP IN GULF MINEFIELD. IRAN'S MINES BLAST US TANKERS.

All through the evening the television networks developed their stories, bringing in experts to discourse on the dangers of that part of the Middle East; recounting Iranian threats over the years; debating the possible involvement of China; discussing the consequences of an oil blockade.

By midnight, the President had called an emergency cabinet meeting in President Reagan's old Situation Room in the West Wing, and there the major brains in the Administration attempted to walk the tightrope between being prepared militarily and creating mass panic at the gas pumps.

Arnold Morgan, whose voice would be heard the loudest since he had been effectively on the case since Friday, was, uncharacteristically, urging caution. He wanted the CVBG in the Strait to protect and assist the Indian Navy's minesweepers. However, he saw no real advantage in making overt threats to either the Iranian or Chinese Navies, save to make them absolutely aware that if any of their warships attempted to interfere they would be sunk forthwith by US naval firepower. So far as the National Security Adviser was concerned, the US Navy had the matter well in hand. With the Strait now well and truly off limits to all world shipping, there seemed little point in looking for trouble until the Indians' Pondicherrys had begun work clearing the mines. In order to clear a three-mile-wide safe passage on the Omani side, Admiral Morgan estimated they might have to sweep forty of them, which might take several days as from Tuesday night (local).

Minesweeping was a thoroughly dangerous business, and it had to be conducted and executed with extreme care. The President wanted to know how it was done and Arnold Morgan suggested Admiral Dickson enlighten everyone.

'Sir,' said the CNO. 'When you locate the mine, it's going to be ten or twelve feet below the surface, attached by its cable to a mooring on the floor of the ocean. Basically it's buoyant and it's trying to float up to the surface, but is held down by its own cable. Well, you sweep them by towing cutting cables from the minesweeper, pulled down to the right depth and out from the side by an otter board. When the sweeper's cable snags a mine's mooring line, it keeps moving until both cable and line are taut. Then the cutter severs the line, allowing the mine to float to the surface. There it can be detonated by small-arms fire from a safe distance. They're easy when they're on the surface but, of course, impossible when you can't see them. However many times you've done it, you're always astounded by the size of the explosion.'

'Hey, that's pretty neat,' said the President.

'And pretty time-consuming,' replied the Admiral. 'How many sweepers are the Indians bringing?'

'Six,' replied Admiral Morgan. 'That'll help speed things up.'

'Cost?' asked the Secretary for Defense, Bob MacPherson predictably.

'I told the Indian Navy Chief that we would arrange for all affected nations to share the costs. Between us, the UK, the Japanese, Germans, France and some of the Middle East exporters, it'll come out as peanuts.'

'No problem,' said MacPherson.

'Look, Arnold,' said the President, using his Adviser's first name for the first time in months, 'I know you want to play this down right now. But I'm not sure we shouldn't go straight into Beijing and demand to know if they have played any part in this whatsoever.'

'Sir, they will simply deny any knowledge, whatever we say, which brings me to a very serious point.'

'It does?'

'Yes, sir. From our observations it looks very much as if the mines were transported to Iran in Chinese warships. Now we have a situation where for the next couple of weeks the Iranians are going to get pretty rich and, to an extent, so are the Chinese. They seem to have a way through the minefield, in Iranian national waters and the price of oil futures is probably going to $40 dollars a barrel for West Texas Intermediate on NYMEX and the same for Brent Crude on the London market. However, I completely fail to see what the Chinese are doing. How could it possibly be worth it?'

'Maybe they just want to show us they can be real world players in the oil game with their new Kazakhstan pipeline,' offered Harcourt Travis.

'Maybe,' replied Arnold Morgan. 'But that's a hell of a dangerous card to play for such a slim moral victory. Christ, for all they know we might get seriously pissed off with 'em. It just doesn't make any sense to me.'

'Well, Admiral, perhaps the political minds at the table can offer something that may have escaped you?'

'Beats me, sir,' said Harcourt.

'All I know is this,' said the National Security Adviser. 'The Chinese are very devious, very patient and utterly insincere when it suits them. What they are not is very stupid and, so far, everything in the Strait of Hormuz is plain stupid. What the hell are they doing, getting mixed up in something like this?'

'I guess they have their reasons,' said the President. 'But even more worrying is what the hell are the Iranians playing at? I know they believe the Gulf of Iran is, by its very name, theirs by rights and that the West has no real business in there at all. But they also know that if they attempt a blockade of the Gulf, we'll dismantle it and probably them with it. They're not stupid either, so what are they doing?'

'Six weeks ago I could not have answered that question, sir,' said Arnold Morgan. 'But things are coming to light and we are seeing a new rise in Muslim fundamentalism. Again the balance of political opinion is swaying against the West and every damn time that happens you get a new militant resurgence in Iran. All those pictures we got from Tehran a month ago, the street riots, the new calls for elections. They were all shouting for the same thing – total separation from the West, the right to their own oil, the right to make the Gulf private, the enduring vision of Islamic world domination. It's a phase, but it's worrying. Meanwhile, the present blockade of the Iranian Gulf is a giant-sized PITA – pain in the ass, that is. We gotta get it cleared or we're looking at world economic chaos.'

Tuesday morning, May 1.
PLAN HQ
Beijing.
Admiral Zhang Yushu had just walked into his new office, where his Navy C-in-C, Admiral Zu Jicai, was already

waiting. 'What do the satellites tell us today?' he asked.

'Excellent news all around, Yushu. Two American CVBGs are closing the Strait. The *Harry Truman* is plainly preparing to leave Diego Garcia today and the US carrier *John F. Kennedy* is under way, heading west out of Pearl Harbor.'

'That leaves just the *Ronald Reagan* Group still in San Diego, correct?'

'Yes, sir, and all the signs are that she is accelerating her overhaul, planning to leave in the next few weeks. There is truly the most thunderous commotion in the United States. Every newspaper, every television network. They're becoming hysterical about this threat to their national interest in the Strait of Hormuz.'

'Perhaps we should offer to sell them some very fine Russian oil, direct from our refinery in Iran, very cheap, fifty dollar a barrel. Ha ha ha!'

'Yushu, you are a hard man. Although I admit the prospect has great appeal, I would counsel silence. Say nothing. Do nothing. See nothing.'

'Meanwhile, to more important matters, Jicai. Are these military estimates accurate? We still have sea-lift capacity for only 12,000 troops? And 250 main battle tanks?'

'Yes, sir. But the turnaround time for our amphibians will be short.'

'Are the ships on their way back from the Indian Ocean?'

'Yes, sir.'

'Excellent. That's the three guided-missile frigates, plus two Kilos?'

'Correct. They're all on their way home, sir. And as you know, the destroyer is making its way back towards Bandar Abbas, just as a warning to the USA that we don't want them to attack our friends in Iran under any circumstances.'

'Ah, but it's a mission well achieved, eh, my Jicai?'

'In the ancient tradition of the great Admiral Zheng He, sir. Just as you always dreamed.'

'And such a dream, my Jicai. Remember the words we all learned, the words written by the immortal Admiral 500 years ago? "*And we have set eyes on barbarian regions far away . . . while our sails, loftily unfurled like clouds, day and night, continued their course as rapidly as a star, traversing those savage waves.*"' Zhang paused for just a moment. Then he said quietly, 'That's our tradition and it's only been dormant. Not dead. We will rise to rule those seas again.'

0955 (local) Tuesday, May 1.
The International Petroleum Exchange
London, England.
No day in the entire twenty-six-year history of Europe's principal oil futures trading floor had ever been awaited with more dread, trepidation and alarm. Here in the shadow of the Tower of London, bounded by streets with echoing names like Thomas More, hard by the waters of historic St Katharine's Dock, the industrial world's fate hung in the balance.

Five hours before New York's NYMEX oil trading gets under way on Wall Street, the London Exchange opens for business, setting the world's pricing benchmark for the day, maybe the month. The commodity is Brent Crude Futures, and the price per barrel of North Sea oil is the one upon which the major international traders and investors are prepared to speculate. If the traders think there's likely to be a glut of oil in the foreseeable future, the price may go below $15, trading narrowly, varying by just a few cents either way. Any sign of a shortage and the price may rise to around $30. A serious shortage can cause this swerving, volatile market to lose all sense of caution. When Iraq invaded Kuwait back in 1990, everyone thought the roof had caved in and, on one lunatic day at the IPE, Brent Crude hit $70 a barrel.

Today the atmosphere was fraught. Captain Tex Packard's ship was still on fire in the Strait, and in London nervous representatives of the big oil producers, refiners, shippers, distributers and marketers mingled with other major users. Brokers representing the power generators, airlines, truck fleet operators, chemical companies and even supermarkets were on tenterhooks. The world's most eminent money men from houses like Morgan Stanley were massed along with everyone else on the packed hexagonal-shaped trading floor, with its tiered pits, video surveillance and colossal security.

The previous night, Brent Crude had closed at $28 a barrel, up three bucks. And West Texas Intermediate in New York was tagged at a few cents below. Today cell phones were running up massive bills connecting the US traders with London, long before the opening bell at NYMEX. What mattered right now was the opening bell in London and the traders, wearing their identifying colored jackets, red, yellow, green or blue, thronged above the pits as the clock ticked on to ten o'clock. Bang on time it rang, signaling the floor was open for business, trading at first in natural gas futures, the prices for which would explode before this day was done.

One minute went by, then the clock hit 1002 and the second opening bell rang sharp and loud, for the initial trades of Brent Crude Futures, the world pricing benchmark; at which point, on this day, the entire system of international oil commodity trading went berserk.

Pandemonium broke out as buyers yelled '*Plus Two. Plus Two!*' But these weren't cents, as in the regular cries of '*Brent Plus Two!*'. These were whole dollars: $30, then $32, then $35, then $40. Bedrock prices for a barrel of oil had jumped thirty-three and a third per cent in nine minutes. 'Mother of God!' breathed the broker for Shell and the trader for a New York bank roared '*Plus Five. Plus Five for 500,000*', which pegged the price of Brent Crude Futures at an astounding $45 a barrel.

Dealers left behind in the stampede for the best prices surged forward as rumor swept the pits that the price was going to $70. Brokers for the big finance houses huddled together, uncertain whether to chase the price up further or whether to wait for the retreat some thought might not come. At least not on this day.

Snatches of conversation fired the desperate atmosphere. Yelling, classless British voices from London, interspersed with louder American tones: '*Jesus H. Christ! This can't last. Bullshit it can't. They've just closed the fucking Gulf of Iran. It's only three ships, for chrissakes! It doesn't matter a flying fuck if it's only one. Right here we're talking fucking minefields! That's one step from global war. The US Navy's moving* three *aircraft carriers into the Strait. You think this market's fake? Forget it. There might be no more oil out of the Gulf for six months.*'

Five minutes later the price hit $50 when a Rotterdam trader bid on a precious cargo of Shell crude currently on its way to Scandinavia. For a brief four minutes the price hung, then faltered at around $50. Then a rumour swept the floor that a major fleet of minesweepers from the Indian Navy was under escort moving up the Arabian Sea to the Strait. The price of Brent Crude Futures hit $55 in forty-two seconds and by now it was impossible to hear anything above the thunder of the pits as the traders piled in, bellowing bids for any available crude oil already free of the confines of the Gulf of Iran. On a normal trading day, 50 million barrels change hands in this room. In today's uproar, almost 30 million were traded in the first forty-five minutes. There was only one thing worse than paying through the nose for oil and that was not having any.

'PLUS TWO. PLUS FOUR. PLUS WHATEVER IT TAKES.'

By eleven o'clock that morning the price of world fuel oil had doubled. By the close of trade it stood at $72. Up over 150 per cent. No one in the International Petroleum Exchange had ever seen anything like it. In New York, West Texas Intermediate had *opened* at $60 a barrel. Gas oil futures had gone through the roof and natural gas futures, thanks to the exploded *Global Bronco*, were even higher.

1630 (local) Tuesday, May 1.
The White House.

Admiral Morgan stared at the pile of data before him. The minesweepers were in action in Hormuz and there was no doubt the field was comprised entirely of Russian-made PLT-3s. So far as the Indian commanding officers were concerned they were looking at three lines, less than half a mile apart. Inshore on the Omani side, they were in deep water and it looked as though the same three lines stretched clean across the Strait to the Iranians' Sunburn missile site. Lieutenant Ramshawe had thus far been correct in all his assumptions.

But now the tasks facing Fort Meade were different. Question one was where is China now deploying the warships? The Kilos seemed to have disappeared from the face of the earth, but the two frigates which had been flying the national flag of Iran had been picked up by the overheads traveling towards China's Burmese base in the Bassein river. The *Shantou* had already left there and was making her way towards the Malacca Strait. But of China's big Sovremenny destroyer there was no sign.

Quite frankly, the Chinese completely baffled the President's National Security Adviser. For a start he had no idea what they had hoped to achieve by providing the hardware for the ayatollahs to mine the Strait of Hormuz.

Nonetheless, they had plainly done it, and the Western world along with Japan and Taiwan, and to an extent South Korea, was presently in deep trouble. The world would run out of oil in a matter of weeks if the Gulf of Iran was not opened up very quickly. The Chinese obviously thought they were immune to this chaos and in Arnold Morgan's opinion they must be taught a very sharp lesson. It might be possible to tweak and irritate the United States, but when you start tampering with the national interest of the world's one superpower you might very well end up in deadly serious trouble. Nonetheless, Admiral Morgan was determined not to overreact until he could ascertain what the men in Beijing were doing.

Not so the President. He went into a complete dither as world oil prices went into some kind of meltdown, or rather a meltup. Constantly on the line to his Energy Secretary Jack Smith, he kept asking, over and over, 'But what's this going to mean for the average American at the gas pumps?'

As early as mid-afternoon, answers were coming in fast and furious. And they were all the same. Up, up and up again, as the big gas station chains found themselves paying fortunes for every barrel of crude oil on either side of the Atlantic. West Texas Intermediate looked set to close even higher than Brent Crude Futures and still big Tex Packard's mighty tanker blazed alone out in the Strait, lighting up the waters. When the gusting wind swung back round to the north-east it sent a gigantic black oil cloud into the night skies above Arabia.

In a week when gas prices could very easily hit $3 a gallon at the pump, or even $3.50, President Clarke faced rampaging inflation on a scale which would send the Federal Reserve into shock. Every commodity and product in the USA was going to suffer because of drastic increases in transport costs. Taxis, buses, diesel freight trains, interstate trucks, airlines – especially airlines – anything that moved was going to be hit. And that was not the worst of it. President Clarke had a vision of the ultimate national uproar: the United States starting to run out of oil, with no time to tap its own reserves. High gas prices were one thing. No gas at any price was another entirely. If the country ground to a halt, his name would surely be remembered as one of the most ineffective presidents in the entire history of the nation. And what the hell was his oh-so-brilliant National Security Adviser doing about it? So far as he could see, a big fat zero. He picked up his phone and asked a secretary to have Admiral Morgan report to him instantly.

Two minutes later Arnold came growling in through the open door to the Oval Office. 'You wanted me, sir?'

'Admiral, what the hell are we doing about this stand-off in the Gulf?'

'Sir, we got a minefield across the Strait of Hormuz, as I explained. The Gulf is now shut. The Iranians are saying nothing, admitting nothing, and they sure as hell aren't about to clear it. Neither are their buddies in Beijing. That means we have to clear the minefield ourselves and the Indian Navy, working on our behalf, began that process several hours ago. They have six minesweepers, under our protection, locating and exploding the mines. But it's slow and there's a lot of them. I understand they have attended to three so far, and my guess is there's still forty to go, in order to secure safe passage for essentially defenseless tankers. There's already an environmental nightmare of spilled oil in the Strait.'

'Well what are we doing about the goddamned Iranians? That's your area, Arnold.'

'Sir, you want me to declare war on 'em? Or at least advise you to do so?'

'I don't know, Arnold.' The President's voice was

rising. 'I just know this could be a major national crisis and we seem powerless.'

'Well, we're not that, sir. However, I do not want to make any kind of extravagant move until we clear the mines, quietly and with as little rancor as possible. A hot war raging around the minesweepers would clearly be absurd. When the field is cleared, though, I'm happy to station a lot of muscle in the Strait and warn both Iran and China that one false move means we'll sink 'em.'

'Well, why not issue that warning right now?'

'I just did, sir, three hours ago.'

'You told 'em we'd sink them?'

'Sir, I just sent a joint communiqué to Tehran and Beijing informing them of our anger at their conduct and our intention to eliminate any warship from any nation which tries to interfere with the removal of the sea mines.'

'And what about the future, Arnold? The future. That's what my job is all about. What about the damned future? How do we know the Chinese might not mastermind this kind of stunt again?'

'Sir, as you know, they have a very large petrochemical and oil refinery on the southern Iranian coast. It's tapped right into the heart of the oilfields of Kazakhstan. I was proposing to recommend its elimination.'

'It's *what*?'

'Destruction, sir. A better word altogether. I agree.'

'You mean bomb it?'

'Sir. Please! Let's not be crude, like the oil.'

'Well, what are you saying?'

'I'm proposing an insertion of Special Forces, to put that refinery out of action for ever.'

'You mean the SEALs?'

'Yes, sir.'

'Can we get them in? And out again?'

'Certainly we can. We can do anything.'

'But surely everyone will know it's us?'

'Same as we know who mined the Gulf. But no one's saying anything, at least not in a confrontational way. We make no accusations, at least not publicly. They make no admissions. We just do what we do.'

'But the goddamned Chinese would go bananas if we blew up their refinery.'

'No, sir. They'd feel like going bananas. But they'd get a very quiet message from us: "You guys want to start fucking around with America's oil supplies? We'll show you how to really fuck around."'

'Arnold, your brutality occasionally takes my breath away. But I like it. Makes me feel safe in this big chair.'

'My job, sir, is to make every American feel safe, no matter how big or small their chair may be.'

'Should I now conclude this strategy meeting?'

'Mr President, this is not strategy. This is direct action. Clear the Strait. Protect the sweepers. Then guard the Strait with all the menace we can. By that I mean four CVBGs on station between the area inside the Gulf and our base on Diego Garcia. Any foreign warship moves in that area without our express permission, that warship's history.'

'Arnold, please go ahead as you think fit.'

'That's not quite all, sir.'

'It's not? What else? You planning to conquer Russia or something?'

'No, sir. But I am distressed by China's plain and obvious naval expansion. It's no secret they want a Blue Water Navy for the first time in more than 500 years, and it's no secret they are expanding at a rapid and apparently sustainable rate. In the past few years they've created a new submarine fleet. They've bought two aircraft carriers, three Russian destroyers and a ton of hardware from the old Soviet missile outfits. They're reaching out, sir. And we really don't like it.'

'We don't?'

'Sir, we are staring a major problem bang in the face. China is on the move. They have cozied up to us for a lot of years and they'll go on doing so for as long as it suits them. But when they feel they're good and ready to challenge us, to dominate the East and to swing the balance of power their way, that's when you'll see the real face of China. Trust me.'

'Well, what do you plan to do about that?'

'I plan to stop that global expansion dead in its tracks. I want that damned great Navy of theirs back in the China Seas.'

'But how do we do that without starting a shooting war?'

'Sir, how do we keep us our own global presence? How do we keep our own Navy roaming the world's oceans making sure no one steps out of line? Right here the world enjoys *Pax Americana*. Like it once enjoyed *Pax Romana*. That was peace on the terms of the Romans. Now it's peace on the terms of the Americans. And we do it by insuring we have a succession of US bases all over the place – in the Pacific Ocean, the Indian Ocean, in the Japanese islands, with our buddies from London in the Atlantic. That's the only way. A chain of supplies and allies. That's what China does not have. Yet. Except for one place. Burma.'

'You mean that new base of theirs in the swamps west of Rangoon.'

'That's the one, sir. The one on the island in the Bassein river. It's huge. Massive facilities for servicing and refueling warships of all sizes, including submarines. The Chinese once dominated the entire Indian Ocean and my instinct is they want to do so again, because that would give 'em control of the main eastbound oil route through the Malacca Strait. Right now that narrow, shallow freeway, with its goddamned granite bottom, is just too far from China to allow them any influence over its tanker traffic.'

'Well, how do you propose to discourage them from using their new Burmese base?'

Arnold Morgan smiled. 'Not too hasty right now, sir. We got bigger problems. But if you've got any shares in China's naval operation on Haing Gyi Island in the Bassein river, sell.'

Four

020330MAY07. The Indian Ocean.
USS Shark. *Speed 30. Depth 400.*
By the start of the final half-hour of the midnight watch,
Lieutenant-Commander Headley was mobile, moving
quietly through the thirty-year-old 5000-ton nuclear boat,
thirty minutes before he was due to take over the control
room from Commander Reid. He had already been down
to the main propulsion room where Lieutenant-
Commander Paul Flynn was watching a very minor seal
leak on the main shaft. The pumps were operating
efficiently and dealing with the incoming fine spray with
relative ease. 'Damn thing wouldn't want to get any
worse, though,' said the dark-haired engineering officer
from south Boston. 'Still, the rest of the stuff's looking
good, reactor's smooth, shaft's steady. At twenty-nine
knots she feels like she's cruisin'. No problems, sir.'

Dan Headley made his way up to the navigation
officer's corner of the ops room. He had only just met
young Lieutenant Shawn Pearson, but he knew he had
been rescued with the crew of *Seawolf* when that massive
nuclear attack boat had been lost the previous year in the
South China Sea. 'Hi, Shawn,' he said, leaning on the big
table and staring down at the chart. 'What are we? 'Bout
700 nor'nor'-west of DG?'

'Accurate, sir. Accurate. I like that in an XO, gives me
confidence. I just sent for coffee. Want some, sir?'

The Lieutenant-Commander had immediately liked

Shawn Pearson because he was sharp, amusing and never lacked respect for more senior officers. Whatever his part had been in the *Seawolf* debacle, he had been highly decorated for it. An honor Dan Headley assumed must have been well deserved. 'Good idea, Lieutenant,' he said. 'Keep me awake for the next four hours.'

'Right now I have us five degrees north of the equator, on line of longitude six-five-zero-zero. As a matter of fact we're running fast beneath about a zillion square miles of absolutely nothing. Maybe 500 miles west of the Maldives, still way short of the most southerly latitude of the Indian continent. But we're gettin' there, sir.'

'Any ships around?'

'No, sir. Just our immediate escort, the frigate *Vandegrift*. She's steaming about three miles off our starboard beam, sir, same course: three-five-two. We're just about five miles off the carrier's port bow and she's got a destroyer off each beam – *Mason* to port, *Howard* to starboard.'

'How about *Cheyenne*?'

'She's way off the carrier's starboard bow, maybe four miles east of us. Same depth.'

Dan Headley sipped his coffee. 'Mind if I take this with me?' he asked companionably.

'Not at all, sir. It'll keep you sharp, while I'm sleeping gently.'

'Well, remember you've still got fifteen to go. So long, Lieutenant. Don't get us lost now.'

'No, sir. I am right on top of this.'

As he wandered towards the control room, Dan Headley thought again of the reality of the situation – this huge jet-black steel tube, forging north through the Indian Ocean, hundreds of feet below the surface, in complete secret, a lethal weapon of war, terminally deadly to any opponent. The *esprit de corps* in an attack submarine was like no other feeling in any other ship. He felt that he and

Shawn Pearson were somehow friends for life, after an acquaintance of just a few hours. US Navy submarines do that. They fling people together, causing them to see only the best points in each other.

Dan Headley was proud to serve in this old ship and so far he had been impressed with every one of his crew. He especially liked Drew Fisher, the Chief of the Boat, a big blond former center fielder from the University of Georgia. The Master Chief Petty Officer had dropped out of college to try his luck at professional baseball, but failed to make it through a constant ankle injury. He had ended up with no university degree, no money and no career, in or out of sports. 'Sir, I didn't even have a bat,' he had told Dan Headley. 'So I just joined the Navy and kept right on going.' Drew had risen steadily up through the ranks and in Lieutenant-Commander Headley's opinion was not finished yet. It was widely rumored that the former Georgia Bulldogs left-hander was on the verge of accepting a commission and that full command might not be that far away.

Drew was only thirty-six years old and, in addition to his onerous duties on board, he had pushed himself through course after course, gaining qualifications in navigation, weapons, hydrology, electronics, marine engineering. Right now he was working on combat systems and spent a lot of time with Lieutenant-Commander Jack Cressend from New Orleans, *Shark*'s CS Officer. In fact, the two men were together outside the control room directly up ahead of Dan and they greeted him cheerfully. The Master Chief, like Dan, was early for his watch and had already ascertained that *Shark*'s new XO was some kind of an expert on thoroughbred horses. In the small hours of the morning, running hard above the towering underwater mountains of the Mid-Indian Ridge, he wanted to know precisely which colt was going to win the

Kentucky Derby at Churchill Downs this Saturday.

Four hours before, Dan Headley had been non-committal on the big field, four of which in his opinion held live chances. This was not good enough for Drew who wanted heavy inside information in fine detail, so he asked the *Shark*'s second-in-command again, 'Come on, sir. Give me your real, true selection.'

'Well, Drew, my daddy raised one of the runners from a foal, big gray colt named White Rajah, trained in New York for Mr Phipps.'

'Can he run?'

''Course he can run, otherwise he wouldn't be entered for the Derby, would he?'

'What did he win?'

'Three races as a two-year-old. Got beat a nose in the Hopeful at Saratoga. But he improved over the winter. They sent him down to South Carolina for a spell, then he came out and damned nearly won the Florida Derby off a bad draw.'

'That his last race?'

'Hell no. He came back to New York, won the Wood Memorial over nine furlongs. That's the best Derby Trial in my view: been won by some of the greats, the real big guns of the horse game. Christ, Secretariat got beat in it before his Triple Crown.'

'Jeez, sir. You really know that horse stuff, right?'

'Guess so. It's in my blood. My family been raisin' racers out in the Blue Grass for about five generations.'

'Ah, but you still ain't told me one bit of real sensitive information about the White Rajah.'

'Oh, that's easy,' replied Lieutenant-Commander Headley. 'His grandaddy damned near bit my right arm off when I was a kid. Vicious sonofabitch.'

'Seriously? Jeez, I didn't know thoroughbred horses were savage.'

'This particular bloodline is very difficult. Got a lot of temperament in there.'

'Then why do people breed to it?'

'Because the suckers can run, that's why. And a lot of 'em can *really* run. Like the Rajah.'

'Well, that settles it. I'm bettin' him.'

'You think they got an OTB in the Arabian Sea?'

'Hell, I forgot about that. Do you think I could borrow the satellite link to San Diego?'

'Oh, sure. We're heading for the front line, in the middle of a world oil crisis and our overhead link is somehow out of action because the Chief of the Boat is trying to back White Rajah in the Kentucky Derby.'

'Shit, it's a cruel world, sir.'

'Crueler if he wins, Chief, and you're not on.'

All three men laughed. There was no doubt that Lieutenant-Commander Headley was already extremely well-liked and now he strolled into the control room, wished the commanding officer 'Good morning' and added, 'Ready to take over whenever you say, sir.'

Commander Reid looked at his watch. 'Seven more minutes, XO. I like to serve a full four hours.'

'Fine, sir. I'll be right here. No change in the satellite contact, sir, 0600 as scheduled?'

'As scheduled, XO. That's the way I like it.'

Dan Headley continued to familiarize himself with the control room, which was smaller than he was used to. His last tour had been, fortuitously, in USS *Kentucky*, one of the huge Ohio Class Trident strategic missile submarines and he had been under the impression that he might be awarded a full command in one of these 19,000-ton nuclear giants. But, quite suddenly, he had been posted to USS *Shark*, on positively her final tour of duty, to assist Commander Reid on his last tour of duty. Dan assumed this was because of the rising unrest in the Iranian Gulf area and there was plainly some concern about the mental steadfastness of the veteran CO. Thus far Dan had found Commander Reid to be reserved, polite, a little rigid in his thoughts for a submarine commander and punctilious in the extreme. But he could work with that. So long as they did not come under serious pressure.

At 0400 precisely Commander Reid handed over the control room. 'You have the ship, XO,' he said formally.

'Aye, sir. I have the ship.'

Lieutenant-Commander Headley checked *Shark*'s speed, course and position. He checked with comms the 0600 satellite contact and ordered, 'Maintain speed twenty-nine, depth 400. Course three-five-two.' Then he picked up his telephone and checked in with the propulsion engineer. The leak on the shaft was no worse. The pumps still coped easily and the big Westinghouse PWR was running sweetly. The sonar room was quiet. Lieutenant-Commander Josh Gandy reported no new contacts of any kind, not that this was likely at such speed.

All through the night they ran north towards the Arabian Sea, until dawn began to break over the eastern waters, way off their starboard beam. Lieutenant-Commander Headley ordered them to periscope depth and accessed the satellite. There was no change in their orders: *Proceed to the eastern waters of the Strait of Hormuz in company with the aircraft carrier* Harry S. Truman. *Then replace on station the* John C. Stennis *Group when it clears the area and runs back south to Diego Garcia.* Both Lieutenant-Commander Josh Gandy and Master Chief Fisher were with the XO when he checked the orders.

'Sorry, Chief,' Dan muttered. 'Nothing from OTB. Guess the Rajah's gonna run without your money to handicap him.' That was the last joke of the watch and the rest of it passed slowly, as did the next two days. By 0400 on Friday morning, May 4, the *Shark* was almost at the gateway to the Gulf of Oman, which leads to the narrow waters of Hormuz. They had crossed the twenty-four-degree northern line of latitude and were currently running 100 feet below the surface with another 250 feet of water under the keel. It would be light in a couple of hours and, presumably, with the Gulf closed except for Iranian ships and very occasionally Chinese, the seas would be empty, with an inbound queue of empty tankers way over to the west.

1730 (local) Thursday, May 3.
Fort Meade, Maryland.
The first night pictures from the overheads which passed over the Arabian Sea and southern Iran arrived on Lieutenant Ramshawe's desk from late on the previous afternoon. Unsurprisingly, they were packed with information, starting with a myriad shots showing the Indian Navy's Pondicherrys still working across the line of the minefield. They were making slow progress, just five knots with long GKT-2 contact sweeps, still with their 5600-ton landing ship *Magar*, which was acting as 'mother ship' to all six of them. An Indian Navy tanker was also in attendance, plus two 6700-ton Delhi Class guided-missile destroyers, built in Bombay and sent on by Admiral Kumar to guard his precious Pondicherrys. Warships from the *Constellation* carrier battle group were in the area, patrolling somewhat menacingly along the line of the minefield inside the Strait.

Out on the outside edge of the line, US frigates rotated patrols, under orders from the carrier *John C. Stennis*, which was calling the shots from ten miles astern of the picket line. No six ships were ever more thoroughly guarded than those six Pondicherrys and they swept the line assiduously, trying to free up an area three to five miles wide to open up the seaway on the Omani side to the world's oil tankers. Every few hours the waters of the Strait erupted to a shuddering explosion, as they located, cut and blew one of the PLT-3 Russian-built mines. More than 11,000 miles away, Lieutenant Ramshawe studied the strange unfolding scene, making detailed notes, writing up his reports, blowing up photographs, extracting details, laying it all out for the thoroughly discredited Admiral Borden, who now had a great deal in common with Commander Tex Packard careerwise.

He put copies on the network to the Pentagon, attention CNO. Other copies were made for electronic transfer to Pacific Fleet Command in San Diego, from where they were scanned via satellite to Pearl Harbor, then Diego Garcia. By private, secure telephone, Jimmy Ramshawe kept Arnold Morgan up to speed on every possible development. So far, to the satisfaction of both men, the Iranians had not dared send so much as a second-hand felucca into the waters beyond Bandar Abbas.

It was 1830, when two grainy, poor-quality satellite pictures of the inshore waters of south-eastern Iran sud-denly caught the eagle eye of Jimmy Ramshawe, because there, like a ghost ship in the fog, was the unmistakable outline of some kind of warship. He reached for his glass and peered at the image. He could see a little more, but not enough. The ship was running north towards the coast of Iran in 300 feet of water. According to the grid, the ship had just crossed 25.10N and was thus sixty-odd miles short of the minefield line. The lines of latitude suggested it was moving slowly, just seven miles in the half-hour between the two images. Jimmy hit a button, summoning a staff member from the developing room and requesting an immediate blow-up of the top left-hand corner of the first green-tinted night photograph.

When it came back twelve minutes later, the quality was not better, just bigger, and again Lieutenant

Ramshawe peered through his magnifying glass. He could tell from the for'ard and aft guns the scale of the ship, which he calculated was in excess of 7000 tons. If it was that big it was a destroyer and if it was a destroyer the range of countries which might own it was relatively small. It wasn't American because he knew precisely where all the US destroyers were in the area. It wasn't British and it certainly wasn't Russian. The Iranians did not own a destroyer, nor did the Egyptians, nor the Omanis. The Indians had two working in the area and five more Russian-built Rajput Class were all accounted for.

Could it possibly be the Chinese Sovremenny, the mine-laying *Hangzhou*, now returning for whatever reason to Bandar Abbas? Jimmy Ramshawe looked again and pulled up the Sovremenny pattern on his computer. The helicopter was in the right position for a start. He could see that. It was parked way forward and higher than the aft deck, right above the ASW mortars. He could also make out the distinctive gap between the fire control front dome (F-Band) and the air-search radar top plate. 'If I'm not very much mistaken,' muttered Jimmy, 'the bloody Chinks are back and the bloody *Hangzhou* is creeping up the coast towards the gap in the minefield. I wonder what the hell their game is?'

He checked the pattern over and over. The quad launchers for the Sunburn missiles, the two aft-mounted Gadfly surface-to-air launchers. All in the right places. This was her, no doubt about that, the most capable warship in China's new Blue Water fleet, *Hangzhou*, built brand-new in the cold Baltic, North Yard, St Petersburg. Here she was again, in much warmer waters, returning to the scene of her plain and obvious mine-laying crimes. Lieutenant Jimmy Ramshawe did not like it. The heavily armed warship would make a fair match for anyone. He could not see the point in talking to Admiral Borden, who would probably remind him of her right to be in Iran's waters, if that was okay with Iran. But it was not okay with Jimmy Ramshawe. *Bloody oath, it wasn't.* He picked up the secure line to Admiral Morgan in the White House.

'How sure are you, Lieutenant?'

'Certain, sir. This is the *Hangzhou* and no bloody error. Looks like she's headed back to Bandar Abbas.'

Arnold Morgan was, for a change, hesitant. He had already ensured the US Navy had issued a formal warning to all countries not to interfere with the minesweeping, but he had not been prepared for the sudden arrival of the most important warship in the Chinese Navy, the one which had helped lay the mines in the first place. 'When do we get new pictures, Jimmy?' he asked.

'Probably in three hours, sir.'

'God knows where she'll be by then. She's fast and she's dangerous. Leave it with me and don't forget to get a decent report in to your boss.'

The President's National Security Adviser was concerned and paced his office, pondering the intent of the commanding officer of the *Hangzhou*. If she was there merely as an observer, the US might have to put up with that. But she was so big and powerful that she would simply have to be warned off while the Pondicherrys were working.

Arnold Morgan knew the two admirals commanding *Constellation* and *John C. Stennis* Groups would be flying off their decks F-14 Tomcats and the FA-18E Super-Hornets. That's what they did on patrol. That's what they were there for, to intimidate any enemy, and these supersonic strike fighters found no difficulty in doing that. The Admiral had not yet asked for details, but he was certain the Tomcats would be making their presence felt. What the Navy did not need was a large Chinese warship prowling around in those waters, with its massive anti-aircraft capability – the two aft-mounted SA-N-7 Gadfly

SAMs. Not to mention its two twin 130mm guns and its four 30mm/65 AK 630 guns, the ones that fire a withering 3000 rounds a minute. No. The US Navy and its fliers could not put up with that. Particularly since the *Hangzhou* also sported two twin heavyweight 533mm torpedo tubes below the fire-control radars for the Gadfly missiles. She was also equipped with a strong anti-submarine capability, two 6-barrel RNU 1000 ASW mortars. Her principal surface-to-surface weapon was the SS-N-22 Sunburn (Moskit 3M-80E), a supersonic Raduga, fired from port/ starboard quad launchers, range: 60 nautical miles at Mach 2.5.

She was a formidable ship, no doubt about that. And Arnold Morgan guessed she had been detailed to escort the original mine-laying Chinese frigates, and possibly even the Kilos, out of harm's way. He also guessed, correctly, that she had been refueled from a tanker out of the Bassein river, which he found, frankly, infuriating. 'And now, where the hell's she going?' he growled to the empty room. 'It had better be far away from any of our current operations. I don't expect the Indians will be too pleased to see her either.'

The question was, what to do? *I guess we can't just sink the biggest ship in the Chinese Navy without risking a world-class uproar, which will send gasoline prices even higher,* he pondered. *But she has to leave the area. That's for sure. Before someone gets trigger happy.* He picked up his secure line to Admiral Dickson and outlined the problem.

'Sir, I do agree. She cannot be allowed to remain in our area of operations. I have warned the Chinese and everyone else to that effect. I think we have to take the view that the Chinese and the Iranians, in the absence of any denials, are plainly in breach of every world peace convention in mining the Strait. I propose to issue one more formal warning, direct to Beijing. Either they get that destroyer out of the area, or we'll do it for them.'

'You saying sink it, Alan?'

'No, sir. I'm saying cripple it. With minimum loss of life.'

'Using?'

'A submarine, sir. Stick one of those Mk 48s right into her stern. Blow the shaft, steering and propulsion all in one hit. Probably take out her missile launchers too with a couple of shells. Then let their friends from Iran come out and tow her in. That way we hold on to world opinion, with very few casualties and a well-deserved warning to China to stay the hell out of the Strait.'

'What if she returns fire?'

'Sink her, sir. Instantly.'

'Good call, Alan. Let's go.'

040500MAY07. USS Shark. 24.40N 50.55E
Speed 25. Depth 100. Course 352.
Lieutenant Commander Dan Headley, his early watch one hour old, called for a transcript of the new orders just in from the carrier. 'Hard copy twice, Jack,' he called down to comms. 'One for the CO.'

Five minutes later he read the instructions to USS *Shark*, ordering them to locate and track a Sovremenny Class destroyer, probably flying the flag of the People's Liberation Army/Navy. It had been picked up by the overheads moving slowly up the southernmost coast of Iran, course approximately two-seven-zero. According to Fort Meade, right now at 0530 it should be somewhere to their nor' nor' east, maybe twenty-seven miles up ahead. *Shark*'s sonar room had already located a ship in that area and the ESM had reported an occasionally transmitting Russian radar. The Flag was correct. She was going slowly. The Sturgeon Class American submarine would catch her inside ninety minutes. Their orders were simply to get in

131

contact with the destroyer, track her silently and await further instructions.

Lieutenant-Commander Headley ordered flank speed, course three-six-zero, which should put him in the correct position some time before 0700. He had someone wake the CO to apprise him of the situation and was mildly surprised when Commander Reid did not show up in the control room within the next forty-five minutes. 'Guess he trusts me,' thought the XO. 'Even though he has known me for only five days.'

In any event they rushed on north, remaining just below periscope depth, leaving a wake on the surface, which no one was around to see. At 0640 Lieutenant-Commander Headley slowed down to come to PD and took an all-round look at the surface picture. Sure enough, out on the horizon, on their one o'clock, was a large warship. Dan Headley had already memorized the profile of the Sovremenny and this was her, large as life, steaming on six miles off the coast of Iran, as if she owned the place. The engine lines on the 8000-ton double-shafted destroyer matched the GTZA-674 turbines on the computer model. He went back below the surface, dictated a signal to the Flag and had it transmitted, announcing he was in contact and was proposing to track the destroyer two miles astern pending further orders.

Dan ordered a course change: *come right seven degrees, down all masts.* At which point a frisson of excitement ran through the submarine, as it always does when any potential quarry is sighted, even in exercises. With the most dangerous warship in the Chinese Navy in their sights, USS *Shark* came unmistakably to life.

At 0700 the Commander came into the control room. He talked to his XO for a few minutes, bringing himself into the picture. But he did not assume command. Rather he left 'to find some breakfast' and asked Dan to let him know if anything important occurred. By now they were running line astern to the destroyer, four miles behind. But the Chinese ship was moving faster, still heading north-west along the Iranian coast. So far as Dan could tell she was not transmitting and did not even have her sonars switched on, which the Kentucky-born officer thought was 'kinda eccentric'. *Given she's just mined the Strait of Hormuz and the business half of planet earth was seriously pissed off with the ship and all who sailed in her.*

Nonetheless, the *Hangzhou* ran on at a steady twenty-knot speed, which again Dan Headley thought was ridiculous. By varying her rate of knots between, say, four and twenty-five, it would have been much more difficult for a submarine to track her. Alternatively, at her quiet, low speed, she might have actually heard the submarine, charging along astern, trying to catch up, making a noise like a freight train. *Beats the shit out of me where they train these guys. Some Chinese laundry, I guess.* So the *Shark* slipped into a classic sprint and drift pursuit, running as deep as she dared in the fifty-fathom waters along the coastline for fifteen minutes, then coming up for another visual set-up, to update the operations plot for the fire controller, just in case they should be ordered into action. Naturally, every time they came up they lost speed, 'drifting' quietly forward at five knots, losing ground all the time.

Six miles short of the minefield the *Hangzhou* made a course change, swinging more westerly, as if to run along the line of the minefield. It was light now, and Lieutenant-Commander Headley immediately accessed the Flag to inform them of the change in direction.

Admiral Bert Harman, in the group ops room high in the island of the *Harry S. Truman*, was uncertain, although his orders were clear. He instructed his comms room to alert the destroyer she was straying into a prohibited area where US warships were supervising a mine-clearing operation. She was to be warned in no uncertain terms to leave forthwith, to resume her course to Bandar Abbas and to remain in harbor right there until further notice.

But the Chinese commanding officer had been instructed to observe proceedings and to bow to no threats from the US Navy or any other. The CO, Colonel Yang Xi, thought this might have been perfectly feasible from a desk in Beijing, but out here it looked very different. He could see US Navy ships out on the horizon, steaming along the line of the minefield in which he'd just seen a sizeable explosion. He decided to ignore the warning, since he considered the Americans were unlikely to open fire. Rather, he would slow down and go in closer for two more miles. He was now in international waters and he could take his time with his turn. Meanwhile he would place his surface-to-surface Sunburn missiles on full alert.

The carrier ops room observed the Chinese CO make no attempt to obey their warning. Admiral Harman picked up his orders and read them carefully: *Should any warship of any nation insist on straying into our prohibited area, you will order the tracking submarine to disable her, not sink, but put her out of commission.* There was nothing ambiguous about that and the *Hangzhou* was a hugely dangerous enemy to both US ships and aircraft. Admiral Harman thus sent his signal in to USS *Shark*, instructing the submarine to disable the Chinese warship should she fail to turn round.

Lieutenant-Commander Headley read the signal and ordered the conn to take a long left-hand swing at flank speed in order to come up on the port side of the Chinese warship. He planned to fire one torpedo, well aft of her beam from range 2000 yards. This meant, essentially, that the Mk 48 would strike the stern and cripple the propulsion of the ship, leaving her helpless in the water until assistance arrived. He sent an immediate message to the Captain, who arrived in the control room at 0745. He seemed agitated, uncomfortable with the decision, not at all keen to open fire on a major Chinese warship. He questioned the intelligence of the orders, wondering if they might not have been changed. If there had been some mistake.

Lieutenant-Commander Headley brought *Shark* to PD once again and requested the CO took a look for himself. 'The Chinese CO has ignored our warnings, no doubt about that,' said the XO. 'And these orders make our duty clear. We are to cripple it, put it out of action with minimum loss of life.'

'Yes, I understand that,' said Commander Reid, declining the periscope. 'But the *Hangzhou* is not doing anyone any harm, maybe just taking a look.' He repeated absent-mindedly, 'Maybe just taking a look.'

'These orders don't tell us to speculate, sir,' replied Dan. 'They tell us to hit the destroyer hard when we are told to do so. And this piece of paper says right now.'

The Captain of the USS *Shark* looked unenthusiastic. 'It doesn't say how long we give it to turn round,' he said. 'I think we might check that with the Flag, XO.'

'As you wish, sir. But I would prefer you do it, because in my view these orders are specific. The Chinese ship has been warned, it has not turned round and I have a piece of paper here ordering us to open fire.'

'This is your watch, XO. I would like the writer to record my unease and my wish for a second opinion on the orders. But if you are certain as to the orders, you have my permission to proceed as you see fit.'

'Thank you, sir. Now, Torpedo Room–XO, prepare tubes one and two. Mk 48s.' Lieutenant-Commander Headley turned to Master Chief Drew Fisher who had materialized at his side. 'Check that out, Chief, will you.

I'm only preparing a second tube in case of malfunction. I intend to fire just one.'

'Aye, sir.'

Inside the sonar room the operators could still hear the steady beat of the *Hangzhou*'s propellers, rising and falling in the ocean swell, making the same soft *chuff-chuff-chuff* sound in the water, now less than 2000 yards away, dead ahead.

Dan Headley ordered *Shark* to periscope depth and his hands grabbed for the handles at knee level as the 'eyes' of the submarine rose up out of the deck of the control room. He scanned the ocean, called out bearing, then range: 'Zero-seven-zero, twenty-one thirty yards, down all masts, make your depth one hundred.'

Seconds passed, then the sonar room operator called it: 'XO-sonar, track three four, bearing zero-six-zero, range two thousand.'

Down in the torpedo room, both tubes were loaded and the guidance officer was in direct contact with Lieutenant-Commander Headley, speaking quietly into his slim-line microphone.

Dan Headley ordered the Officer of the Deck, Lieutenant Matt Singer, to take the conn: 'Hold your speed at three knots.'

The sonar team checked the approach, calling out the details softly to the XO. The rest of the ship was stone silent as they crept forward, preparing to fire the shot that would most certainly be heard in the Great Hall of the People.

Lieutenant-Commander Headley took another fast look at the screen. Then he ordered: 'STAND BY ONE, stand by to fire by sonar.'

'Bearing zero-six-zero, range two thousand yards, computer set.'

'*SHOOT*!' snapped Dan Headley.

Everyone felt the faint shudder as the big Mk 48 swept out into the ocean, making a beeline towards the Chinese destroyer.

'Weapon under guidance, sir.'

At forty knots, the torpedo would run for less than two minutes before hitting the utterly unprepared Sovremenny Class destroyer. It hit in the precise spot Dan Headley had specified, bang on the stern. It slammed into the long low aft section and detonated, blowing the main shaft into three pieces, the propeller into the deep water, and the rudder into a split and twisted mess of steel. The *Hangzhou* could no longer maneuver, couldn't steer, couldn't move. As the pall of smoke began to clear away from her stern area, she looked more or less normal, but in truth she was powerless. Her crew could hear the ship's tannoy blaring instructions and the medical teams were already making their way aft to tend the wounded, but by the standards of torpedoed warships there was relatively little blood shed.

The communications room was still intact and the ops room was unharmed. In fury, Colonel Yang Xi was thrashing around looking for a target at which to lash back. But he could see nothing short range for well over two miles. He had missiles, shells and torpedoes, but nothing close at which to aim any of them specifically. Nor could he see what had hit his ship – if, indeed, anything had. For all he knew it was just an explosion. But he realized that was stretching the realms of coincidence. Three minutes after the impact he received yet another signal from the American carrier, again ordering him out of the area, but offering to request assistance from the Iranians if the destroyer's comms were down. The Colonel did not answer. Neither did he consider it prudent to open fire with his missiles, because if he did the Americans would surely sink him. In his present situation he was the epitome of a sitting duck. Instead, he relayed a signal to the Iranian

Naval Command at Bandar Abbas requesting assistance.

Meanwhile Lieutenant-Commander Headley turned USS *Shark* round and returned to his position on station twenty miles off the port bow of the *Harry S. Truman*.

0100 Friday, May 4.
The White House.

Admiral Morgan sat alone in his office in the West Wing. He had promised Kathy he would be home by 11 p.m. but that was before the *Shark* had planted a torpedo in the stern of the *Hangzhou*. He had been on the line to the CNO almost every moment since.

The *John F. Kennedy* Group was five days out of Pearl Harbor and making a swing to the south from her normal route up to the coast of Taiwan. Admiral Dickson had ordered her straight to Diego Garcia. The increased tension in the Hormuz area had also caused the CNO to tell the Atlantic Commander-in-Chief to move the sixth operational US CVBG, that of the *Theodore Roosevelt*, out of the Mediterranean and on to the Indian Ocean. Like Admiral Morgan, he had no idea what the Chinese were up to and he had a bad feeling about that new Chinese base in the Bassein river. Within a few days they would have four carrier groups conducting a *roulement* between Diego Garcia and the Hormuz Strait, with the *Roosevelt* free to roam the Indian Ocean with her consorts anywhere it looked like the Chinese might cause more trouble.

So far as Arnold Morgan was concerned, he had seen enough. Always completely mistrustful of the men from the Orient, he now believed their true colors were being shown. They had cold-bloodedly caused a massive world oil crisis, they had caused scenes of chaos in the Gulf of Iran and no one dared to bring a big tanker across Jimmy Ramshawe's line, which defined the essential contour of the minefield. The oil market frenzy had abated slightly, thanks to soothing words from the American President that free and clear passage through the Strait of Hormuz would soon be resumed. But Americans were paying $3.50 a gallon at the pumps and Texaco, along with three other US-based corporations, were threatening to put the price up to $4 next week. The President was at his wits' end, demanding the Strait be reopened immediately, apparently unable to grasp the consequences of another tanker being blown up and the global uproar which would surely follow if the USA had declared the route safe to resume trade.

The weekend passed more or less uneventfully. White Rajah was made hot favorite, before losing by a half-length at Churchill Downs after closing on the winner all the way down the stretch. But at 0530 (local) on Monday morning, May 7, at the northern end of the Malacca Strait, an even more unexpected event happened. A 300,000-ton, virtually empty Japanese-registered crude carrier literally blew itself to pieces: went up in a colossal fireball right off the northern headland of Sumatra, within a few miles of the open ocean.

Like Hormuz, this is a very busy oil route, the seagoing highway to the Far East, the route of almost every tanker coming out of the Gulf of Iran, or even from the oilfields of Africa – straight across the Indian Ocean towards the Nicobar Islands, then through the Great Channel into the Malacca Strait, which divides Sumatra and the Malayan peninsula. The Strait is close to 600 miles long and the tankers use it for their outward and inward journeys. Almost 100 per cent of all the fuel oil and gas requirements in the Far East is carried on the big tankers through that narrowing seaway, the short cut to the South China Sea. It saves over a thousand wasteful miles, for without the Strait ships would have to travel right round the outside of the old East Indies.

Arnold Morgan heard the news with an undisguised groan as he and Kathy sat down to dinner on Sunday night, twelve time zones back. 'This', he grated, 'is getting goddamned serious.' No word of complaint had been heard from the Chinese since their destroyer was damaged. Nor, of course, had there been any word of admission for their part in mining Hormuz in the first place. Ms O'Brien had actually heard the report on the news while Arnold was cooking some pork chops on the grill. They had been out all day, sailing along the Potomac in a friend's yacht, and for some reason there had been only drinks and potato chips on board. The President's National Security Adviser rarely, if ever, touched alcohol during the day, and both he and Kathy had concluded the voyage, cold after the sun went down and hungry *in extremis*, as the Admiral put it. They declined to go to a restaurant with the other guests and sped home in Arnold's staff car. With heavy sweaters on and glasses of wine from the Loire Valley, they had fired up the grill and were just moving into Arnold's favorite part of the day, when Kathy reported the demise of the giant VLCC. 'Now how the hell did that happen?' he asked Kathy's labrador, Freddie, who made no reply, but continued to look, with eyes like lasers, at the pork chops.

Kathy returned with the wine bottle but little information. 'They just said the tanker was unladen,' she said. 'No information was available how the accident happened. They did draw a parallel with the ships that blew up in Hormuz last week and the newscaster mentioned there seemed to be a jinx on the shipping of heavy crude oil these days.'

'Yeah,' he muttered. 'A jinx wearing a goddamned lampshade on its head and eating its dinner with a couple of painted sticks.'

Kathy laughed. No one had ever made her laugh like

Arnold Morgan, especially when he was being sardonic. She threw her arms round him, and kissed him softly and slowly. No one that agonizingly beautiful had ever kissed Arnold Morgan. Certainly not like that. 'If it wasn't for about a billion tons of shipping blazing away in the Far East threatening to cause an end to civilization as we know it,' he said, 'I could get very involved with that kissing business.'

'Well, you should think about it more often,' she said. 'Get a kind of rota system going, you know, save the world, make love to Kathy, save the world, kiss Kathy for a few hours, then save the world again. If necessary. Meantime I'll take you just how you are.'

'Thank you,' he said, grinning. 'How about eat the chops, make love to Kathy, drink the Meursault, kiss Kathy?'

'I'll buy that,' she said. 'But how about saving the world?'

'Screw the world,' he said, putting his arm round her. 'Can't the goddamned world see when I'm too busy?'

The Admiral removed the chops from the grill with a pair of long silver tongs. One of them broke and the meaty part fell to the flagstone patio. Freddie dived at it as if he had not been fed this century and retreated sneakily into the bushes. 'Has that greedy little character got any Chinese blood?' he asked.

Kathy giggled, took the plate of chops from the Admiral and told him, 'Sure he has. Freddie, honored grandson of Dalai Lama.'

'That's Tibet, dingbats,' he said.

'Same thing, if you ask the People's Republic,' she stated.

It took only a few more moments for them to turn off the new gas grill and move inside to where the Admiral had lit a log fire in the study. This was a rather grand house and Kathy had been awarded it, amicably, by her husband in the divorce settlement. He had been a fairly rich man, and his pride and joy had been his book-lined study, which was situated through a beamed arch from the dining room. Kathy assumed he had another such set-up in his new house in Normandy, France, where he now lived with his French wife.

A studious diplomat, with a family grain business in the Midwest, he was always described by Kathy as kind and lovely, totally preoccupied with the problems of the world and 'about as much fun as a tree'. He had been much older than she, as Arnold was. But the laughter she shared with Arnold, his willingness to talk to her at all times and the sheer joy of their being together made up for any age differential. They were as devoted as it was possible to be and one day she would marry him. When he retired.

Meanwhile, she served the pork chops, salad and the French loaf, sat down and asked him, 'How do big ships burn when there's nothing in them? What's to burn? The newscaster said it was returning unladen to the Gulf.'

'Well, I didn't really hear it, but that sounds right. You see, those big tankers never really get rid of that crude oil when they unload at the terminal. I'm not sure what's left, but in a vast holding tank there's probably several inches still slopping around after the pumps are turned off. It's not the actual crude oil, which is like a black sludge, that burns. It's the gases rising up from it. So you can very easily have a situation where a full-loaded tanker is a lot less inflammable than an empty one. Because the holding tanks in the empty one are full of gases and those babies will go up real fast. It's the same with gasoline. If you could somehow plunge a lighted match into the gasoline without igniting the gases that are evaporating the liquid would put the flame out, like water. You probably won't remember, but twenty-five years ago, when the Brits fought the

Argentineans for the Falkland Islands, a bomb came into a ship – actually I think it came in low, and traveled right through and out the other side. Anyway, it started a minor fire, but hit a big diesel gas tank on the way through and tons of ice-cold fuel cascaded out and extinguished the fire. That's how it works and that's what caused the explosion in this latest tanker. The gases going up with a major bang.'

'Thank you, sir. Nicely explained. What do you think caused it?'

'I'm afraid to think about that right now. But I know one thing. It's not another minefield. Both Singapore and Sumatra get rich on the pilotage fees through the Malacca. They're high and getting higher. Last thing they want is a blockade. The Chinese would get no help from them. That means we're looking for something else. But not tonight. We're having dinner, then I'm not going to save the world and we'll go to bed quietly together. Tomorrow will be different. I'll be in the office early. So will you. And Admiral Borden wants to fasten his goddamned safety belt.'

'I'm just beginning to feel a teeny bit sorry for the poor Admiral.'

'Well, don't be. He's a negative guy. Which is bad in Intelligence. In Fort Meade you gotta stay right on top of the game. Also, Borden's obviously been very awkward with the excellent Lieutenant Ramshawe. I don't like that. Young men that sharp ought to be encouraged, not made to feel frustrated so they have to phone the goddamned White House in order to get someone to pay attention.'

'Well, you were pretty short with him when he did make the call.'

'Kathy, there are formalities of command in the United States Navy and they have to be observed at all times. Quite often they soothe troubled waters, even soften the truth. What they never do, however, is *hide* the truth. Jimmy Ramshawe knew that when he called. He probably knew I'd be kinda dismissive. But he also knew I'd hear him. That's why he called. He never had to tell me his boss was being pig-headed stupid. He understood that I'd get it and he was right; more goddamned right than even he knew at that point.'

'I guess it was pretty impressive how he got on to the Chinese involvement?'

'Sure was. He was a couple of jumps ahead of me and we were running on the same track. I'm not real used to that.'

'Do you feel a little resentful . . . someone that young?'

'Hell no. I was pleased. Saved me a lot of thinking time. That boy just laid it right out, almost.'

'What d'you mean, almost?'

The Admiral leaned back in his chair and took a deep sip of Meursault. 'Kathy,' he said. 'There's something real strange about this whole damned thing. Lemme ask you a question. What's the first thing any halfway decent detective wants to know about a murder?'

'Whodunnit?'

The Admiral chuckled, leaned over, took her hand and told her he loved her. Then he stopped smiling and said, 'Motive, Ms O'Brien. Motive. Why was this crime committed?'

'Okay, Sherlock, go for it.'

'Kathy, I cannot go for it. Because I cannot for the life of me see one motive the Chinese might have had for getting heavily involved in a blockade of the Gulf of Iran. I have racked my brains and every time we make a big move to protect the mine clearance I get a damned funny feeling about the entire scenario.'

'You do?'

'Well, we got a Navy which has to protect the Indians'

ships. But right now we got battle groups standing by to relieve battle groups. We've even got battle groups coming out of the Med in order to get into the Arabian Sea. Do you know how many ships that is – in the five US battle groups?'

'What are they, a dozen each? So I guess around sixty?'

'Kathy, that's enough naval hardware to conquer the world about three times over. That's more US warships grouped together than there's been since World War II. So what the hell's going on? There's no hostile threat. The mines which blew three tankers are essentially passive, just sitting there in the water and the Pondicherrys are quite steadily getting rid of them. Neither China nor Iran has opened fire on anyone. Christ, we just banged a hole in China's most important destroyer and they never even fired back, never protested. I just got an awkward feeling I might be missing the big picture right here. Seems to me we got too much naval hardware in one place. I know that's because we've also got a President whose only real concern is the price of gasoline at the American pumps. I'm wondering, too, if we're overreacting to the oil threat to civilization. Could someone be very seriously yanking our chain?'

1700 Monday, May 7.
Headquarters, Eastern Fleet
Ningbo, Zhejiang Province.
The streets were always crowded at this time in the ancient harbor town which lies 120 miles due south of Shanghai across the great Bay of Hangzhou. Ningbo traces its roots back to the Tang dynasty, through more than a thousand years of trading and every day in the early evening a commercial stampede seems to break out, as if the entire population were racing to sail before the tide. Throngs surged across the old Xinjiang Bridge in the main port

145

area. Traders bought and sold all along the old central throughway of Zhongshan Lu. Yet it was a curious place to see a senior naval officer, in uniform, hurrying through one of the oldest parts of town, along Changchun Lu.

Nonetheless, moving swiftly between the merchant houses along the crowded sidewalks was the tall, lean, still upright figure of the Commander-in-Chief of the People's Liberation Navy, Admiral Zu Jicai. He was no stranger to this city. He had been born here more than sixty years before and his naval career had begun in the dockyards of Zhejiang Province and ultimately, before he was thirty years old, in Shanghai. Following him closely among the shoppers were four uniformed Navy guards with sidearms. Even for a mission as unorthodox as this, Admiral Zu was not permitted to travel so far from the dockyard without protection.

He reached a building on the left-hand side of the street and paused briefly to confer with his guards, instructing them to wait outside and to have a staff car ready in forty-five minutes. Then he walked up the steps and entered through one of the wide, folded screen doors of *Tianyige*, the oldest private library in all of China, dating back to the sixteenth century, to the height of Ningbo's prosperity during the Ming dynasty. A member of the family bowed formally to him and the Admiral returned the courtesy, before he was led through the book-filled paneled main room into a smaller inner sanctum, dimly lit and plainly designed for thought and as a home for reference books.

There was a single table in the room and it stood beneath a deep, paneled, beamed ceiling, divided into wide squares, each decorated with intricate inlays of light wood and ivory of an entirely different pattern. Seated at the table, in the shadows beneath this great mosaic of ancient Chinese art, was the powerful figure of Admiral Zhang Yushu, senior Vice-Chairman of the PLAN's Council.

'Ah, Yushu, you found my childhood hideaway,' said Admiral Zu.

'Hello, Jicai. You were right. One of the most secretive rooms in China. We can talk here. But we must be swift and careful and so, quickly, what can you tell me about the destroyer?'

'Very little. The Americans warned her away from the area of the minefield, which she ignored as agreed. Then one of the American ships opened fire and essentially crippled her. Blew both shafts, both props and rudder. There was no way of returning fire and in any event she could not really see her assailant. Which makes me think they may have hit her from a submarine.'

'Yes. Precisely. But the loss amounts to very little. Are the Iranians towing her in?'

'Yes, sir.'

'And the tanker at the end of the Malacca Strait?'

'Our Kilo hit it with a torpedo and vanished. Apparently it was a good choice. Nice and big, and nice and empty.'

'Excellent. Have the Americans panicked?'

'I'm not certain, sir. But they just diverted yet another CVBG towards the Indian Ocean. It's on its way through Suez now.'

'And the carrier *JFK*?'

'Plainly on its way to Diego Garcia, taking a southerly route – a long way south from its normal route up to the Japanese islands and Taiwan.'

'Which leaves them where?'

'With *five* carrier battle groups either in, or heading for, the Indian Ocean, Diego Garcia or Hormuz.'

'And the *Ronald Reagan* Group? Still in San Diego?'

'Yes, sir and non-operational for a good two months yet. My guess is they'll call the *JFK* back for Taiwan.'

'Then we'll have to deal with her, I suppose. But I don't think that will be beyond us. Not with our Kilos.'

'No, sir.'

It was a very Chinese relationship. Formal to a degree when the subject involved the Navy's business, Commander-in-Chief to the Biggest Chief. But when the conversation slipped from report to discussion and opinion, it instantly lapsed into the kind and understanding conversation of two lifelong and beloved friends.

'And now, Jicai, do we see any improvement in our amphibians' capacity?'

'Not really, sir. I think we have to accept 11,000.'

'And are we ready?'

'No, sir. But we are preparing every day.'

'Where do you see our critical paths?'

'Certainly the Kilos, sir. We will have them routinely overhauled and ready. Most other ships are on standby. Airborne troops I understand are training with some success but with more to learn. The infantry commanders have forgotten nothing. Tanks are ready. In the air I fear it will be costly.'

'Do we have a date?'

'I'm looking at ten days, sir.'

'A feint to the outer island first?'

'Absolutely, sir.'

'Are you confident, my friend?'

'With great reservations, sir.'

'That's good, my Jicai. All commanders must be a little bit afraid.' With that, Admiral Zu walked to the door of the little room and called softly to his friend, a member of the twentieth generation of the family to own this library.

Moments later the librarian returned and handed each of his guests a small porcelain cup containing sweet, heavy Shaoxing red wine, served warm. 'A toast, Jicai,' said Admiral Zhang. 'To the immortal memory of the ruler of all the seas, Admiral Zheng He.'

Arnold Morgan wanted answers and he wasn't getting any. At least not from Admiral David Borden. The Acting Director of the NSA was unable to grasp how urgently the Big Man in the White House wanted to know who hit the tanker in the Malacca and with what.

Admiral Borden actually said, 'Sir, we do not I believe have any proof the tanker was hit at all.' Which was tantamount to telling Evander Holyfield that nobody just bit a hole in his ear.

Admiral Morgan was furious. He banged down the phone, just as news came in that Brent Crude had gone to $78 a barrel in London on rumors of a worldwide strike by the masters of the big tankers. Right now America was looking at $5 for a gallon of gasoline at the pumps. Worse yet, if things did not shake loose very quickly, there could be shutdowns at some of the nation's major electricity generators which ran on fuel oil or natural gas. 'KATHY!'

She came in through the open door, closing it hastily in case someone else heard the anger of the President's top military adviser.

'Get George Morris on the phone right now.'

'Arnold, he had surgery early this morning. You know that. He must be asleep.'

'Well, wake him up.'

'Don't be ridiculous. We can't wake him up. He's very sick.'

'He'll be a whole lot sicker if the goddamned lights go out and his iron lung shuts down.'

'Arnold, they do not use iron lungs in modern surgery any more.'

'Try not to bore me with this high-tech crap. Electricity is the lifeblood of all hospitals, including George's. Okay, okay, don't wake him up till later but tell him to get into

Fort Meade tomorrow and kick that asshole Borden out of his office.'

'Arnold, I guess you could arrange to bomb Shanghai, but you cannot instruct the head of surgery at the naval hospital in Bethesda to discharge probably his most important patient.'

'Kathy, forget all I've just said. But please ensure I speak to George the moment he regains his senses. Because this clown in Fort Meade is unlikely ever to regain his.'

'Yes, sir. Meanwhile, anything I can do?'

'Yes. Get that good boy, Jimmy Ramshawe, on my private secure line. Hop to it and don't tell me he's asleep or anything.'

'Of course, I may murder you one day, my darling,' she said, stalking out of the room, head high, trying not to laugh.

National Security Agency
Fort Meade, Maryland.
Lieutenant Ramshawe's phone rang angrily, reflecting precisely the general demeanor of the caller.

'Hello, sir. Yup, this is Jimmy, sir, I've been on it since I got here at 0300 this morning. You want my opinion? I think the Chinese fired a torpedo into that tanker from one of those Kilo Class submarines.'

'What makes you think so?'

'Sir, I've had full coverage of those coastal waters, all the way down from the Rangoon delta to the northern headland of Sumatra, right down from the Nicobar Islands. And I'm here to tell you there's not a warship in sight in those waters all through the weekend and then suddenly, BAM! Another tanker goes up at 0630 local time. And where does it go up? I have it at 06.10N 94.50E. That's six miles south-east of Point Pygmalion, the southern headland of Great Nicobar. It's also 600 miles south of the

Chinese navy base in the Bassein river. I'd say less than three days' running for a Kilo moving at twelve knots through waters without a serious naval presence. At least nothing that's looking for them. They don't even have to be careful. Anyway, sir. That's not all.'

'Go on.'

'Sir, I got two satellite shots right here, showing a Russian-built Kilo on the surface, heading right for the Mergui archipelago, that's right off the Burmese coast . . .'

'I know where the hell the goddamned Merguis are, for Christ's sake. Keep going.'

'Yes, sir.'

Arnold Morgan smiled to himself.

'She's about 180 miles from the burning tanker and that's fifteen hours from the hit. So she could have done it, but they don't seem to care too much who knows.'

'Very strange, Jimmy. What do you make of it?'

'Not a great deal, sir. I can't see the point of it, except to cause chaos. All I know is this does not look like casual maritime vandalism.'

'Keep thinking, Jimmy. Write your reports and keep me right in the game.'

Ten minutes later Admiral Morgan was standing in the Oval Office informing the President of the United States that the Chinese had, without question, been responsible for yet another tanker explosion, the fourth. And so far as he could tell there was no reasonable motive for harming any of them, except to cause a massive hike in world oil prices, which would damn nearly bankrupt Japan and knock the hell out of the USA's burgeoning economy. 'As for Europe, with their North Sea oil beginning to run out, sitting there with virtually no resources except a lot of damned expensive people and welfare programs big enough to stop the earth on its axis, well, hell, God knows what's going to happen to them without Arab oil.'

'Arnold, I have to make a move. I have to do something. I cannot let this all go unremarked by the United States. Do we have the Gulf under control?'

'It's under control but not yet safe. We got enough forces in there to conquer anything up to World War III, including the sun, the moon and the planet of the fucking apes.'

The President laughed, but his concern overrode any humor there might have been in his mood. 'Arnold,' he said. 'We gotta show a major presence. We gotta frighten everyone to death, show 'em we mean what we say.'

'Sir, we could show 'em we mean what we say with one CVBG. Christ, they carry eighty fighter aircraft and right now we don't have a damn thing to shoot at. We've also got *five* carriers either in, or on their way in. If the oil starts flowing again those warships could almost suck the place dry.'

'Arnold, there has to be something very odd about this Sino-Iranian pact. I just cannot tell what they're up to. I only know we cannot drop our guard.'

'Maybe. But I have a feeling there's a goddamned hidden agenda that we are not tuned into. There simply is no obvious motive for this action by the Chinese. But I do still think there is one thing we must do: lock 'em right out of the Indian Ocean.'

'You mean what we discussed before?'

'Yes, sir. We've gotta get rid of that oil refinery they just built, and then that navy base in the Bassein river. Send the little bastards back home to the South China Sea.'

'Arnold, I think to do that we will need the support of at least one ally and I don't know where that might come from.'

'Jesus, that's an easy one. We don't even need to frown over that.'

'We don't?'

'No, sir. The Indian Navy would give their eye-teeth to get China out of the Bay of Bengal and all points west of there. Remember, that old animosity is as ingrained as Iraq and Iran. The Indians do not want the Chinese Navy prowling around in their backyard. Remember too, India is very nearly bigger than China in terms of population, and richer. I have thought for years they should be our best friends in the East.'

'Hm. You think they'll support us kicking some Chinese ass?'

'Basically I think we tell no one what we're about to do, except to tip off Admiral Kumar about our approximate plans. He's gonna love it. So's his Prime Minister.'

'You still root for the actions of your favorite troops, the cut-throats of the Navy SEALs using their world-famous techniques of solving all problems with high explosive.'

'Those are my methods of choice, sir. Mainly because no one quite knows what's happened. Yet they can't fail to know it must have been us.'

'Well, Arnold, since I've been in this chair I've allowed you to unleash these guys on several targets and I'm obliged to say they always bring home the bacon, some of it nicely fried.'

'This time it's gonna be stir-fried. I'm sick to death of this Chinese crap.'

'Okay, Arnold, do your duty as you see it. Send 'em in, the silent destroyers.'

'That's the way, sir. Maximum effect, minimum blame. We'll give 'em seventy-eight bucks a barrel. Crazy pricks.' He turned away from the Chief Executive and walked slowly out of the Oval Office, his thoughts cascading in on him as his rich imagination took him into the hot, dark recesses of the sprawling refinery on the Strait of Hormuz. He thought of the guys, coming in hard and silent, out of

153

the sea, moving across the sand, watching for armed sentries, and in his mind he felt their fear and their strength, and their patriotism.

He walked right by Kathy O'Brien's desk without stopping, snapping out briskly just one command as he opened his office door, 'Get me Admiral John Bergstrom on the line. SPECWARCOM, Coronado Beach. Secure Line. Encrypted. We're talking Black Ops, Kathy. Usual procedures.'

Five

Admiral Morgan's call to SPECWARCOM was essentially a request to Admiral John Bergstrom to put two
teams of Navy SEALs on twenty-four-hour notice in
Coronado, prepared to embark immediately for Diego
Garcia. That conversation took less than four minutes.

'Just one thing: degree of danger?'

'High. But your guys probably won't work up a sweat.'

The next call was likely to be more complex, since even
Arnold Morgan could not take the United States to war all
on his own. He asked his sole serving non-commissioned
officer, Kathy O'Brien, to sequester President Reagan's
old Situation Room in the lower floor of the West Wing.
Then he ordered her to summon the Secretary of State,
the Defense Secretary, the Energy Secretary, the Chief of
Naval Ops, and the Chairman of the Joint Chiefs to a
meeting, top priority, classified, in ninety minutes' time.
He excluded the President since he already had verbal
Oval Office clearance to mount whatever military
operation he saw fit. He assumed this particular President
would deny all knowledge if the operation went wrong,
which it had better not.

It was 1500 when General Tim Scannell came hurrying
through the big wooden doors flanked by two saluting US
Marine guards. The door was closed firmly behind him
and he walked to his place at the head of the big table, at

155

Admiral Morgan's right hand. 'I'm sorry to hold you up, gentlemen,' he said politely. 'It's just that we got more going on in the Middle East than we've had since Saddam got above himself seventeen years ago. We got more ships out there too.'

To the left of the Chairman of the Joint Chiefs sat the Secretary of State, the steel-haired veteran diplomat Harcourt Travis, and the Energy Secretary Jack Smith, probably the best CEO General Motors ever had. Opposite them were the recently appointed CNO Admiral Alan Dickson, former Commander-in-Chief Atlantic Fleet, and the Defense Secretary Robert MacPherson. Because the meeting was convened and chaired by Admiral Morgan himself the seating of the military men always placed them in some kind of ascendancy. *Civilians have their place, of course, but when you need to get stuff assessed and then acted upon in a serious hurry, the military leave 'em standing.* The Admiral's view on that subject was both uncompromising and generally accepted, since he was unlikely to change his mind. 'Gentlemen,' he growled, frowning deeply, 'we've got a major shit fight on our hands.'

Jack Smith, attending his first effective war cabinet, smiled at the Admiral's poetically worded appreciation of the situation and added formally, 'There's reports of $4-a-gallon gasoline in the Midwest.'

'Jesus Christ,' said Admiral Morgan. He shook his head and muttered, 'If we're not damned careful, this could get right out of hand.'

He then called the meeting to order and proceeded to outline the stand-off in the Gulf, and approximately what he proposed they should do about it. 'You all know roughly what's happened. The Iranians and the Chinese between them have constructed a deep, we *think* three-line, minefield clean across the Strait of Hormuz, distance

156

of about twenty miles. So far three tankers have hit and burned. We have the Indian Navy in there sweeping the field, trying to open up a seven-mile-wide freeway for the world's tankers to start entering and leaving the Gulf. But it's slow and somewhat perilous.

'Right now we have five US CVBGs either deep in the area or on their way. That's essentially to protect the Indians, and make those seas safe again for the continued orderly conduct of the world's oil and gas trade. Most of that's routine and under control. However, in the early hours of this morning there was a development which I did not like. An unladen Japanese-registered tanker suddenly blew up at the north end of the Malacca Strait. I have reason to believe it was hit by a torpedo from a Chinese Kilo Class submarine. I further believe that Kilo was refueled at the new Chinese navy base in Burma in the Bassein river delta. I also believe it's on its way back there. But that's just a sideshow. The real problem is China. Her intentions. The depth of her involvement in the mining of the Strait, and her ambitions in the Arabian Sea, the Gulf area, the Indian Ocean and in particular the Bay of Bengal.'

He paused and no one spoke. 'Gentlemen,' he continued, 'I am quite certain that if we do not chase China out of those oceans we will live to regret it. Remember, they have been passive in terms of sea power for more than 500 years, just running a coastal Navy to protect their own shores. But not any more. They're plainly in expansionist mode, acquiring submarines, destroyers and a couple of aircraft carriers from the Russians. They're building a new ICBM submarine platform and they are pushing westwards. That new oil refinery of theirs south of Bandar Abbas gives them an excuse to send protective warships into the Arabian Sea. The new Burma base has given them a home port from which they could essentially control the oil routes through the Malacca Strait. That's all the oil routes to the west and north Pacific.'

Admiral Morgan paused again, then he growled, 'Gentlemen, these guys are not just stepping lightly on our toes. They're running us over with a fleet of fucking rickshaws and I'm not having it.'

Jack Smith and General Scannell both smiled, and Harcourt Travis laughed out loud. 'Arnold,' he said, 'you have such a way with words. You really should have considered the diplomatic service.'

Everyone in the room knew the suave Secretary of State was not entirely enamored of the President's crusty National Security Adviser and some thought the diplomat's calm, thoughtful intellect was a very good foil for the irascible ex-nuclear submarine commander. But the Admiral's mind was inevitably superior and he had won almost every one of their exchanges down the years, even if he did occasionally sound like a master-sergeant in an ugly mood. 'Hey, Harcourt, old buddy. Glad to hear you're still sharp, because I want you to give me an assessment. If you wanted to chase the Chinese out of the Indian and Arabian Seas, what action would you consider taking?'

'You mean as an American?'

'Christ, no. As an Ethiopian.'

This was too much for both Jack Smith and General Scannell who burst out laughing. Bob MacPherson and Admiral Dickson tried to control themselves, and even Harcourt permitted himself a deep chuckle – restrained, of course.

'You see, Harcourt,' Arnold Morgan smiled, 'that's the trouble with you foreign service guys, you're always looking for the extra half-sentence, to give yourselves a few more seconds to think. It's just a habit. Yes, Harcourt, as an American, you got it first time.'

'Well, to begin with I'd go and pray at the tomb of my

former Emperor Haile Selassie, the Lion of Judah. Then I guess I'd come back and advise you to blow the bastards right out of the water. Is that sufficiently primitive?'

'Harcourt,' replied the Admiral, unsmiling, his bright blue eyes narrowing dangerously, 'I like it.'

At which point everyone laughed some more, but it was edged with nervousness, like telling a joke before an oncoming disaster. The Navy are good at that. In World War II no US ship was ever blasted by bombs or torpedoes without one of the survivors observing, 'Guess you shouldn't have joined if you can't take a joke.'

The Admiral quickly regained his stride. 'I'm talking politically. You know our problems – the Iranian naval base at Bandar Abbas, the new Iranian refinery, right there next to the warships, the Sino-Iranian refinery, effectively owned by the Chinese, just along the coast, and the new Chinese naval base and refueling docks in the Bassein river. All four of those installations represent a giant pain in the ass, not just for us, but for all nations which require oil and gas.'

Harcourt Travis nodded, an air of caution written right across his face. 'Arnold,' he said, 'I do not think we could just cold-bloodedly take out the Iranian base at Bandar Abbas. However covertly we moved, everyone would know it was us and I think it would be construed as a blatant act of war. However, I think we would hold on to world opinion if we hit any warship we judged to be a threat to the free passage of shipping through the Gulf.'

'Uh-huh. How about the Iranian refinery?'

'Bad idea. If the situation in the Gulf turned really ugly we might just need the oil out of that refinery. We might even need to seize it. Let's not destroy it, however pissed off we might be at the ayatollahs.'

'And the new Chinese refinery?'

'That's different. Because that refinery gives the

People's Liberation Army/Navy a reason to be operational at the western end of the Indian Ocean and the Arabian Sea. I'm not saying we go in and blast the place to smithereens, probably starting World War III. But if that refinery were to . . . er . . . become dysfunctional after some kind of . . . er . . . problem, well, I guess a lot of people would be pretty relieved.'

'And the base on the Bassein river?'

'That,' said Harcourt flatly, 'has gotta go.'

'Any drift on the state of mind of the Burmese government? Or Myanmar, or whatever the hell they call it?'

'Well, you know it's a military junta, Arnie. It's in power regardless of the results of democratic elections and recently they appear to have become much less friendly towards the Chinese. But the Big Dragon sits right against their back door and the Big Dragon has built roads and even railroads right through the country to the port cities on the Bay of Bengal. The Chinese have armed the Burmese military, sold them God knows how much hardware on long lines of credit. I'm afraid the Burmese are in too deep to get out. We'll get no help from them. You want to get rid of that Chinese base, you're on your own. But you'd have some cheerleaders in India.'

'They still pissed off about the tracking station on Great Coco Island?'

'Very, very pissed off. The Chinese installed it with extreme cunning and furtiveness. Then they put an airstrip in there. Now they can pry deep behind India's eastern coastline. Myanmar says the 75 AF Radar Squadron is theirs, but everyone knows it's Chinese. They probe straight across the Bay of Bengal and record all take-offs from Calcutta airport and any military airport along the coast. The Indians call them the Chinese Checkers.'

Bob MacPherson, another veteran of this Republican administration, interjected here in support of the Secretary of State. 'There's more trouble in that region than even we realize. The Chinese have spy ships all over the Bay of Bengal and that's thanks largely to their base on Haing Gyi Island. It would be a hell of a lot more difficult for them if it weren't there.'

'Trouble is', said Harcourt, 'that Burmese coastline is so damned strategic. The Coco Islands are only just in Burmese waters, right on the Coco Channel, the main seaway for *every* merchant ship bound for eastern India ports and Bangladesh. Immediately to the south, around ten miles, we have the northernmost islands of the Indian archipelago, you know, the Andamans and the Nicobars, stretching 500 miles to the south towards the Malacca Strait. No one in the area feels safe with Chinese warships constantly on patrol there.'

'I'll tell you something else,' added Jack Smith. 'On average there are 300 ships passing through the Bay of Bengal every day. A lot of them are tankers to and from the east. There's some new economic projections which suggest that in the next twenty years, fifty per cent of all world trade will center on the Pacific-Asian countries. God knows how many more ships that will mean.'

'And China sees itself as the great controller of those seaways,' said Bob MacPherson. 'But the elimination of the base in the Bassein river would set them back a quarter of a century.'

'So what are our priorities?' asked Admiral Morgan.

'I think we make it plain to the Chinese that we will sink any of their warships in the clearance zone in the Strait of Hormuz. We then quietly mastermind a problem in their refinery in Iran and cause it essentially . . . er . . . not to work. That gets them out of the western waters of the Arabian Sea and the Indian Ocean. The oil issue is irrelevant because it's from Kazakhstan and the Chinese are going to get it anyway, probably via a pipeline into their western territories, and on to Shanghai.'

'Christ,' said Admiral Morgan. 'That's – what? – five thousand miles or something? They can't do that.'

'With respect, Honorable National Adviser,' said Harcourt in his best Cantonese accent. 'They built a very long, very high wall. They'll probably manage to dig a fucking hole.'

Arnold Morgan chuckled. But he was very pre-occupied. 'And our next priority?' he asked.

'I think you know the answer to that. Let's chase them out of the Bassein river. Somewhat secretly. And probably earn the thanks of many millions of people.'

Admiral Morgan sat thoughtfully. He and Harcourt Travis had been through a few run-ins, but despite everything, he liked the Secretary of State. And he liked him for one overriding reason: *smooth sonofabitch really knows his stuff. He's a scholar, a realist and a cynic. A guy you can count on for important opinions.* 'Harcourt,' he said. 'I thank you. I thank all of you. Civilians may consider the meeting concluded. CNO, Tim, I'd like a half-hour more to discuss tactics.' He stood and shook hands with the departing Chiefs of Foreign Policy, Defense and Energy. 'I scarcely need to remind you of the hugely classified nature of the matters we have discussed,' he added. 'There is no one who needs to know, save for ourselves.'

Then he walked to the end of the room where Kathy had pinned up a large chart of the Strait of Hormuz, showing the coastline all the way from Bandar Abbas to the desert town of Kuhestak, way over on the long, near-barren eastern shore, forty-eight miles south of the Iran Navy HQ. 'Come up here and take a look at this,' he said. 'You see this place right here, Kuhestak? The Chinese refinery is situated here, two miles along the coast to the south. It's big. There's a massive pipeline system running in here, all the way from the oilfields in Kazakhstan, 1000 miles right across the heart of Iran. This precious Iranian seaport is soon going to give China its energy from the heart of the second-largest oil producer on earth. Because it can run tankers in here of virtually unlimited size, then drive out straight across the Indian Ocean, through the Malacca Strait and into the South China Sea. In my view that's basically what the trouble is all about. That is precisely why China wants this growing military presence in the region and why we cannot allow it.

'You just heard the assessments of Harcourt and Bob. Now I want you to tell me how a dozen SEALs can take out that refinery. I say a dozen because the water's shallow and well patrolled. We're going to need an SDV, I'm certain of that, and we only have one in the area – the one stowed on the deck of good old *Shark*. The good news is it does not take a whole lot of high explosive to blow up an oil refinery. Sonsabitches are apt to blow themselves up if you give 'em a head start.'

'Guess you're referring to the big bang in Texas City back in 1947, eh?' said General Scannell. 'I had an uncle lived somewhere out near Galveston. He told me when I was just a kid you coulda heard that explosion from 150 miles away.'

'I was about three years old at the time and we didn't live that far from the disaster,' said Arnold. 'I remember my daddy told me the ship that blew it exploded with such force its one-and-a-half-ton anchor was flung two miles and embedded itself ten feet into the ground at the Pan American refinery.'

The recollection of the Texas City disaster reminded all three men of the enormous problems involved in taking out a major refinery, with its attendant sites of sprawling petrochemical plants; just about every square foot of such

163

industrial time bombs is filled with highly volatile, flammable materials, including vast pressurized storage tanks for natural gas. The new Chinese installation at Kuhestak had all of that and more.

Hundreds were killed, thousands injured in Texas City, buildings all over town were blasted beyond recognition. The devastation was not restricted to the waterfront, nor to the refining towers and storage areas. It just about ripped the entire town apart. A radio announcer simply yelled, 'Texas City just blew up!' The mushroom cloud rose 2000 feet into the air. Massive, white-hot steel parts from the French merchant ship SS *Grandchamp* were hurled into the holding tanks hundreds of yards away, setting off secondary explosions, which in turn caused immense damage. The burning *Grandchamp* with its heavy cargo of ammonium nitrate fertilizer was responsible for what was still, some sixty years later, the worst industrial catastrophe in US history. At the time, so soon after World War II, there were few modern safety precautions in place and, of course, there was none of the grim voyeurism of late twentieth-century television, with its voracious, insatiable appetite for agony, heartbreak and disaster, which it finds so helpful in its endless, somewhat childlike quest for drama and action.

Nonetheless, even without archive footage from television, Texas City 1947 remains a milestone in United States industrial calamity and Admiral Arnold Morgan, a native-born Texan himself, had no wish to involve civilian casualties in the little Iranian town of Kuhestak, even though he gave not one jot for the lives of the Chinese technicians at the refinery – *you guys wanna fuck around with the free passage of world oil and gas? Guess you should have thought about that real deeply before ordering those mines from Moscow.*

In any event the Chinese refinery had to go. The

remaining questions were how quickly, and how to get the SEALs out before the whole shooting match went up in smoke and took our guys with it.

Meanwhile, Admiral Dickson stared at the little numbers on the chart, checking out the water depth, turning over in his mind the equation. *Shark can't operate in depths of less than 150 feet. How near can she go before the guys have to leave in the little electric SDV, running until she touches the sand and then unloading the SEALs to swim in the rest of the way?*

'What d'ya think, Admiral?' Arnold Morgan was stepping aside to allow the CNO some space.

'*Shark*'s gonna need passageway through the minefield. Then she's got a twenty-mile submerged run nor'nor'-east up to this point right here, 'bout twelve miles off the Iranian coast. She'll be in at least 180 feet of water all the way there, say 26.36N, right on 56.49E.'

'That's precisely where I had the rendezvous point, Alan. Great minds, right?'

'Realistic minds, at least, sir. *Shark* wouldn't want to move inshore any further. She starts leaving a wake that's asking for trouble. Iran's got a few fast attack craft with ASW mortars. We wanna stay real silent.'

'How many guys does the SDV hold?'

'Well, the old ones carried only ten. That's the one on *Mendel Rivers*, crew of two and eight SEALs. This new one holds fourteen, so we got twelve active SEAL demolition guys. We're just lucky the SDV is on the deck of *Shark*, otherwise we'd be all over the damned place. Still I guess we're due for a bit of luck. Haven't had much for a while and I gotta real gut feeling about getting Beijing out of Arabia.'

'You and me. What d'you say, General?'

Tim Scannell looked thoughtful. 'I was just thinking, something goes wrong, say the submarine gets hit and crippled, any thoughts on back-up? You need a carrier in the area to frighten everyone away, or you want me to order up some fighter aircraft we can deploy out of Oman, with the Brits' help?'

'Good call, General. Anything hits our submarine, I mean a surface ship, we vaporize it, right?'

'Yes, sir, Arnie. But how about an Iranian or Chinese Kilo Class submarine in the area? Both nations have 'em and as you know they're little bastards under the water.'

Admiral Dickson responded immediately. 'I'll order a coupla LA Class nuclear boats to ride shotgun on *Shark* while she goes in. They'll pick up a Kilo if it's close enough.'

'And then?' Arnold Morgan looked quizzical.

'If it's under the surface we sink it. No questions asked.'

'Thank you, CNO. That's my language you're talking. You can only fuck around with these towelheads and Orientals for just so long, right?'

'Right, sir.'

'No bullshit,' added Admiral Morgan by way of emphasis.

'Matter of fact, sir,' said Alan Dickson, 'I'd say our biggest worry was getting the guys in, once they leave the SDV. You see the twenty-meter depth line is all of five miles offshore. The ten-meter line's only about a half-mile further in. Then they got a coupla miles in about four feet of water on flat sand. Terrain's fine, but there is a risk of detection, and it's a long way back to deep water and safety.'

'A long way for you and me, Alan. But not these guys. They'll slide through those warm shallows like a shoal of Florida bonefish – fast, sleek, unpredictable and likely to fight like hell.' Arnold Morgan made a curving forward motion with the palm of his left hand. 'Death to the Chinese oilers, right?'

'Actually, I'm more worried about pursuit than anything else, Arnie, especially if they keep a fleet of helicopters at the refinery.'

'Alan, if that place goes up like I think it will, there's not going to be anything even resembling pursuit. Bergstrom has the charts and his top instructors will be involved in the planning. I expect Commander Rick Hunter will lead the squad, but I'm not sure if he'll go into Iran or Burma. Not both.'

'You have real faith in those SEALs, don't you?'

'To one extent. If they can't do it, it can't be done. I know that a group of the most highly trained demolition killers on this planet can blow up a goddamned oil refinery. Gimme a book o' matches and I'll blow the fucker up myself.'

Both Alan Dickson and Tim Scannell laughed at the President's top military adviser: always just the right combination of steel and intellect, respect and contempt, fortitude and laughter. Arnold Morgan really was anyone's idea of the perfect keeper of America's front line.

Both the Admiral and the General now stood back and watched as Arnold once more stepped up to the chart, this time holding a grainy black-and-white photograph in his left hand while making a tiny drawing on the chart, a small pencil line five miles offshore right on the twenty-meter depth line. 'See that?' he said. 'That's the loading dock. Just completed construction. That's where the big Chinese VLCCs will be landing. The pipeline's already in but we have no evidence of trade yet. Pity the sonofabitch is so far from shore, otherwise we could just hit some combustible merchant ship and give 'em Texas City Two. But, as the proprietors of the refinery might put it, no can do. So we'll just have to slam the fucker, bang in the middle of the plant. Then maybe take out the loading dock on the way back, if there's ships on it.'

'Okay, sir. Sounds good, if a bit tricky. You wanna talk some about the Bassein river hit?'

'Not now, Tim. I'm judging that to be a lot more complicated. We'll have John Bergstrom in before we finalize and possibly a couple of his commanders – maybe forty-eight hours. Wednesday morning.'

He saw the two Service Chiefs out and then walked slowly back to the chart of the Strait of Hormuz, muttering to himself, 'They must know that goddamned refinery is vulnerable. They must know there will be some form of retribution if the US finds out they helped lay that minefield. Or maybe they figure we'll never find out for certain?' He paused for a full minute, then mumbled, 'Nah, they're just not that stupid. They must know we'll find out.' *And if that's the case*, he pondered, *there's only one question left. What in the name of Christ are they up to?*

072200MAY07. Strait of Hormuz
Flight Deck USS Constellation.
26.30N 56.50E. Course 225. Speed 30.
She was turned along the south-westerly run of the minefield now, the US Navy's beloved forty-five-year-old *Connie*, plowing forward into the hot wind of this sweltering Arabian night. She was about five miles north of the field and the area seemed quiet, as the Indian Pondicherrys moved steadily about their hazardous business, cutting the mines free and then blowing them on the surface.

But still the howling F-14D Tomcats, courtesy of US fighter wing VF 2 – the fabled Bounty Hunters – gunned their aircraft off *Connie*'s 1000-foot-long flight deck, up and into the black skies which now blanketed the most lethal stretch of ocean in the entire world. Each pilot wore on his right sleeve the Bounty Hunters' triangular emblem, the yellow delta-winged fighter-bomber on red, white and blue stripes. Most of them also sported the jaunty gunslinger patch, the cowboy tomcat leaning on a big D, with the new stitched lettering, *Any time, Pal*. They flew right out on the edge of the envelope, banking in hard over the Iranian coastline and then back out to sea. This really was *Any time, Pal*, because right now the US Navy meant business and everyone knew it. One squeak out of an Iranian anti-aircraft battery, one illumination, one suggestion and that battery would be obliterated by a phalanx of missiles with an accuracy record of around 100 per cent.

Navy pilots are used to being accused of 'US bullying'. But they were not bullies tonight, while the whole world awaited the reopening of the Gulf to oil tankers. Tonight the Navy fliers were the fearless White Knights of the Skies, the way they mostly saw themselves anyhow, and they hurled their Tomcats through the high darkness of Islam, the single most threatening airborne cavalry ever assembled, on a mission to shut down the menace of a known aggressor. *Any time, Pal*. The patches said it all.

Back on *Connie*'s flight deck in the controlled chaos of a hectic night's flying the twenty-two-ton Tomcats were slamming down in batches, because the carrier has to keep making ground downwind, altering course, between landings and take-offs. Swarms of flight deck personnel surrounded each aircraft as it thundered in, a team ever ready to rush forward and ram the Sidewinder safety pins into the pylon firing mechanisms. The hot swirling air, stinking of JP-4, burned rubber, searing hot metal and salt water, assaulted everyone's senses as the air boss snapped out commands through the 88,000-ton ship's tannoy system. This was *Connie*'s last tour of duty.

Out on the stern, oblivious to the ear-splitting shriek of the incoming jets, the duty arresting-gear officer, a lieutenant junior grade, sweating in his big fluorescent yellow jacket, was in contact with the hydraulic operators one deck below. The wires were ready to withstand the 75,000lb force of the Tomcat hitting the deck at 160 knots, the pilot's hand still hard on the throttle just in case the hook missed. The twenty-eight-year-old Lieutenant, Bobby Myers from Ohio, could feel his voice rising now and he snapped down commands to the hydraulic men: 'Stand by for Tomcat one-zero-seven, two minutes.' He looked back over the stern, ninety feet above the water, straining to catch the lights of the fighter-bomber. He knew the pilot personally and, as it did every single time, his chest began to tighten and his heart was racing. Nothing ever dismisses the nerve-twisting tension that grips the arresting-gear officer when a fighter-bomber is on its final flight path. Every arresting-gear officer who ever lived, that is.

Bobby had him now, five miles out, and he checked the wires again, checked on his radio phone the huge hydraulic piston was ready to take the strain in the forthcoming controlled collision between deck and plane. 'GROOVE!' he shouted into the phone, the code word for, 'She's close, stand by!'

Two miles out now, bucking along in the warm erratic air currents of the Gulf, the Tomcat pilot fought to hold her steady, watching the landing lights, always watching the balls of light, an iron grip on the stick. He could see the carrier's stern rise slightly on the swell and the precision required for the high-speed landing would be measured in inches rather than feet. Every pilot knows he is a split-second from death every carrier landing he makes, knows that one in five Navy pilots die in the first nine years of their service.

Seconds later Bobby Myers snapped, 'SHORT' – the critical command for everyone to stand right back away from the machinery. And now Bobby saw the Tomcat right above, screaming in. '*RAMP!*' he bellowed and every single eye on the flight deck was lasered in on the hook stretched out behind. The blast from the jets shimmered the night air. The ear-shattering din of the jet engines made speech impossible. One mistake now and it would not be just the pilot who died. A pile-up on the flight-deck could spark a jet fuel fire that could put the entire ship out of action.

Hundreds of battle-hardened flight deck technicians, already swarming forward, silently breathed 'Thank God' as the hook swung and then grabbed the wire, hauling the Tomcat to a standstill. Just as they would all breathe 'Thank God' again, one minute from now, as they coaxed yet another F-14D out of the sky to safety, refueled her and prepared her to go again.

So it is, out with the front-line steel fist of the US Navy, where men face danger every minute, where they operate in harm's way every single day, always under orders, always working for the cause. Their rewards are modest, at least financially. But in a sense they have the biggest pay-checks of all, not written out on some bank transfer but on their own hearts.

Meanwhile, 200 million citizens back home grouse and moan about the rising price of gasoline.

'*Tomcat one-zero-six, one minute. STAND BY!*'

080600MAY07. USS John F. Kennedy
10.00S 137E. Course 270. Speed 30.
The 88,000-ton carrier was halfway between Pearl Harbor and Diego Garcia, steaming at flank speed through the Arafura Sea south of the Indonesian archipelago, heading for the near-bottomless waters above the Java trench. They were well through the narrows of the Torres Strait, there was almost no wind off Australia's Northern Territory and it was hotter than hell. *Big John*'s 280,000 hp

171

Westinghouse turbines were working. The giant four-shafter was fully laden with more than forty fighter attack F-14A Tomcats, F/A-18C Hornets and a dozen more radar spotter aircraft, prowlers and ASW squadrons.

The flight wing patches worn by the aviators bore legendary US Navy outfits, the Black Aces, old Fighting 14 the Top Hatters, and VFA-87 the Golden Warriors. There might not yet be a full-scale war raging in the Gulf of Iran, but you'd never have known it watching *Big John*, armed to the teeth, driving forward on the second half of its 10,000-mile mission to Jimmy Ramshawe's minefield. Now 5000 miles of the Indian Ocean stretched before them. They would be the fifth US CVBG to arrive on station, almost certainly to move north from Diego Garcia immediately, up to the Gulf to relieve the *Constellation* Group.

On the bridge of the carrier Rear-Admiral Daylan Holt was studying the plot of his group, one cruiser, two destroyers, five frigates, two nuclear submarines and a fleet tanker. At this speed they were burning up fuel fast. But his orders were clear: *Make all speed to DG and stand by for Gulf patrol.* That was one way to send someone on a 10,000-mile journey across the world. But Admiral Holt was prepared, even though it was difficult to get a handle on how serious things really were in the Strait of Hormuz.

He sipped black coffee in company with his Combat Systems Officer, Lieutenant-Commander Chris Russ, as the sun began to rise blood-red out of the ocean over the stern of the massive warship. There was an air of apprehension throughout the carrier, had been since they had cleared Pearl a week before. The pilots were predictably gung-ho. A bit too gung-ho and now, for the first time, Lieutenant-Commander Russ posed the question to the Admiral: 'Do you think we might actually have to fight this, sir? I mean a proper hot war?'

'I think it's possible but unlikely, Chris. Look at our perceived enemies — Iran, who put down the minefield, and China, who made it possible. Well, for a start Iran's not going to fire a shot in anger. They know we could ice their entire country in about twenty minutes. They have not fired yet and in my opinion will not fire at all.'

'How about the Chinese?'

'They might attack if the action were in the South China Sea where they have their main fleet and we have many, many fewer. But they won't attack in the Gulf. They're too far from home and anyway they know we'd wipe out their ships in about twenty minutes.'

'That's a kinda busy twenty minutes, sir,' said the Lieutenant-Commander, grinning.

'That's a lot better than a kinda dead twenty minutes,' replied the Admiral, not grinning.

0600 Tuesday, May 8.
HQ SPECWARCOM, Coronado Beach
San Diego, California.

Commander Russell Bennett, one of the most highly decorated US Navy SEALs ever to serve in the squadron, was relishing his new job as the senior instructor for combat-ready men. The ex-Maine lobsterman, lionized in Coronado for his daredevil role as forward commander in a sensational attack on a Chinese jail the year before, was back home on the beach, running through the cold surf, driving his men ever onwards, before the sun had fought its way above the cliffs. They'd been out there since 0430 and some of the newer guys, fresh out of their BUD/S course, were finding it tough going. Rusty's methods were brutal in the extreme. He parked six Zodiacs a half-mile offshore and ordered all fifty of the men into the surf to swim out and get on board. Then he had them drive forward with their paddles, beach the big rubber landing craft, turn it round and then fight it back out through the crashing breakers, again using paddles only.

One half-mile later they all jumped once more into the freezing water, wearing only swimming shorts, and fought their way back to the beach leaving only the six boat drivers behind. Tired, freezing, still in the dark, the men were then ordered to run four more miles back along the beach to a point where the Zodiacs were again waiting a half-mile offshore.

They'd done the exercise twice now and all they heard was Commander Bennett's voice urging them onwards: 'Keep going, son. I'm probably saving your life.' They were precisely the same words Rusty's own instructors had yelled at him fifteen years before. More important, they had been prophetically correct, which was, essentially, why the hickory-tough Rusty Bennett was still breathing, after an operational career which had six times seen him square up and stare down the Grim Reaper. The carrot-haired ex-SEAL combat Team Leader was just a bit too tough to die and today he was making sure that also applied to the men he was now training. Every last one of them.

Three times in the past fifteen minutes young SEALs had fallen flat down in the sand, too cold, too exhausted to care. Each time Rusty Bennett had stood above the man and roared abuse, swearing to God he'd blow his head off if he didn't *get up and move forward*. Two of the men were almost unconscious. One of them was sobbing. But all three reached down again and found more, and got up and moved forward in a combination of agony and defiance. At the end of the exercise Commander Bennett took each of them aside and told him quietly, 'That's what it's all about, hanging in there when you have nothing left. That's a great job you did. I'm proud of you.'

Back in the SEALs headquarters, Commander Bennett was summoned to the office of the SEAL Chief, Admiral

John Bergstrom. 'Morning, Rusty,' he said. 'How do they look?'

'Good, sir. Very good. Six of the veterans are already excellent leaders and some of the new guys have terrific potential. We got great swimmers, good radio technicians, demolition guys and marksmen. Plus a few obvious hard men.'

'Can we get two teams of twelve out of the group for a couple of critical missions?'

'I'm sure we can, sir. I really like what I'm seeing from them. But I wouldn't mind knowing roughly where we're going.'

'Well, you and I are leaving for Washington shortly after midnight for a final briefing. We'll be there all day. I guess we'll know then.'

'Are we seeing the Big Man, sir?'

'In person.'

'Jesus. Are you sure I'm ready for this?'

'You're ready. Just as long as you remember his bark's bad, but his bite's worse. Just kidding. The Admiral loves SEALs. Thinks we're the most important guys in the US armed services. Anyway it's pretty obvious where we're going, isn't it?'

'I'm afraid so, sir. Middle East. But I just wonder what we're supposed to be doing.'

'Probably not public relations. If Arnold Morgan wants us, he wants something either flattened, or just plain obliterated. Trust me.'

'Hell. I hope it's not the big Iranian naval yard down on the Gulf. It's swarming with military personnel.'

'Of course, you're an expert, eh, Rusty?'

'Yes, sir. A very fair description. Damn place gives me the creeps.'

'If I had to guess, I would say it's certainly not Bandar Abbas the Admiral wants to talk about.'

'Why not, sir? He said to have two teams of twelve on twenty-four hour battle notice. That's two targets. Separate.'

'Even Arnold Morgan could not possibly think twelve SEALs could take out an entire naval base, with several thousand men on duty.'

'We might have a shot if we went at night!' said Rusty, grinning. 'But I agree. He's got something more passive in mind.'

John Bergstrom walked across the room to a large-scale electronic chart of the ocean along Iran's south-eastern coast. He stood staring at it as if checking reference points. Then he muttered, almost inaudibly, 'What about that damn great Chinese refinery?'

'Sorry, sir. I didn't quite get that?'

'Oh, nothing, Rusty. Just a thought. Let's wait until tomorrow. See you here tonight zero-zero-thirty. Civilian suit. We're meeting Commander Hunter at the White House.'

'Aye, sir.'

0859 Wednesday, May 9.
The White House Lawn.

Admiral Morgan turned his head sideways to the wind and stared into the skies to the south-east, searching like an air traffic controller for the big Navy helicopter bringing John Bergstrom and Rusty Bennett in from Andrews Air Base. He checked his watch, one minute before touchdown and no sign yet of the US Marines Super Cobra clattering across the eastern bank of the Potomac. 'If I could *see* the sonofabitch right now they'd still be a minute late,' he muttered. 'Standing out here on the grass like some fucking rose pruner. Goddamned disorganized sailors. Where the hell are they?' He had to wait two more minutes. Then he spotted the Marine guided-missile gunship, with its brand-new four-bladed rotor, bearing down on the White House. The pilot swung over the building, banked the helicopter to its port side and dropped gently down on to the landing pad.

Seconds later the loadmaster had opened the passenger door and the US Navy's Emperor SEAL, Admiral John Bergstrom, stepped down into a bright spring morning in the capital. Behind him, dressed in a dark-gray suit, with gleaming black shoes, came the powerful figure of Commander Bennett. He wore a white shirt with a dark-blue tie. His principal distinguishing feature was pinned on his left lapel, the combat SEAL's gleaming golden Trident. Rusty Bennett's colleagues swore he pinned it on his pajamas each night without fail.

Arnold Morgan walked towards them with a welcoming smile. 'Hello, John,' he said. 'Good to see you again.' He shook the hand of the Commander-in-Chief of SPECWARCOM, then turned to the junior officer, who was hanging back in the presence of a legend, and said solemnly, 'Come and take me by the hand, Commander Bennett. This is a moment to which I have looked forward for a long time.'

Rusty walked towards him and said quietly, 'Admiral Morgan, it's my pleasure to meet you.'

As their hands clasped, the Admiral found his imagination roaming out of control. Before him stood a clean-cut well-presented naval officer, but in his mind Arnold Morgan saw a warrior, face blackened, machine-gun cocked, leading his men out of the water, up the beach, face to face with unimaginable danger. He saw in Rusty's deep-blue eyes the icy glance of a born leader, a veteran of three brutal SEAL missions, a tiger among men, and he shook his head and said, 'Commander, I don't often get a chance to shake the hand of a real hero. I just want you to know I regard it as a very great privilege.'

177

Rusty nodded and said without emphasis, 'Thank you, sir. Thank you very much indeed.' In the background he could see the White House, the very citadel of American power, and he wished with all his heart that his widowed father, Jeb Bennett, the Maine lobsterman from Mount Desert, could have seen him right now, just for a few seconds.

They walked companionably towards the main door to the West Wing and the agents handed both SEALs special passes, before they set off down the corridor to Admiral Morgan's lair. Kathy O'Brien greeted them as they arrived and informed the Admiral that Alan Dickson and General Scannell were waiting inside. She had just received a signal from the base at Quantico that Commander Hunter was in the area and that his helicopter would put down on the White House pad in five minutes, direct from the SEALs' east-coast HQ at Little Creek, Virginia, home of Teams Two, Four and Eight.

Inside the office the introductions were made, principally for the benefit of Rusty. The rest of the officers knew each other. Kathy ordered coffee for everyone but returned almost immediately to announce the arrival of Commander Rick Hunter, a titanic SEAL team leader who had operated under deep cover in a murderous attack on Russian naval hardware in the late Joe Stalin's northern canals; and who had been in overall command of the attack on the Chinese jail the previous year. Commander Hunter would lead the SEALs into the Chinese-occupied base in Burma, less than six weeks from now. He walked through the door, a massive, hard-muscled warrior, standing 6ft 4ins tall and tipping the scales at a zero-body-fat 220lbs. He was dressed like Rusty in a dark-gray suit, with a white shirt and highly polished shoes. Like Rusty, he wore the gleaming golden Trident of the combat SEAL on his left lapel.

Admiral Morgan vacated the big chair behind his desk and walked across the room to meet the battle-hardened SEAL leader from the Blue Grass State. He told him, as he had told Rusty, that it was an honor finally to talk to him.

'Sir,' said Rick Hunter. 'I had no idea you had even heard of me.'

'Rick,' replied Arnold Morgan. 'For me to refer to you as one of the finest combat commanders our Special Forces ever had would be to damn with faint praise. I know who you are and I know what you have done. Please go over and sit in my chair, behind my desk and allow me to bring you a cup of probably disgusting coffee. It's the best I can do.'

Everyone laughed, and the big SEAL went and sat in the Admiral's chair.

'If you only knew, Commander, how many hours I've sat there, wondering about you and your missions, and whether you could possibly succeed. Well, you ought to feel right at home. That's my Rick Hunter worry-myself-to-death seat.' Admiral Morgan poured coffee for everyone and directed their attention to the electronic chart he had pulled up on a big screen at the end of the room. It showed the south-east coast of Iran and it was highlighted by three dotted lines, close together, joining the Omani coastal town of Ra's Qabr al Hindi to a point twenty miles east on the Iranian shore. It stretched like a wall across the Strait.

'That the minefield, Arnie?' asked Admiral Bergstrom.

'That's it. And we should have a pretty good-sized seaway through it in a few more days. The Indian sweepers have done well. We're looking for a cleared gateway of three or four miles.'

'Tankers start moving this week?'

'We're not that clear.'

'Okay, boss,' said the SEAL Chief. 'Lay it on me. What do we hit?'

'Up here, John. Twenty-nine miles to the north. See where it says Kuhestak? The new Chinese oil and petrochemical refinery is two miles south of that little town. It's huge.'

'You want it put out of action?'

'Uh-huh. I want it vaporized.'

'Jesus,' said Rick Hunter.

'What's the water depth inshore?' asked Rusty Bennett.

'Damn shallow,' replied Arnold Morgan. 'We got about five miles under nine feet, the last two miles are under four.'

'Can we get a submarine in close?'

'Probably seventeen miles, then an ASDV into the shallows. The last five miles you have to swim, walk or wallow. Water's warm. No military presence that we know of. A deserted coastline.'

Commander Hunter nodded. 'We got the new ASDV, the one that holds fourteen guys?'

'You have. It's on board *Shark* right now. Two-man crew, twelve SEALS.'

'Range?'

'Sixteen hours at six knots.'

'Will it wait, using zero power. Or come back for the guys later?'

'It'll wait.'

Commander Hunter nodded again. He turned to Admiral Bergstrom. 'Am I going in, sir?'

'Not this time. You're leading Mission Two. That's two weeks later. If you agree. You've served your time on active duty, as you well know. I'm not ordering you in. But I'd be grateful if you'd answer in the affirmative.'

'But I don't know the nature of the attack.'

'It's on a Chinese naval base in the Bassein river in Burma,' interjected Arnold Morgan. 'It's going to be dangerous, but highly organized. Failure is unthinkable.'

'Well, sir, I'm not too bad at wiping out Chinese military.'

'You're also the best Team Leader the SEALs have had since Vietnam, according to John. Except, of course, for the now-retired Rusty here. Quite honestly, Commander, I'd be real unhappy with anyone else in charge.'

'Will it be my last active mission, sir?'

'It will. And it will guarantee you make Admiral in the shortest possible time. Admiral Dickson here will give you that personal guarantee. Ask him, John.'

'Commander Hunter, will you accept command of Mission Two, the forthcoming attack on the Chinese base in the Bassein river?'

No hesitation. 'Affirmative, sir.'

The three Admirals nodded curtly in the time-honored naval code of recognizing a big decision, well made. Then they turned back to the screen, where John Bergstrom was pointing at the course *Shark* would steer up to the ops area. Arnold Morgan had already coded in the rendezvous point at 26.36N 56.49E where the submarine would wait in 180 feet of water, seventeen miles south-west of the Chinese refinery.

By now Commander Bennett was assiduously taking notes. Two big blue, yellow and white charts had been provided for him and John Bergstrom to take back to Coronado. Rusty had drawn in the lines of the minefield and was now marking water depths. 'That's a darned long way in those shallows,' he said. 'Is there any radar down there?'

'Not that we can see. Certainly no Chinese radar. We detect no military presence whatsoever by the Chinese. Nearest radar is down by the missile sites at the end of the minefield. That's around thirty miles away. If the guys are kicking in along the surface, even in three feet, there's no way they'd get picked up.'

'It's the last coupla miles I'm concerned about,' said Rusty. 'Water's just about ankle deep, then a kinda swamp area, then flat, rough, sandy terrain. No cover.'

'SEALs can move across that in under twelve minutes,' replied Admiral Morgan. 'It's gotta be 10,000 to 1 against a towelhead with a radar screen picking anyone up thirty miles away while the guys are going in.'

'It wasn't that I was so much worried about, sir.'

'Sorry, Commander. How do you mean?'

'My guys can get in,' said Rusty. 'I'm more worried about getting them out.'

'Okay, Commander. I have given this thought,' said Admiral Morgan. 'Let's take a worst case. The refinery blows before your guys are clear. Let's say you did not hit the control tower hard enough and the non-military guards hit the buttons to their Iranian Navy buddies at Bandar Abbas. That's nearly fifty miles away. Too far for a patrol boat. Their only shot at catching you is helicopters and by the time they've saddled a couple of them up, that's twenty minutes. Flight time at 170 knots is, say, fifteen minutes. By which time you've had thirty-five minutes to get into deepish water. It's pitch dark and they gotta find you. Right out there I got two guided-missile frigates. Your guys have radios. Those fucking choppers get too close I'm gonna have them blown right outta the sky and blame the goddamned refinery explosion. Matter of fact I might blow 'em right out of the sky on take-off. Fucking towelheads.'

'How about they happen to have a helicopter or two down by the minefield missile sites?'

'Anything moves into the sky anywhere near that minefield, it's toast,' growled the Admiral. 'Remember, right now the US of A is in sole naval control of the Gulf, the Strait of Hormuz and the northern Arabian Sea. No one moves there unless we say so. *No one.*'

'Thank you, sir,' said Commander Bennett.

'Any time, Commander. Glad to be of help.' Arnold Morgan smiled thinly. He was loving this. Talking to real fighting men. Guys who knew something. Proper people. He gazed at the SEAL, a veteran of more dangerous situations than most people could even imagine. Rusty stood there, still looking at the chart, still writing in his notebook, his bearing upright, his luxurious dark mustache perfectly trimmed, his gaze steady. Arnold Morgan could have talked to him for a week. At this moment he suddenly asked the SEAL from the coast of Maine, 'Commander, may I ask you a question? A rather personal question?'

'Of course, sir.'

'When you hit the island in the South China Sea, at the head of your team last year, were you ever afraid?'

'Yes, sir.'

'Did your fear subside once you got into action?'

'No, sir. I was afraid all the time.'

'Did any of your men realize that?'

'No, sir.'

'Were they afraid?'

'Yes, sir.'

'Did anyone give in to their worst fears.'

'No, sir.'

'How do you know?'

'Because they all wear the Trident, sir. We don't give in to anything.'

Arnold Morgan just nodded and said, 'Of course.'

It was plain that the Admiral was quite moved by the short conversation, and John Bergstrom stepped in and said, 'Rusty, you will be going on the mission, I believe? Not into combat, but you are going to be there?'

'Yes, sir. I was unclear before what it entailed. I would like overall command, until they go in. Then I'll hand over to the team leader. I'll go with them in the submarine as far as the rendezvous point. That way I'll be close if something should . . . well . . . happen. Something . . . er . . . unexpected, I mean. I'd like your permission for that, sir.'

'You have it, Commander.'

Admiral Morgan said now that he considered the insertion of the SEALs, plus the getaway, were clear to everyone and that it was time to take a look at the refinery itself. He clicked off the electronic chart and replaced it with an excellent color transparency, thirty inches by twenty-four, taken by the satellite of China's vast new petrochemical plant on the Iranian coast. He told them it had cost close to $2 billion to build and would generate product worth more than $10 million a day. It refined petrol, kerosene, jet fuel, heavy fuel oil, liquefied petroleum gas, tar and sulphur. After just a couple of months operational it was refining 250,000 barrels a day.

'You guys hit this hard, there's gonna be a lot of very, very angry Chinamen running around. It's a big place with a lot of pipes and towers and valves. However, it's no good just blowing holes in things. Bust pipes and bent towers can be shut off and repaired, with little lasting harm done. That's not our objective. We intend to blow this place sky-high and I'm looking for ignition, right? Pure combustion.'

'No bullshit,' said Admiral Dickson, in an undisguised parody of Arnold Morgan's favorite phrase.

'Precisely, CNO,' confirmed the National Security Chief. 'No bullshit.' He walked to his desk, picked up his thirty-six-inch long steel ruler and came back to the screen. 'Right,' he said, 'I'm going to stand off to the side here so you can all see the area I'm referring to. That way Rusty here can use a yellow marker on one of these prints I had done. OK, now I'm assuming you are not all experts on refining and I'm going to explain what you are looking for. By the way, twenty-four hours ago I knew none of this, but I do now because I had Jack Smith come down and explain it to me.

'I have had notes on this prepared for everyone to take back and study, but I do want to go over it. For a start, we should be clear; a refinery converts crude oil – in this case from Kazakhstan – into a whole range of products. The crude is really just a combination of hydrocarbons, which are separated inside the refinery into various groups, or fractions. It's actually called "separation, conversion and chemical treatment". The stuff basically gets distilled, but it's complicated because some fractions vaporize, or boil, at very different temperatures – gasoline at 75F, some heavy fuel oils at 600F. They also condense at different temperatures. What happens is the crude gets pumped via pipes, through a furnace, which heats it to maybe 725F. The resulting mixture of belting hot gas and liquids then passes into a vertical steel cylinder, called a fractioning tower or a bubbling tower.

'This little bastard is what we're after. Because inside that tower we got a lot of shit happening – the heavy fuels condense in the lower section, light fractions like gasoline and kerosene in the middle and upper section. The liquids, all highly inflammable, are collected in trays and drawn by pipes along the sides of the tower. Some fractions never even cool enough to condense and these get passed out through the top of the tower into a vapor recovery unit. I'm talking high-test incendiary. One of these towers goes up because of a bomb stuck on its lower casing, can you imagine? It blows the heavy fuel oil into a blizzard of fire, which hits gasoline, kerosene and then liquified gas in the vapor unit. That tower, so far as you're concerned, is potentially one of the world's biggest fireworks.'

He rapped the screen with his ruler. 'See this group

here at the north end? There's ten towers. So far as I can see, the biggest may be a hundred feet high. We wanna bomb this one, this one and this one, out here on the right by these holding tanks. According to Jack, they're full of gasoline. I'd say if the towers blow, they'll take the storage tanks with 'em. They might even take the entire local landscape, so I'd prefer you guys to be well clear before you detonate.' He paused for effect. But no one spoke. So he pressed on. 'This tall building here', he said, 'is the control center. It is essential you hit this and hit it hard. Because in there they can turn off the flow of oil through literally miles of pipeline. We don't want that. We want that stuff flowing in, feeding the fire, keeping it raging.

'Finally we come to this group of holding tanks. Jack says this is where they store thousands of tons of deep-frozen liquified natural gas. Looks like there's around thirty of them and they are strategically well placed from our point of view. They are nowhere near the towers and far from the control center, so we're not wasting any of our explosive assets. You can see from this picture the tanks are huge, maybe fifty feet high and forty feet in diameter. I'd guess if we hit five of them that'd send the lot up. It would also give us a triangle of fire and explosions, the towers, the control center and the holding tanks, which will certainly take out this middle storage area which lies between them.'

He looked at his audience and noticed he still had their attention. 'Gentlemen,' he said. 'Out here on the north-west of the plant you can see yet another large grouping of tanks. Jack thinks this is the chemical area, maybe a lot of ammonium phosphate for fertilizer. I realize that you are going to be short-handed, only twelve of you can go in. But if you found yourselves with some spare time, with a little spare explosive, you could do a lot of damage out there with the stuff that once blew up Texas City.'

'Arnold,' interrupted Admiral Bergstrom, 'were you proposing to nail down the entire plan here for us to go away and . . . er . . . well, refine?'

'Absolutely not, John. I'm done. I just wanted us to be singing from the same hymn sheet for the seaward insertion and getaway, and for the extent of the mission, the amount of TNT required and the main targets you must attack. The number of SEALs going in is dictated by the size of the ASDV. The rest is up to you: how and when you break through this high wire fence to get in, how you deal with possible alarms and guards. I'll have any and all information from Fort Meade fed into Coronado at all times during the next few days. The Navy will be ordered to supply *anything* requested by either Commander Hunter or Commander Bennett during the missions. By that I mean, of course, heavy back-up firepower. Whatever it takes.'

'Okay, Arnold. Now, how about the Bassein river? Mission Two?'

'I'm in the process of taking some heavy-duty advice on that, John. But I have prepared charts for you and Rick to take back to California. I've also got a few godawful black-and-white pictures of the place, but NRO are working on some better, clearer stuff which I'll get to you. This whole operation is strictly Navy. That's why Alan Dickson is taking overall command of it personally. Especially during this extremely classified stage. He and I will be in constant communication, but I'd prefer you two to work directly together. Depending on the advice we get, we may have to change tactics. I just don't want to get into anything that might be obsolete next Thursday.'

'Understood, sir.'

By 1145 the meeting was over. The three SEALs declined lunch and left to board their helicopter immediately: White House lawn to Andrews Air Base, Andrews direct to San Diego. Military aircraft. As Admiral Morgan would have phrased it, 'No bullshit.'

As things were, he phrased only one other scenario as they walked through the West Wing corridors: 'Remember, guys, bang out that refinery and the Chinese are out of the western Indian Ocean, because they have no further reason to be there. And we're not having it – fucking rickshaw drivers bringing the goddamned free world to a standstill. And we're not having it at the eastern end either. I want that Burmese base of theirs wrecked and I want their Navy back in the China Seas where they belong. When the Bassein facility is slammed, I'm gonna tell the little pricks precisely why and they can stick that in their fucking rice bowls.'

He was still standing, glowering, beside the helicopter pad, long after the Cobra was up and over the river towards Andrews. Still muttering, 'It's been 500 years since China had a big fleet in the Middle East and that's not long enough.'

1000 (local) Thursday, May 10.
Headquarters, Eastern Fleet
Ningbo, Zhejiang Province.
Admiral Zhang was puzzled. Here was the United States with the biggest concentration of naval power assembled since the war with Iraq seventeen years ago and they had made absolutely no communication with either of the nations which laid down the minefield in the first place. 'You think they may not know who the culprits were?' he asked the C-in-C, Admiral Zu Jicai.

'They know,' he replied. 'They saw our warships down there. Indeed, they just crippled our leading destroyer. At least I think they did. No proof, of course.'

'Well, if that's the case we have a rather strange silent war going on, wouldn't you say? Two of the most powerful nations, plus the guardians of the old Persian Gulf, grappling in some three-way Sumo headlock without one word being spoken by the protagonists.'

'And, unhappily, no referee,' said Admiral Zu.

'It's bizarre. The Americans have uttered no formal protest about the minefield. But they have moved a staggering line-up of naval power into the area and it's standing there like that ridiculous·ape they all admire so much, King Kong, fists flailing, but no one to strike.'

Admiral Zu chuckled. 'The trouble with the Americans is they always have a hidden agenda. We cannot drop our guard and we don't want our warships anywhere near them.'

'You think they have an agenda for striking back at us? We have, after all, been responsible for the total destruction of four extremely expensive oil tankers.'

'It's hard to know, Jicai. I don't think they would come after us and attack one of our cities, or even a naval base. So what's left?'

'Well, we do have a very large oil refinery in Iran.'

'Oh, yes. But the Americans won't attack that. They revere money too much and oil is currently the world's most precious commodity. They might one day try to buy shares in it, but they wouldn't destroy it. That would just turn them into reckless cowboys like Saddam Hussein, ignoring the ecology of the region, not to mention a lot of civilian deaths.'

'Nonetheless, Yushu, I think we should strengthen the guard at the refinery, perhaps borrow some of those attack dogs the Navy has at Bandar Abbas.'

'It certainly could not be harmful, Jicai. I agree with you. We ought not to underestimate the innate viciousness of those men in the Pentagon.'

'Even if, for the moment, their actual agenda remains hidden, Yushu.'

'As, indeed, does ours, my Jicai.'

189

Six

101200MAY07. 10.40S 146E.
USS John F. Kennedy

On the face of it, *Big John* was not making much progress. The giant carrier was back in warm waters 200 miles off the Australian state of Queensland, having passed once more through the narrows of the Torres Strait. There was still no wind, they were still running at flank speed and it was still hotter than hell. The only difference from one week ago was they were heading east, rather than west. *Big John* had been diverted. No one had given a reason. There was just a terse signal from the Third Fleet HQ in San Diego to come about and head back the way they had come. Forget Diego Garcia. Make instead for the Pacific, steer east of New Guinea and head on north, taking up station off the east coast of Taiwan.

There was a widespread suspicion on board that China must as usual have been growling around too close to the independent island in which the USA had such a major investment and for which she was pledged to fight, very nearly to the death.

However, the truth was more mundane. The Nimitz Class carrier *Ronald Reagan*, just out of major overhaul in the San Diego yards, was simply judged to be in need of a considerably longer work-up period than one week. And with *Constellation, Truman, Stennis* and *Roosevelt* all in the Hormuz area, it was decided the *Reagan* ought to take the proper time to get into front-line shape and that the *JFK* could perfectly easily swing round and make the Taiwan patrol, leaving the other four CVBGs to take care of the oil problems at the gateway to the Gulf. Those four battle groups packed enough of a punch to deal with any problem in the entire history of the planet. The mere presence of *Constellation* and *Truman* had frightened away the Iranians, the Chinese and anyone else wandering around trying to make a buck.

Which still left *Big John* thundering along towards the Coral Sea, with everyone sweating themselves half to death, wondering what the hell the Chinese had done and what the hell, indeed, they themselves had done to deserve making this lunatic circular route south of Indonesia, in seas which were of no interest to anyone.

0800 Thursday, May 10.
US Navy Base, Coronado.
Even in the shadowy, unlit inner sanctum of SPECWARCOM this was as secret as it gets. Deep in one of Coronado's underground ops rooms, behind locked doors and armed guards, twenty-four hand-picked Navy SEALs were undergoing a two-day briefing by three of the toughest men who ever wore combat boots: Admiral John Bergstrom, Commander Rick Hunter and Commander Rusty Bennett. The task before them was relatively compact by SEAL standards – the destruction of two foreign installations, one of them loosely guarded. But the overall intent of the operation was Herculean: to drive the Republic of China out of the Gulf of Iran, the Strait of Hormuz, the Arabian Sea, the Indian Ocean and, in particular, the Bay of Bengal. In that precise order.

Twenty-four members of America's most elite, ruthless Special Forces, against the collective will and determination of 1.3 billion Chinese citizens and their 300,000-

strong Navy. The odds, by any standards, were not in any way promising. For the Chinese, that is.

In fact, there was a total of twenty-eight battle-ready SEALs in the ops room, four 'spares' should anyone be injured. Commander Hunter himself was one of the main group and would personally lead in his team of twelve on Mission Two.

Right now, Commander Bennett was going over the initial insertion of troops, the final four or five miles which Assault Team One would swim/wade, en route to the sprawling Chinese refinery on the shores of Hormuz. Before him was the chart of the shallow waters all along the beaches. 'Well, guys,' he said, in the usual, informal SEALs method of command, 'you can all see these depths. If you're lucky, the ASDV will get in to within four miles, but this damn chart is obviously not reliable. If the submarine can make it right in here to the ten-meter line, that's about the best you can hope for. That'll be a three-mile swim in warm water no more than nine feet deep. Then it looks like you may have to wade the last mile. But the good news is there is no formal military surveillance. We've swept and surveyed it thoroughly and found nothing. The nearest foreign military is thirty miles away. Also, you have tremendous cover offshore, a US Navy presence which, for the past couple of weeks, has plainly frightened everyone else to death.'

Rusty paused and asked for questions. There were none. He flicked off the chart of the seaward approaches and zoomed in on the Chinese refinery. 'Right here I want you to start making notes,' he said. 'Each of you will be provided with a clear 10 × 8 print of the objective you see on the screen. Obviously you will make your approach from the west, through this marshy area, up the beach and across these sand dunes. You'll see from the satellite shots that there is cover in here, within 400 yards of the perimeter fence, and that's important. Because we want you to make two separate entries. First night, you'll reach the perimeter fence at around midnight. I want you to cut it cleanly on three sides, a gap big enough for two men at a time to go through. I want a team of four, each armed with ordnance, to go to work right away on this near group of storage tanks.'

He pointed at what looked like a cluster of twenty-eight giant white tin cans, thirty feet high, sixty feet in diameter. 'I want you to place the explosive at the base of three of these,' he said. 'They're made of cast concrete, with steel casing on the outside. Each one is full of just-refined petroleum. See this pipeline? You can follow it due west and then pick it up out near the new offshore loading bay. It's gotta be gasoline which, as you know, burns up pretty good. This is not a time-consuming task. I'm talking twenty minutes' work maximum, from the time you get in through the wire. Of course, if you should be caught or attacked, the entire mission is cancelled.'

Rusty paused again, took a long swig of iced water and proceeded: 'Three more of you will take care of cutting the wire on the outer fence, then folding and clipping it back into position at the conclusion of the first night ops. That team will also be responsible for observing and avoiding guard patrols. For obvious reasons we do not want to be detected, because our main assault will be on the following night. Questions?'

'How many bombs do we carry in, sir?'

'Six for the holding tanks, three for each of the two groups. Three for the towers, which could be overkill since I suspect one would blow the hell out of ten square miles of oil pipelines. And three more for the control center, two ground level, one higher up if possible. If there's time you'll need another couple for the petro-chemical area, but I realize there may not be. That's a total of fourteen – one each for most of you. However, three mines go in through the wire the first night, eleven the second. I know that's a lot to do, with your own personal weapons, plus the Draegers, the attack boards and the detonation kit, but it's not that bad, except for the long wade-in through the shallows.'

'Are we taking in any heavy weapons, in case we get into real trouble?'

'No. Nothing real big. If anything unexpected happens, you're one radio shout from help. We'll have helicopters ready to take off from *Constellation* at one minute's notice, get you the hell outta there.'

'How about the goddamned Iranians get helos up if we're detected?'

'Anything takes off from any Iranian military or Navy base we take it out instantly. So far as I'm concerned, your safety is not an issue. You're protected by the heaviest front-line muscle we have, Danny, it's secrecy we're interested in. Just don't get detected.'

'Okay, sir,' replied Lieutenant Dan Conway, another decorated veteran of the South China Sea operation the previous year. 'Softly softly, catchee Chinese monkey.'

'Never mind Chinese monkey, sir, how about Chinese woofer – attack dogs? If they've got Dobermans or shepherds, we'd have to shoot them or they'll try to tear us to pieces. We'd be into a goddamned uproar at best.'

'Okay, Bobby. We've seen no evidence of any guard dogs in the refinery. In fact, we've not even located formal guard patrols. Langley tells us there are no guard dogs. However, I agree we should consider the matter, because one damned dog going berserk and barking like hell could wreck the secrecy of the operation. Which would not be fatal, because our main objective is destruction. But we would very much like to get in, and out, unseen and unknown.'

'If we shoot any dogs, they gotta know we're in there, right?'

'Correct. But we might find a way to silence a couple of Dobermans without killing, if we were unlucky enough to run into them on the first night. Second night doesn't matter so much, since I don't plan any survivors.'

The intricate details of the SEAL attacks wore on through the whole of that Thursday and, after dinner, into the night. They reconvened on Friday morning and concluded late in the afternoon, each man now fully acquainted with his task and how to carry it out to the letter. No one ever suggested it was going to be easy.

0930 Saturday, May 12.
200 miles west of San Diego.
30,000-feet altitude.
The huge US Navy Galaxy, which carried the SEAL assault teams, was making 400 knots above the Pacific, bound for Pearl Harbor, Hawaii. After a short refueling stop there and the unloading of several tons of marine spares, the remainder of the 13,000-mile journey to American's Indian Ocean base at Diego Garcia would be non-stop.

The SEALs sat together in the rear of the aircraft, their personal gear stowed in packing cases with the rest of the combat equipment they would haul into the Chinese oil refinery. Each man had carefully packed his flexible, custom-made neoprene wetsuit. His big SEAL flippers, for extra speed, were also custom-made. On the instep of each was the lifetime identification number awarded to him after passing the BUD/S course. All of them had picked two modern scuba-diver's masks, the bright Day-Glo colours for amateurs carefully obscured by jet-black water-resistant tape. The attack boards which the lead swimmers would use on the swim-in had been carefully stowed. To a marauding SEAL, this piece of equipment represents almost certain life or death. The leader holds it out in front of him with both hands, his eyes constantly flicking between compass and small clock, neither of which betrays even a glint. No SEAL ever goes into the water wearing a watch, for fear a shaft of light off its bright metal casing might reflect back and alert a sentry or a harbor wall lookout. Thus the leader goes forward, kicking with his big flippers, counting between each forward thrust: kick-two-three-four-five, kick-two-three-four-five. Five-second intervals, ten-foot distance covered every time, 100 feet in fifty seconds, 1000 feet in a little over eight minutes, 1000 yards in twenty-five minutes, a mile in forty-five minutes, three miles in two and a quarter hours.

It was plainly critical they get the ASDV as close inshore as possible. A two-hour-plus swim, even at a quiet, steady pace, even by the iron men from Coronado, is a strength-sapping exercise and they would need high-energy food, water and a half-hour rest before moving into their target.

There were a dozen SEALs among the group with combat experience. Several of these men had made a swim-in before. They all knew the feeling of tiredness in the water. But they also knew they could dig deep and overcome that. The fresh ground for all of them would be the last mile, when it was too shallow to swim, possibly too tiring to wade fast, carrying a lot of gear, including the flippers.

The twelve-man assault team for the attack on the refinery was essentially one and a half SEAL squads, from Group One, Coronado, the numbers being governed by the number of men who could fit into the ASDV. They would be led by the near-legendary combat SEAL, Lieutenant-Commander Ray Schaeffer, from the seaport at Marblehead, Massachusetts. Ray had taken part in two of the most lethal peacetime SEAL missions ever mounted:

a submarine attack deep in the interior of northern Russia and the harrowing assault on the Chinese jail the year before, for which he had been highly decorated. In SEAL tradition, he was not required to accept another order to go into combat. But there was no need for any order. Lieutenant-Commander Schaeffer not only volunteered, he insisted, and his old boss Rick Hunter was delighted to have him aboard. The attack on the refinery would be Ray's first, and last, overall field command, before he returned to the east coast as a senior BUD/S instructor at Little Creek, Virginia.

Ray was eminently qualified for this command. Aside from his experience both under fire and under cover, he was a superb navigator, an expert seaman and yachtsman. He was the son of a sea captain and a former platoon middleweight boxing champion. He was not as big as Rick Hunter, nor as brute-force strong. But then neither was anyone else. Ray Schaeffer was, however, an ice-cold operator, ruthless with a knife, deadly with any firearm and, under attack, a trained, merciless killer. His men would follow him into hell.

His 2 I/C would be Lieutenant Dan Conway from Connecticut, who had performed with absolute distinction in the attack on the Chinese jail. He was thirty now, a tall, dark-haired demolition expert from the submarine base town of New London. He'd finished in first place after the BUD/S 'Hell Week', the murderous SEAL indoctrination which breaks one in two of the applicants. A superb athlete, Dan had very nearly gone for a career in professional baseball, but Annapolis beat out Fenway Park for his services and the ex-college all-star catcher had never looked back. Everyone knew he was destined for high office in the Navy SEALs and his promotion to lieutenant-commander after this mission in the Hormuz Strait was a foregone conclusion.

One other lieutenant would be included in the first group, the twenty-eight-year-old Virginian John Nathan, making his first combat mission. John, the son of a prosperous Richmond travel agent, had elected to become a SEAL specialist in high explosive and its various detonators. He was thus in overall charge of the eleven limpet mines stowed in the hold of the giant Navy freighter. Six of them, with specially aimed charges, would be attached to the massive holding tanks in the gasoline and petrochemical areas. Another three to the bases of the 100-foot-high steel bubble towers which separated the crude. All eleven were fitted with backpack straps for the swim-in and large magnets to grip the target surface.

John Nathan had sat in on the meeting with Admiral Bergstrom and Commanders Bennett and Hunter while they discussed tactics to take out the control center. At first the Admiral had toyed with a plan to hit the center with Mk 138 satchel bombs, just hurl them through the windows and run like hell for the fence, right at the last minute, leaving the Chinese to deal with the chaos for a couple of hours before the main charges went off and, hopefully, blew the place to pieces. The destruction of the control center would, of course, render it near-impossible to turn off the valves and isolators, which regulated the flow of crude oil through the main pipelines.

But Rusty was skeptical of this strategy. The SEAL Leader from Maine thought the explosion in the control center would cause the Chinese instantly to summon assistance from the Iranian base at Bandar Abbas to conduct a thorough search of the entire refinery. It would be, said Rusty, a search which would surely reveal the limpet mines on the tanks and towers. 'They'd only need to find one,' he said, 'and they'd go through the place, searching every square inch until they found the rest.' In his opinion that would be 'kinda silly'.

No, the control center would have to go off bang with all the other stuff, using a delayed charge of a couple of hours to give the SEALs time to get clear, out into the deep water. John Nathan recommended the plastic explosive C4, which looks like modeling clay and can be made into any shape. It works off an M-60 time fuse lighter, which burns through regular green plastic cord loaded with gunpowder at around one foot per forty seconds. John preferred this fuse because it's a spring-loaded pin like a shotgun, no matches, no bright light and extremely quiet, just a dull thud. Also, there was a new timing device which could delay it several hours and, in John Nathan's experience, was just about 100 per cent reliable.

The last details for the second SEAL mission, to the Bassein delta, were not yet finalized, but all the necessary fuses, plastic explosive, mines and detonators were loaded into the Galaxy for storage at Diego Garcia. There was enough C4 alone in the hold to 'blow up half the world', according to John Nathan, who carried with him the complete list of ordnance throughout the long flight. 'Something combustible hits this baby,' he said in his deep Virginian drawl, 'guess we'd wobble the goddamned rings of Saturn.'

Nathan had started his Navy career as a navigation officer in a frigate, and still liked to pontificate about astrology, the universe and the solar system. The heavy-set, fair-haired Southerner answered to the nickname of 'Clouds', which everyone thought was hysterical, given its obvious proximity to his present field of expertise, with a progression to the word 'mushroom'.

Sitting next to Clouds in the rear bench was another Southerner, Petty Officer Ryan Combs from North Carolina. He was a tall, athletic outdoorsman, expert with a hunting gun and a fishing rod. Ryan was only twenty-six, but he was a tremendous swimmer and as good with a machine-gun as anyone on the Coronado base. He could handle the 500-round-a-minute M060E4 single-handedly and he would carry it under the wire into the Chinese refinery. Commander Bennett had personally requested his appointment to the SEAL combat mission on the shores of Iran. It would be Ryan's first.

Rusty had also requested personally the big, beefy Pennsylvanian Rob Cafiero, the platoon's heavyweight boxing champion, who was as big and almost as strong as Commander Hunter himself. Rob was a mild-mannered giant, with dark, close-cut hair and not an ounce of fat on his 220lb frame. At thirty-two he had made Chief Petty Officer, but Rob was ambitious and was studying to take a commission as soon as possible. Like Lieutenant Nathan, he was an expert on high explosive, but his best field of expertise was in unarmed combat. He was a veteran of the conflict in the mountains of Kosovo.

These were the five key players in the twelve-man assault force, which would slide into the warm shallows along the coast of Iran less than five days from now.

111600MAY07 USS Shark *with* Harry S. Truman *CVBG South of the Hormuz minefield.*
Lieutenant-Commander Dan Headley could not make up his mind whether he was being trivial or not. The new orders had arrived this Friday night, while he and the CO had been together in the control room. Dan had read them out to the Commander, whose comment had been, at best, absent-minded. The orders specified a critical new mission, the insertion of a SEAL team, a precision task which always heightens tension in a submarine. But Commander Reid had merely said, 'I really must take my shoes off,' and had proceeded to do so.

Lieutenant-Commander Headley had thus found

himself for the first time in his life, next to a commanding officer who was standing in the control room in his socks. It wasn't much, but it was new and Dan Headley did not really do new. He was a devotee of the tried and tested ways of the United States Navy. He liked and expected his fellow officers to act in a predictable, cautious but determined way: though sometimes with an added dash of daring, the way most senior warship officers are trained to view an often hostile world. He particularly liked his commanding officer to react in a calculated manner. *I really must take my shoes off.* 'Jesus Christ,' muttered Dan.

The trouble was he could not get it out of his mind, though he knew it to be insignificant. The CO had swiftly returned to normal, even suggested they have a private talk about the insertion later in the afternoon. But he had left without really acknowledging the seriousness of the forthcoming Black Op next Tuesday night. Dan Headley found it curiously disconcerting.

Now, as the submarine cruised slowly at periscope depth twenty miles off the gigantic port bow of the *Harry S. Truman*, he made his way down to the confined privacy of the Commander's personal cabin and tapped on the door.

'Come in, XO,' called the CO. 'I've got us some coffee. Let me pour you a cup.'

'Thank you, sir,' said Dan, heading for the second chair at the little desk and noticing for the first time a small framed print hung on the wall, a portrait, really, just a head and shoulders of an obviously eighteenth-century nobleman. While the CO splashed the hot black coffee into their mugs, Dan Headley leaned over and took a closer look at the portrait. The gentleman wore a tri-corn hat, with a sash across his chest. Beneath the picture were the words, *L'Amiral, le Comte de Villeneuve*. Dan found that unusual and he said cheerfully, 'Nice little picture, sir. But why a French admiral?'

'Oh, you noticed that? It belonged to my grandmother. She was French, you know, my mother's mother. Lived in a small town called Grasse in the South of France, up in the hills behind Cannes. I went there a coupla times as a kid. Pretty part of the world.'

'Yes, sir. I was in Nice once, just along the coast. It was crowded, but kinda warm and cheerful. My dad and I went together, trying to buy a racehorse. Little provincial meet down there in the spring.'

'I didn't know that was horseracing country.'

'It's not really, sir. But they have a meeting down there before the weather gets warm further north in Paris. We went especially to buy back a mare we'd sold as a yearling. She'd won about four races, one at Longchamp.'

'Long way to go to buy a horse.'

'Yes, sir. But she was from a family which'd been real fast back in Kentucky. My daddy's the senior stud groom on a very big farm out there and the owner just wanted her back as a brood mare.'

'Did you get her?'

'Yeah, we got her. Probably paid too much, what with the shipping and all. But when Mr Bart Hunter – that's my daddy's boss – wants a mare he'll usually pay the price.'

'Was she worth it?'

'Not really. She never bred a stakes horse. But one of her daughters was very good, produced a couple of hot-shot milers in New York. Then her next foal, by a top stallion called Storm Cat, fetched $3 million at the Keene-land sales. He couldn't run worth a damn, but I guess that sale probably quadrupled ole Bart's money in the end.'

'I find that very interesting, Dan. The way the talent of a fine family just keeps coming back, sometimes skipping a generation, but still hanging in there, ready to surface.'

'That's the way it's always been in the horse-breeding business, sir.'

'And it's not a whole lot different with people, if I'm any judge,' replied Commander Reid.

'I'm not sure that's altogether politically correct, sir. Breeding people's a tricky subject – aren't we all supposed to be born equal?'

'Believe that, XO, you'll believe anything.'

'You got any hotshot ancestors yourself, sir?'

'Well, we never delved real carefully into it, but I certainly have some deep connections with the French Navy. Very deep.'

'Not Admiral Villeneuve?'

'*Non.*' Commander Reid paused, almost theatrically raising his head. 'We have a connection to the man who effectively won the American Revolution, Comte Françoise-Joseph de Grasse, victor of the Battle of the Chesapeake.' Commander Reid dipped his head, as if in deference to the memory of the French admiral who had held off the British fleet at the mouth of Chesapeake Bay on September 5, 1781.

'Hey, that's really something, sir,' said Dan. 'Was your grandma named de Grasse?'

'Oh no, the family of Françoise-Joseph merely adopted that title and named themselves after the town.'

'Good idea, eh, sir? We get those SEALs in and then out of Iran, I might do the same. How about Lieutenant-Commander Dan of Lexington?'

Commander Reid never even cracked a smile. Le Comte de Grasse was clearly a man about whom he did not make jokes and this Friday afternoon was plainly a time when he did not make plans. The two men finished their coffee more or less in silence and the CO suggested a more formal planning meeting at 1100 the following day.

The new XO left with two unimportant but nagging questions in his mind. One, what was this '*non*' crap all about and, two, what the hell was the CO of a US attack submarine doing with a picture of the ludicrous Admiral Villeneuve on the wall? This was a man who had narrowly escaped the annihilation of the French fleet at the Battle of the Nile and then commanded the new fleet at the absolute catastrophe of the Battle of Trafalgar, where he was taken prisoner, escorted to England and six months later committed suicide. Dan Headley walked back to the control room confirming to himself that he was a loyal XO, resolved to support his immediate boss under any and all circumstances. But in his deepest, most private thoughts it occurred to him that *this Reid weirdo might be a half-dozen cannon balls short of a broadside.*

0400 Monday, May 14.
US Navy Base, Diego Garcia, Indian Ocean.
The Galaxy freighter came thundering into the runway in the small hours of the morning, thirty-four hours after leaving the North Island Air Base in San Diego. Most of them had slept during the second half of the journey from Pearl Harbor, but they were all tired, in need of a stretch, and the stifling heat of the island, only 400 miles south of the Equator, took them by surprise.

Unlike most arriving passengers after a trans-Pacific journey, the SEALs had to supervise their own cargo. Crates which were accompanying them on the next leg of their journey, up to the flight deck of the *Harry S. Truman* 2600 miles to the north, had to be carefully separated for reloading, while the rest of the explosive, which would ultimately be used at the far-eastern end of the Indian Ocean, were taken on fork-lift loaders to the main storage area. Lieutenant John Nathan and Commander Hunter took care of this task, and Rusty Bennett checked off the material being reloaded into a much smaller aircraft for this afternoon's flight up to the carrier.

They were escorted to especially prepared quarters,

fifteen small rooms set aside for the men who were going to work in Iran, fourteen more for those who were waiting in Diego Garcia for their orders to embark for the Bassein river. The SEALs hung around only for a half-hour, during which time they demolished about 7000 ham, cheese and chicken sandwiches and several gallons of sweet decaffeinated coffee. By 0600 they were all asleep and would remain so until 1300, when they would eat a major lunch of New York sirloin steak, eggs and spinach, as much protein as they could pile in, before boarding the aircraft for the northern Arabian Sea. That journey was of almost seven hours' duration and the Navy pilot put down on the *Truman*'s deck in a light sub-tropical sou'wester just before 2200 on that same Tuesday night.

The carrier was busy that evening and the howling Tomcats were coming in in clusters every two minutes. The Admiral had ordered a separate crew to disembark the Special Forces fast and then move their gear down to the hangar for storage, before being ferried with the SEALs by helicopter to USS *Shark*, which would be waiting a half-mile off their port beam at 1600 the next day, Tuesday, May 15.

Their ranks were thinned out now. Commander Bennett and Lieutenant-Commander Ray Schaeffer supervised the opening of the crates and removing the personal kit each SEAL would require before the short thirty-mile submarine run up to the rendezvous point. Lieutenant John Nathan took care of the separate interior boxes which contained the weapons, breathing apparatus and attack boards, before carefully marking the containers of high explosive which would take down the Chinese oil refinery.

Forty minutes later the three officers joined their colleagues in a corner of the huge ship's dining room for what carrier men call MIDRATS (mid-watch rations).

Tonight they ate specially prepared Spanish omelettes, french fries and salad, and they all ate together, no separation of officers from men. SEALs always ignore this distinction, particularly on the eve of a truly lethal operation, such as this one might very well become.

They retired to bed soon after midnight but for most of them it was a fitful night. The first four hours of sleep were easy because of general tiredness after the endless journey. But by 0400 the SEALs were awake, each man wondering what the next twenty-four hours would hold for him. The younger first-mission SEALs would not sleep again this night and even the veteran Lieutenant-Commander Ray Schaeffer was anxious. He climbed out of bed and walked around his room, flexing his muscles, as if taking comfort from his enormous strength. But the mission weighed heavily upon him and he could not take his mind off the warm shallows through which he must lead his men in the darkness of the following night.

Commander Bennett was sharing a bigger cabin with Lieutenant John Nathan and the younger man was unable to sleep. Three times he stood up and walked over to the door, finally pulling on a sweater, waking Rusty and leaving to find a cup of coffee. Fortunately a big carrier never sleeps and the dining room was full, mostly with Navy flyers. By some bush telegraph they seemed to know the broad-shouldered young stranger in the corner nursing a plastic coffee cup was one of the SEALs going in later today. None of them was a stranger to fear and daring, but there is an aura surrounding a combat SEAL on the brink of a mission and no one approached him. No one, that is, until a cheerful twenty-four-year-old pilot from Florida, still in his flying jacket, showed up. He collected a tall glass of ice-cold milk and walked straight over to Lieutenant Nathan's table, stuck out his hand and announced, 'Hey, how you doin'? I'm Steve Ghutzman.'

The SEAL explosives chief looked up and nodded. He shook hands and said, 'Hi, Clouds Nathan.' He felt awkward, sitting here in the middle of the night with this robust stranger, but in truth he was glad of the company.

Steve swiftly regaled him with details of the hot, gusting south-west wind out there. 'You don't wanna take your eye off the ball tonight, I'm telling you. The air's like a goddamned switchback coming in. It wouldn't be no trouble to slam one of them Tomcats bang into the ass of this fucking airfield. Gotta stay right on top of it, yessir.' Steve was unable to distinguish the rank and station of his new companion, and he was talking fast, in the slightly high-adrenalin way Navy pilots do after a tense landing on the flight deck. But he was a nice guy, born a mile from the runway at the navy base in Pensacola, a flyer all his career, just like his father before him. He imbibed the milk, got up to get another glass and brought back a second cup of coffee for his new buddy. Winding down a little, he asked finally, 'What's that first name of yours? I didn't quite catch it?'

'Oh, it's just a nickname. The guys all call me Clouds because I'm interested in astronomy. I used to be a navigator. I got kinda used to it.'

'Hey, that's cool. Clouds. I love it. You just arrived? Didn't see you around before?'

'Yeah, I'm pretty new. Got in a while before midnight. And we'll be gone by 1500.'

Steve Ghutzman hesitated. Then he dropped his lower jaw in mock astonishment. 'H-O-L-E-E-E SHIT!' he said. 'You're one of 'em, right?'

'Guess so,' said Lieutenant Nathan, smiling. 'Guess I'm one of 'em.'

The pilot knew better than to ask details of a classified SEAL mission, but like most of the 6000-strong crew of the gigantic Nimitz Class carrier, he knew there was a

SEAL team on board for less than twenty-four hours and that they were going into Iran later today. He knew nothing of the mission, the objective, or when they were due to return. Just that they were 'going in', God help them.

Throughout every corner of the US Navy the SEALs were regarded as men apart. *Jesus Christ, I'm sitting here with one of 'em, right now.* Steve Ghutzman was hugely impressed and didn't know quite what to say. This was a condition to which he was utterly unused and he just muttered, 'You having a little trouble sleeping tonight?'

The SEAL nodded. 'Some,' he said. 'This is my first mission. Guess it's on my mind.'

'You been in the platoon a while?'

'Oh, yeah. Five years now. And I've done a lot of training, but you always think of this day, the day you're going in. For me that's today, right now, and I can't sleep worth a damn.'

Steve nodded. 'They tell you a lot about it before you go?'

'Everything there is to know. I've never even been to the Middle East, but I know what I'm headed for. I know every hill and every rock. I know how warm the water is and where to be careful. But it doesn't stop you thinking about it. Can't get it off your mind.'

'You think it takes courage, or is it just the training?'

'Well, I guess it's mostly the training. But in my case it's gonna take courage. I don't know about the others.'

'Shit, Clouds, you scared?'

'Damn right, I'm scared. Wouldn't you be?'

'Damn straight I would. But you guys are the best. What do they say, one SEAL, five enemy, that's fair odds, right?'

'Seven.'

Steve laughed. 'Hey, you guys are indestructible.'

'Not quite. We bleed. And we hurt like everyone else. We're just a bit tougher to get at.'

Steve Ghutzman drained his glass. 'I gotta go. I'm back up there at 0800.' He stood up, stuck out his hand and said, 'Hey, it was good to talk to you, buddy. Good luck tonight, wherever the hell you're going.'

'Thanks Steve. We're staying the hell out of hell, that's for sure.'

1500 Tuesday, May 15.
The Flight Deck, USS Harry S. Truman.
For the short run out to USS *Shark*, the fifteen-strong SEAL team embarked in one of the last of the Navy's old warhorses, the HH-46D support/assault Sea Knight helicopter. The explosive and other gear had been airlifted in a cargo net four hours previously, and now Rusty Bennett stood at the loading door and saw each of his men aboard. They all wore just light pants and olive-green T-shirts. They carried their heavy-duty welder's gloves for the hot-rope drop to the deck of the submarine. It was too hot for them to wear wetsuits and an area had been set aside in the submarine for them to change and prepare for the swim-in during the final hour of the journey up through the partially cleared minefield. There were, as ever, the flight deck crews on the take-off area as the two rotors on the big white US Marines Sea Knight roared into life. The SEALs had already blackened their faces with waterproof greasepaint and were just about unrecognizable.

Among the crowd was Steve Ghutzman and he yelled a solitary, '*Go, Clouds baby!*' His voice stood out in the general serious hush that surrounded this departure. But big Lieutenant Nathan heard him, and he half raised his right hand in response, smiling to himself at his new twenty-minute friendship with the Navy Tomcat pilot. For all he knew he might need Steve's fighter attack

209

aircraft not too long from now. The Navy had mounted rescue attacks for missions a lot less dangerous than this one.

They flew low, out over the calm blue water towards the waiting submarine. It took less than fifteen minutes and, as the Sea Knight hovered above the deck, they all saw the thick rope unravel downwards to a point in front of the sail, right behind the long deck shelter on the right, where the miniature submarine awaited them. One by one the SEALs grabbed the rope and dropped fast, away from the aircraft, sliding down thirty feet before gripping hard with the big rough leather gloves, their brakes, and coming in to land gently on the casing of the *Shark*. Lieutenant-Commander Schaeffer led the way, followed by Lieutenant Dan Conway, then Lieutenant Nathan, then Petty Officer Combs, then the big Chief Petty Officer Rob Cafiero. The next seven combat rookies came sliding in right behind them, with Commander Rusty Bennett bringing up the rear.

They were greeted by the Officer of the Deck, Lieutenant Matt Singer, who hustled them quickly through the door at the base of the sail and on down the ladder. The hatches were slammed shut and clipped behind them, and Commander Reid ordered *Shark* to periscope depth heading north. 'Steer course three-six-zero, make your speed one-five for fifteen miles, then stand by for course change to zero-seven-zero.'

They all felt the submarine's gentle turn to due north, settling on a course which would allow them to cleave right through the middle of the now three-mile-wide 'gateway' through the minefield and on up the Strait until she turned in towards the shore of Iran.

Lieutenant-Commander Dan Headley led them down to a more or less empty area in which they could prepare for the mission. He fell into conversation with Rusty

Bennett and mentioned he had a good friend in the Squadron: 'Guy named Rick Hunter, Commander Hunter now, I believe. He and I grew up together.'

'Hey, you gotta be from Kentucky, right?' said Commander Bennett. 'Rick's a real good friend of mine. Just left him, matter of fact, down at DG.'

'That right? I didn't know he was anywhere near here.'

'Oh, just Rick and about seven-eighths of the entire United States Navy,' Rusty chuckled. 'I'm telling you, someone in the Pentagon's awful jumpy about whatever the hell's going on in the Gulf.'

'Guess so. All we know is what everyone else knows. The Iranians somehow mined the Strait of Hormuz and shut down most of the world's oil supply.'

'Big minefield, I understand. That's gotta be a major worry.'

'It ought to be,' replied Dan Headley, smiling. 'Specially for you. We're just about in the middle of it right now.'

'Shit,' said Rusty. 'I knew I shouldn't have come. Your CO any good?'

'I don't really know him well enough to say. But I don't think he's hit anything recently.'

'God forbid he starts now.'

Both officers laughed. And *Shark*'s XO asked what Rusty's men needed between now and the 1900ETD.

'They had lunch, steak and eggs, at 1400,' said the SEAL commander. 'Maybe you could fix a few sandwiches, slices of pizza or something. Just in case anyone's hungry. But I don't think many of them will be. They'll need a lot of cold water, though. They got a two-hour journey in the ASDV, then a long swim. Don't want them to get dehydrated.'

'Okay. I'll get that organized. By the way, you're not going yourself, are you, sir?' The XO paid due deference to Rusty's higher rank.

'Not this time. But I'm gonna help your boys get the ASDV moving, if you think I could help. I've done it a few times in my life and this is a very big vehicle.'

'I'm sure my crew would appreciate that, sir. The damn things are always difficult and this one's the biggest we've ever had.'

'Anyhow, right now I want to talk to the guys while they're getting ready – so we'll catch up in a little while.'

'Good enough, sir. My watch starts in a few minutes. I'll be in the control room, you need to find me.'

By now the twelve combat SEALS were sorting out their gear. Each man had his own custom-made wetsuit and numbered flippers. Each of them had a Draeger oxygen supply, the SEAL special air bottle which leaves no tell-tale bubbles on the surface. Each would carry a knife and Heckler and Koch's superb light sub-machine gun, the MP-5, a close-quarters weapon, best inside twenty-five yards, but perfect for an assault on a non-military establishment. Only Petty Officer Ryan Combs would carry in a bigger weapon, the lethal M-60E4 machine-gun. They would carry in, between them, fourteen ammunition belts, each containing 100 rounds. Ryan himself would carry the gun, plus two belts to give him a total weight of 40lbs to carry. The gun would be used only in a dire emergency if they had to fight their way out of the refinery. Ryan would also carry on his back a limpet mine, which he could manage just fine. It was the walk through the shallows that was so worrying. The Draeger is just about weightless in the water, but it weighs 30lbs in the air and that gave Ryan Combs very nearly 100lbs in weight to haul to the beach, which would probably prove too much after a quarter of a mile.

Rusty Bennett had ordered big Rob Cafiero to step up and share the load of the gun and ammunition if Ryan could not cope. All the SEALs were heavily laden, a bomb or mine for eleven of them. Two for three of them. The fusing wire and detonation devices would be carried by John Nathan. Between them the SEALS would also haul camouflaged ground sheets, two shovels, wire cutters, clips, plus night binoculars, the lightest possible radio for emergency only, water, high-protein bars and medical supplies. The return journey would be one hell of a lot easier.

In Rusty's final briefing, back in the carrier, they debated making a request for the crewman of the ASDV, not the driver, to accompany them in, strictly as a beast of burden, until they reached dry land. But that ASDV was priceless, the only one of its kind and the CO of the *Shark* probably would wish to take no chances by leaving it in the hands of just one operator. However, if push came to shove, Rusty would insist and no CO wants to go against the express wishes of a SEAL commander on the edge of a dangerous mission, probably on orders direct from the White House.

So they prepared for their final talk together. Spread out before them were the chart and the map. As they pulled on their wetsuits in a temperature deliberately turned down to 50F, they listened to Rusty, who was saying the ASDV driver would take the vehicle in as far as possible, until the keel touched the sand. 'Right then we'll move into the dry hatch, one at a time, as soon as it floods each man will drop straight through. The man with the attack board goes first, then his partner drops through and they move immediately, swimming east, bearing zero-nine-zero, until the water gets too shallow to swim comfortably. The six two-man teams rendezvous in the shallows. They should be around five minutes apart. After that you know what to do.'

For forty minutes more the SEALs made their final preparations and at 1750 they began to embark the ASDV, dragging in the gear, each man slipping expertly up through the hatch finding his allotted seat and placing his equipment in the tight overhead space. The loading took all of half an hour as the SEALs struggled to find a reasonably comfortable position for the two-hour ride inshore in this sturdy sixty-five-foot-long electric submarine.

Down in the control room Lieutenant-Commander Headley had the ship, assisted by the sonar officer, Lieutenant-Commander Josh Gandy, and the navigator, Lieutenant Shawn Pearson.

'Right now I have us at our destination, sir. That's 26.36N 56.49E on the GPS.'

'Okay, Lieutenant. Depth?'

'I was just coming to that, sir. We've still got plenty of water. I'm showing ninety feet below the keel and we're sixty-five feet below the surface. You wanna save the battery on the ASDV, I'm certain we could run in maybe another three miles. This chart's kinda pessimistic about depth.'

'You agree with that, Sonar?'

'Yes, sir. I'm showing total depth of just over 200 feet and Shawn's chart gives 170. We could certainly go on.'

'Okay, conn-XO. Make your speed eight, steer zero-four-five, depth six five, call out fathometer reading every five feet.'

'Aye, sir. We just saved the ASDV a half-hour's battery each way.'

'Good call, Navigator.'

At which point Commander Reid entered the control room, looking less than thrilled at the way the submarine was being run. 'Did you just countermand my orders, XO?'

'I adjusted our rendezvous point by three miles north-east, sir, because of clear and obvious discrepancies in the chart. We're still in deep water and we can save the battery on the ASDV.'

'The battery on the ASDV is not your concern, Lieutenant-Commander. What is your concern is a set of orders issued to us by the Flag and signed by me as your Commanding Officer. I do not permit leeway in orders such as those.'

'As you wish, sir.' Dan Headley looked bewildered. But he replied with a calm demeanor.

'XO, turn the ship round and return to 26.36N 56.49E. The rendezvous issued by the Flag.'

'Sir, with respect, could we not let the guys out right here, a couple of miles nearer their objective?'

'I think you heard me, Lieutenant-Commander. Turn this ship round immediately and return to our correct place. I have no desire to take my ship any nearer the shores of Iran than is absolutely necessary.' With that he turned on his heels and walked out of the control room, leaving all three of the ship's operational officers speechless.

Shawn Pearson spoke first. 'Now that, gentlemen,' he said, 'was rather interesting.'

'If you meant that the way I think you meant it, I do not want to hear any more,' replied the XO somewhat severely.

Lieutenant-Commander Gandy just shook his head.

They all felt the slight lurch as USS *Shark* made an underwater U-turn and began to transport Rusty Bennett's SEALs *away* from their target area. Nonetheless, within twenty minutes they were back on station at 26.36N 56.49E, facing the right way, seventeen miles south-east of the Chinese refinery, and the underwater deck crew was wrestling with the ASDV out of the flooded shelter and clear of the big submarine's casing.

Rusty Bennett proved an enormous help to the four-man team and they shoved the miniature submarine out in near record time. It was on its way before they blew out the dry deck shelter and up in the bow Lieutenant Brian Sager was conning the little ship in, on instruments only, assisted by his navigator. Behind them the SEALs were dry but cramped and they traveled mostly in silence. The journey was made at six knots all the way and Brian Sager kept on going well beyond their estimated point of departure at 26.45N 56.57E. He pushed on for another mile and a half, just below the surface, until they gently brushed the soft, sandy bottom, less than three miles from the beach. The sonar on the ASDV had picked up no vessel within ten miles.

It was exactly 1900 and growing dark when Lieutenant-Commander Ray Schaeffer, wearing his wetsuit, hood up, goggles and flippers on, Draeger connected, attack board in his left hand, slid down into the dry compartment, ready for the flooding. Three minutes later he dropped through the hatch into the warm waters of the Strait of Hormuz. Ray stared at the compass, breathed steadily, and was grateful that his limpet mine, Draeger and weapons seemed to weigh nothing. He tried not to think of the abrupt difference there would be when they hit the shallows.

Moments later one rookie combat SEAL, 'Charlie' to his colleagues, knifed downwards through the water next to him. Breathing carefully, he placed his right hand on Ray's wide shoulder. The Lieutenant-Commander from Marblehead swung round until the attack board compass told him east, then the two SEALs kicked towards the oil refinery owned by the People's Republic of China.

The extra distance covered by Lieutenant Sager meant the swimmers would essentially run aground inside two miles. The two lead SEALs kicked and breathed steadily, swimming about nine feet below the surface covering ten feet each time they snapped the flippers. After thirty minutes Ray estimated they had covered 1200 yards, two-thirds of a mile, and for the moment nothing was hurting.

Behind them, on Attack Board Two, came Lieutenant Dan Conway, guiding another rookie; Clouds Nathan swam powerfully five minutes back, then Rob Cafiero, then two rookies, both ace swimmers. Last of all swam the tall Petty Officer from North Carolina, Ryan Combs, both hands on his attack board, leading his rookie, who dragged the machine-gun in a special waterproof container, which made it nearly weightless.

The entire operation would have been a thousand per cent easier if they had been able to row inshore in a couple of big eight-man inflatables. But senior management at SPECWARCOM had dismissed that possibility out of hand. *One alert Iranian patrol boat moving through its own waters four miles offshore could, legally, have blown the US Navy SEALs to pieces.* As Admiral Bergstrom had mentioned at the time, 'Guess I'd rather have a dozen tired SEALs wallowing around in the surf than twelve dead ones floating face up in the fucking Strait of Hormuz.'

Ray Schaeffer had sat in on that meeting, and he smiled to himself as he thought of the diabolical difference between planning in an air-conditioned room in Coronado and making a swim like this, thousands and thousands of miles from home. Ray kicked and counted, kicked and counted, keeping his eye on the compass, staying on zero-nine-zero. They'd been going for an hour and a half now, and by Ray's reckoning that spelled 3600 yards covered, which was two miles, give or take the length of a submarine. There was a rising moon and phosphorescence in the water. He thought he could make out the ocean bottom right below, but he was unsure and he did not want to waste energy, or his precious air, on finding out. Also, he was asking serious questions of his granite-hard body and there was a nagging pain high up in both thighs. His calves and ankles were mercifully fine, because that was where the pain usually hit on a long swim and there had been times when it had hurt like hell.

The kid behind him was only twenty-one years old and there was no way Ray was going to betray tiredness, so he gritted his teeth, dug ever deeper and forced himself forward, ignoring the lactic acid now flooding into his joints and muscles making every yard an ordeal. Seventeen minutes after the two-mile mark, Ray felt his board sliding through sand. Instinctively he straightened up and was surprised to find himself standing up to his chest in about four feet of water, still holding the attack board. Charlie bobbed up right beside him and they both shut down their Draegers, reclining back in the water, resting their aching limbs. They took the mouthpieces out and stored the airlines neatly.

'You all right, sir?' asked Charlie.

'No problem, kid,' replied the Lieutenant-Commander. 'Let's take five, then walk forward slowly for another five and wait for Dan to show up.'

'Sounds good. Can you see anything up ahead, sir?'

'I thought I could just then, a dark shoreline directly in front, maybe a half-mile. But the moon's gone behind that cloud and I can't see a fucking thing.'

By now the lead SEALs had removed their flippers. They were walking slowly forward and were quickly in less than three feet of water. The Draegers were beginning to weigh heavily, so were the mines. They were comfortable with the rest of their gear.

About 100 yards back, Dan Conway and his team-mate broke the surface and began to walk forward. By the time they caught up with Ray and Charlie, Clouds was in, then the rookies only two minutes behind. Big Rob Cafiero and his rookie were in next, but they had to wait ten minutes for Petty Officer Combs, who was of course carrying the M-60 machine-gun which might save all of their lives in an emergency.

Ray Schaeffer aimed them east and they set off on the stretch they had all been dreading, wading in eighteen inches of water through the long shallows, each man hauling 80lbs plus. After 100 yards it was like walking through glue. No one complained but it was a muscle-throbbing exercise and there was no efficient way to do it except to keep pushing forward, lifting your feet just enough to take the real 'tug' out of the water. However, it was pleasantly warm, there was no surf to speak of and up ahead they could see the shore. That was the good news. This walk could have been a mile and a half. As things looked it would be only a little more than 1000 yards. Ray ordered them to fan out and draw their weapons, which made a long line of black-hooded figures thirty yards apart. When they reached the beach, assuming it was deserted, they would close in to Lieutenant-Commander Schaeffer's central position to check the GPS. The numbers they were looking for were 26.47N 57.01E.

The last 100 yards was easily the worst and they struggled through a kind of kelp field, knee deep and clinging. But eventually they walked up on to a completely empty beach of coarse sand and occasional rocks. There was not a light and certainly not a person to be seen. The numbers on the GPS were spot-on, which explained a lot. Nothing on this particular stretch of wasteland had been picked up after a hundred satellite passes carefully logged and studied at the top-secret National Reconnaissance Office in Washington. The even more beady-eyed operators at Fort Meade had found nothing either. One mile dead ahead, across slightly hilly terrain, was the sprawling Chinese crude-oil refinery.

It was 2130, and Lieutenant-Commander Schaeffer ordered the SEALs off the beach and into the rougher

219

ground behind. With exquisite timing the moon came out again and they could more or less see where they were headed without using night goggles. Up ahead they would be approaching the south-western corner of the refinery and somewhere before that they would make the rendezvous point, dumping most of their gear.

Four SEALs only would enter the refinery tonight. Two more would cut and fold back the wire, and Petty Officer Combs would ride shotgun over the operation with the big gun and also join the wire cutters as lookouts. No one knew what to expect in the way of guards, or even lights. They knew only that Ray Schaeffer, Dan Conway and Clouds Nathan were going through the wire perimeter fence, assisted by Charlie, to lay down the pile-driver explosive contained in the limpet mines, which they would attach to the inside-facing walls on the big gasoline-holding tanks.

Chief Petty Officer Rob Cafiero would take charge of the base camp, when they found it, unloading ground sheets, setting up the radio, posting sentries, preparing the mass of explosive for the main assault tomorrow night. But it took another hour before they found a three-corner outcrop of warm rocks, five feet above the ground at its highest point. It provided protection from the north and from the seaward side. The SEALs used the wire cutters to cut scrub and cover the camouflage nets. It had to be 1000 to 1 against anyone stumbling across their 'hide' and from the sea it was totally invisible.

They all removed their wetsuits, and wore only light camouflage combat trousers and jackets. They pulled on their desert boots and the warriors going in tonight increased the greasepaint on their faces, tied their matching green-and-brown 'drive on' rags around their heads, in the style chiefly popularized by Willie Nelson.

They ate a couple of protein bars and drank water.

Then, shortly after 2300, Lieutenant-Commander Ray Schaeffer led Assault Group One forward, a total of seven SEALs, carrying the three limpet mines and all the detonation equipment required to take out the group of holding tanks hard against the fence in the south-west corner of the refinery. No explosions until tomorrow, but a lot of the groundwork completed with, hopefully, a thorough knowledge of the defense system the Chinese operated in their new refinery.

'Don't expect us back before 0400, Rob. We wanna make a very careful recon of this place and it will take time.' Lieutenant-Commander Schaeffer's words were almost inaudible and a light breeze from the ocean scarcely ruffled the poor, rough, brown grass which grew sporadically on this warm moonlike landscape.

They drew their weapons and marched forward, moving softly over the ground. Up ahead there was a glow in the sky and they all knew what that was. The main surprise as they pushed east away from the ocean was the amount of light there was both inside and around the refinery. Within ten minutes they had a clear view of the western perimeter, which Ray Schaeffer knew was two miles long. They could see a line of lights, set high on steel pylons every 200 yards. But they were aimed into the refinery and cast almost no light on the dark wasteland around the outer edge. This was good and bad, because it made their approach easy. But one of the lights was throwing a lot of illumination right into the group of storage tanks to which they were headed. They lay flat on the ground, staring at the fence twenty yards in front of them.

'Christ,' said Clouds. 'It's gonna be like the stage of the New York Ballet in there.'

'Great,' muttered Dan Conway. 'We'll probably get a round of applause.'

'Shut up, comedians,' whispered Lieutenant-Commander Schaeffer. 'That light second from the end has gotta go. Guess we could shoot it, but I'd rather cut it.'

'That would sharpen up the guards if they found the cut,' said Dan.

'Yeah, it might,' replied Ray. 'But I've been looking down the line of lights. There's one every 200 yards but I'm only counting fifteen not seventeen. That means there's a couple out already. Those bulbs go all the time, I'd say, and one more isn't going to put the place on red alert. These guys are civilians. They'll probably send a couple of electricians out, maybe tomorrow, to replace the bulbs. So we want to make a cut they won't notice.'

'Okay, sir,' said Charlie. 'I'll do it. I'll slice down six inches and pull the inside stuff out. One little cut puts the bulb out. Then I'll fold it back inside the rubber casing. They might not notice it at all.'

'Don't worry,' said Ray Schaeffer. 'I have a little roll of electrician's tape in my pocket and we can thank Rusty for that. He told me before we left Coronado we will almost certainly have to take out a couple of lights and a little roll of black tape does a lot to cover your tracks.'

'Beautiful,' said Clouds. 'Pity about the applause, though.'

They moved in towards the fence, staying low, crawling over the ground on elbows and knees, the time-honored approach of the killer SEAL. Dan Conway and Charlie went to the base of the light pylon and the two rookies began to cut a hole in the chain-link fence. There was no sign of guards, none of life in this remote part of the refinery in the small hours of the morning. The only sound was the *snap* of the wire cutters as they carved a doorway through the fence.

At 0017 the big light went out, plunging the storage tanks into darkness. The SEALs lay silently, waiting for a

Chinese patrol to show up. But none did and, at 0035, they pulled back the wire and Ray Schaeffer with Clouds Nathan wriggled through, followed by Lieutenant Conway and Charlie. Clouds had the detonator, fuses, time clock and cord, plus one of the shovels. The other three carried the big limpet mines on their backs and they raced for the cover of the storage tanks, three lines of ten, all owned by the China National Petroleum Corporation. All now in deep shadow. It did not look far on the aerial photographs they had been studying for several days and they all knew the precise route to take. But it was a long fifty yards over flat ground and they were glad to know that Ryan Combs was right inside the fence with his trigger finger on the machine-gun.

Once in among the tanks they worked fast. They made for the middle one in line five and the two outer ones in line six, which formed a triangle bang in the center of the group. Clouds removed the mines from their straps and clamped the magnets on to the lower inside-facing surfaces of the three tanks. He wired up the detonators and ran cord from each one to a central point at the western edge of the untargeted middle tank in line six, where he wired up the clock which would dictate the time of the explosion of all three mines. Then he took the shovel and buried the det-cord in the soft sand. When he arrived back at the clock, he wrapped it in a plastic bag and buried it too without setting it. That would take about one minute on the way out tomorrow night, if their luck held. Right now they were 'outta here' and they flew for the fence, unnoticed by anyone, and made their way back through the wire.

It took another ten minutes to clip the fence back into shape and the SEALs retreated into the rough ground twenty yards back, from where they would watch whatever movement there was inside the refinery. It was a long,

223

boring wait. The only sign of life was almost a mile away inside the control center. Occasionally they caught a glimpse through the binoculars of a door opening and once they saw some kind of a jeep move from the control block up towards the main refining towers, but it was too far to see if anyone got out or in. By 0330 Lieutenant-Commander Schaeffer concluded the refinery was just about devoid of any security whatsoever and he declared the recon at an end. By this time tomorrow night they'd be on their way out to the submarine. God willing.

They arrived back at base camp at 0400, reported on the distinct lack of armed guards, at least in that remote part of the refinery, and drank a lot of water. Lieutenant-Commander Schaeffer and his men would sleep first, and Chief Petty Officer Cafiero organized the sentries.

They were all awake by 0800 and spent the day lying low, under the camouflage, eating very occasionally one of the high-protein bars and studying endlessly the layout of the refinery's interior.

Tonight there would be three targets: the towers, the control center and the middle group of storage tanks. If there was time, Lieutenant Dan Conway and Clouds Nathan would also attempt to insert high explosive into the more remote petrochemical compound, but that would be touch and go. It was almost 800 yards from the towers along a well-lit road.

Ray Schaeffer had divided the SEAL squad into three teams of four, one led by himself, one by Lieutenant Conway and one by CPO Rob Cafiero. Lieutenant Nathan would join Ray in the critical attack on the giant separating towers, Dan Conway and Charlie would take the central storage area, while Rob Cafiero and Ryan Combs would place the high explosive on the walls of the control center. Two young SEALs would accompany each team, acting as guards, lookouts and radio operators, should there be a need to communicate. Each time clock would be set to detonate at 0300. They would all go under the wire together at 2300 and the watchword of the operation was 'stealth'. At least for the first hour it was. Thereafter the SEALs would feel free to fight their way out and down to the beach using whatever means were necessary. Ryan Combs would bring two belts of ammunition and the M-60ES machine-gun with him.

They dug and buried all their surplus gear, including groundsheets. They left the wetsuits, flippers, Draegers and attack boards under the camouflage nets. Because of the twelve-man limit on the team, they did not have the luxury of leaving anyone in charge and at 2230 they all set off towards the refinery. It was warm and windless, with no moon. High cloud drifted in from the sea and they marched in silence, in three lines of four, through the desolate area behind the beach towards the refinery. The first thing Ray Schaeffer noticed was that the light they had deactivated the previous night was still deactivated. The second was a jeep moving swiftly along the outer perimeter along the narrow black-top track they had crossed to get to and from the storage tanks. The vehicle did not stop or slow down in this remote corner of the plant, but there were four people in it and they were carrying weapons, a direct result of an instruction from the Chinese Navy, received forty-eight hours previously. The guards were, in fact, military personnel from the People's Liberation Army and they had been in residence for two months, although they had not found it necessary to mount any form of patrol. The area was, face it, deserted.

The SEALs flattened themselves into the ground as the jeep drove past, but then they moved quickly to the fence and the clips were removed to open their own personal gateway. Once inside, they placed three clips back on the wire to hold it more or less in place, to attract no attention.

At this point they checked again their synchronized black pocket watches and the time clocks, which would be adjusted as the charges were put in place. Then they fanned out into three groups. They would meet again ninety minutes from now, at 0030, in the dark, deserted area of the towers.

The first team on station was Dan Conway's. He and Charlie led the two rookies deep in the shadow of the hot crude-oil pipes, which cleaved a gantry right down the middle of the refinery. They moved slowly, creeping quietly along, directly beneath the great three-foot-diameter pipes. They provided excellent cover all the way to the central storage area. The four SEALs waited for fifteen minutes until they were certain they were alone, then they bolted across the flat, well-lit ground to the left and dived into the shadow of the first tank, remaining motionless on the sand for ten minutes, heads down, but knives drawn.

Meanwhile Lieutenant-Commander Schaeffer and his 2 I/C, Lieutenant Clouds Nathan had made it to the tower area. They had crossed two sets of railroad tracks, well to the right of the central pipeline system, and were now crouched in the dark on the south side of a giant holding tank. The towers looked massive, but there were three very close together in the center of the separating plant and these were the targets.

The problem was four Chinese technicians, who had plainly arrived in a parked jeep, testing what looked like a large valve halfway up the biggest tower. 'Oh, Jesus,' said Ray. 'If they're not outta here in thirty minutes we'll go and place the two mines out in the petrochemical area and then come back. We can't risk being seen, not yet, not until the stuff's in place.' They waited. So did the technicians. Finally Ray whistled up both of the other teams on the little radio, and announced he was going to the distant chemical area and would use two of the mines. Dan Conway was instructed to get among the towers as soon as possible with the two extra mines his team were carrying.

They carried out their regular mine placing on the tanks in precisely the swift, efficient way Clouds had worked the previous night. The time was precisely 2345 and they set the time clock for three hours and fifteen minutes. Then they rushed back across the open ground into the shadow of the pipeline and began working their way up to the tower area. Meanwhile, Ray and Clouds were jogging along the eastern perimeter fence, in the shadow, directly under the lights, headed for the wide area of the plant owned by the China National Petrochemical Corporation. When they arrived the place was not only silent, there were huge dark areas to the west of the tanks and they worked here, shoveling a shallow six-inch trench in which to lay the det-cord. By the time they'd finished it was 0015, and Ray set the clock for two hours and forty-five minutes. Then he buried it lightly in a plastic bag.

By the time SEAL Team One was out of the chemical area, Rob Cafiero and Ryan Combs were making steady progress around the control center. They had placed one mighty charge of plastic C4 explosive hard on the wall below the main downstairs window, and they had seen four white-coated technicians enter the building and four come out. Both SEALs could also see there was a basement in the building and realized this was the place to set a major C4 charge because it would surely bring the entire construction down, wrecking all of the control systems and allowing the hot crude to keep on flooding through the pipes, feeding the fires, just as it had done in Texas City sixty years previously.

Now they were ready. The center was plainly staffed by the minimum number of people, and Ryan Combs told the two rookies to take the machine-gun and cover them while he and Rob went through the front door, which had been unused for at least twenty-five minutes. They raced across the yard, Rob carrying the explosive, detonator and plastic, Ryan now with a silenced, even lighter machine-gun, the regular MP-5, right behind him. They pushed open the door and moved into the hallway. In front of them was a down staircase and they took the steps four at a time, swinging hard left at the bottom and going to work under the stairs setting the plastic bomb for a timed detonation.

It was just 2350 and they set the clock for three hours and ten minutes. They swung back out of the stairwell at exactly 2351, just as two Chinese staff members came out of a lower-floor operations room. The four men stared at each other in total disbelief and the two refinery workers, confronted with two armed green-and-brown-faced monsters, turned to run back into their room. One of them shouted one word in Chinese before Ryan Combs cut them both down in cold blood with a burst from his MP-5. Instantly the two SEALs dragged the bodies back under the stairs, before there was too much blood to clean up. They made sure the two victims would not be easily seen, then they bolted back up to the main hall, opened the front door and raced back to the shadows where the two rookies waited.

'Everything okay, sir?'

'Except for a couple of Chinamen.'

'Christ, did they see you?'

'Not for long.'

Right then the radio light flickered and Ray Schaeffer was on the wire informing them of the new meeting point at the first tower at 0100. He was also on the line to Dan and Charlie, checking their progress. Shortly after midnight the SEAL Team Leader knew that all of their objectives were now achieved, with the exception of the giant towers.

By 0030 Rob and Ryan had placed their third and final plastic bomb right under a nest of incoming electric wires, and the Chief Petty Officer considered this wrapped up the entire operation very tidily. He set the clock for two hours and thirty minutes and, safe in the knowledge that this particular control center was not going to control anything after 0300, led his men back towards the main pipeline for the shadowy 500-yard journey towards the refining towers.

When they arrived there they found a scene of silent consternation. The Chinese were still there, still up the tower, still working. At least, two of them were. The others had gone.

'There's no way we can place the mines on that metal without those guys seeing us,' said Ray Schaeffer. 'The risk is too great. We'll have to shoot 'em and that's not easy either.'

'Well, they don't have a phone up there, how about a diversion, something to get 'em down? Suppose we set fire to their jeep? That'll do it.'

'Yeah and it'll bring a lot of other guys out here as well. Fire in a refinery is a goddamned nightmare.'

'You don't say.'

Then the SEALs received what looked like a slice of luck. Both the Chinese technicians began to climb down the ladder from the refining tower.

'How about that? They're going.'

And so they were. They stepped into their jeep and departed, leaving the entire area to the three teams of US Navy SEALs, who instantly split up and clamped the magnetic mines on to the designated towers and primed the fuses. Lieutenant Nathan raced between them, paying out the det-cord, splicing it into place and running it out for the three strands to meet at a central point in the shadows of the Number Two tower. Behind him two

SEALs carefully buried the cord in the sand and Clouds checked his watch. It was 0150 and he set the timer for one hour and ten minutes. It was time to leave.

For the SEALs, that is. Not a two-man patrol of Chinese guards hanging on to the leashes of two huge, brown and black, straining Doberman pinschers. They were just arriving. They had been especially briefed, direct from Shanghai, to be on the lookout for US Special Forces inside the refinery and alert they were. They came round to the edge of the main tower and were confronted with eight big men, two of them with shovels, four with MP-5 machine-guns and all of them with hideously camouflaged green-and-brown faces.

At the moment of sighting there were forty yards between the forces of China and the US SEALs. The guards reacted in strict unison, unleashing the dogs at the touch of a button and both blowing whistles loudly. Dan Conway moved first, as the lead dog leapt at the throat of Lieutenant Nathan. He raised his unsilenced MP-5 and almost blew its head off.

The second dog swerved towards Lieutenant-Commander Schaeffer and Dan Conway almost cut it in half with a short burst into its neck. By now the guards had their hands on their own weapons, but like the dogs they were too late and Ryan Combs aimed a withering round of fire from the M-60E4 straight at them. Both died instantly, but the whistles had done their job and all twelve of the SEALs could hear the roar of a jeep heading from the main pipeline straight towards them.

'Cover!' roared Lieutenant-Commander Schaeffer. 'Get right down in the dark. Ryan, let 'em get out and then let 'em have it.'

The light was poor, but they all saw the lights of the jeep as it came screeching into the clearing between the towers. They saw the two new guards jump out. Ryan

Combs opened up again with the machine-gun and, as the guards went down, Ray Schaeffer and Charlie charged forward. But they did not see a third guard in the back seat who swung his Kalashnikov on them and shot Ray Schaeffer through the head at point-blank range. His second burst caught Charlie high on the right-hand side of his chest and both SEALs fell to the ground together. Again Ryan Combs opened fire and instantly took out the third guard, leaving just the jeep running noisily, with one dying SEAL on the ground and another unconscious beside him. There were also five dead Chinese.

Lieutenant Conway took command, ordering the rookie SEALs to get the two wounded men into the jeep. He jumped into the driving seat himself and told the rest of them to get in or on, anywhere, but to hold tight while he drove for the south-western perimeter. Somehow they all hung on, as the ex-Connecticut baseball catcher gunned the jeep forward, slamming it over the railroad tracks, swerving through the sand, going for the dark pylon, second from the end. Fifty yards from the fence he rammed on the brakes, and Clouds Nathan scrambled out and bolted into the holding tanks to their right, where he swiftly set the timing clock on last night's mines for sixty-one minutes. At this time an eerie siren went off loudly in the control center, just as Clouds came charging round the corner and reboarded the jeep.

'Time?' yelled Lieutenant Conway. 'What the hell's the time?'

It was just about 0200. The action had taken less than five minutes and their Team Leader was down. Dan Conway rammed the jeep right up against the fence and two more SEALs opened up their private doorway. They piled out and dragged the two wounded men through the gap in the fence. Then the Lieutenant reversed the jeep against the gap, jumped out and crawled under it to safety on the other side of the wire. Before they left he tossed their one grenade into the vehicle and blew it to smithereens, covering the gap in the wire with red-hot metal and burning fuel.

Then they set off on their longest journey, carrying their leader and the rookie Charlie between them. They no longer had the mines and the explosive. But their burden was heavy and pursuit was inevitable, and their chances of survival were not much better than 60–40. They reached base camp, administering morphine to the badly wounded Charlie and desperately trying to stop the blood seeping from Lieutenant-Commander Schaeffer's shattered skull. But they all knew it was hopeless. Ray was breathing very erratically and he died in the arms of Lieutenant Dan Conway, who was unable to stop the tears cascading down his camouflaged face.

The task of carrying the body back out through the ocean was plainly Herculean and might even result in their capture, if the Chinese had a further squadron of guards. But the SEALs would not leave him. They changed into their wetsuits, and big Rob Cafiero hoisted the Lieutenant-Commander over his shoulders and began walking steadily to the beach. Clouds Nathan and Dan Conway carried Charlie, who was losing blood at a serious rate. They were unable to stop it, but they got him into a wet suit and just kept going forward. At the beach, they regrouped. They had no option but to drag the body of Ray Schaeffer into the water and tow it out to the submarine. The time was 0240. They had to move and they had to get their big flippers on, and it took too long because of the trauma, despite their training to deal with death. But they made it to the shallows and Dan Conway led the way, pulling Ray behind them, much lighter now as the water grew deeper.

Twenty minutes later they were in about four feet, a

half-mile offshore, and they stopped to look back and witness whatever damage they had wrought. For a few moments nothing happened, then an unbelievable explosion ripped into the night air as the big refining towers went up, every last one of them, sending a bright orange and purple sheet of flame into the heavens. Seconds later the ocean seemed to shake as sixty massive gasoline storage tanks blew up like an atomic bomb. They heard the distant rumble as the control center exploded in a crashing, rolling fireball of flame and falling masonry, and the sky seemed to light up as the oil fire took a hold, thousands of barrels of prime crude from Kazakhstan thundering into the inferno, fueling a fire which would burn for six days. They could feel the heat out there in the water, almost two miles away.

'Jesus Christ,' said Ryan Combs. 'Whatever they wanted, I guess we've done it.'

'But it wasn't damn well worth it, was it?' said Dan Conway.

'Steady, Dan,' said Rob. 'I don't think Ray would have wanted you to say that.'

The new Team Leader just nodded. The two SEALs turned out to sea, to the west, where the ASDV awaited them and kept swimming just below the surface, towing the still and silent body of Lieutenant-Commander Schaeffer between them.

Seven

160500MAY07 USS Shark.
26.36N 56.49E. Gulf of Hormuz.
PD. Speed 3. Racetrack pattern.
The message from the communications room was not very
clear. 'XO-comms. We're getting something on VHF.
But it's kinda shaky. I'd say about twelve miles away, from
the ASDV. I guess they've surfaced and may be using a
hand–held aerial. But they keep breaking up. We're still
trying. Whatever it is doesn't sound good.'

'Comms-XO. You're not dealing with a MAYDAY,
are you?'

'No, sir. But they're in some kind of trouble. Wait a
minute, sir. There's something right now. Oh, Jesus,
they've lost a man, sir. Wait a minute, I'll be right back.
Stay on the line, sir.'

Lieutenant-Commander Dan Headley could hear the
background noise in comms: 'Say again? Over. Say again?
Over.' He heard *Shark*'s radio operator repeat twice,
'You're saying "dead" right? D for delta? Right? Please say
again. Over.'

Three minutes later the comms chief was back on the
line. 'So far as I can make out, sir, Lieutenant-Commander
Ray Schaeffer has been killed and one of the rookie
SEALs, Charlie Mitchell, is very badly wounded. They're
afraid he might die and they're asking if we can get the ship
in any closer. You know, of course, the ASDV makes only
six knots flat out . . .'

By now Commander Rusty Bennett had materialized in the control room and Dan Headley repeated to him the extremely bad news. No one heard the mission commander mutter, 'Oh, no. Not Ray.' He just said formally, 'Are they sure it's Ray?'

Dan Headley added, 'They were broadcasting from the ASDV. It wasn't very clear, but I'm afraid we better prepare for the worst.'

'Did they say how bad Charlie Mitchell was hurt?'

'Badly. They're afraid he might die if he doesn't get attention soonest. They want us to bring the ship in to meet them and I'm happy to do so. But you know about the CO last time. He nearly had a heart attack when I changed the orders in even a minor way.'

'Where is he now?'

'I guess asleep.'

'Do we wake him?'

'No. Fuck him. Let's go get the guys out.'

'Okay. Down all masts. Conn–XO, make your speed twenty knots. Steer zero-three-four. Fathometer report the depth. Navigator XO, report to me immediately.'

The submarine surged forward and everyone who was awake heard the distinct change in the rhythm of the ship. Lieutenant Pearson came hustling through the doorway, holding a chart. 'Right here, sir,' he said. 'We're in 200 feet of water and we can go at least six miles on this course without even thinking about it.'

'Thanks, Shawn . . .'

But he was cut off from further communication by the sudden appearance in the control room of Captain Reid, wearing his pajama trousers, shoes, socks and a Navy sweater. 'XO, might I ask where precisely you are taking this ship when our orders are perfectly clear to remain on station?'

'Sir, we are on a rescue mission. The ASDV just radioed

in. The SEAL Team Leader, Lieutenant-Commander Schaeffer, has been killed and another of the twelve is badly wounded. They called to request we come in and meet them. They are afraid the second SEAL might also die. We're going in six miles to a probable depth of 150 feet. If I have to, we'll continue on the surface until we find them.'

'Lieutenant-Commander Headley, you do, of course, realize that your orders are directly countermanding both mine and those of the Flag?'

'Sir. There are ample provisions in Navy Regulations to provide for emergency actions in order to save life. Especially one of our own.'

'XO, DO NOT REMIND ME OF THE NAVY'S REGULATIONS. I KNOW A GREAT DEAL ABOUT THEM AND THE ONE I SUGGEST YOU CONSIDER IS THE ONE THAT GIVES THE COMMANDING OFFICER ABSOLUTE POWER IN HIS OWN SHIP.'

'I am well acquainted with that one, sir.'

'Then, for the second time in as many days, I am ordering you to turn this ship round and return to our correct waiting position at 26.36N 56.49E.'

'Sir,' interrupted Commander Bennett. 'As you are well aware, I outrank Lieutenant-Commander Headley and it was at my request he agreed to go on a rescue mission, possibly to save the life of one of my most valuable men.'

'Then I must remind you, sir, that you have no rights whatsoever in this ship and I will not have this inter-ference. What exactly is this? Some kind of damned conspiracy? Well, you've picked the wrong man to make a fool of, waiting until I'm asleep and then flagrantly disobeying my orders.'

'Sir, may I just . . .'

But Rusty was cut off in mid-sentence. 'N-O-O-O.

YOU MAY NOT. TWENTY-SIX THIRTY-SIX
NORTH, SIR. FIFTY-SIX FORTY-NINE EAST,
SIR. THAT'S OUR CORRECT POSITION AND
THAT'S WHERE WE'RE GOING. YOU CANNOT
RUN A NAVY FOR A GUY WHO'S PROBABLY
CUT HIS GODDAMNED FINGER. RETURN TO
OUR DESIGNATED POSITION AND THAT'S AN
ORDER, XO!'

Midnight Wednesday, May 16.
Office of the National Security Adviser
The White House, Washington DC.
Admiral Morgan had been alone for two hours, since
Admiral Dickson had returned to the Pentagon. Both
men knew the SEAL team had gone into Iran and that
the attack on the refinery was scheduled for the small
hours of Thursday morning, an eight-and-a-half-hour
time difference from Washington. Both men were aware
that it had already happened from several different
sources, the satellites, the CIA, the embassy in Tehran,
the Brits via Oman on the other side of the Strait and a
very sketchy item on CNN. The flight deck crew and
almost everyone else on board USS *Constellation* had seen
the fireball from twenty miles offshore. The US Navy
knew comprehensively, from Diego Garcia to Pearl
Harbor, from Coronado to Norfolk, Virginia, that a
twelve-man team of SEALs had just destroyed the
world's biggest and newest Middle Eastern oil refinery.
What no one knew was the fate of the SEALs and
Admiral Morgan paced his office awaiting some news. In
his mind he guessed they'd be back in the *Shark* by
around 0800 their time.

That, he estimated, was a half-hour ago and so far he'd
heard *nothing*. *What the hell's going on?* That was Admiral
Morgan's question. He'd kept Kathy on duty, watching

237

her e-mail screen, sitting by the phone, ever ready to bring in the message that everyone was safe. It was a curious trait in his character, since he was now, at least in job description, a political adviser. But he was not a political adviser in the place that counted. In his heart he was still a Navy commanding officer and that did not permit him to leave the bridge until he was absolutely certain that the men were home unscathed. *So why was no one telling him they were safe? Maybe they weren't safe? And if not, why not? Again, What the hell's going on?* 'KATHY!'

The door opened and the spectacular figure of Ms O'Brien came through it, still quite incredibly glamorous despite the late hour. 'I do wish you wouldn't yell like that,' she said. 'It's so . . . so . . . well, uncool.'

'Who the hell else would hear me in this goddamned graveyard?' he rasped.

'Only everyone.'

'Like who? You think they could hear me in the Oval Office, if the President's still working?'

'My darling, they could hear you in the Rose Garden.'

'Oh, of course. I forgot we got that midnight pruning crew in there, snipping away until breakfast.'

'Arnold, I am merely suggesting that it must be unnecessary for you to sound like a drill sergeant, in the White House, in the middle of the night. And by the way, sarcasm does not become you.'

'Yes, it does. It becomes me better than anyone I ever met. Anyhow, where the hell's my SEALs? Answer that, Miss Decibels 2007.'

Before she could reply with something suitably pithy the phone rang at her desk outside the main office. Secure line. She walked quickly out through the doorway and instantly put the call through to the Admiral.

'Yup. Morgan. Speak.'

'Arnie, it's Alan Dickson. Good news and bad news,

I'm afraid. The SEALs wiped out the refinery, but only ten of them got back.'

'Are they inside the *Shark* right now?'

'They are. But they lost the Team Leader, Lieutenant-Commander Ray Schaeffer. They also lost one of the new guys, young Charlie Mitchell.'

Admiral Morgan was stone silent for at least a half-minute while he gathered himself. 'They didn't die in the fire, did they?'

'No. There was some kind of battle inside the refinery. The Chinese had a military guard patrol, which we were not expecting. With attack dogs. The guys were cornered, but they took out all five guards and both dogs, blew up their jeep and then the entire oil plant. Apparently the guards managed to get a couple of bursts out of their old Kalashnikovs. Hit Ray and Charlie at less than twenty feet, point-blank range. They never had a chance.'

'They didn't leave our guys behind, did they? Not in that godforsaken country?'

'No, they did not. They brought the body of Ray Schaeffer out. At the time Charlie Mitchell was still alive, but he died in the ASDV about fifteen minutes before they got back to the submarine. It was a long journey at only six knots and they couldn't save him.'

'Thanks, Alan. Let's talk in the morning.'

'Good night, sir.'

Arnold stood up from his desk and walked to the window. He stared out into the darkness, and before him he saw the half-lit refinery and imagined the SEALs, out there alone, trapped in a firefight, and he imagined the gallantry of the young Americans, the terror, the air alive with bullets, Lieutenant-Commander Schaeffer, the Leader, charging forward trying to save his men. *Ray Schaeffer. Goddammit. He went into Russia for me. He went into China for me and he's gone into Iran for me. Now he's dead.*

Admiral Morgan heard Kathy return to the office. But he just stood with his back to her, staring out into the pitch black of the White House garden, because he could not bear her to see him this upset.

'I've ordered us some coffee,' she said. 'How many did they lose?'

'Two.'

'I guessed from your voice it was bad.'

She saw him wipe the moisture from his eyes with his shirtsleeve before he turned to face her, and she noticed his voice was tight when he said, 'Please make sure that both Admiral Dickson and I attend the funeral in Marblehead for Lieutenant-Commander Ray Schaeffer.'

'What about the President?'

'I don't think so. He wouldn't understand.'

'He'd understand the death of a Navy officer, wouldn't he?'

'Possibly. But he'd never understand the courage. The duty. The honor. The mind of such a man.'

'Well, I'm sure the people of Marblehead would like to see the Lieutenant-Commander given the honor of the President attending his funeral,' replied Kathy. 'Couldn't you explain it to him?'

'That, I am afraid, would be like trying to teach a pig to speak. You would succeed only in irritating the pig. I'm afraid the simple truth of a military officer prepared to lay down his life for his country will forever remain a mystery to men like President Clarke. Because they do not do it for money. It's not for glory, either. Most of them find it impossible even to talk about it. It's not for power. It's for something else. Something very private, to people like Lieutenant-Commander Schaeffer. Believe me, there aren't many of them and I guess you can see how upset it makes me when we lose one.'

'Yes. Yes, I can. I've never seen you like that before.'

'Guess not many people have. They think of me as some kind of civilian SEAL in a gray suit, but inside I'm like everyone else. So are the SEALs. They get scared, they feel pain and they bleed from their wounds. Sometimes I guess I bleed for them.'

'Yes, my darling. Don't you.'

The coffee arrived and Kathy poured it. The Admiral sat at his desk saying nothing. But suddenly he stood up and told her, 'I'm not paid to sit around worrying about yesterday. I'm paid to start figuring out tomorrow. In my game you gotta keep going forward or the bastards will trample you to death.'

He came and put his arms round her, but she could still see the sorrow in his face, as he privately mourned the dead SEALs. She did not think it possible that anyone had ever loved anyone more than she loved Arnold Morgan.

0900 Thursday, May 17.
Southern Fleet Command HQ
Zhenjiang, South China.
News of the total destruction of the Chinese refinery hit Beijing at around 0800 local. By 0900 the world's media had put something together on the lines of 'yet *another* diabolical oil fire in the Strait of Hormuz – this time a massive refinery'. The world's oil markets were about to go collectively berserk for the second time in a month.

Admiral Zhang believed, correctly as it happened, that the price per barrel might go right back to $85, off its week-long low of $65 when the major trading market in Tokyo opened. Surprisingly, he remained calm. 'Well, Jicai,' he said to his friend. 'I suppose we might have expected something like this.'

'You mean you believe someone did this to us, that it was not just an accident?'

'Jicai, the Pentagon just blew up China's most

241

important oil refinery in revenge for the minefield we helped to create in the Strait of Hormuz.'

'You mean they bombed it, or hit it with a guided missile? Surely not. They would not dare instigate such an act of war so publicly.'

'Jicai, it is entirely possible that no one will ever know what happened to our installation in the Strait of Hormuz. It is also possible that the world's media will never even consider such an act was perpetrated by the oh-so-high-and-mighty United States. But I shall always know differently.'

'Do the media sense there may be something sinister? Are they linking the other fires?'

'Not so far. But of course they are not tuned in to our involvement in the minefield yet. Though I am quite certain the American military knows. That's why they just blew the refinery.'

'Do we hit back?'

'We cannot. There's nothing for us to hit in the immediate area of the refinery. Anyway, it would not be in our interest to do so. The Americans would then start to destroy our entire Navy and I am afraid we could not stop them. I'm rather of the opinion that our days in the Arabian Sea and the Gulf of Iran are over. For the moment, anyway. The Americans are in charge there now.'

'This is so unlike you, Yushu. So accepting of such terrible events.'

'Well, I did remind you I was half expecting something of this kind to happen. Now I should remind you that the essence of all war throughout our long history has been attrition. We can afford losses, both physically and emotionally. The rule is that we never take our eye off the main objective and that grows ever nearer. We must let the oil fires burn and later this morning we will have our own light in the sky.'

Admirals Zu Jicai and Zhang Yushu were now joined by the recently appointed Commander-in-Chief of the Southern Fleet, Vice-Admiral Yang Linzhong, a short, stocky ex-frigate captain from Canton. 'Gentlemen,' he said, entering his own office and bowing his head. 'I have just been visiting our sonics laboratory and they are ready to demonstrate for you their work over the past six months. I think you will be impressed.'

The two most senior Admirals in the entire Chinese armed forces rose and followed Yang out to a waiting Navy staff car, which drove them immediately a distance of less than a mile to the domain of Lieutenant-Commander Guangjin Chen, the PLAN's Mr Underwater, their great mastermind of deep-sea listening counter-measures. His rank of Lieutenant-Commander was honorary. Mr Guangjin was essentially a scientist, more at home in a white laboratory coat than a naval uniform. In fact, no one had ever seen him in a uniform, even though it was rumored he was the highest-paid officer in the Chinese Navy below the rank of rear-admiral. His kingdom was under water in the strange, eerie caverns of the oceans. He marched to the orders of the tides, he listened to the evidence of the echoes and he acted on the lingering ping of the sonic pulses. Much of his work had been in the field of decoys, disguising, hiding the beat of the engines of the warships, seeking always to confuse and deceive the enemy.

What very few people knew, however, was that Guangjin Chen had masterminded a private project of such brilliant deception it almost took Admiral Zhang's breath away. He had heard about it only a year ago while he was still Commander-in-Chief of the Navy and he had heard about it just by chance. Great was his fury when he found out that Mr Guangjin had offered the idea to the Navy for development ten years previously, four years

243

before he even joined the Senior Service. Guangjin had been turned down flat, probably because he was merely a civilian. In any event, Admiral Zhang knew brilliance when he heard it, even if it might not work. So last August he had summoned Mr Guangjin to his home for dinner and there he conducted an interrogation, to the great glee of the scientist.

Like all scientists, the lean and earnest Guangjin adored talking about his work, especially a project he had believed to be long dead. He shyly admitted to the great Chinese Admiral that he had continued working on the project, at his home, these past several years.

The night proved to be magical. They had sat outside Admiral Zhang's beautiful summerhouse on the island of Gulangyu, just across the Lujiang Channel from the South China seaport and navy base of Xiamen. The air was warm, a light south-west wind drifting across the great estuary of the Nine Dragon river and Guangjin in company with the Zhangs sipped fragrant tea out on the stone patio beneath the curved red roof. The scientist was on his feet, answering questions and pointing with a cane at the stone squares upon which he walked.

'But where's the carrier now?'

'Right here, sir. In this stone square.'

'So where's our Kilo?'

'Right here, sir, in the middle of this paler stone square.'

'Is it transmitting?'

'No, sir. Not yet.'

'Well, when will it?'

'When I tell it to do so.'

'But how will you know when?'

'I'll be watching all the time.'

'How?'

'Via the satellites, sir. It's very easy to track a large ship in the open ocean. You can hardly miss it.'

244

'How long is the transmission?'

'Oh, just a few seconds. Long enough to be heard.'

'Then what?'

'Well, if the US Admiral has a modicum of sense, he'll bear away and make a more northerly course.'

'I suppose he will.'

'And he'll keep going until I frighten him again.'

The Admiral remembered just shaking his head in amazement and he had said, 'Chen, I am deeply impressed. I want you to continue your work on this as a priority. Move it to a secure area in your working block and perfect it. Essentially you will answer only to Admiral Zu or myself. I regard it as our personal mission and I'm going to codename it right away, in memory of this evening. From now on, it's Operation Pavingstone.'

Admiral Zhang would never forget the conversation. It had been on his mind for months. This very brilliant person, who had joined the Navy strictly as a sonics expert, was on to something. Now he was going to find out just how big and whether it would work.

The three Admirals climbed out of the staff car and two guards escorted them into an inner office of this highly classified laboratory. There before them stood Lieutenant-Commander Guangjin, who bowed politely, never having quite mastered the traditional Navy salute. 'Welcome, gentlemen,' he said, 'to my humble quarters.' He'd never quite got to grips with the normal greeting of 'Sir' from a two-and-a-half to an admiral. But great scholarship has a dignity of its own and no one noticed. 'Yushu,' he said, with an earth-shattering lack of formality to the highest-ranking admiral in the world's biggest nation, 'it is especially nice to see you again – and I think you will be very pleased with me.'

Admiral Zhang smiled and patted his prodigy on the shoulder. The project belonged, of course, to the scientist, but Zhang had made it possible and if it worked, history would judge them both kindly.

Mr Guangjin walked to the rear of his long, bright work area and led the way into a darkened room, lit only by the back lighting of the computer screens, in almost every respect a replica of a warship's ops room. He paused before a screen upon which there was an illuminated grid. 'That's it, Yushu, just as we planned it. Operation Pavingstone, eh? Ha-ha, and now, as you know, we have two test sites ready for us. We have a towed-array frigate way up in the north in the Yellow Sea and another in the Pacific, 600 miles off our southern coast. Both ships have in the last hour thrown the device over the side and are ten miles distant. The device is at present passive. But now I am going to activate the one in the Yellow Sea. You, Yushu, will speak personally to the sonar room in the frigate.'

He handed a telephone to the senior Admiral, who spoke into it. 'This is Admiral Zhang. Will you please inform me what is happening?'

'This is Lieutenant Chunming, sir. Right now we have nothing on the screen. Just the usual waterfall. Please stay on the line.'

Guangjin moved to the control keyboard, which was set before the grid screen. 'Activating now,' he said, pressing the keys.

The room was silent, as the electronic pulses flashed to one of two Chinese satellites. Then Admiral Zhang heard down the phone, 'Lieutenant Chunming, sir. I'm getting something and it's engine lines, transient contact, just seven seconds, but I'm certain it's a submarine making a turn. One moment, sir, the computer's trying to match the lines. It's coming up, sir, this is a Russian-built Kilo Class diesel-electric. No doubt. The pattern fits precisely.'

The Admiral replaced the telephone. He turned to the

scientist and held out his hand. 'Remarkable,' he said. 'Quite, quite remarkable.'

'Now we shall try the second one, way out in the Pacific. Please hold this telephone and I will attempt to activate . . .'

Four minutes later an almost ecstatic Zhang Yushu heard another sonar officer in a distant Chinese frigate say to him, 'Here it comes, sir. We've caught a transient on a Russian–built Kilo Class submarine.'

201300MAY07 20N 125E.
USS John F. Kennedy
Speed 20. Course three-one-five.
Big John was steaming over 3000 fathoms of water. All flying had been cancelled for two days because of a severe storm and the personnel of the Black Aces, Top Hatters and Golden Warriors were bored by the inactivity. Nonetheless the forecast was good, the storm had abated and the carrier was currently in the Philippine Sea, 180 miles north–east of Cape Engano. That put her 270 miles south-east of the Taiwan coast, but just 150 miles short of her ops area.

These were the usual patrol waters of the US Navy, the world's policeman, protecting the rights of the citizens of the nation of Taiwan. The area was a triangle, its shortest side ninety miles long facing the central eastern coastline of the island, around fifty miles off the beaches. The other two sides were each 150 miles long, joining at a point close to the 125-degree line of longitude. Most of the water inside that triangle was 15,000 feet deep.

The *JFK* was steaming straight towards it, high, wide and handsome, no secrets, no subtlety, no intent to deceive. Just one thunderous iron fist, the same one which had warned Red China for more than half a century, *stay out of our buddies' backyard*. Here they came again, pushing through the long Pacific swells, cleaving through thirty-foot waves, 88,000 tons of steel-clad power, daring anyone to raise an objection. The new emblem patch of the Tomcat pilots uttered a thousand words in just three: *Any time, Pal*.

On a bright computer screen 570 miles away in the Southern Fleet HQ in Zhanjiang there was a replica of the op area of the *JFK*. It showed a line 100 miles long, 50 miles off the eastern seaboard of Taiwan and it fell back 150 miles into an oblong rather than a triangle. Essentially it represented the guesswork of a dozen Chinese ex-warship commanders and it was not a bad guess at that. The *JFK* triangle fitted very neatly in Guangjin's 'box' and the positional accuracy of the 100-mile line opposite the Taiwan beaches was nearly uncanny. It was, of course, the result of years of study of US Navy patrols and all around the Chinese version of *JFK*'s op area was a 600-mile-long line in the shape of a sloped roof on its side, representing Admiral Zhang Yushu's assessment of the Americans' likely line of approach. That was the line they were now watching for the carrier and, in precisely three hours from now, *Big John* would breach that line at 20.41N 124.18E. The Chinese Navy satellites would relentlessly track her wherever she went.

Back in Zhanjiang, Lieutenant-Commander Guangjin made another adjustment to his screen and over his US op-area chart there was now a much bigger square, 240 miles long north to south, 240 miles wide west to east. It was divided into grid squares numbered 1 to 6 and A to F. At almost every corner of each of the thirty-six squares there was a black circle and every one of those circles of course had a number, A-5 or C-4, just like any map reference. The US ops area into which the *JKF* was headed was bang in the middle of this computerized grid.

Big John steamed on, now making just twelve knots

since Admiral Daylan Holt had cleared the flight wings to begin operations at 1500. The deck once more came alive to the howl of the jets and the surge of the deck crews, as the fighter-bombers screamed into the bright skies above the deep Pacific Ocean.

The course of the carrier now became erratic, certainly on the distant Chinese chart in Zhanjiang, because the *JFK* had to keep changing course to east–south–east, into the wind, for the landings and take-offs. But her basic northern track up to the ops area remained steady. She crossed Admiral Zhang's outer line of approach at 1900. The busy flying evening wore on in the great water-borne fortress of *Big John*. The Admiral's ops room was receiving no reports of foreign warships anywhere in the area. Nothing from either of the two nuclear submarines riding shotgun off his port and starboard bow. Not a thing from the S-3B Viking ASW aircraft ranging out in front, dropping sonobuoys into the water, seeking any foreign submarine which might be lurking in these deep waters. Behind this fast, powerful, deep-field ASW screen the rest of CV-67's battle group, two destroyers and five frigates, moved safely through seas which had been 'swept' by possibly the world's sharpest ears.

At the current low speed, with a lot of course adjustments, *Big John* and his men were about eight hours short of their op area. Though Lieutenant-Commander Guangjin did not need them to be in it, just heading up that way. At 2200 he activated, via the satellites, the Chinese decoy station B-5. Floating in the water, identifiable only by its ultra-thin aerial wire, B-5 was just about invisible at fifty feet. It made one short, sharp transmission from approximately 100 miles north-west of the carrier and three of the sonobuoys dropped by the Viking picked it up instantly at range fifteen miles and under.

Lieutenant J.G. Brian Wright had the signals on the

aircraft screen immediately and assessed a rough position of a patrolling submarine at 21.20N 122.21E. The engine lines fed into the Viking's onboard computer and moments later Brian Wright was contemplating the presence of a possible Russian-built Kilo Class diesel-electric in the water 100 miles from *Big John*. He guessed the submarine had just made a 'dynamic start' of her engines, probably to charge her batteries. Everyone connected in any way with a big carrier is wary of a diesel-electric underwater boat because of their stealth at low speed. Lieutenant Wright punched in his signal to the Admiral's ops room: 'Dynamic start possible Kilo Class position 21.20N 122.21E. Transient contact. Attempting to localize.'

The Viking, heading north, banked back hard to the east in search of the 'intruder', sweeping the sea with radar, looking for a submarine, which did not exist. It was just a brilliantly invented transmitter with a slim aerial wire jutting three feet out of the water, almost invisible by day, totally invisible by night. It was being activated at will by Lieutenant-Commander Guangjin Chen 600 miles away in Zhanjiang – activated to transmit the uniquely chilling engine lines of the Kilo Class Type 636.

Admiral Daylan Holt received the signal from comms at 2220 and instantly ordered a course change: 'Come right as soon as you can to zero-three-zero. Cancel all flying.'

The *JFK* quickly retrieved two more fighter aircraft, then slewed slowly round in the water, settling thirty degrees east of north. It took the ship a full fifteen minutes to make those maneuvers and, five minutes later, the Viking picked up a new transmission from one of the sonobuoys. Again it was transient. To the sonar operator thundering through the dark skies above the Pacific it looked like a dynamic stop. He could see just a little curl at the base of the tiny bright 'paint' near the bottom of his screen. It looked no nearer than the first contact and he recorded it in essentially the same spot, suggesting in his signal to the Flag that it was almost certainly the same contact they had located twenty minutes previously.

There the minor drama seemed to end. Nothing more was heard from anyone. Flying continued unabated, *Big John* held her zigzagging course for the landings and take-offs, and another forty-five miles of water slipped beneath her keel.

But out over that pitch-black water, at 0145 in the morning, another Viking picked up another transient contact off two sonobuoys. Again they judged it to be a Kilo, but no one was certain whether or not it was the same one, because its position was roughly fifty miles north-east of the last one, which meant it must have been making over ten knots; unlikely, because the American sonar would have picked it up. For the second time that night a big US Navy Viking banked round again to the east and never caught a glimmer of anything. At least, not for a half-hour, when a different buoy picked up what appeared to be a dynamic start. Neither of the two US submarines, both deploying towed arrays, picked up anything and the signal from the Viking to the Flag was similar to the others: 'Transient contact. Kilo-Class 636. Possibly same as Datum One. Rough position 21.53N 122.45E. Attempting to localize. Prosecuting.'

Guangjin Chen's C-4 was proving as elusive as B-5 and now both of these devilish decoys, being instructed from the satellites, remained silent. The entire US Navy could have set off in pursuit and they would have found precisely nothing. Nonetheless, Admiral Holt was obliged to move his carrier further east from his northern course, because a Kilo is simply too dangerous a ship to risk going close to and, anyway, easy to sidestep.

Once more the ocean world beyond Taiwan's east coast

went more or less silent. *Big John* steamed on approximately towards her ops area, but her present course would carry her right past the triangle, past the point to the east, unless she could turn in. But that seemed very doubtful at present, since there appeared to be at least one and possibly two Chinese submarines somewhere off her port beam, patrolling where *Big John* wanted to be. The US submarines were picking up nothing on the towed arrays.

Then, at 0545, the patrolling Viking tracker picked up the signal again and this time it was appreciably closer to the carrier. In fact, it was still C-4 transmitting but the *JFK* was only 75 miles from the decoy now, instead of 100. Admiral Holt did not like it. He edged east again away from his op area. He simply could not go in there if there should be one or more Chinese Kilos awaiting him. Particularly since everyone in the Navy now knew the SEALs had just banged out a $10-billion Sino investment down in the Strait of Hormuz. The Admiral pressed on north for another thirty miles, and at 0804 on Monday morning, May 21, Guangjin Chen hit the computer buttons to activate C-3. A new field of US sonobuoys picked up the transmission immediately and the patrolling Viking's signal to the Flag caused major consternation. They assessed this was an entirely different Kilo and it was waiting bang in the center of CV-67's op area.

Admiral Holt had the distinct feeling he was being pushed around by the Chinese Navy and he was beginning to sense a feeling of rising frustration. He had only one option: to make a swing right round the north-east end of the triangle and try to move in some time in the next few days when the Kilos had tired of this game of cat-and-mouse. Nonetheless, he could not take any risks and he ordered a course change to the north-east, with his submarines moving out to his west and the Viking pilots scanning the ocean with ever more vigilance.

For a long time there was nothing and then, just before midday, the Viking picked up a new contact and again it was a Kilo. It could have been the same one they heard at 0804, but it might very well have been a different one. The Chinese only own four Kilos and privately Admiral Holt thought there were probably two of them out there. However, at 1200 (local) that was not quite the point. What mattered was that the Viking operator put the transmission only fifty-six miles off *Big John*'s port beam and that was not good. Worse yet, it was continued, but not localized, by either of the SSNs.

In Admiral Holt's opinion, this was becoming quite serious. There was, it seemed, at least one Chinese Kilo possibly as close as fifty miles from the carrier and it seemed to be extremely elusive, which was a shuddering thought for a US admiral accustomed to controlling the ocean on, above and below the surface for 200 miles in any direction wherever he roamed. No admiral commanding a carrier battle group wants to go anywhere within 300 miles of a foreign, unfriendly, land-based air force and he certainly wants no part of a marauding submarine. The Chinese ploy to have two Kilos on permanent patrol in the Taiwan Strait is based on the simple assumption that no US admiral would drive a carrier down the Taiwan Strait if this were so. Neither would he. The steel-haired Daylan Holt, a Texan from Mesquite on the western edge of Dallas, was face to face with a brand-new brand of hardball international politics out on the northern edge of his own op area. Of course, he could sink the Kilo if he could catch it below the surface. If he could find it.

But no one could find it, or even them, if there were two, despite having flooded the probability areas with radar, ESM, and active and passive sonar from his sub-marines, aircraft and towed-array frigates. It was beginning to look as though the *JFK* would have to continue north-east into the deep water at the southern end of the lonely Sakishima Islands, where Japan finally peters out into the Pacific. This is a very remote corner of the ocean, 300 miles south-west of the American base at Okinawa, the farthest outpost of a far-lost empire. The Sakishimas stand 120 miles west of Taiwan, sixty miles from the op area of *Big John*. Admiral Holt had an uncanny feeling he was being herded away from his objective by the demonic, near-silent Chinese submarines.

The Chinese, for their part, not only tracked the Americans all the way, at 1400 they activated E-1, some eighty miles north of the carrier, undetected by the outriding nuclear submarine. The Viking picked it up and signaled the Flag. Admiral Holt briefly changed course and, as he did so, Guangjin activated D-2. Just a transient, a seven-second transmission, which had the effect of pushing the carrier towards the waters south of the tiny island chain, to Ishigaki, where the water was deep and which, by a grand design hatched in distant Zhanjiang, lay neatly in two outer squares of Lieutenant-Commander Guangjin's grid.

Admiral Holt was forced to turn north again and he reasoned that the Kilo force, however many, was now to his left and right, but falling astern. If they wanted to get at his carrier they'd have to transit north-west through the massive ASW barrier he'd set up. The decoy Kilo buoys were indeed on either side of him, but the wily Zhang had stationed two real Kilos just thirty miles ahead of the CVBG and he'd done it seven days ago. For the moment they were almost stationary, transmitting nothing, preparing to launch a copybook attack on the US carrier, identical to that of Commander Ben Adnam when he destroyed the Nimitz Class carrier USS *Thomas Jefferson* in the Arabian Sea five years previously. They had chased and pursued nothing. They had just waited, silently, for the prime moment to fire, when Lieutenant-Commander Guangjin's ingenious invention had done its work. Unlike Ben Adnam, they had not needed to assess the wind and the carrier's time of approach. The very occasional transmissions from the floating electronic buoys had 'herded' *Big John* into the appointed place like so many sheepdogs.

The Chinese submarines were in there, in 600 feet of water, the Kilo Class hulls 366 and 367, jet-black 3000-ton diesel-electrics built in Russia's Admiralty Yard at St Petersburg. They were each armed with eighteen TEST 71/96 wire-guided passive-active torpedoes, homing at forty knots to fifteen kilometers. But the Chinese COs would fire their two torpedoes, with their 205kg non-nuclear warhead, from a lot closer than that.

Admiral Zhang, however, was not out to create world havoc and mass destruction. He just sought, quietly, to cripple the great US warship, despite all the difficulties that would involve. At 2100 that Monday evening his underwater commanders drew a bead on *Big John*.

Same time (0800 local) Monday.
The White House.
Everything about the *goddamned Chinese* baffled Arnold Morgan. He had no idea why they would have wanted to infuriate the entire Western world, not to mention much of the Eastern world, by assisting the *goddamned towelheads* in mining the Strait of Hormuz. Maybe just for money. Maybe they really thought they could make a huge financial killing by selling their oil from Kazakhstan at the massive world prices which would follow the blockade of the Gulf of Iran. Maybe. But maybe not. It made some sense to the President's National Security Adviser. But not enough. Well, the USA had slammed back hard, as China must have known they might, and no one had complained to anyone. Certainly the USA knew there was no point

remonstrating with the Chinese over the minefield, because they would say nothing. Equally the Chinese had said nothing to anyone about the destruction of the oil refinery.

Admiral Morgan knew he was not going to receive any answers to anything, which was why he had summarily requested the presence of the Chinese ambassador to Washington, the urbane Ling Guofeng. Arnold might not be getting any answers, but he was about to deliver one or two home truths.

Kathy O'Brien politely ushered the ambassador into the main office at 0815. The two men knew each other, of course, but it was always a cool relationship. The Admiral had passed one or two withering broadsides across the bows of the Chinese ship of state in the past few years and Ling Guofeng had frequently been obliged to keep his head well down.

In another life they might actually have been friends. Both of them knew more about the world than was good for anyone, and both knew implicitly where their loyalties were. Arnold Morgan, a natural aggressor, was constantly issuing warnings, making threats and, occasionally, carrying them out. The veteran Ambassador Ling, in his role as China's chief appeaser in Washington, was thus obliged to absorb a substantial amount of grief from the Admiral. But the diplomat from Shanghai knew how to roll with the punches. 'Good morning, Admiral,' he said, bowing. 'What a very kind invitation. It's been too long.'

Arnold Morgan raised his eyes heavenwards. *Too long! Never mind the blown-up tankers, never mind the minefield, the world oil crisis, Japan almost going bankrupt because of it. Never mind the blasted refinery still spouting flames 100 feet into the air. Will someone ever save me from this Oriental bullshit? Too long, he says. Jesus Christ.* 'Ambassador, the pleasure is, as always, mine,' replied the Admiral. 'Please sit down. I have ordered a pot of Lapsang Souchong, your favorite China tea, I believe – at least your favorite in this country.'

'Now that is very kind of you and I hope it will smooth our way during our discussions.'

Arnold slyly congratulated himself on Kathy's call to Ling's secretary on Friday afternoon to establish the subtleties of the ambassador's tastes. He had no recollection that Kathy had made the call without even asking him.

Anyway, the tea was delivered and poured by a polite and attentive waiter, and Arnold Morgan stepped up to the plate. 'Ambassador, there is much that cannot be said at this discussion. Much, possibly, that never will be said. I have asked you here because I believe that you and I understand each other.'

'I think and hope that we do,' replied Ling in his impeccable English accent.

'Well, let me begin by saying that we are very well aware of China's complicity in the placing of the minefield in the Strait of Hormuz.'

'Oh, really?' replied Ling. 'I have not been so informed.'

'I guess, if I wanted, I could inform you myself. Of the origin of the mines, the date they left Moscow, the times of the refueling stops for the Andropov freighter which delivered them and the date the PLAN assisted the Iranians in laying the fields.'

Ambassador Ling said nothing, betrayed nothing, not a flicker of understanding, the precise way all great ambassadors are supposed to operate under this kind of pressure in a foreign capital.

'But there is no need for me to do so, since we both understand the . . . er . . . rather heated game we are playing. But I would like to mention the fire which is still raging in the Strait at the Chinese refinery. That,

Ambassador, represents the collective wrath of the entire industrial world. So I would warn you about the danger of writing it off as an accident and blithely rebuilding it.'

'Am I hearing *an admission* that the United States of America actually attacked and destroyed the $10-billion Chinese refinery in the Strait?'

'No more than I am hearing *an admission* that China purchased hundreds of sea mines at vast expense from Moscow and then tried to shut down the principal power supply of every oil-consuming country in the world. Damn nearly all of them, that is.'

Ambassador Ling said nothing.

Admiral Morgan continued, 'So, my good friend Guofeng, I would like to conclude with this piece of advice for you and your government. In our opinion, and in the opinion of all our allies, you have committed a crime of vast proportions in the Strait of Hormuz. It is a crime which must not be repeated. It is therefore my rather sad duty to advise you' – here his voice rose to its familiar growling quality – '*to stay the fuck out of the Middle East oil routes.*'

'And if we should insist on our right to trade in any international waters?'

'You would find no objection from us, because your ships are welcome to visit us at any time. But if you continue to put Chinese warships anywhere near the north reaches of the Arabian Sea, inside the Strait of Hormuz, or indeed in the Gulf of Iran, we shall have no hesitation in sinking them. Your nation has committed a terrible crime, for reasons best known to your masters in Beijing. But the rest of the world will not permit you the leeway to repeat that crime. Ling, old buddy, your Navy is on its way right back to the South China Sea.'

'I shall indeed report your views to my government. But do I have your permission to inform them that the

United States wilfully destroyed the Chinese refinery?'

'No, Ambassador, you do not. You may tell them that the elimination of the refinery was in your opinion an act of retribution against your government for crimes committed by China in the Strait. You may also say that the US government was not unsupportive of the action against the Chinese oil. But as to who perpetrated the destruction, that may never be known. But if I had to guess, I'd say you should look to some of those Arabs, who are currently unable to sell their oil because it's all trapped in the Gulf.'

'Yes, of course,' replied the ambassador. 'How foolish of me not to have identified the culprit at once.'

'Well, for the time being that would appear to be all. But heed what I say, Ambassador. Because I would not want things to become any more tense between us and you guys have done quite sufficient damage for one month.'

'Quite frankly, Admiral, so, might I say, have you.'

Same time (2145 local).
Off the island of Ishigaki.
Hardly moving through the water, both Kilos waited silently, ten miles apart, in the path of the carrier's approach from the south-east. The *JFK* was clearly identifiable by her noise signature and at 2215 the westerly Kilo assessed the Americans would pass within 3000 yards. The Chinese prepared to fire, while the easterly Kilo decided to wait, just in case an attack by her consort should cause *Big John* to swerve her way. It is almost impossible to co-ordinate a torpedo attack by two submarines. Only one would open fire, since charging in at high speed would simply give the game away. The westerly Kilo's two torpedoes would come in from the carrier's stern arcs on predictions from the last known bearing. The big TEST

weapons would be launched quietly at thirty knots, staying passive all the way, which at least would give them a chance of avoiding a full frontal smash into the hull. The Chinese wanted only the shafts and there would be nothing *Big John* could do. There would be no time.

2150. 'Stand by one.'

'Last bearing check.'

'SHOOT!'

The Chinese torpedo came powering out of the tube, hesitated for a split second, then whined away into the dark waters.

'Weapon under guidance.' Kilo 636 was right on top of her game.

'Arm the weapon.'

'Weapon armed, sir.'

Ninety seconds go by. 'Weapon now 1000 yards from target, sir.'

'Weapon has passive contact.'

'Release to auto–home passive.'

Moments later, Kilo 636 loosed off a second torpedo which, like its colleague, was now streaking through the water towards the lights on the stern end of the carrier's flight deck. It was a classic submarine attack, conducted with ruthless professionalism in a manner which would tolerate no comeback. There simply was no time.

Inside the ops room of the carrier the sonar men picked up the torpedoes. At least they picked up one of them. 'Admiral – sonar. TORPEDO! TORPEDO! TORPEDO! Bearing Green 198 – Torpedo HE tight-aft. REAL CLOSE, SIR. REAL CLOSE.' Real close now meant no more than 500 yards. Which put the lead torpedo thirty seconds from impact somewhere on the stern of the carrier. Firing back was out of the question. An 88,000-ton carrier is not built for close combat of this type.

Someone yelled: 'DECOYS!' But that was about two

minutes too late. The combat systems officer alerted all ships that the Flag was under attack. But before he could even utter the words 'Chinese submarine', the first TEST 71/96 smashed into the port outer propeller, blowing it off and buckling two of the four shafts. Moments later the second torpedo, undetected, slammed into the port inner propeller and blew up with staggering force, causing distortion to the starboard inner as well. *Big John*, even if he was still floating, was not going anywhere for a while.

The *JFK* was well compartmentalized and she would not sink. But with her massive shafts damaged she was no longer capable of operating aircraft. The great leviathan began to list slightly. Damage control teams were right on to work on the flooding. Engineers stared in horror at the extent of the harm done to the shafts. The Admiral, still wondering where the next torpedo would come from, launched two more Viking trackers from the flight deck. He recalled the LA Class submarines from deep water out to the south-west, bringing in one destroyer and a frigate for a close ASW hunt near the carrier.

The signal being sent to Pearl Harbor was as shocking to the communications room as the Japanese attack had been to the naval staff sixty-six years previously:

212155MAY07. Position 24.20N 124.02E. To CINCPACFLT from US Carrier *John F. Kennedy*. Hit by two torpedoes, passive homing unknown origin. Two explosions in shaft area. Three shafts out of action. One shaft remains serviceable. Max speed available ten knots. Fixed wing flying not feasible in less than twenty-five-knot headwind. Initial assessment damage severity: requires early docking.

Same time (0800 local).
Office of the CNO
The Pentagon.
Admiral Alan Dickson was aghast. The signal from
CINCPACFLT Headquarters left no room for doubt. The
People's Republic of China had unquestionably fired two
torpedoes at a US carrier, 125 miles off the east coast of
Taiwan. Worse yet, they'd both hit and the carrier had
been powerless to stop them and, so far, take any form of
retaliatory action. Further attacks had to be expected but
had not yet materialized. Admiral Dickson decided that if
the Chinese could torpedo the ship, they could also bomb
it and he ordered the immediate evacuation of all aircraft
currently stationed in the carrier. Whatever crew could be
spared and moved to Okinawa should go too. All other
manpower surplus to the essential running of the crippled
ship should be removed to the *JFK*'s accompanying
destroyers and frigates.

He hit the secure line to Admiral Morgan and broke the
news to the incredulous but thoughtful National Security
Adviser. 'The thing is, Arnie, I am going to get the carrier
back to Pearl – might have to tow it. Sounds too big for
Okinawa. Anyway, she's effectively out of action.'

'Yes. That's a big ship to try to fix, so far from a major
US base,' replied Admiral Morgan. 'Anyhow, I guess you
better get over here. Bring all the information you have
and we'll try to decide what the hell to do.'

Same time (2300 local).
Southern Fleet HQ
Zhangjiang.
'Well, Jicai, very satisfactory,' purred Zhang Yushu.
'That's all of them, I believe. The *Roosevelt*, the *Truman*,
the *Constellation* and the *John C. Stennis* all so very busy
7000 miles away in the Strait of Hormuz. The *Ronald*

Reagan stranded nearly 9000 miles away in San Diego. The *John F. Kennedy* out of action. Which leaves us entirely free to conduct some local business of our own.'

At 2200 on the clear, moonlit evening of Tuesday, May 22, 2007, deploying the most massive display of military power since the UN's 1991 advance on Saddam Hussein, The People's Republic of China attacked Taiwan.

Eight

It was too quick even for STRONG NET, the brand-new multi-billion dollar air defense early-warning network. Taiwan's Hawk surface-to-air missiles remained in their launchers as the Chinese onslaught came in. There was not a bleep out of the new ultra-sensitive Tien Kung medium-to-long-range system based on the old US Patriot and deployed around Taipei. Everything about the attack from the mainland was utterly unexpected. Even the target was essentially way out in right field. But in the small hours of May 22, China was undeniably bombarding, presumably with a view to capture, the picturesque archipelago of the Penghu Islands, sixty miles off Taiwan's eastern shores. Of course, the Penghus are not entirely picturesque. Taiwan maintains a 17,000-strong offshore island command army on Penghu. There is an airport and outside the city of Makung a big navy base, home of the 154th Fast Attack Squadron.

Now, at these mid-ocean marks, China was literally hurling short-range ballistic missiles (SRBMs) launched into the night from the opposite shore from bases in Fujian and Jiangxi Provinces. And high above the Taiwan Strait an armada of China's newly built B-6/BADGER long-range bomber aircraft, laden with land attack cruise missiles (LACMs) was preparing to strike the Penghu naval base.

It was six minutes before Taiwan could respond, by which time the Makung shipyard was ablaze, with two

3000-ton Knox Class guided-missile frigates, the *Chin Yang* and the *Ning Yang*, burning ferociously alongside the jetties. Taiwan launched her opening batteries of Tien Kung missiles from the west coast of the main island straight at the incoming BADGERs and downed nine of them in fifteen minutes. But they could not prevent the first wave of SRBMs screaming into the outskirts of Makung, almost demolishing the entire Hsintien Road to the north of the base, in the process reducing both the Martyr's Shrine and the Confucius Temple to rubble. The precision bombardment hit the airfield, blitzed the telephone company at the north end of the main Chungching Road and the main downtown post office. Within ten more minutes Taiwan had a squadron of US-built F-16 fighters in the air, howling out of the night in pursuit of the BADGERs, which were no match for them, and the US-supplied deadly accurate Sidewinder missile blew eight more of them out of the sky.

Below the opening air battle a big flotilla of Chinese warships was moving in on the Penghus, led by the second of their Russian-built Sovremenny destroyers, in company with four Jangwei Class guided-missile frigates and six of the smaller heavily gunned Jianghu Class, which had been conducting regular fleet exercises in the Strait for the past five days. Shortly after midnight they opened fire with a long-range shelling assault on the tiny islands of Paisha and Hsi, obliterating the three-mile-long bridge which joins them. They slammed two missiles into Hsi's spectacular Qing dynasty Hsitai Fort from which, on a clear day, you can see the mountains of both Taiwan and China. Then they turned south-west and battered the islands of Wang'an, Huchang and Tongpan.

The Taiwan High Command in Taipei was forced to the opinion that China was in the process of capturing all sixty-four of the Penghu Islands, with their 147 historic temples, mostly dedicated to Matsu, the goddess of the sea who would always protect the islanders, but who was not having that much effect right now. The Penghus have been, for centuries, permanent home mostly to fishermen and farmers. Walls of coral, built to protect large crops of peanuts, sweet potatoes and sorghum, form a unique landscape. The endless beaches and blue waters have made the Penghus one of the great tourist attractions in the East.

However, at this precise moment the beautiful Lintou Beach, on the seaward side of Makung, resembled Dunkirk, 1940, more than anywhere else. Batteries of China's CSS-X7 missiles – a new version of the Russian-designed M-11 with a 500kg warhead – were detonating everywhere. Ocean-front bars and restaurants were flattened, huge spouts of salt water and sand blasted over the city.

In Taipei the President, in conference with the Premier and his military Chiefs of Staff, ordered an immediate defence of the islands, 'before the Chinese attempt a landing'. Lieutenant-General Chi-Chiang Gan, Commander-in-Chief of the Army, ordered 25,000 troops from all military bases on the north-east coast to head south by road and rail. At 0200 the government commandeered every fast train on the electrified west-coast line, particularly the Ziqiang and Zuguang expresses. The General ordered an airlift of 20,000 troops from the Taipei area to the big southern Navy base at Kaohsiung. Admiral Feng-Shiang Hu, Commander-in-Chief of the Navy, ordered the 66th Marine Division based in Kaohsiung to embark and sail immediately to reinforce the island garrison at Makung. He put three Newport Class troop-landing ships, and a 9000-ton Cabildo Class LSD on four hours' battle notice. The *Cheng Hai* docks down three small Japanese-built LSUs, each capable of carrying 300 men right into the beaches.

In the small hours of the morning the Taiwan High Command desperately signalled the US Seventh Fleet HQ requesting immediate military assistance, informing the United States that Taiwan was under attack from the forces of mainland China. Admiral Feng-Shiang personally told Admiral Dick Greening, Commander-in-Chief Pacific Fleet (CINCPACFLT) in Pearl Harbor that he feared for his country's existence, that an air battle was raging over the Taiwan Strait and that his pilots were winning it. But on the sea, China had a major flotilla of warships both bombarding and preparing to land on the strategically important Penghu Islands, which everyone knew China had *always* wanted to own. 'We badly need a carrier battle group, anything to get them away.' Admiral Feng-Shiang was almost pleading. But there was nothing CINCPACFLT could do. Nothing anyone could do. The United States did not have a CVBG available except in the Middle East, which was nearly two weeks away from the Taiwan Strait and anyway, it could scarcely be spared.

Powerless in Pearl Harbor, the Admiral knew now why *Big John* had been hit in such a brutal and unexplained manner. 'Holy shit,' breathed Admiral Greening. 'The bastards are gonna take Taiwan and so far as I can see there's not a damn thing we can do about it – we don't even have the hardware to attack China.' He promised to get back to the distraught Taiwanese Admiral, but right now he had to call Washington and inform Alan Dickson precisely what was happening. They patched him through to the White House, where the CNO was with Arnold Morgan. Kathy put the secure call on the conference line and both Washington-based Admirals listened aghast as Admiral Greening informed them that China had militarily invaded Taiwan. At the conclusion of the call Admiral Dickson requested thirty minutes thoroughly to appreciate the situation.

But Arnold Morgan stood up and there was a strange smile on his face. He shook his head, over and over, and kept saying, 'Those little bastards. Those cunning little pricks.' Finally he turned back to the CNO and said, 'Alan, old buddy, did you ever hear the phrase "checkmate"?'

'Guess so.'

'Good. Because we're in it.'

Every piece of information he had absorbed in the past several months, every twist and turn of the plot in the Gulf of Hormuz, now sprang into place, all the way back to that moment when Lieutenant Ramshawe had called him in the restaurant. Arnold Morgan could remember the young Lieutenant's words verbatim: *It is my opinion that there may be a serious minefield out there, maybe running from the Omani coast, place called Ra's Qabr al Hindi right across to Iran, and I think we ought to find out.*

The Admiral was cogitating aloud now: 'Jimmy was right and he ought to be promoted for brilliance. Borden is going to be relieved of command at Fort Meade. George Morris is gonna get better in the next twenty minutes or he's fired too; so are all his fucking doctors. I'm about to admit I've been outwitted by the goddamned Chinese pricks. They never wanted to screw up the oil, never gave a flying fuck about the oil, they just wanted to tie us up, at least tie up the carriers, thousands of miles from the South China Sea. I guess we threw 'em a curve when we diverted the *JFK* back to Taiwan. So by some damn clever means they crippled her. *And then there were none.* Hours later they attack Taiwan, *knowing* beyond any doubt there is nothing on earth we can do about it, save for starting World War III with nuclear missiles. And even Taiwan ain't worth that.'

'Holy shit,' breathed Alan Dickson. 'You mean there's nothing we could do to save her?'

'There's plenty we could do. But not in time. Taiwan

will fall inside two weeks. That's how long it would take the *Truman* Group or the *Roosevelt* Group to get there. The fight would be all over before they could get out of the Indian Ocean.'

'But so far they've only taken a few shots at the Penghu Islands.'

'Alan, that news is gonna be so out of date by tomorrow morning it'll make the Washington Monument look like Stonehenge.'

Admiral Morgan checked his watch. It was already 5 p.m. – six o'clock the following morning over the Penghu Islands, where suddenly the rumble of battle grew steadily more faint and the surviving Chinese bombers swung back towards the mainland. The flotilla of warships ceased their bombardment but closed rapidly, effecting a complete blockade of the islands. Anyone wanting to get in would have to fight the Chinese Navy.

With half the armed forces of Taiwan already well on their way south, Admiral Zhang, who had assumed command of the entire operation, moved to Phase Two. As the sun rose blood red out of the Pacific Ocean, he unleashed the massive missile bombardment of the west coast of Taiwan he had been planning for six months. It started in the north with Chiang Kai-shek International Airport, the powerful SRBMs blasting craters in the runways, but surprisingly taking out only the air traffic control tower. The regular passenger terminals were not targeted.

Zhang's ballistic missiles slammed into the road system, blasting huge chunks out of the coastal highway. They hit the town of Chungli where the main south-running freeway crosses Route 1. They obliterated that junction and took out 400 yards of the railroad track. They blew apart a freeway road bridge west of Hainchu. They hit the Mingte Dam, west of Miaoli, and three times more they knocked serious hunks out of the south-running roads, freeways and railroads before they reached the majestic bridges, which span the estuary of the Choshui river. There, with a withering salvo of missiles, the Chinese took out all four of them, blasting steel and masonry into the water, stopping Route 17 in its tracks, ending the long winding path of Route 19, splitting assunder the great north-south freeway and closing down the south-running railroad.

The entire transportation system which crosses the pancake-flat rice-growing plains of west-central Taiwan was in ruins. And that was before the Chinese missiles reached the south-western city of Tainan, Taiwan's provincial capital for more than 200 years until 1885. Zhang's missiles completely destroyed every runway on the airport. They hammered Routes 17 and 19 north of the river and blasted yet again the main highway south. There were three massive separate hits on the most important road-freight artery in the country as it swept west of the city towards the port of Kaohsiung, thirty miles further south. It was just about impossible to move troops or anything else back to the north. Admiral Zhang's brilliant feint to the Penghu Islands had drawn half the Taiwanese army 235 miles away from his main objective, Taipei.

The Chinese warlord had not even begun. Again he launched his remaining 120 B-6/BADGER aircraft. They headed out over the coast in three great waves of forty, once more loaded with the new land attack cruise missiles. This time their targets were strictly military, Taiwan's air defense installations, air force runways and naval bases, places the PLAN had been watching and checking for years. The BADGERs were accompanied by air force fighters, the Q-5B Fantan, and more bombers, the newer JH-7s and the SU-30MKKs. Air superiority aircraft, J-10 and J-11 Flankers, flew sortie after sortie, trying to protect the bomber force and downing several Taiwanese fighter aircraft in a sustained attempt to gain air superiority over the Strait.

The opening attacks hit the brand-new, but untried, Modified Air Defense System (MADS), with its super-PATRIOT anti-ballistic missiles, which had been installed all around the capital. They slammed the airfields of the new Indigenous Defense Fighter aircraft in Taoyuan County and further south in Yunlin. All along the flat west coastal plain they took out the Tien Kung air defense systems. They hit the high slopes of the central mountains where the Taiwanese military had major west-facing air command and control centers, built especially to deal with a massive incoming attack from the mainland, as this most certainly was. For years Chinese agents had reported to Beijing every detail of the Taiwanese key logistic centers and the military Intelligence headquarters (C-41). Now the land attack missiles, launched from the air, were aimed at every one of them, backed up by the huge short-range ballistic missiles, which were still thundering into the sky every few minutes from their launchers 100 miles across the Strait in Fujian and Jiangxi Province.

Brave little Taiwan shuddered under the withering onslaught of the Dragon from across the water. But they conceded nothing. For hour after hour, their pilots had fought those F-16s into the sky, attacking the incoming missile bombers. By midday it was apparent that China had made an error of judgement in not locating Taiwan's mobile short-range air-defense systems, CHAPARRAL, STINGER/AVENGER and ANTELOPE. CHAPAR-RAL consists of four modified AIM-9C Sidewinders mounted on tracked vehicles; the STINGER/AVENGER SAMS is a pedestal-mounted system with two pods, each containing four STINGER missiles, mounted on the back of a High Mobility Multi-Purpose

Wheeled Vehicle (HMMWV). ANTELOPE, developed and perfected at Taiwan's Chung Sang Institute of Science and Technology, fires from an HMMWV, four Tien Chien-1 missiles with a fourteen-mile range. A deadly, low-flying intercepter, it has an outstanding target acquisition system. The Taiwanese moved these three systems along their west-coast line to lethal effect, launching their missiles doggedly and accurately from anywhere they found cover. They fired from the rice fields, from behind barns, woods and coral walls. They fired from any of the foothills of the coastal mountains they could reach. By mid-afternoon they had devastated the Chinese fleet of BADGER bombers. Of the 120 which came in from the mainland, less than 70 made it back.

But they had only stopped the aircraft, not the missiles, and by nightfall the entire transportation system in the west of Taiwan was wrecked. The communications systems, both civilian and military, were non-operational. Their permanent air defensive systems were essentially destroyed. There was nothing left of the much-vaunted SKYGUARD installations. The AIM-7M/SPARROW anti-aircraft missiles had scarcely left the ground. In the history of aerial combat, the monstrous struggle for supremacy above the Taiwan Strait was right up there with the Battle of Britain, except that both Admiral Zhang and Taiwan's Air Force C-in-C, General Ke-Chiang Wong, had it all over H. Göring and Adolf.

By nightfall on May 23, China had achieved the destruction of many of its objectives, but somehow Taiwan had fought them off. In addition to the battering of the BADGER fleet, China had lost ten Fantans, plus twelve more bombers and nine Flankers. The Taiwanese had lost a total of forty-three combat aircraft, which meant, in a sense, they were somehow winning the air battle. But China had 2200 fully operational fighter and bomber aircraft, while Taiwan had a total of only 400 combat aircraft. As in every war in its long history, China was perfectly prepared to suffer massive attrition in pursuit of her goals, safe in the knowledge that ultimately they had more of everything, especially people and, these days, aircraft and ships. The fact was that at this rate of killing, China could go on losing this air battle twice as long as Taiwan could go on winning it. The absence of the always-expected heavy US air support was a death blow to the island, which suddenly found itself fighting for its life.

The situation at sea was, if anything, worse. The Chinese Navy comprised 275,000 personnel, with over fifty destroyers and frigates, sixty diesel–electric and six nuclear submarines, nearly fifty landing ships, plus several hundred auxiliaries and smaller patrol vessels. Taiwan had an excellent Navy of twenty-two destroyers, twenty-two frigates, fifty fast attack craft, but only ten submarines. Their forty landing ships were plainly not required in a conflict with China.

Unsurprisingly first blood on the water went to China. In the middle of the afternoon a PLA naval aviation long-range maritime patrol aircraft, a Y–8X Cub, flying down the center of the Strait, picked up the small flotilla carrying the first wave of Taiwanese Marines going in to reinforce the Penghus. The Cub signaled back to Southern Fleet HQ and, two hours later, two Chinese Kilos moved in and made a fierce underwater attack upon Taiwan's warships. They slammed a torpedo into each of the Newport Class LSTs, and hit the *Cheng Hai* with two more, leaving the big LSD on fire and listing, with more than 400 casualties on board. With every hour, more and more Chinese warships arrived on station around the Taiwan coast, securing their sea lanes, plainly preparing to protect the Chinese landing force, which everyone now knew was inevitable.

0730 (local) Wednesday, May 23.
The White House, Washington DC.

The atmosphere in the Oval Office was subdued. Indeed, an air of melancholy hung over the entire capital, as America's friends, colleagues and partners on the other side of the world fought for survival. The President was worried, mainly that he might somehow be blamed, and he was beginning to see himself as some kind of Nero figure, fiddling around in Washington while Taiwan burned. 'There must be something we could do,' he kept saying. But Bob MacPherson, the Defense Secretary, kept telling him that as far as he could see there was nothing. The Secretary of State, Harcourt Travis, thought the less said to anyone the better, although he knew the USA was bound to defend Taiwan 'under the Taiwan Relations Act, Public Law 96–8'.

Arnold Morgan paced the room, racking his brains for a solution. He concentrated now on trying to spell out the situation for the President. He knew it would be difficult, because this President these days saw the world only in terms of himself and his reputation at the end of his second term. Finally he was prepared and said, 'Sir, as I have already explained, the Chinese have pulled off a stupendous act of deception, forcing us to put eighty per cent of our available sea power into a false, but dangerous, situation in the Strait of Hormuz. In the process they have sunk three VLCCs and caused the death of several seamen, most of them American, inside the Gulf of Iran. They have further hit and sunk a Japanese tanker north of the Malacca Strait and plainly torpedoed a US aircraft carrier in the Pacific. They are now moving ahead and conquering Taiwan, the *only* objective they have ever been interested in.'

He paused to allow this catalogue of Chinese transgressions to be fully appreciated, then continued, 'In return, we have smashed their oil production in the Gulf area and I have warned their ambassador that we see no purpose to Chinese warships entering the area of the northern Arabian Sea in the future. Should they ignore this warning, they understand we will not hesitate to hit and sink any and all Chinese ships anywhere near the oil sea lanes of the Middle East. They have done quite sufficient damage to the world oil market already and the international community simply will not put up with their presence in the area any longer. The Chinese understand that. I think.'

'Arnold, I kinda know all that,' said the President. 'I want you to deal with Taiwan.'

'Very well, sir. But you'll forgive me for reminding you that all of these matters are very closely connected.'

'I'll forgive you. Taiwan.'

'Okay,' said Admiral Morgan, declining to mention what he actually thought about the conversation – *some cheek, this fucking ignoramus trying to keep ME on track*. But he rose above it, more or less effortlessly, and continued, 'Sir, this attack on Taiwan has been very carefully planned. We thus find ourselves watching a rather ungainly giant swatting and whacking his way to victory. But he is well prepared, he's in his own waters, he doesn't give a damn about the attrition of ships, aircraft or people and he wants the prize of Taiwan more than any Chinaman has ever wanted anything. We cannot intervene, mainly because we don't have anything to intervene with. Even if we did, I'd be inclined to advise against. Because we would find ourselves in a very serious sea battle, and the upshot might be that we could lose three or four major ships and a couple of thousand American crewmen. They, on the other hand, might lose twenty ships and 10,000 crewmen. The difference being that they wouldn't care a fuck and would just go on fighting. We, however, could not put up with that. We'd have riot conditions at home, you'd be swept from office along with the rest of us and we'd all be accused of deliberately starting a new Vietnam on account of some goddamned no-account Chinese island which is about a mile and a half from Shanghai anyway. That's how the public and the press would react.

'It's all very well us patrolling the waters, like we've been doing for years, and frightening everyone to death whenever we had to. But it's quite another thing to be prepared to go to war, to send our young men to fight and die, thousands of miles from home. Sir, if we took this country into armed conflict with China over a bunch of fucking pottery makers in this goddamned island right off their coast, you could wind up with another civil war in this country and I'm not joking.'

'But we always were able to drive the Chinese off before.'

'Yeah, but they were only goofing around then. This is entirely different. This is a nation on a war footing, perfectly happy to fight and die for their belief that Taiwan is a part of China, an offshore province that needs to be brought back into the motherland. On the other hand, we are really prepared only to posture over Taiwan. No president of the USA is going into a real shooting war with China over their goddamned island. We'd fight 'em over Middle Eastern oil, if we had to, because that's in our national interest and the public would understand that. But they would not understand American sailors being blown to pieces over the territorial claim of one Chinaman over another.'

'I guess you can understand the Chinese wanting this offshore island back,' said the President. 'Same as they wanted Hong Kong, which was even further inside their own backyard. I just never understand this obsession. Never understand what they really want.'

'What they *really* want, sir', replied Admiral Morgan, 'is

the National Palace Museum of Taipei.'

'The museum?'

'Correct. Because it contains the most priceless collection of Chinese art and history. It is without question the greatest museum in the world, the greatest museum there has ever been.'

'Is that right?'

'That, sir, is right.'

'Well, I thought the Chinese regime hated culture. Didn't Chairman Mao and his wife try to destroy every vestige of their country's culture, burning books, destroying university libraries and all that?'

'They sure did and that was a big part of it. The entire heart of China, every ancient book, manuscript, tapestry, sculpture, painting, porcelain, silver, jade, gold, whatever, dating right back to the ancient Shang Kingdom, thousands of years ago, was contained in one collection. About 10,000 cases of it. Held for 500 years in the Forbidden City in Beijing.'

'Well, how did it get to Taiwan?'

'Basically, Chiang Kai-shek took it.'

'Christ! All of it?'

'Nearly. It was just about the last major act he undertook before he and the Kuomintang were exiled to Formosa. He just felt that Mr and Mrs Mao might destroy the entire thing, so he packed it all up and somehow shipped fourteen trainloads of Chinese tradition across the water to his new home.'

'Did anyone care? I mean back on the mainland?'

'Not for a while. But then Formosa had its name changed to Taiwan and its capital Taipei became a world financial power. So Chiang Kai-shek decided to build this fabulous museum in a park to the north of the city, kinda showcase to display this colossal record of the cultural history of China.'

'Don't tell me, Arnie. Right then the Chinks wanted it all back?'

'That's right. The museum opened some time in the mid-sixties and the Chinese almost immediately started to lay claim to the entire collection, ranting on about the cultural tapestry of China being displayed in this offshore island, which somehow claimed to be nothing to do with the mainland.'

'And what did Chiang Kai-shek say to that?'

'Plenty, sir. He said plenty. He told them that in his view they were nothing more than a murderous communist rabble who would probably have burned the history of China and never given it another thought. He told them he, Chiang, was the rightful ruler of China, that Taiwan was the rightful cradle of the Chinese nation, and that one day he and his armies would return and reclaim the mainland, and he'd see 'em all in hell before he'd submit to their barbarism.'

'And the collection of Chinese history?'

'That was even easier to deal with. Old Chiang Kai-shek told 'em to go fuck themselves.'

'And the stuff's been there in the museum ever since?'

'Right. They even called it the National Palace Museum after the original in the Forbidden City.'

'And did the stuff survive all this turmoil?'

'By some miracle not one piece was ever broken. Which, in the opinion of the Taiwanese people, proves that the collection is precisely where it's supposed to be; and they do have the unanswerable argument that Mao and his wife would most certainly have destroyed it.'

'And what does the modern Chinese regime have to say about that?'

'Nothing. Except to stamp their feet and shout, "Want treasures back! Want treasures back!"'

Everyone in the room chuckled. They would have

laughed out loud if the situation had not been *quite* so serious.

'Jeez. There must be literally thousands of pieces,' said Bob MacPherson.

'I think there's more than 700,000,' Admiral Morgan explained. 'I went to see it once a few years back. But they can only display 15,000 pieces at a time. They rotate every three months. So if you lived in Taiwan and went there four times in a year, you'd still only see 60,000 pieces, which is less than ten per cent of the collection. It'd take twelve years to see everything.'

'But where do they keep all the stuff which is not on display?'

'No one really knows,' Arnold continued. 'But it's supposed to be hidden in some vast network of vaults in the mountains behind the museum. They say it's all connected by tunnels.'

'You'd think with all that stuff they could do some kind of a deal, wouldn't you? Display half of it in Beijing or something.' The President slipped automatically into the politician's instinct for compromise.

'The Chinese mindset does not work like that,' said Arnold. 'Mainland China wants this irritating little rebel island to hand over the culture of China which, they say, Chiang Kai-shek stole from the people.'

'And the Taiwanese are still telling 'em to go fuck themselves?'

'Exactly,' Admiral Morgan confirmed. 'And before we're a lot older I'd say there's going to be a ferocious battle over that museum. You can bet the Taiwanese have put in some very thorough security systems. Even if Taiwan falls, which it plainly must, there's no guarantee that collection will not be wiped out. The Taiwanese may even use it as a bargaining card.'

'You mean, *if we can't have it, nobody's having it?*'

'Possibly. But more likely, *We have the power to destroy it, at the touch of a button. If you go and guarantee to leave us alone for ever, you can take it with you. Failing that, no one shall have it.*'

'Meanwhile, gentlemen, what are we going to do about the situation militarily? I ask this in the full knowledge that my National Security Adviser has already spelled out the plain and obvious truths of the matter. There's no possibility that the United States of America is going to all-out war with China over Taiwan. The most we would ever have done would have been to place a lot of very heavy muscle in the area and dare anyone to take us on. Today, however, that is not an option. China is, as Arnie has said, on a war footing, prepared to fight and die for her cause, which she is already doing. We're not going near the place.'

'And how do we answer Taiwan's cry for help?' asked Harcourt Travis.

'We offer to negotiate for them,' said the President. 'We threaten to make China into a pariah in world trade. We threaten to withdraw all trade with anyone who trades with China. We rescind their most-favored-nation status. We ban their exports. Call in their debts. All that and more. But we're not trading missiles, shells and bullets with 'em.'

'Nor torpedoes,' said Arnold Morgan.

'You mean, really, we just sit back and let the battle play out?' asked Bob MacPherson.

''Fraid so,' said Arnold. 'But I am working on a plan to make them pay a very high price for what they have done and I think we can confine their future activities to the China Seas.'

'Sounds like a particularly ambitious plan,' said Harcourt, 'since we're dealing with a nation which has just stood the world on its head, and apparently has no qualms about wrecking economies and then going to war.'

'It is an ambitious plan,' Admiral Morgan agreed. 'It's a plan which I like a lot for two reasons. First of all because it involves a large amount of dynamite and second because it will create a multitude of hugely pissed-off Chinamen.'

'I like it too,' said the President. 'Don't know what it is, but I like it.'

The meeting continued for the rest of the morning and still made no headway with regard to military discouragement towards China. It was agreed the State Department would send the most strongly worded communiqué to the Beijing government 'deploring in the extreme the vicious military action undertaken this week by China against their peace-loving neighbors, an independent state now recognized by the United Nations'.

Harcourt Travis pointed out that no civilized single country had undertaken any such unprovoked action in the past quarter of a century, save for Serbia and earlier Argentina against the Falkland Islands. In Harcourt's opinion, the Chinese would do well to take note of the fate that befell the leaders of these countries, and would be advised to *cease and desist* this totally unwarranted bullying against a small island neighbor. He did not anticipate a reply, nor did he get one.

Harcourt had been reluctant to put American threats of any kind into writing and that afternoon Admiral Morgan had the Chinese ambassador brought in to answer some hard, searching questions. But the ambassador merely stalled and said that China was simply answering a request from the Taiwan government 'to stabilize the situation in their country, with a view to normalizing relations with the mainland, which would be in everyone's interest'.

Arnold Morgan, who by now had pictures of the burning naval base in the Penghu Islands, produced them and asked if that was China's way of 'stabilizing the situation'.

Somewhat uncharacteristically, Ling Guofeng produced two pictures from his own briefcase and offered them to Arnold, who stared in amazement at the 500-foot-high inferno, which was still blazing from the oil refinery in the Strait of Hormuz. 'Might I assume this is your way also?' asked the ambassador.

'You may assume anything that makes you happy,' growled Admiral Morgan. 'I'll accept, if you like, that persons unknown blew up a few barrels of your oil. But that's a whole hell of a lot different from going to war with another much smaller country, killing the civilian population, hitting them with bombs, cruise missiles and your entire Navy. That's not even comparable. I want you to express to your government our horror at your actions and to warn them in the strongest possible terms that there will be consequences, which none of you will much enjoy. That's all.'

Ambassador Ling considered himself lucky not to have been expelled from the United States forthwith. He wished the National Security Adviser goodbye and hurried from the West Wing of the White House.

All week long such meetings would take place as the USA argued, cajoled and threatened the People's Republic of China in any way they could. They recruited support from every one of their allies, from Britain, France, Germany, Russia, Canada, Australia and Japan. They cancelled China's most-favored-nation status, banned imports from China and had their allies do the same.

Meanwhile, on the seas beneath the endless air battles, the Chinese Navy continued to deploy their warships, running them down from the Northern Fleet to form a silent blockade of the great port of Chi-lung, home of Taiwan's 3rd Naval District and the northern patrol squadron. The Taiwan Air Force, its airfields and runways severely damaged, half their pilots now dead or missing, spent the nights licking their wounds, repairing airstrips, fueling fighter aircraft ready to face the Dragon again on the following day. All the while the Chinese warships moved into control positions, dominating the Strait, establishing safe lines of communication and supply. Overhead, to the north of the island, Special Forces were packed into aircraft dropping behind Taiwan's beaches to the west of Chi-lung, the remote area chosen by Admiral Zhang and his senior commanders for the opening beach-head of the conflict.

This Chinese strategic planning had taken many months to finalize, but ultimately the tactics had evolved almost of their own accord. The vast majority of Taiwanese people live on the coastal plains on the western side of the island, principally in the north around Taipei and in the major population centers in the south around Tainan and Kaohsiung. Inland, the country is mountainous and forbidding, and the east coast is guarded by towering cliffs rising up from the sea. Any attempt to attack from the east would have been absurd and the prospect of serious operations in the mountains would have been daunting to any invader. China's objectives were clear: to bring about the total surrender of the island without having to fight for every inch of territory or for the outlying islands.

Plainly the objective had to be secured in the shortest possible time, at all costs to avoid unnecessary collateral damage. The Chinese military had no wish to destroy what they wanted before they even laid hands on it. There was also a determination to avoid excessive casualties to both sides, and an unspoken need not to damage China's political world standing any more than was absolutely necessary. Nonetheless, they had to get troops in there and all through the week they landed Special Forces under the cover of darkness by parachute and from the sea. They were delivered by submarine, small merchant vessels and fishing boats, dropped into the shallows along Taiwan's 1000 miles of coastline on suitably lonely beaches; made more lonely by the near-total destruction of the island's military communications systems.

Shortly before midnight on Saturday, May 26, the land attack began. An armada of massive transport aircraft protected by squadrons of jet fighters, began roaring over the Taiwan Strait, slightly north of the island itself. An entire Division of China's 15th Airborne Army rumbled eastwards, packed into recently acquired Russian-built IL-76MD/CANDIDs, specially configured for airborne operations. Flying astern of them, low over the ocean, was a fleet of Y-8/CUB transporters, likewise packed with troops, the entire fleet under the control of their Airborne Command, a gray-painted A-501 Mainstay.

Taiwan's air defenses were all but useless now and the massed ground forces of the Army, which had been swept to the south in the false panic over the Penghu Islands, was now unable to get back because of the wrecked roads, bridges and railroads. This effectively allowed China's first landing force to hit the beaches from out of the night unchallenged. One by one, the huge low-flying aircraft climbed to an altitude of 1000 feet and disgorged their live loads into two separate dropping zones seven miles apart, two miles behind the glorious white sands of Chinsan beach, a spectacular tourist area thirteen miles west of Chi-lung on the north coast of Taipei County. Hundreds and hundreds of paratroopers came thumping into the soft sand behind the wide shoreline, several miles from the nearest urban districts. By 0230 there were 3000–4000 on each landing beach, and the Chinese commanders were rallying the Division quickly and efficiently, ordering the airborne troops to move off as soon as they were formed, heading inland away from the sea, forward of the landing area, for almost a mile.

The Chinese began to dig in, establishing, well forward of the beach-head, two crescent-shaped screens, which would become the first line of defense Taiwanese troops would encounter should they attempt to attack the forthcoming amphibious force from the mainland.

Taiwan's problem right now was communication. The military systems were in such bad shape that it was near impossible to transmit a message, never mind a detailed conversation or report. Certainly there were small units stationed near Taipei which were aware of air activity out on the northern region. They may even have assumed there were troop drops being made. But they had no forces in contact, no Intelligence, no way of knowing what the invasion force was doing, certainly no way of assessing whether a beach landing was in any way imminent.

Meanwhile the Chinese were thundering forward with their two steel defense perimeters, one astride the road from Taipei, just north of Yangmingshan, the other astride the main approaches to the beach landing areas from Chi-lung – clean across the road from Feitsuiwan.

They strived in pouring rain all through that Sunday, digging trenches, preparing ammunition, setting up machine-guns. The ground mission of China's 15th Airborne Division was to stop a Taiwanese counter-attack at any and all cost. They had to be ready to protect the landing craft of the big Chinese marine division when it hit the beaches, complete with its own armor, artillery and air defenses, early on Monday morning, May 28.

And ready they were. While the main forces had been digging in, a small Chinese marine force, similarly trained to the US Navy SEALs or Britain's Special Boat Squadron, had checked out and cleared the landing area, marking the lanes, staking out their own positions to supply local machine-gun cover while they guided the landing craft in. By 0300, three hours before the sun would clear the distant horizon, the sea was suddenly alive with the unmistakable signs of invasion, tiny black landing craft, packed with armed troops streaming in towards the shallows. As the sky brightened and long pink fingers began to form among the pre-dawn rain clouds, the sound of the ramps echoed along the shoreline: big, clanging ramps, manhandled by shouting troops. Down those ramps came the big tracked vehicles, engines howling as they drove down the steep gradients and splashed into the surf, driving forward, looking for their lane lines on the beach. Out beyond the waves, in the calmer waters a half-mile offshore, there was a kind of controlled chaos, as ships maneuvered into position, the hydraulic docks opening up to allow more and more of the landing craft to break cover from the LCDs. This was D-Day Normandy on only a slightly smaller scale and if any Taiwanese units were watching, they were looking at the opening round of an unwinnable fight. Six hours later everyone who was going ashore had gone ashore. The ships were turned back across the Strait to reload with thousands more troops and this time they would be joined by dozens of civilian ships, all making their way to the northern beach-head out on the Chinsan sands.

Rarely had a capital city the size of Taipei experienced such mass confusion. Its three million inhabitants – and three million more in the surrounding district – knew, of course, that their island was under attack from the People's Republic of China. But the Chinese had thus far gone to extraordinary lengths to avoid harming even one building in the great northern metropolis. They had attacked, exclusively, military installations and military

286

communications, with the exception of the international airport, which they completely disabled even though the passenger terminals were untouched. Taiwan's television news broadcast hourly reports on the continuing air battles over the central waters of the Strait. There were reports of the destruction of the Navy base in the Penghu Islands, and there were further reports of the Taiwanese Navy preparing to defend the shores against a mass invasion from the sea. But nothing was being reported from the beach-head and there were no signs of bombs, rockets, shells or missiles. Save for the tension and fear, the city seemed normal. It was as if China had decided to shut down the military effectiveness of Taiwan, but possibly nothing further.

Taipei itself continued to function. Shops opened as normal, schools and universities remained active, traffic was its usual hideous mess, but buses ran and people went to work. Hotels stayed open and thousands of tourists trapped in the city booked in for extra weeks. It was impossible to leave Taipei, but equally impossible to travel to Taipei. The major long-distance freeways were virtually deserted, the railroad station was dead, the airport was dead, the runways wrecked.

The United States had informed the government it would begin an evacuation of its citizens caught in the entanglement of the Chinese invasion, but it quickly became apparent there was nowhere in the north of the island where a US passenger aircraft could land and, of course, there were no proper foreign embassies in Taipei, because of the problems of upsetting mainland China. There were just the 'pseudo-embassies' where diplomats operated under the cover of the 'American Institute' on the Hsinhyi Road, the 'British Trade and Cultural Office' on the Jenai Road, the 'France-Asia Trade Association' on Tunhua Road, none of which had any serious clout with anyone. So, as the first waves of Chinese troops splashed ashore seventeen miles to the north-east, Taipei continued to function, both citizens and visitors alike, with no option but to await the inevitable arrival of the conquering hordes from the mainland. There was no escape and life moved precariously forward for all of them.

Five days later, on the morning of Saturday, June 2, the National Palace Museum was busier than usual. It was somewhere interesting to go for the new prisoners of the city and the tourist buses were full, wending their way across the Chi-lung river, up through the northern suburbs to the Waishunghsi neighborhood at the foot of the Yangming Mountains.

The museum, set in elaborate parkland, with tree-lined gardens, is probably the most imposing building in Taiwan. The sweeping, extravagant approach leads to a massive flight of wide stone steps, like those at the Capitol building in Washington. At the top of this giant stairway stands an unmistakable Chinese palace, built in traditional style with white walls and green-tiled roofs. Curiously, there is never much sign of security in the outer grounds, save for the occasional uniformed guard, and today there was absolutely nothing. The military garrison two miles down the road was almost deserted since three-quarters of its entire force had been swept south along with most of the northern Taiwanese army.

By 1.30 p.m. there was a line of six buses creeping up to the disembarking area. Five of them carried a normal passenger load of men, women and children, husbands, wives, schoolteachers and tour guides. The sixth bus, a regular number 213, fourth in line, was transporting only men, fifty of them, each dressed in light civilian clothes. Forty-two of the seats were occupied by bored-looking men reading newspapers. But the eight passengers in the rear of the bus were sitting on ammunition cases in front of the back bench-seat upon which rested the big machine-guns and boxes of hand grenades which might very well be required in the next twenty minutes, depending on the level of resistance. The bus driver, a lean, hard-eyed Chinese agent, had spent all morning rounding up his passengers, collecting them from a series of safe houses in the Sungshan district, where they had been lying low since the first parachute drops of the Special Forces five days previously. These were the elite of the Chinese army, supremely trained Oriental SAS men, and now they were poised to strike, each man armed only with a concealed machine pistol or a folding sub-machine gun, as bus number 213 crept slowly up to the base of the wide stairway to the palace.

It stopped, leaving its engine running, and the doors slid swiftly open. Forty-two men stepped slowly out into the rain, gathering in groups of six, separating on various levels of the steps. Slowly, without urgency they made their way to the top and walked through the huge doors into a somewhat grim, drab and unspectacular interior main hall, in almost shocking contrast to the grandeur of the exterior. On either side of the hall was a towering wing, filled with spectacular treasures, and the groups of Special Forces, unsuspected, unrecognized, moved up to the ticket office and paid their entrance fee. In their original groups of six, they dispersed among the crowds into various great rooms, to the left and to the right, and to the upper floor. No one made a move, until the final group moved up to the counter and requested six tickets. The young lieutenant leading the group handed over a NT$500 bill with a tiny machine-gun painted on it. As he did, he told the cashier, 'Right now, Lee, GO!'

Lee, who had been in place on behalf of the PLAN Intelligence Service for the past five years, swung out of his booth and walked swiftly across the hall to the information desk and disappeared into a door marked 'Emergency Exit Only'. Still no one betrayed anything until, two minutes later, every light in the building went out. Great pictures were no longer illuminated, the glass cases full of treasure went suddenly murky beneath the limited natural light still filtering in through the windows of this dull June day. The National Palace Museum was without electric power, and deep beneath the stone and marble floors Major Chiang Lee flew along the underground corridor, a flashlight in his left hand and a hand grenade in his right. He reached the giant automatic generator with just twenty-five seconds left before it kicked in, and he ripped out the pin and hurled the grenade straight at the big 600-gallon gas tank to the right of the main machinery. He dived back round the corner of the massively reinforced concrete walls and flung himself to the ground. Four seconds later the thunderous explosion and contained fire insured that not only was the museum without power, it was going to stay precisely that way for the foreseeable future.

Every secure door both inside the museum itself, inside the labyrinth of underground tunnels and inside the echoing vaults which held the treasures of 5000 years, was suddenly useless. If they were open they would stay open. If they were closed they would open up easily enough without the power-locking devices. Major Chiang Lee, after hundreds of hours of study, a million deceptions and the patience of a Buddha, had done his work. He moved back through the dark passage towards the area where the elevator from the main floor emerged. In the fire-control doorway, right opposite, he retrieved his Kalashnikov machine-gun and walked back up the emergency stairs into the wide foyer where there were now scenes of some disquiet, though nothing resembling panic. The building had been constructed to such a heavy-duty standard that the rumble of the explosion, 100 yards away deep below ground, had scarcely been detected.

Major Lee fired a short burst from his machine-gun into the information desk by way of attracting attention. Then he blasted a volley at the six high-security cameras which he knew would operate for several hours on emergency batteries. Then he ordered everyone to stand back against the walls. He seemed a small, insignificant figure to be issuing such a command, but suddenly he was joined by two groups of six men all leveling smaller but just as deadly weapons.

The Taiwanese guards, indoctrinated for years as to the Jihad seriousness of their responsibilities, immediately moved as a trained unit of four men, racing into position behind two huge stone pillars and opening fire at the aggressors in the lobby. But they were not in time. At the first sign of movement, Admiral Zhang's commandoes hit the ground, returning fire towards the pillars. No one hit anyone, but behind the museum guards there was a team of six Chinese Special Forces. Now, with their weapons drawn, and firing from the rear, they cut down the security men in five seconds flat.

Just then, nine uniformed guards from the upper floors, pistols drawn, raced down the wide interior stairs. But this was like the St Valentine's Day massacre. Women screamed as the Chinese Special Forces, crouching beneath the benches along the walls, opened up with a sustained burst of fire, which left no survivors, only nine bodies sprawled on the wide staircase, their blood pouring on to the gray stone steps.

Up on the overlooking balcony a further troop of museum guards had seen the appalling situation and retreated into the main exhibition rooms, slamming shut the massive wooden doors and locking them by hand with their six-inch-long master keys. They used mobile phones, desperately trying to raise the military in the nearby garrison. The Taipei Police were on the line swiftly and assured them of assistance within ten minutes. Down in the tunnels the underground guards, and those who protected the doors into the vaults, gathered in the dark, twenty-three of them, heavily armed and massively confused.

By now there were several dozen tourists trying to open the outside doors, and Major Chiang Lee and his men began to herd the crowd inside the foyer towards the main entrance, which was guarded by Special Forces. Each visitor to the museum was searched. All mobile phones were confiscated. The double doors were opened just a couple of feet and each visitor was dispatched out into the crowd with instructions to leave the area immediately. At this point it was obvious that the National Palace Museum had been captured, at least temporarily, by a small squadron of Chinese Special Forces. Lines of tourists returned to the waiting buses and the eight men remaining in number 213 were now outside their bus, brandishing Kalashnikovs and ordering the drivers away.

Inside the main foyer another gun battle broke out when guards from the tunnels broke through the emergency exit and began shouting orders to the crowd. Unaware of the gravity of the situation, they never had a prayer when the Special Forces gunned them down at close quarters. Six of them died instantly, the rest retreated back down to the dark tunnels, which was going to pose a substantial problem for the Chinese.

Ricocheting bullets had already injured four American tourists, one of them a young boy aged around eight. The four-man medical unit which was integrated into the attacking force was attending the wounded, using their own supplies, and as they worked the large crowd was slowly exiting the building and moving down to the buses.

Now the Chinese moved to secure the museum. Two bigger machine-guns, plus ammunition, were brought up to the foyer from the waiting buses. All outside doors were locked by hand and a dozen sentries were posted. The remaining twenty-eight attackers split into three groups of six and one of ten, the main assault force which would storm the exhibition rooms where there were still armed security guards. They hit the one on the upper left first, blasting the door open with machine-gun fire, then spraying the room with fifty rounds, calling for total surrender. A stray bullet shattered a glass case and smacked straight through an early seventeenth-century Qing dynasty helmet used by a long-dead emperor for reviewing troops. The bullet cracked open the head of one of the three decorative dragons, split a large ruby in half and probably did about a million dollars' worth of damage. But the helmet survived and it fared better than a black pottery wine jar, fashioned in the shape of a silkworm cocoon, dating back to the Warring States period of around 300 BC. This shattered on impact with another Kalashnikov bullet and joined the remnants of a priceless three-thousand-year-old, foot-high, jade Juei Tablet from the early Shang Kingdom.

The four cowering guards plainly realized that if the Chinese Special Forces were prepared to inflict such damage on the contents of these rooms, their own lives were not worth four cents. They came forward, unarmed, with their hands high and as they did so they heard the thunder of the second machine-gun as it obliterated the lock on the door, which guarded the room across the wide stone corridor on the upper right. Again the Chinese Special Forces came in low and hard, the machine-gun ripping bullets into the room, from a floor-level position. The two central glass cases were blown apart, glass from the taller flying everywhere. But the principal casualty was a large carved ivory Dragon Boat from the Qing dynasty, again early seventeenth-century, perfectly created, right down to the eight oars, with sixteen pennants and the deck canopy, all set in a gold-painted lacquer box. The Russian-made bullets hit it broadside on, reducing it to shards of split white ivory: a destruction of history sufficient to reduce any curator of any museum to unashamed tears.

The machine-gun fire also ripped across two magnificent paintings set high on the west wall above a colossal stone table. The larger one, *Late Return from Spring Outing*, an acclaimed picture in ink and color on silk by the sixteenth-century Ming master Ch'iu Ying, had been ripped by two lines of bullets. To its left, the slightly smaller *Early Snow on the River* was even older – a tenth-century masterpiece by Chao Kan, one of the greatest painters of the Southern T'ang court. The serene beauty of the two paintings had been utterly desecrated by the Special Forces attack. Both were priceless, and both were now completely destroyed.

Two of the security guards, sheltering under the stone table, were hit and killed, the others begged for mercy and were permitted to surrender. They trooped outside to join their colleagues with their faces to the wall, hands high above their heads, under the scrutiny of the Chinese raiders. Room by room, the Special Forces took the museum. The staff were taken prisoner, the last tourists were ejected from the building and machine-guns were placed strategically on front and rear balconies.

At 1445 the sound of helicopters could be heard, out over the surrounding park. The Special Forces commander, in conference with Major Chiang Lee, knew they must be Taiwanese reinforcements, because the signal had not yet been sent back to the beach-head at Chinsan that the museum was secure. Instantly they ordered all prisoners out on to the steps with instructions to clear the area and radioed bus 213 to open fire at will on the incoming helicopters. Crammed with special police and the remnants of the army still in the area, the choppers came clattering in over the trees and immediately flew into a hail of bullets from the high front balcony and the area to the rear of the bus.

The lead aircraft took the brunt of the heavy fire from the balcony. It exploded, erupted into flames and veered over almost in a full somersault before crashing, rotor first, bang into the green-tiled roof. The second helicopter was hit from below and its main engine stopped dead. It dropped like a stone from 100 feet, obliterating itself on the stone forecourt and then exploding, killing fifteen tourists and injuring thirty-nine others. The third banked left across the trees and flew swiftly back to the nearby Army garrison. Meanwhile, Major Chiang Lee sent in the signal to the beach-head that the National Palace Museum was safely in Chinese hands for the moment, save for the underground tunnels and vaults, which still contained resisting security forces of an unknown number.

Twenty minutes later the first of two waves of Chinese airborne battalions came in over the park, the big helicopters and transporters containing two anti-aircraft detachments carrying QW-1 SAMs, a new, modified missile with a 35lb warhead, equipped with a lethal IR homing device accurate to three miles. The incoming battalion was also armed with portable anti-tank weapons and light mortars. The troops began to jump out into the park, swarming out of the aircraft on to the wet green grass below and forming an instant steel ring around the museum. They tied up with the Special Forces commandos who had originally taken the museum and swiftly moved their missile defenses into position.

The museum was not yet completely secure from attack. But it would need a formidable modern force to break through. Taiwan had no chance of recapturing the palace and only a remote shot at destroying it from the air at this point, because its air force was tragically weak and its missile defenses just about spent. The treasure trove of the Chinese centuries was firmly under the control of Beijing for the very first time since Chiang Kai-shek's fourteen trains, bearing the very soul of his vast country, had rumbled down to the east-coast ferries almost sixty years previously.

Nine

News of China's tightening stranglehold on the island of Taiwan was emerging with leaden slowness. Beijing, unsurprisingly, was releasing nothing, and there had been no time for any of the Western media's Far Eastern correspondents even to reach Taipei before the iron grip of the Chinese military took hold of the region. With the complete rupture of all Taiwanese military communications, the West was left with no sources, no information and no prospects of obtaining any. The only news emerging from the island was the occasional sly undercover dispatch from the pseudo-embassies and they had access to very few hard facts. The air battles which had now been fought over several days had taken place more than sixty miles from mainland news reporters, out of sight, out of earshot, basically out of reach.

On this Wednesday morning the mood in the West Wing of the White House was very somber. The hard men of the United States armed forces, Admiral Arnold Morgan, Defense Secretary Bob MacPherson, the Chief of Naval Operations Admiral Alan Dickson and the Chairman of the Joint Chiefs, General Tim Scannell, had been proved powerless to fight two enemies in two separate theaters. They were tied up in the Strait of Hormuz, guarding the world's main oil routes, and China was effectively left to do whatever it liked.

297

News was trickling in of a very large Chinese force landed on Chinsan beach. It was already moving south-east to the port of Chi-lung. It had taken three days to muster and the Chinese airborne troops had accepted very heavy casualties as the depleted but still determined Taiwanese forces constantly attacked them on the ground. Nonetheless, the tide of warriors sweeping across the Strait from the mainland, by both air and sea, was too great, too engulfing for the Taiwanese to stop. Tens of thousands of Chinese troops made the beaches from the vast flotilla of civilian boats, merchant freighters and Navy ships. This was a mission that had all of China behind it, and all the efforts of the remaining battalions of Taiwan's northern army proved unable to break through the 'screen' of Chinese marines who fought doggedly to protect their beach-head from attack.

Now they were on the move and Admiral Dickson considered they would swiftly attempt to capture the port of Chi-lung. Early reports, telephoned in secret from the pseudo-embassies, had the Chinese growling along the road, marching behind tanks and armored vehicles. But the Admiral offered a ray of hope here, because there was a major Taiwanese defensive force in this area. It had been formed six years previously with the express purpose of holding off a Chinese attack on Chi-lung and the invaders would have to fight for every inch of ground in the port city. It would perhaps come down to attrition, like most of China's wars. If so, there could be only one winner. In Arnold Morgan's opinion the Taiwanese would be suing for peace within ten days.

This was Black Wednesday, no doubt. At 0915 a White House agent entered the office of the National Security Chief to inform all four men that the Navy helicopter taking them to Andrews Air Base was on the lawn. From there they were flying up to Cape Cod, landing at the sprawling Otis Air Force Base, then heading on by Navy helicopter to Marblehead, Massachusetts, twenty miles up the north shore from Boston, for the funeral of Lieutenant-Commander Ray Schaeffer. Admiral Morgan himself had insisted the SEAL Team Leader be given, posthumously, the highest possible decoration in the United States Armed Forces, the Medal of Honor. As a SEAL, Ray Schaeffer's award was for many, many services rendered to his country. It would be awarded with no public announcement whatsoever.

In California 3000 miles away, the funeral of US Navy SEAL Charlie Mitchell was also taking place and it would be attended by Admiral John Bergstrom and the Pacific Fleet C-in-C, Admiral Dick Greening. CINCPACFLT had personally recommended the rookie combat SEAL quietly be awarded the Navy Cross.

In Marblehead there was an air of terrible sadness. The Schaeffer family had lived there for generations and Ray's wife, Wendy, with their two little boys, Ray Jr aged nine and Bobby, six, were returning to live in the old family house down by the water, where Ray's widowed father now lived alone. The church was packed, with crowds lining the narrow street outside, and General Scannell read a moving eulogy, regretting that the Lieutenant-Commander's area of operations was classified to such a degree that no one would ever know precisely where he had served and with what 'unfathomable courage' he had carried out his duties. 'I hope', he continued, 'that his Medal of Honor and the presence here of the senior military figures in America will offer some testament to the regard in which he was held in the United States Navy.'

Eight naval officers carried the casket bearing the fallen SEAL to his last resting place and the church bell tolled out over the little seaport as they lowered the body of Ray Schaeffer into the ground. Admiral Arnold Morgan read the final prayer, offering the sentiment that 'ordinary people like ourselves may sometimes find it difficult to understand what drives a man like Lieutenant-Commander Schaeffer forward, to comprehend that selfless gallantry which is bestowed upon so few. I don't suppose Ray would have been able to explain much either. So we will just have to accept that God granted him an inner light and we now wish him farewell, sure in the knowledge that light will guide him home. Amen.'

At the graveside Wendy Schaeffer was erect and brave, with her arm round Ray Jr. But little Bobby wept uncontrollably for his lost father and Admiral Dickson knelt down to comfort him.

The only good news throughout the day was the formation of a Schaeffer family trust, which was begun with a massive $100,000 personal donation from the former Chairman of the Joint Chiefs and Boston banking heir, Admiral Scott Dunsmore. The rest was a catalogue of sorrow and remembrance, and the four military chiefs from Washington took their leave as soon as the burial was over. They were back at the White House by 1630 and it quickly became clear that the flight had done nothing to lessen their fury with the People's Republic of China.

Admiral Morgan had uttered the word 'bastards' about thirty-seven times and it was clear that his mind was made up – China's conquest of Taiwan could not now be prevented, but China – 'Chinese pricks', to quote him more accurately – was going to pay for its crimes. 'We can't make 'em retract or retreat, but we can sure as hell make certain their ambitions go no further offshore than Taiwan.' It was also clear that the Admiral fully intended to drive the Chinese Navy out of the Indian Ocean, all the way back to the South China Sea. 'We already have them out of the Gulf area because they know we'll sink any of their warships which show up there and we'll have overwhelming world opinion with us,' he said. 'The problem on the eastern side, the Bay of Bengal, is likely to be a bit more complicated. But we're gonna have them the hell outta there, and they're not coming back. Okay. They got Taiwan, but they're gonna pay a price for it.'

He yelled, formally, for Kathy to order them some fresh coffee, with cookies, and answered his telephone as it tinkled effeminately on his desk. 'Faggot phones,' he muttered, snatching it up and growling. 'Morgan. Speak. I'm busy. So make it quick.'

Kathy's dulcet voice murmured sweetly, 'Outside desk to home base. Message received about the coffee and cookies. I have one incoming signal, oh rudest of pigs, Admiral George is ready for duty tomorrow.'

'Beautiful,' replied the Admiral and, turning to Tim Scannell without breaking stride, he snapped, 'Fire Borden. Get him the hell out of there. George is coming back.' Then, as if doubting the possibility that his thin pastel-green phone would be man enough to transmit a message, he replaced it and yelled through the door, 'KATHY!' Make sure that coffee's *hot*!'

General Scannell told the Admiral he would indeed arrange to have Admiral Borden transferred to somewhere more amenable with his talents.

'Christ, Tim,' he rasped. 'Don't do that. We can't have someone of his seniority driving the harbor launch.'

The General grinned. 'I'll take care of it,' he said. 'But to return to our subject, you really do intend us to move forward and either destroy or disable that Chinese naval base in Burma and then warn them out of the area?'

'In one, Tim, old buddy, that's our plan.'

'Timing?'

'I think right now. Give the little bastards something to think about while they're strangling Taiwan.'

'Is John Bergstrom up to speed on this, Arnie?'

'As far as he can be. He has the charts, but no decent satellite pictures and he knows we're moving on it. He has a SEAL team in place in Diego Garcia and we got the right SSN available with the biggest ASDV we have. Same one we used to get the guys into the refinery.'

'So this meeting now constitutes the finalization of the attack?'

'Guess so, Alan. We have to start somewhere. So let's get into it – let's hit these commie bastards hard. One for the Schaeffer, right?'

'One for the Schaeffer it is, Arnie.' General Scannell was not smiling.

Admiral Morgan pulled up a big computerized chart on a wide screen at the end of his office. 'Come on over here, guys,' he said, striding forward. 'Let's take a good look at the position.'

The chart showed the vast delta area between the port of Rangoon and the coastal mouth of the Bassein river, 125 miles to the west. This is the fabulous rice bowl of Burma, intercepted by rivers, streams, canals and tributaries, which irrigate millions of acres of farmland. Through here the mighty 1350–mile–long Irrawaddy river (today it's Ayeyarwady) splits and meanders to the ocean, packed with freshwater fish and monsoon waters, which originated hundreds of miles to the north towards the Indian and Chinese borders. It is a sprawling, wet, tidal basin, with great promontories of land jutting out between the estuaries of nine rivers, all of which flow into the hot, steamy corner of the Bay of Bengal known as the Gulf of Martaban. The agricultural produce from here feeds much of the nation and much of China too. The endless paddy fields are interrupted by mango swamps and the occasional monsoon forest, but this land is f-l-a-t.

Admiral Morgan frowned and pointed his ruler at the far left section of the chart. 'This last wide stretch of water right here', he said, 'is the Bassein river delta. It's the widest of the south-flowing waters in this area and you'll see that this island, the long triangle here, on the left-hand side of the estuary, is called Haing Gyi. You will also notice that the goddamned place sits in about six inches of water, which is a pretty fucking crazy area to build a naval base, even if you happen to be a Chinese prick.'

General Scannell came very close to blowing his coffee clean down his nose, so unexpected was Arnold's swift turn of phrase. But he moved in closer and observed the wide area of green swamp, which stretched all the way along the northern shoreline of Haing Gyi, almost joining it to the Arakan peninsula. 'Well, we ain't going in that way,' he said unnecessarily. 'What about this light-blue area which stretches right across the southern approach?'

'Oh, it's much better in there,' said the Admiral sardonically. 'There is a maximum of nine feet shelving to about nine inches and, on the face of it, gentlemen, we have to assume the Chinese are nuts.' But his face relaxed and he continued, 'But nuts they ain't. This is a very strategic corner of the ocean. As we have discussed before, warships from here have the capability of controlling the Malacca Strait. If I pull up this chart a bit, get us in closer, you'll see what the little bastards are up to. Right here, in this central stretch of the island's east coast, we got water, see? More than forty feet right up to the shore and it stretches out here into what looks like a natural but narrow channel, all the way up from the mouth of the estuary, minimum depth forty feet, maximum fifty-five feet.

'However, if you follow it down here, about four miles, the whole damn place goes shallow again. So if you're trying to get in from the ocean you got a ten-mile stretch with only twenty feet of water. Which you'd think would be impossible. Here we got a deepish water throughway into deepish water jetties. You cannot, though, get a big ship in there. But I know they can, because I happen to have located on a very poor photograph a Chinese Kilo Class submarine right in there, moored alongside. And that little bastard draws thirty-five feet on the surface. They didn't carry the sucker in, did they?'

'Probably not,' replied Admiral Dickson with mock seriousness.

'What they've done is dredged a channel, which does not appear on any Navy charts,' said Arnold. 'What's more, it isn't going to appear on any because they're not about to allow anyone in there. There's been a major building program by the Chinese on that eastern shore and they have a very neat little situation – a fully equipped naval dockyard, in an area where there are very few other facilities for overhauling a ship or even refueling. They got it all to themselves and they're going to be an even bigger pain in the ass than usual if we do not, gentlemen, get 'em the fuck out of there ASAP.'

'What do you use for power?' asked the CNO.

'I'm not absolutely certain, but Lieutenant Ramshawe's on the case. I appreciate the question. That island is in a remote place and it's difficult to see what they are using. But the area is well lit and plainly operational. It's possible they are using the reactor of a nuclear submarine, but we can't find it and the water is not deep enough for it to hide. Ramshawe thinks they have a major power plant, but we can't yet tell the source. Anyway, when we do, I think we should destroy it. Gentlemen, we have to get them outta there.'

'Do you think China has a major single objective in all of this, Arnie?' Bob MacPherson looked pensive.

'I think it's pure expansion, Bob. For so many years they've restricted themselves to their own area of the world, which ought to be big enough for anyone. But they increasingly see themselves as powerful global players.

They are envious of us and consider themselves our equals. They covet our influence, our allies and, above all, our muscle. But what they really covet is the world's oil supplies. Because as China gets rich, it's going to require more and more fuel, and most of that fuel is in the Middle East and south-central Asia. Of course, there's a ton of it in Siberia, but that means negotiating with Russia, which is not about to trade away one of its very few natural resources.

'Which brings us back to the Malacca Strait, the single great throughway of all oil to the Far East. If we allow China to dominate the Malacca, we give them the power to force some tankers right round Indonesia and that's going to cost the Japanese a vast amount of money. All their fuel costs will rocket upwards, natural gas, propane, jet fuel and gasoline. The key to China's domination of that Strait is their new base in Burma. Without it, they're damn nearly helpless, because they simply live too far away. Gentlemen, right now we have world opinion on our side. We can force them out of the Bassein river delta and no one would support any of their claims of US bullying. That's what we're going to do.'

'Anyway, who's to know what happened if the SEALs pull it off?' asked the CNO.

'China will know, because we'll fucking tell 'em. But they have made the mistake of striking the first blow against the West with that minefield in Hormuz, then literally conquering Taiwan. Everyone knows they deserve whatever the hell's coming to them. My guess is that if we hit Haing Gyi, the ole Chinks are going to go real quiet for several years.'

'But how the hell do we get in there to hit it?' asked Bob MacPherson. 'And since we're going to tell them what we've done, what's wrong with just bombing the sonofabitch?'

305

'The USA does not bomb people, without a drastic and just reason,' replied Admiral Morgan. 'However, we may justify an attack on China's Indian Ocean east base. It is no more than a power play. The superpower bangs the pretender into his rightful place: second place. But it's so much better that the guy with the busted nose is the only one aware of who's whacked him. That way it goes quiet. Some accident, on some remote island, off the Bay of Bengal. That's the way to run the world these days. Keep it quiet, keep it tight, but make it count.'

'Well, you were right about the refinery in Hormuz,' said Admiral Dickson. 'We've heard nothing from China by way of complaint.'

'That's because they know,' said Admiral Morgan. 'They know and they understand. Quite honestly, I don't think they care. Their objective was Taiwan and they were prepared to pay the price for it. I doubt they'll ever bother to rebuild that refinery. But in the next several months you're gonna see the start of a trans-Sino pipeline, all the way from Kazakhstan to their eastern seaboard. It's the Chinese way. They'll build the world's longest ditch, containing the world's longest pipe, like they built the world's longest brick wall and the world's greatest dam at Three Gorges. They have the labor and they're not afraid to use it. A lot of it, one suspects, slave labor.'

'Meanwhile,' said Admiral Dickson, 'how the hell are we going to get the guys into Haing Gyi and what are they going to do when they get there?'

'First question, how to get in.' Admiral Morgan moved closer to the chart, zooming back a little to show the water depths out in the Bay. 'That's a problem. You can all see the fifty-meter line out here, fifteen miles from the central seaway into the estuary. I'm not completely crazy about this chart, but they have the fifty-meter line well defined. It follows the coastline very accurately, all the way down from the narrow border with Bangladesh. Anywhere you look it's showing depths of around 165 feet to the left and 120 feet to the right. So we gotta assume it's more or less correct. Hence our submarine is going to have to make a rendezvous point somewhere on that line, where she can still hide in 150 feet of water.

'But that's up to the SEALs and to *Shark*'s CO. More important is the insertion of the troops. I've given it a lot of thought, because that ASDV is so damned slow. Fifteen miles is a long way at six knots and that only gets us into the mouth of the estuary. It's another ten up to the deeper water off Haing Gyi. That's a total running time of more than four hours and it leaves us with the ASDV in a pretty vulnerable spot. My conclusion, therefore, is that we bring the guys into the estuary, which will take two and a half hours, then creep up the new channel as far as Rocky Point, here on the southern-eastern headland of the island, and let 'em swim in. We then have the ASDV return to the *Shark*.'

'Leaving the guys alone in there?'

'For a short while. Because I think we have to get 'em out with fast rigid inflatables. The possibility of pursuit by the Chinese is high and they may have fast patrol boats out searching. If they locate the ASDV crawling through the mud, in a channel less than forty feet deep, with nowhere to maneuver right or left, we could be light one boatload of very precious guys and that would not be good.'

'You mean we set up a rendezvous point somewhere along the island beaches?' asked General Scannell. 'Then get 'em out fast, running all the way back to the submarine at high speed on the surface?'

'No alternative. ASDV in, for maximum stealth, when we're not expected. Top-speed run out, when the Chinese Navy is searching around in the dark, but may not catch us. Those fast inflatables make twenty-five knots.

307

The guys will obviously get a good start, maybe fifteen minutes, and that way they have a real shot no one's gonna locate 'em.'

'Okay, Arnie. Sounds good, so long as they don't get caught in the base. We got a contingency to rescue if the crap hits the fan while they're still working?'

'No, Alan. No, I'm afraid we don't.'

'Nothing?'

'How can we? We wouldn't know if they were in trouble. The only thing we can do is have an accurate rendezvous point on the island, with fast boats waiting to evacuate. The ASDV cannot fight and the submarine is too far away.'

'Jesus, that's a tough call for the guys. Who's in charge?' asked Tim Scannell.

'Commander Rick Hunter.'

'That makes me feel better. But it's still tough. I hate to send the guys in with no back-up.'

'So do I. But they will be armed to the teeth and very thoroughly prepared. Chinese guards wouldn't have a prayer against them if push came to shove.'

'They didn't have one against Ray Schaeffer either,' replied Admiral Dickson. 'But shit happens.'

The four men were thoughtful for a few moments. As they contemplated the horror of discovery while the SEALs were ashore, plying their devastating craft, the door swung open and Kathy O'Brien came in bearing a brown envelope addressed personally to Admiral Arnold Morgan, delivered by hand from Fort Meade to the White House.

'Just a moment,' said the Admiral. 'This might be just what we need. If it is, it should have been here two hours ago. But if Borden's taken my advice the newest observations are gonna be real thorough.'

And thorough they were. Fort Meade had apparently

solved the mystery of the power source of the sprawling naval complex on Haing Gyi Island.

REPORT ON HAING GYI ISLAND POWER SOURCE

Comprehensive overheads have revealed no external power sources or supplies to Haing Gyi base. This includes possibilities of the use of a generating ship or nuclear power plant.

Power supplies for operation of the base facilities all appear to emanate from a single large building in the center of the base.

Detailed examination of the foundation area of this building, in particular its size and scope beyond the building itself, suggest a possible geothermal source of power. This is confirmed as entirely consistent with local geophysical characteristics, supported by the known existence of mud volcanoes within fifteen miles of the Haing Gyi facility.

An attachment is a full engineering statement of how geothermal energy is tapped. It indicates its vulnerability and opportunities for disruption/accident.

Arnold mumbled about another cup of coffee and asked his three colleagues to 'hold everything' while he skipped through the notes on geothermal power. Bob MacPherson poured and Arnold yelled 'KATHY!' once again, and asked the goddess of the West Wing to have three copies made of the photograph of Haing Gyi. Three minutes later the Admiral looked up, complained that his coffee was half cold and told his guests that the principal mission of the SEAL attack on the Chinese base would be to destroy a power station, and with it the entire electronic network that runs from it. There would also be some other naval hardware which had to go, but basically they were knocking out a major power supply, which would shut down the base entirely.

The four colour photocopies arrived and were duly studied by Admiral Dickson, General Scannell and Bob MacPherson.

Admiral Morgan pointed out the building in the center and asked if anyone knew how a geothermal power station worked. No one did. 'Well, what you're always looking at is an area where heavy rainfall has filtered through the earth's surface for millions of years and right here we have such an area. It's sandy in a lot of places and it gets a lot of sudden fierce rain from the monsoons in a very flat basin, where it can hang around and filter through. Here we have an area with volcanic activity, where the earth's plates can prise apart, shifting way below the surface, forming giant hollow caverns thousands of feet deep. Now in these caverns we get huge underground lakes and the bottom is so deep the water becomes colossally hot from the earth's core. If you drill down in exactly the right place, you hit one of these lakes and the compressed, boiling water flashes off into steam. If you let it, it will blast 3000 feet into the air, in a clean, clear, white plume of steam. The Nevada Desert is the big steam-well area in the USA. Some of 'em light half of San Diego and occasionally Las Vegas.'

He paused to let everyone absorb what he was saying. 'Right,' he went on. 'Got that? Now look at the picture. See that building? Well, here's how it got there. The Chinese geologists located the steam lake and capped the drill hole. Then they dug deep and poured a solid concrete foundation, probably fifty yards by fifty yards by fifty yards deep. Clean down the middle of this they sank their main shaft into the vast cavern which contains the lake. They capped it with a massive valve at the top, right on the concrete, and then they built their power-generating station all around it on that big concrete cube. They installed the electric turbines to run on steam power and when they completed their electronic grid for the whole dockyard they opened the valve. The steam surged straight up the shaft in the middle of the fifty-yard cube, into the system, and began to rotate the turbines. The clever little Chinks thus had virtually free, endless electric power for years to come. It sounds complicated but it's not really. It's just a kinda upside-down dam with the force coming upwards from the earth, rather than downwards from released water. One thing about electric turbines: the only thing you have to do is turn 'em.'

'And our guys have somehow to get in there and blow it up?' asked the General.

'I think that would do very nicely,' replied the Admiral, 'because that would shut down the base indefinitely.'

'Is John Bergstrom on side?' asked the CNO.

'He is. They're consulting their main demolition guys and I have to get this stuff to Coronado right away. Then two main SEAL explosives officers will leave immediately for Diego Garcia to brief Commander Hunter and his team.'

'Do we have any handle on how well this place is guarded?'

'Fort Meade's been watching it carefully for some weeks and there is some security. But not overwhelming. Haing Gyi is in such a strange, inaccessible place. It's literally surrounded by Burma, whom the Chinese have been financing. It looks to me as if they have not even considered the possibility of an attack on the base. But of course it is a military installation, and there will be patrol boats and guard patrols on the jetties. But we have not found any sign of patrols in the interior of the base. Just some activity close to the visiting ships. The trick is to get in there nice and quiet. Then cause absolute havoc and get out while everyone's trying to find out what's going on. It nearly always works. Surprise. You can't beat surprise.'

'Meanwhile, where's the SEAL team?'

'They're all in Diego Garcia, waiting. The refinery team are all there too, waiting to fly back to Coronado. They made it back from Hormuz in one of the carriers. The *Shark*'s in there too, waiting to embark the SEALs for the coast of Burma.'

All four men took a break from the charts to watch the CNN evening news and the lead item was more or less what Admiral Morgan had expected. The Chinese were fighting fiercely for the port of Chi-lung and according to the news had swiftly secured the actual dockyard area with a team of Special Forces, which had overpowered the mainly civilian security guards. Most of this information had leaked out through merchant ships' radios via Hong Kong.

But the rest of the picture was very blurred. The Chinese had breached the wire fences and now controlled the container docking areas, but the surrounding town was still very much Taiwanese. The local garrison was well equipped and was backed up by continuing air strikes from a remote strip in Hsinchu County. The Chinese assault force thus found itself badly bogged down, sustaining heavy casualties out on the Yehliu Road, four miles from the town. The Taiwanese had somehow managed to conserve eight of their most modern ground-attack aircraft. Armed with cluster bombs and cannon, the Taiwanese pilots came in groups of four from the south, constantly harassing the great mass of Chinese troops, tracked vehicles and artillery moving ponderously towards Chi-lung.

CNN had found access to satellite photographs which showed a mass of fire out along the western approaches to the seaport and, in some ways, the Chinese were in a very difficult position. They had a Special Force in control of the port area, but it could not hold out for ever and the advancing army from Chinsan was at a standstill. The Taiwanese had found the range with a battery of cruise missiles, which were currently smashing up the entire road system from the west. They had forty M–48X medium tanks on that side of the town, arranged defensively, and the Chinese commanders knew beyond doubt they were in a serious fight for this seaport and they were not winning it. The problem was they had to win it. Otherwise this local war might drag on for weeks. The Chinese needed heavy reinforcements. They needed possibly 300,000 men on the island of Taiwan in order to secure it, and they could not land that many without capturing a major container port and bringing in major transport ships which could land men in their thousands. They needed the jetties, they needed the docking facilities. They needed Chi-lung.

Out on the Yehlui Road things were going from bad to worse. The Chinese army was having constant problems with its surface to-air missiles, and after sixteen hours of sustained attack from Taiwan's brave fighter pilots they had hit only one and had themselves sustained hundreds of casualties. It was impossible to evacuate them all back to the beach-head and their hospital capacity on the long sands was negligible. The fact was, China had to take Chi-lung, not just to give them a proper inbound port for her massed armies, but to give her a proper mechanized base for supplies of both food and ammunition, treatment of the wounded and communications. At present they had no base on the island of Taiwan.

Admiral Morgan stared at the screen, trying to read between the lines. He was a military officer attempting to picture the scene in his mind, as were General Scannell and Admiral Dickson. It was the CNO who spoke first. 'They don't get ahold of that goddamned seaport in the next two days, they could find themselves in serious trouble,' he muttered.

'Think they might switch the attack altogether, maybe go south to Kaohsiung?' asked Bob MacPherson. 'That's as big as Chi-lung.'

'I wouldn't have thought so,' replied Admiral Dickson. 'According to our information, the bulk of the Taiwanese army is trapped in the south, can't get back north. But that army is probably in pretty good shape, mainly because they're kinda stranded, with nothing to fight. By the look of this the Chinese are determined to win the battle in the north and right now they're in some trouble.'

'They are that,' interjected Arnold Morgan. 'They got a foothold in the container port and another in the museum, which is what this war is at least partially about. But they have to consolidate and that does not seem to be happening.'

'You know what their real problem is?' said General Scannell thoughtfully. 'They are bound and determined *not* to knock down Taipei. You take that option away from an invading army, you cut its balls right off. You render them unable to use the ultimate force. If they rolled up their sleeves and began a bombardment of the capital city, flattening major buildings, destroying the downtown area, Taiwan would surrender inside an hour. It's not like the London blitz, or Berlin. It's different. More like a civil war. Faced with imminent death, or normal life under an ultimately benevolent ruler on the mainland, there's only one answer for Taiwan. Until China gets prepared to slam Taipei she's gonna be fighting a half-assed conflict against a very proud enemy. That's gonna cost them a lot of guys.'

'Not that they care about that,' said Arnold Morgan. 'But I'm with you. They have to *take* Taiwan by force of arms, with an army occupying it mile by mile. Until Taiwan formally surrenders.'

'And the longer they take to get their asses in gear at Chi-lung,' said the CNO, 'the worse it's gonna get. In my opinion, they'd be better to knock down Chi-lung to save Taipei.'

'They might at that,' added General Scannell. 'But one thing's for sure. They can't stay long as they are now.'

The second item on the news was a lot more serious. The conflict in Taiwan had again sent the world oil markets into a complete frenzy. The prospect of a war that the United States might be drawn into always does. And here was the CNN newscaster reporting another chronic rise in the price per barrel. Brent Crude was up $10, back to $64, having subsided from its peak of $72 as the Pondicherrys did their work in the Strait of Hormuz. But Americans in the Midwest were paying $4 a gallon at the pumps, and Texaco was intimating this could go to $5 in the weeks ahead, while the world's VLCCs struggled to replenish supplies. Now the latest 'spin' being placed on the news of China's war with Taiwan was frightening the markets all over again. What if the Chinese somehow seized control of the Malacca Strait? What would happen to Japan if the price of their fuel doubled again? They were still the world's second-largest economy and they needed fuel for everything. What price would they pay to survive? Where would this put the West?

Essentially this was a newsroom's dream, free rein to terrify the populace, ratchet up the ratings and look wise. There were frowns, set fair beneath perfectly coiffed hair-styles and pieces. There were expressions of deep concern and superior learning from men who had zero first-hand experience of politics, the military or the world's financial markets, save as onlookers. 'The question is, where is this all going to end?' said one of the network men. 'And what is the US government planning to do about it? That's what's concerning every American here tonight.' He said

315

it as if he had just plumbed the very depths of Socrates.

'What a total asshole,' observed Arnold Morgan.

Nonetheless, the oil crisis remained exactly that. The situation in Taiwan was out of control. Admiral Morgan knew only one thing – the US had to get China out of the Bay of Bengal. The US Navy had to lead the way in freeing up the oil routes both to the east and to the west. He stood up and walked over to the window, staring out into the darkness. He mused to himself in the silence of his profound intellect: *Whichever way you look at it, the financial fate of the modern industrial world lies in the hands of a dozen US Navy SEALs and may God go with 'em.*

1100 Saturday, June 2.
US Navy Base, Diego Garcia.
Commander Donald Reid had temporarily handed over the wardroom in the recently arrived USS *Shark* to his XO, Lieutenant-Commander Dan Headley, and the Team Leader of SEAL Assault Force Two, Commander Rick Hunter. The two lifelong friends, reunited somewhat surprisingly in this remote US outpost in the Indian Ocean, had not yet progressed to their principal business. Far from the steamy Bassein river delta, their talk centered on a cool, sunlit afternoon in Maryland two weeks previously, on Saturday, May 20, when a big gray colt named White Rajah had won the Preakness Stakes by four lengths, over nine and a half furlongs, the second leg of the American Triple Crown.

White Rajah, bred in Kentucky by Rick Hunter's father, Bart, raised from a foal under the supervision of Dan's father, Bobby, thus joined the immortals who had thundered to victory in the 134-year-old Classic: Man O'War won this, so did his son War Admiral. Then there was Whirlaway, Assault, Count Fleet, Citation and Native Dancer. Bold Ruler and his peerless son Secretariat, the greatest of all twentieth-century stallions, Northern Dancer, the Triple Crown winners Affirmed and Seattle Slew. They all won in Maryland. White Rajah would retire to stud with a book value approaching $8 million. Breeders would line up to send mares to him at $50,000 each. According to Rick there was a chance he would begin his new career at Hunter Valley Farms, the land of his forefathers, that of his vicious grandpa, Red Rajah, who had once nearly bitten off the young Dan Headley's arm.

'Been in touch with your dad?' asked the XO.

'Oh, sure. We fixed up some kind of a computer hook-up a few days ago. I watched the race on one of the screens.'

'Hey, Ricky, that must have been really exciting.'

'Sure was. Even though I knew the colt had won. Christ! You should have seen him, heading into the last turn at Laurel Park. You now how damn tight it is. And it was a big field, bunched right up, the Rajah stuck in the middle. But they fanned out like always on that track and there he was, two on his inside, three on his outside, holding his place, waiting for the split. Jorge hit him once and he dug in. Deep in the stretch he hit the front and at the eighth pole he was clear, drew right off. Beat 'em four lengths. No bullshit.'

'Fantastic, Ricky. Just fantastic. How 'bout the Belmont Stakes? They gonna let him take his chance in New York next week?'

'Dad says not. None of that family went twelve furlongs and they think he only just saw it out at Churchill Downs. They don't want to get him beat over a distance too far for him. I think they'll put him away for the Travers at Saratoga and if he wins take a shot at the Breeders' Cup Classic. But they're not gonna run him a yard over ten.'

'Yeah. Sounds right. The family really throws milers.

But how come the owners don't want to keep him and send him to stand at Claiborne?'

'Well, Dad's put in a big offer and of course he knows the bloodline. They been raising those big fiery bastards for years at Hunter Valley. I think the Rajah's trainer thinks he'd be better among people who knew him as a foal. Guys who're aware of the family's tricky temperament. If he comes to Hunter Valley, the owners will probably hang on to four shares.'

'Guess so and I guess my own daddy's gonna end up in charge of him.'

'No doubt of that and that's gonna be real good news for you. If we get him, Bart's giving your dad a breeding right to him. He told me.'

'One pop?'

'Hell no. Every year. First classic winner we've bred since 1980 and your dad gets to share the wealth. The Rajah hits in the breeding shed, your retirement is buttoned up safe.'

'Shit, Ricky. We gonna end up drinking cold beers in the Blue Grass, singing the music and raising the yearlings.'

'Nah, not us. We got bigger things to do. That's an ole man's game. You and me gonna run the goddamned United States Navy.'

'Well, if we are, we better get this next sonofabitch right or we might both end up dead. Specially you.' Dan Headley looked pensive. He stood up and asked the steward for more coffee. 'Have you looked at this mess?' he asked the SEAL boss. 'According to the chart, there's no way in except on a fucking jet-ski.'

Rick Hunter chuckled. He'd spent a lot of his life chuckling with, or at, the son of his father's right-hand man. As kids, Danny had always been the funnier one of the inseparable pair and, when they were old enough to sustain an interest in girls, it had usually been Danny who had attracted them most. Until they realized the potential of one day becoming the chatelaine of Hunter Valley Farms. 'Seriously, Dan, I can't see how we can make it in there on the surface, straight up the middle of the channel. They'll surely have a patrol boat and there's not enough water to bring even the ASDV in submerged.'

'I got a few notes right here, Ricky. Apparently there's an unmarked channel in there, maybe forty feet deep, enough water to get a diesel–electric submarine into the jetties.'

'You mean right in the center of the tidal stream? Jesus, that's only about as wide as the home stretch at Laurel Park.'

'Guess so.'

'I don't need a submarine. Be better off on White Rajah. He knows how to stay straight.'

'Well, at least you're not gonna be driving. Last time you and I tried to stay straight in the middle of the night you hit a telegraph pole in your dad's truck and knocked out half the lights in Bourbon County.'

'Yeah,' said Rick. 'But I was only eighteen years old.'

'Nonetheless, old buddy, your legend lives on. No one's achieved anything like that with that particular pole since Arthur Hancock hit it in the middle of the night back in the 1960s.'

'Keep pretty good company, don't I? The great Arthur Hancock and the future Admiral Rick Hunter. You want someone to put your lights out, you can't do a whole lot better than us.'

'Well, I hope someone's put 'em all out when you get into this Bassein river. You get caught, Chinese sailors slice off balls of aging Kentucky hardboot. First gelded SEAL reporting for duty, yes, sir.'

'Shut up, Dan, for Christ's sake. You're making me nervous.'

319

'Okay. No more jokes. Let's have another look at that chart. Now, see this mark here, this is where your boss Admiral Bergstrom suggests we make the rendezvous point. We got 160 feet of water and we can put *Shark* under the surface with room to spare. That's 16.00N 94.01E, about twelve miles off the Burmese coast west-sou'west of Cape Negrais. We launch the ASDV right there and steer one-two-zero straight into the mouth of the delta. It's all of sixteen miles and it's going to take two hours and a half. That's where it gets tricky, because you have to find the damn channel. We know it's there, because we know they got a submarine in there. But we do not know where the hell it is, so we got a real issue and a big question: does it run north or south of this little island here . . . what's it called? Thamihla Kyun. There's a little deep water to the south, maybe sixty feet plus. But your men in Coronado think they dredged straight across this narrow shoal. It's easier to drag silt out of the shallows. Your guys think the channel's right in there, see? By this fifty-foot trench north-west of Thamihla.'

Commander Hunter stared at the chart. 'Okay, but what if they're wrong? We'll just plow the ASDV straight into the bottom and we might never get it out. How are we supposed to do this?'

'Very, very slowly, my lad. Using your sonar, sounding the bottom, carefully checking the surface picture whenever you dare. See this mark here? That's a red can, flashing light every two seconds. I want you to take a visual on the periscope. The guys think you'll pick up the main entry channel less than a mile east of the can. That's where you alter course. Speed three knots, steer three-five-zero for 2000 meters and change course at 15.53N 94.16E. At this point you are going to be in patrolled waters and you're gonna be awful careful, hear me?'

'Yes, sir, Danny. Jeez, you really know this submarine

crap, right? I can see why your boss handed the insertion over to you.'

'Nearly. I had to ask him. I just didn't want you going in there briefed by anyone except me. Kinda surprising how easy he agreed, though.'

'Guess he recognizes a young master.'

'Guess so. Just keep paying attention to what I'm telling you. We got another hour before lunch. Then the first formal briefing of your guys starts at 1500. I'm sitting in on it, so don't fuck it up. Don't want to have to keep correcting you. So listen.'

'How 'bout you listen for a minute, shithead?'

Dan chuckled at the sobriquet, an ageless boyhood term of endearment. But Rick Hunter continued seriously, 'What happens if we do bump the bottom and we can't find the goddamned channel? What then?'

'Look, I realize you've been rolling around in the dirt throttling guards, killing terrorists and blowing things up all your life. But what I'm going to show you requires careful thought. Now look here. This deep trench is very important because it's a haven for a small submarine, moving through waters which are plainly too shallow to allow it free passage. You want to get a channel into this main lane, which your guys have marked here, you want first to get into the stretch where you don't have to dredge. Got it?'

'Got it.'

'Right. Now there are two ways into the trench. The long way, across here, maybe two and a half miles, dredging all the way, in water only fifteen feet deep. That'll take months. Or, alternatively, you could take this three-mile detour, west of the island, in deeper water, and that way you only need to cut a channel 300 yards long max and you're in the trench. What do you think?'

'I'll take the 300-yard cut any time, any day.'

'That's what our oceanographers think the Chinese Navy will have done. Therefore your driver will take the ASDV round through the deeper water and we think he'll find the hole straight into the trench. When the water settles at, say, fifty feet, you guys go to PD and you'll see the flashing light about a mile up in front. At which point you're headed straight for the channel and that'll take you in to where you wanna be.'

'What happens if some bastard's coming the other way down this narrow ditch?'

'Edge hard to starboard. Drop down to the bottom and sit in the mud, act like a recently drowned pig. Whatever it is will go right by. If you hear anything, just die very quiet on the bottom. Gently.'

'You keep saying "quiet" and "gentle". You suggesting I'm some kind of a gorilla, young Danny?'

'Not really, but you're the Leader and you got a lot more in common with a gorilla than a sea wraith.'

'Well, anyway. I'm not driving.'

'Thank Christ. But what I was going to mention was the utter unlikelihood of your meeting another ship. I mean the latest satellite picture shows only two warships in there, plus a submarine, with two or three patrol boats running around some of the time. We have no pictures of any boats running around after midnight at any time. Personally I think you will find the channel easily and you will make your landing with no trouble. After that, you're in charge. But my guys will get you out, Rick. On that you can trust me. That's a promise.'

'Who's driving the ASDV?'

'The best man in the Navy. He's a specialist. You might even know him. He's Lieutenant Mills and he can maneuver that little ship anywhere. He's calm, expert and very instinctive about danger. Better yet, he's done it before and you could not be in safer hands. He'll get you in and, if there's trouble, he won't get caught. You can't ask for more than that.'

'Yes, I can.'

'What?'

'Just for you and me to be sipping a coupla cold beers on my daddy's side porch, listening to the music, watching the mares and foals moving across the paddocks in the evening. Instead of raising hell in some Chinese dockyard.'

'Yeah, doesn't that sound great right now? Guess it's because we're just around the corner from real danger. But it's too late to think of our own world. It's too late. We're in someone else's world big time and we gotta make it happen.'

Two hours later Commander Rick Hunter stood before the team which would shortly embark for the eastern end of the Indian Ocean. They had taken over a brightly lit, concrete-walled ops room, with a five-foot-wide computer screen placed at the side of a long trestle table. The eleven SEALs who would accompany the Commander into Burmese waters were seated casually along the other side of the table with notepads and pens. Each man was issued with a map of the delta of the Bassein river, plus various views, shot from the satellites, of the Chinese base itself. Everyone had a blow-up of the geothermal power station which sat almost in the center of the dockyard complex.

Behind the SEALs sat the additional, but critical, personnel: the CO, Lieutenant-Commander Dan Headley who would take USS *Shark* in and supervise their escape; Lieutenant David Mills who would drive the ASDV inshore; Lieutenant Matt Longo from Cincinnati, the ASDV navigator; and Commander Rusty Bennett, who would not join the mission but whose guidance would be greatly appreciated. At their back the steel door was shut and locked. Two naval guards remained on duty immediately outside, with four more patrolling the area beyond the main door to the otherwise deserted building. No one, including the C-in-C of the Fleet, was permitted to enter. Even to exit the ops room, each SEAL needed to have his notepad personally signed by the Team Leader. No one was permitted a phone call. There was absolutely no further contact with the outside world. Nor would there be until they were back in USS *Shark* at the conclusion of the mission. They were scheduled to sail at 2200 tonight, Saturday, June 2.

Commander Hunter immediately introduced his second-in-command, twenty-eight-year-old Lieutenant Dallas MacPherson, a wide-shouldered Southerner from South Carolina, who had started life at the Citadel, the state's near legendary military academy, but switched after only a couple of semesters to the naval academy at Annapolis. He rose rapidly in dark blue, making Lieutenant in double-quick time, and serving as a gunner and missile officer in an Airleigh-Burke destroyer before the age of twenty-five. This was good, but not good enough for the restless Dallas, who suddenly, to the surprise of his colleagues, requested a transfer to the US Navy SEALs.

He crashed through the BUD/S course, finishing in third place, complaining he'd probably 'been stitched up' – most SEALs are happy to pass through in the first thirty. Throughout his short, but meteoric career people had been more or less divided on whether he would end up in Admiral Bergstrom's chair, or in a box with a posthumous Medal of Honor. He was tough as hell, brave as a lion and smarter than almost everyone. But there was a daredevil in his soul and that might either save the lives of an entire squadron, or alternatively get them into terminal trouble. Commander Hunter was in no doubt. Lieutenant MacPherson was reputed to be the most brilliant young explosives expert on the base, a progressive naval scientist on the subject of demolition in all its forms. Rick Hunter would take Lieutenant MacPherson any day, on the strength of his swiftness of thought. When he appointed him he had said, 'Dallas, where we're going the only thing that's gonna keep us alive is brains. Keep using 'em and we'll make it out.'

In fact, Lieutenant MacPherson's father was a distant cousin of the veteran Secretary for Defense, Robert MacPherson, and when news of this had seeped through various wardrooms, one senior commanding officer had remarked playfully, 'Well, young Dallas, you can't beat a few family connections in the military to insure you advance your career.'

'Sure can't, sir,' replied the twenty-two-year-old midshipman. 'I taught that Bob MacPherson damn near everything he knows.'

Today, in the most secretive room in the most remote American naval base, Dallas was about to undertake an awesome responsibility, not only to accept command of the entire force, should anything befall the Leader, but to ensure personally the total destruction of the geothermal power station on the island of Haing Gyi. Rick Hunter introduced him carefully, as a young officer in whom he had the utmost confidence and from whom they must take orders unquestioningly while working in the Chinese electricity-generating plant.

He then introduced his personal bodyguard, Lieutenant Bobby Allensworth, with whom he had served on another highly classified mission the previous year. He provided no background, certainly not the information that young Bobby had fought his way out of a life of petty crime in south-central Los Angeles and obtained his commission in the US Marine Corps. He said merely that Lieutenant Allensworth would be personally responsible for the safety of the force, particularly if they had to fight their way in, though he hoped this would not be necessary.

Chief Petty Officer Mike Hook, also from Kentucky, a medium-sized supreme athlete and swimmer, was included as the number-two explosives expert on the team. He would be personal assistant to Lieutenant MacPherson during the time setting of the charges, and the guardian of the special bomb they would carry in – the one Dallas said would split the steam shaft assunder, releasing a massive geothermal force, which might very well blow up the entire base.

'How far in the clear do we want to be when that happens?' asked someone.

Before Commander Hunter could reply, 'one hour', Lieutenant MacPherson remarked that he thought back in Coronado would be just perfect. That was the deceptive side of Lieutenant MacPherson's character. He sometimes sounded merely flippant, but the truth was he was always a few strides in front. He knew 'one hour' was correct, but he'd gone past that and was instinctively trying to defuse the tension, to reduce the fear factor, the prospect of the unknown. Some officers think this approach has no value whatsoever. But you still have to be extremely able to do it and Commander Hunter laughed anyway. Only Lieutenant MacPherson understood the perfect timing required to send that armor-piercing, steel-cased bomb thousands of feet down the main steam shaft, to blast the giant well-head valve apart and release the seismic energy from the core of the earth.

'Gentlemen,' said the Commander. 'Details of the in-base mission will be clarified during the three-day journey to the Bay of Bengal. For the moment I intend to show you precisely where we are going, how we land, where we get off and the main drive of our objective.' Briefly he introduced other key members of the team: two SEALs who had also served under his command the previous year in the South China Sea, Riff 'Rattlesnake' Davies and Buster Townsend, the radio operator. Both were from St James's Parish down in Louisiana's Mississippi delta. Both had served in surface warships. He also brought forward the toughest man in the squad, Petty Officer Catfish Jones, an ex-deep-water fisherman from the coast of North Carolina. Catfish, twenty-nine, was a combat veteran of the Kosovo campaign. He had a nineteen-inch neck and forearms of blue-twisted steel. Bobby Allensworth had instructed him in unarmed combat and these two represented the front line of the assault group's heavy muscle if they came face to face with the Chinese inside the Navy base.

For his opening remarks Commander Hunter played down the danger of the mission. 'We are going into a lightly defended Chinese naval base,' he said. 'It's a relatively new facility and we've had it under observation for several weeks. Our Intelligence conclusion is that the owners do not anticipate a serious attack from anyone, which should give us a reasonable chance of accomplishing our mission. That, incidentally, is to take it off the face of the earth as quickly as possible.'

At this point a ripple of disquiet could easily be sensed in the room and the Commander elected to clear up the problem which was on everyone's mind: why are we doing this? 'As most of you know, we are in the middle of a world oil crisis, caused principally by the Chinese. In the judgement of our colleagues in National Security, China has further plans for disruption at the other end of the Indian Ocean. But she can only instigate this disruption by maintaining a major Navy base in the area. This one, at the mouth of the Bassein river, is the sole means by which China can have a catastrophic effect on the free and peaceful flow of the world's oil. Our instructions come direct from the White House. We are to take out that naval base on behalf of the government of the United States of America. The successful achievement of our objective will not only send the Chinese right back to their home waters, where they belong. It will deservedly earn the gratitude of every person in the industrialized world. Although they will not know, of course, to whom they are grateful. But we'll know and that's what matters.'

Everyone in the room nodded approval. Commander Hunter told them that for the purpose of this initial briefing he wished to demonstrate to the entire group precisely where they were going and how they were going to find their way in, in the pitch dark. 'Okay,' he said. 'Look at your own charts and follow my bigger electronic one as we go.' He used a long ruler and pointed it at the rendezvous point where *Shark* would arrive with the entire mission on board. 'Right here,' he said pointing precisely, 'we get into the ASDV, in about 160 feet of water. We then take this route, down towards this little island here, then according to our experts we take this route, to this slightly deeper water. We believe this flashing light on the red can, marked here, will guide us into a newly dredged channel. Then we pick up the main throughway to the island of Haing Gyi where the base is.

'You'll see on your chart that we adjust our course to zero–two–zero and run on up here in the main channel, as far as the next light – it flashes every two seconds. We'll pick that out probably a mile before we get there. Though we have not absolutely finalized our landing spot, we are leaning towards this area – Rocky Point. It's a headland with deep water in front, right up to the beach. Maybe fifteen feet. We can swim in there and it's far enough away from the base to carry no sentries: about one and a quarter miles. We have to walk that, with our equipment, but there's no hills, no swamps and just a tidal river to cross.

We'll take a look when we get there. This looks like a bridge and if it's quiet we'll use it.'

'We coming out the same way, sir?'

'Absolutely not. Because there's no way we can make our business look like some geothermal accident. The Chinese are going to know it's us very early on. The ASDV's too slow and it'll need to turn round as soon as it drops us. So they're bringing in rigid inflatables to get us out fast. The water's very flat this time of the year. We'll be back in the submarine in fifty minutes.'

'How many buildings are we planning to hit?'

'Probably three, but the big one's the power plant. That's our mission critical. We slam that, the base is useless. There are also a couple of Chinese warships in there. We'll take a crack at both of them if we can. Just a couple of stickies.'

'Any idea of the strength of the guard, sir?'

'Well, our guys have counted only about eight men patrolling at any one time. Four on the main jetties and four back here a little, where this destroyer seems to be further inshore. That probably means if we arrive there at around 0100, there'll be eight guards we may have to eliminate before we enter the power plant. If we're quiet we may not see any more for two or three hours, by which time I hope we'll be on our way out. If we do have to fight again, we may have to eliminate eight more. But I am not sure that will be necessary.'

'How about knocking down the guardhouse with everyone in it, maybe at midnight when they probably change over?'

'We thought about that. But it's awful noisy and we're not quite sure where the Chinese keep reinforcements. We don't want a bunch of Chink helicopters chasing around all over the goddamned place. Especially as one of 'em might locate and kill us. Generally speaking, we think stealth is the best way to accomplish our objectives.'

'Okay, sir. No problem.'

'Final refinements will be made throughout our journey, via the satellites. We got a lot of guys working on this and things will develop before we reach the coast of Burma. Broadly speaking, we think the element of surprise will be decisive in our favor.'

'How about the getaway, sir? Can we board the inflatables up close to the base? Like we don't want to end up running through a fucking paddy field for about ten miles pursued by the goddamned coolies, right?'

'Dallas, no, we don't. Neither do we want to look as if we're running boat trips round the fucking harbor in the middle of the night. We'll have that organized in another day or so. My own view is we take the edge of the swamp in the south.'

'But that's a hell of a distance, sir. Do we have any chance of immediate help if we come under fire, or if we are seriously pursued?'

'No, Dallas. I am afraid we do not.'

Ten

0900 Monday, June 4.
Northern Taiwan.
The battle for Chi-lung had now been raging for five days
and, despite heavy casualties, the Chinese began inexor-
ably to win it. They kept coming forward, landing
thousands more men on Chinsan beach, and calling in
more and more air sorties from the mainland. But they left
over 3000 dead along the Yehliu Road before they finally
forced their way into the inner suburbs of the seaport.
Street by street, block by block, yard by yard they fought
their way towards the docks. The Taiwanese defended
with their courage high and they were never really
defeated. Merely engulfed.

Then, as the Chinese army prepared for the one push
that would drive them into the vast container port area,
the Taiwanese pulled off a master stroke. A team of their
Special Forces crossed the railroad out along the
Chungshan-1 Road, swam into the harbor and severed the
mooring lines of two massive container ships, just as the
tide was turning. Thirty minutes later, with these two
gigantic ships slewed beam on across the entrance to the
docking areas, the Taiwanese scuttled them both with high
explosive, partially blocking the main route both into and
out of the harbor. It would take the Chinese Navy three
more days to drag the wreckage clear and make a free
passageway for their big troopships. Scuttling the containers caused a momentous commotion in the docks and

it allowed the Taiwanese army to escape cross-country, dropping back to Taipei, leaving the invaders from the mainland victorious but in something less than good order.

For a start, Chi-lung was a shambles both in the harbor and in the streets. There was debris and rubble everywhere. No one knew how to get anywhere. In addition there were several isolated pockets of local resistance and the Chinese were desperately trying to avoid killing civilians. This was a serious hindrance, since the civilians were well supplied with grenades, rifles and machine-guns. They fought furiously, night and day, to eliminate the invading army, using ancient tactics of snipers and booby traps against unsuspecting troops. Not in living memory had the Chinese armed forces been so extended, engaged in highly complex combined operations not only beyond their own land borders but overseas. This was an adventure with which they had absolutely no previous experience in modern times. Much of their equipment was outdated and unsophisticated, and their military processes and procedures were full of glaring shortcomings.

It all began to take its toll. Some of the Chinese commanders began to believe the only way to capture Taiwan was to knock it down. Everyone knew China's top Special Forces units were trapped in the museum, without supplies. Their helicopter squadrons had been savagely depleted both over the ocean and in the air above northern Taiwan. Attempts to air-drop food into the museum grounds had been met with vicious rocket, shell and missile fire from regrouping Taiwanese anti-aircraft battalions. General administration of those who had been in battle was very poor. No one was being fed on a regular basis, personal equipment was often inadequate and almost all the logistics systems had fallen apart. Lines of combat resupply were crashing. Ammunition, fuel, lubricants, rations and water simply could not be brought in fast enough to keep up with the thousands of troops on the ground.

There was of course scope for the Chinese forces to requisition water and fuel supplies from local sources, even to scavenge food supplies, but this was a hostile area. Everyone was a sworn enemy and it took a huge amount of time and effort just to stay alive and keep moving. Failure to bring forward munitions for armor, artillery, air defense and attack helicopters took another heavy toll. Chinese progress was thus becoming fearfully slow and the morale of the ground troops was beginning to suffer. By midday on this June morning the High Command, now meeting in Beijing, was being informed that the Taiwanese army was again moving north, throwing pontoons across the rivers, heading back to defend their beloved Taipei. Another ferocious fight through city blocks, having to fight around every corner, not knowing what lay ahead, round any corner – this was too much even to contemplate.

Admiral Zhang Yushu knew about warfare in all of its facets, but specialized street combat in a foreign capital, far from home, against a reinforced enemy, was too much even for him. But, wily old warrior that he was, he came up with the only solution there was. He decided their best strategy was to stretch the limits of the remaining Taiwanese resources and at 1300 on that Monday afternoon he ordered the Chinese Navy to open up another front in the south, with immediate effect. More particularly, he ordered a naval bombardment of the northern beaches of Taiwan's banana-belt city of Tainan, followed by a second full-scale amphibious assault at Luerhmen. In Zhang's opinion this would surely stop the headlong rush north of the Taiwanese army.

Luerhmen had precisely the correct historic credentials to attract a strategist of Zhang's abilities, with his curious

333

mixture of grim reality and flights of *folie de grandeur*. A beach-front suburb of Tainan, Luerhmen was where the great Koxinga had landed 400 war junks containing the 35,000-strong Ming dynasty army and hurled the ruling Dutch out of their Tainan stronghold in 1661. So far as Zhang was concerned the ruling Taiwanese were at least as alien as the Dutch and the vibes about the old provincial capital were all good. He turned the full might of his Navy against the south-western city, sending in his second Sovremenny destroyer with three frigates to soften up the area for the forthcoming landing the following day.

His principal mistake was miscalculating the strength of the Taiwanese air force at the naval air base outside Kaohsiung. They still had nineteen F-16As and they had repaired the long-range radar facility on the outskirts of the base. At first light on the morning of Tuesday, June 5, they picked up China's Sovremenny, cruising six miles off Tainan, making a racetrack pattern in a light-quartering sea.

Admiral Feng-Shiang Hu, C-in-C of the Taiwanese Navy, was on duty himself, pacing the ops room, still determined to fight off the marauders from across the Strait. He instantly dispatched a flight of five of his F-16s, the ferocious little single seaters, converted now to carry a 500lb bomb under each wing instead of their usual Sidewinder missiles. They took off overland at 0620, swung out south of the island and made a long right-hand loop over the Strait, coming in from out of the west, fifty miles off the Taiwan coast at 600 knots, wave-top height, in a formation of three and then two, dead astern. The 8000-ton Sovremenny destroyer was silhouetted against the rose-colored eastern sky and her ops room acquired at 0628. The missile director's fingers flew over the keyboard, sending up four SA-N-7 Gadfly weapons into the launchers.

But the CO of the Sovremenny had no real-time battle experience and he spoke swiftly to his accompanying frigate, which had also picked up the incoming Taiwanese fighter-bombers. They conferred briefly and the destroyer captain ordered his ship to make a hard turn to port in order to reduce his radar echo signature to the incoming bombers. In a grotesque, elementary error he offered them the knife-edge of his narrow bow, instead of the broad beam of his ship. Temporarily the radar control operator lost the F-16s altogether when they ducked down below the radar, but at twenty-seven miles they 'popped up' again and the Sovremenny instantly acquired, the operator calling, his voice rising: '*US radar regained. Track one-zero-four-eight. Incoming 600 knots, bearing two-seven-zero, range twenty-five.*'

Higher now above the waves, the Taiwanese pilots heard the Sovremenny's radar locking on, squealing on their radar warning receivers, but they pressed on grimly towards the Sovremenny. Streaking in over the water, making ten miles a minute, a mile every six seconds, the three leaders aimed their aircraft straight at the huge Chinese warship. They spotted it eight miles out and lined themselves up only just in time. Then they unleashed all six of their bombs in a dead line at the bow of the ship, the one non-variant, the one computer calculation which could not significantly change. The machines were fighting the engagement, but it was men who were directing it. The Chinese missile director, in the same split-second, launched the Gadflies which blasted into the air, even as the bombs flashed across the waves propelled by the colossal speed of the aircraft.

The F-16s tried to bank away, but the one on the left took the missile head-on and blew up in a fireball. The center bomber was also hit right behind the wing and exploded as it made its turn, both pilots dying instantly.

The third and fourth missiles both missed and now the bombs were screaming in, bouncing like flat pebbles hurled across the water. The first one smacked into the waves and leapt high over the destroyer's bow. Had it been the beam, it might have cleared the ship and gone right by, but it was not the beam. It was the bow, and the bomb slammed off the water, shrieked over the foredeck and smashed straight through the bridge windows and down deep into the hull before it exploded. The next bomb came in a fraction of a second later, again clearing the bow in a high arc and down through the middle of the super-structure, wrecking the ops room, the communications room and every missile-control system on board. The third bomb cannoned into the water, thirty yards off the bow and slammed into the hull, just aft, crashed through the plates on an upward trajectory and removed a large slice of the foredeck of the ship.

But it was the fourth bomb which did the real damage, albeit entirely accidentally. This one, dropped from beneath the wing of the escaping F-16 out on the right, crashed into a rising wave 100 yards in front of the Sovremenny, deflected left and rose high, 150 feet into the air. It screamed down into the aft area behind the main superstructure, its descent so steep it slammed straight through the deck, into the engine room and detonated with a shattering blast, close enough to the keel to blow the bottom out of the ship. The Sovremenny, listing sharply to port, capsized within three minutes and, ten minutes later, sank with all hands to the bottom of the Strait.

The two Taiwanese back-up bombers, running in four miles astern, were not acquired by the stricken Sovremenny, and they raced past the already burning warship and banked hard left, straight to the frigate which was supposed to be riding shotgun for the bigger ship, but had made no move to fire her missiles.

The ops room of the frigate, distracted by the carnage on the destroyer, finally launched her shorter-range missiles. But it was too late. One malfunctioned and the other blasted off way after the F-16s had launched their four weapons and turned away. Nonetheless, the CO was well trained and he offered the incoming bombs the beam of his ship, as indeed the destroyer should have done. The first one flew harmlessly overhead, the second flew almost harmlessly, but smashed the mast and radar equipment as it came through. The third came in low, crashed through the hull and went straight out the other side, demolishing almost the entire central deck area.

The fourth bomb detonated in the water before it reached the ship and miraculously no one was killed, though two sailors were wounded, mostly by bomb splinters. Equally miraculously, the frigate was still floating; crippled, largely useless, but still floating. Generally speaking, Admiral Feng-Shiang considered it a very good hour's work by the Taiwan Navy fliers, since it was not yet time for breakfast. But one of the downed pilots was his nephew, aged only twenty, and it was fifteen minutes before he could bring himself to face his senior commanders.

Admiral Zhang was furious. The sheer numbers of the bombs which had hit his Russian-built ship meant that plainly there had been a monumental mistake and Zhang Yushu had been in the Navy sufficiently long to believe the most common mistake by Naval commanders in all of modern warfare: the realization that any bomb, hurled forward at low level by an aircraft making over 600 knots, hardly *drops* at all. It is flung forward with enormous force and, when it finally catches a wave, it slows right down, then ricochets upwards, maybe eighty feet, and onwards. Still on line, but high. In Zhang's view, to stay alive in the path of this ship killer you should offer your beam, which will afford a fair chance of the lethal bouncing bomb whizzing over the top, since the deck is only about fifty feet wide. Offer your bow, especially on a ship as large as the Sovremenny, and you present a target the entire length of the ship, 500 feet from bow to stern, ten times more surface area than its width: a 1000 per cent greater chance of being hit and sunk. Admiral Zhang knew the overriding temptation to turn bow-on, presenting a target so narrow it must be safer. But he remained convinced of his theory, since the incoming bomb's line trajectory is pinpoint accurate to about three inches. Zhang's Law on Bombing said the only issue is the *length* of the target, not the width.

Now his Commanding Officer had paid for his error not only with his life, but he had also paid with the lives of his ship's company. Not to mention the $500-million ship itself. '*What a complete and utter . . .*' ranted the Admiral, employing a Chinese colloquialism normally heard on the lower decks of his ships, rather than in the offices of the military's highest command in Beijing. He simply could not believe the price he was paying for the rebel island of Taiwan. He could not believe the manpower, the death rate, the number of lost ships, the destruction of literally dozens of his aircraft, and now the great destroyer.

Zhang Yushu was going to end this war and he was going to end it fast. *If this goes on, the damned US Navy will get here and then there'll be all hell to pay. I cannot allow this to go on. We have to move and move big.*

Meanwhile, the airborne troops were piling out of the transporters high above the drop zone, three miles north-west of Tainan airport, and the Taiwanese army was awaiting them on the ground, raking the landing fields with a steel wall of ordnance. All attacking armies, down the centuries, have sustained far greater losses than the defensive forces. But this was getting right out of hand. It took a succession of air strikes, sustained for more than two hours, finally to clear the Taiwanese army out of the area.

Windspeed for the airborne landings was around fifteen knots and there were heavy Chinese casualties because wounded men were being blown off-course from the central area. The commander on the ground had set up his 'hospital section' way upwind and several troops became involved in bringing the wounded in for emergency treatment. Eventually they would be transported on for evacuation, to the airport, which was of course China's immediate objective.

The opening assault force was late reaching the airport. It was broad daylight, now, and due to a total failure of communications – as usual, Taiwan's weakest link – the Chinese, by some miracle, achieved an element of surprise. They stormed the perimeter fence and swarmed into the runways, capturing entire sections of the complex. They moved 2000 troops into the roads surrounding the airport, securing the area. They dug in and established their portable low-level air defense weapons, principally the QW-1 surface-to-air missile. They blasted their way into the control tower and occupied it. They also secured the fuel farm, and commandeered a vast supply of gasoline and jet aviation fuel. They seized every airport vehicle and sent a task force back to the drop zone to evacuate the wounded paratroopers.

By midday Tainan airport was in Chinese hands, their first major air-head on the island. Within a half-hour, massive troop reinforcements and equipment began to fly in. Almost two complete divisions were on the ground by 1400, and they were accompanied by thirty attack helicopters, checked, refueled and armed, ready for the assault, first on Tainan and then on to the great Taiwanese port of Kaohsiung.

By this time, a division of Marines was attempting to land on the beaches at Luerhmen and scores of landing craft, protected by warships from China's East Sea Fleet, were driving forward into the shallows, only to be met by a strong, well-disciplined force of Taiwanese militia. Again the Chinese commanders on the landing beach had little option but to fight and the two forces met on the main road at Tuchang. The early advantage went to the home troops and they mowed down the invaders, firing at will from rural positions more in tune with guerrilla warfare than a formal confrontation of twenty-first-century armies. With hundreds more troops pouring into the beaches, the Chinese began to crash forward in a major break-out early in the afternoon. They left more than 500 dead on the field, but the remnants of the Taiwanese militia, bombarded now by Chinese mortars and howitzers, were forced to retreat and the newly landed Marines kept moving up, marching on towards the airport to join the massed divisions of the army, which would surely now capture the southern part of the island.

Meantime, back in Beijing, Admiral Zhang Yushu stared in dismay at the reports coming in from the front. He could see there had been a long delay in the attack on the airport, he could read the reports of more heavy casualties, and what seemed like a carnage both in the drop zone and on the Luerhmen beaches. He weighed all this against the crushing loss of the Sovremenny. With fury in his heart, he ordered a total abandonment of the new beach-head at Tainan and instructed his commanders to maximize the air-head at Tainan airport. He also demanded to know the precise position around the city of Taipei.

From here, things almost went into slow motion. Again, on the outskirts of Tainan, the Taiwanese fought heroically. China's huge army was stopped dead, just as it had been on the outskirts of Chi-lung. Again there was bitter fighting, block by block, street by street, as houses, shops and industrial buildings were systematically cleared. But there was a huge price to pay, both in manpower and a colossal expenditure in ammunition.

Simultaneously, in the north the Chinese army had reached the outskirts of Taipei and they too ran into a fight, which would drain their limited resources. Casualties were appalling. The Chinese lost more than 1000 men in the first two hours. The Chinese commander on the ground was in satellite contact with Beijing and Admiral Zhang himself decided that if he had to knock down Taipei in order to subdue the island, then so be it. He ordered his senior battle commanders to take drastic measures, whatever it took to reduce the level of casualties. As things stood, the invading Chinese would need to capture and control the National Taiwan University Hospital in Taipei and certainly the Chengkung University Hospital in Tainan. So China began to send in an armada of Z-9W Dauphin attack helicopters, heavily armed with anti-tank missiles. These 140-knot monsters cruise at 15,000 feet and, with the air-head established at Tainan Airport and the main airport outside Taipei now under Chinese control, they were free to clatter over the Strait, land, refuel and await deployment.

That happened late in the afternoon. The Dauphins took off and swooped into the western approaches to Taipei. They came in low over the Tamsiu river, through sporadic anti-aircraft fire, and slammed four missiles straight through the granite outer wall of the Presidential Building on the corner of the Paoching Road. They hit the Armed Forces Cultural Center, almost blew apart the Tower Record Building and, for good measure, banged a missile into the great Chiang Kai-shek Memorial Hall. That killed eight people but failed to put a dent in the giant white statue of the departed father of the Taiwanese nation. This was the first attack on the city and members

341

of Taiwan's ruling party were petrified, because from where they stood among the crushed masonry and collapsing ceilings in the Presidential Building it seemed as if China had reluctantly decided to knock down the entire capital.

Things seemed even worse far to the south in Tainan where again the Chinese Navy's Dauphin choppers came in hard and sudden, firing their big missiles at will. They slammed the biggest religious temple in east Asia, the Shenmu, flattened the police station, blew up the Department of Motor Vehicles, knocked down an outside wall of the biggest department store in the city. Right behind this apparently indiscriminate air attack the Chinese sent in their hard-trained Marine and airborne forces. In both cities, they moved forward tactically, behind the air attack. The remainder of the Taiwanese forces began to melt away, some throwing down their weapons. Civilians fled the central areas by the thousands, women and children picking their way through the rubble, accompanied by local soldiers who had discarded their uniform jackets.

The Chinese army kept coming, but there was a subtle change taking place. The massed soldiers and Marines of Admiral Zhang's military had no stomach for killing civilians, especially Chinese civilians, which the Taiwanese still plainly were, and the commanders on the ground knew it. The Army marched on to the entrance to the Presidential Building near the Peace Park and blew open the locked main doors with three hand grenades. The guards fled and six minutes later the President of Taiwan, in company with eight of his senior ministers, sued for peace. They came out with their hands high and were greeted with immense respect by their conquerors. The leaders of both sides went formally to the high cabinet room and the national television station was summoned to hear their government command the Army, Navy and Air

Force of Taiwan to lay down their arms and surrender. Communication lines were immediately opened up to Beijing and Admiral Zhang, with his senior commanders, announced they would land at Chang Kai-shek Airport at 1030 the following morning, to agree the terms of surrender.

Thus, shortly before 6 p.m. on the afternoon of Tuesday, June 5, 2007 the independent Republic of China, known internationally as Taiwan, returned to the rule of the 'other China', the People's Republic, the communist successors to Chairman Mao Zedong. It was the ultimate horror, the endless dread of the peace-loving, profit-worshipping populace of the defiant little island across the Strait. And thanks to the guile of the smiling Admiral Zhang Yushu, Taiwan's mighty friends in Washington had been powerless to raise a finger to save them.

Which left Admiral Morgan in his dressing gown, sitting in the book-lined study in Kathy's house in Maryland at 6 a.m., watching the news, sipping black coffee, in a mood which hovered somewhere between disbelief and rank poison. 'Just so long as they don't think for one moment they're going to get away with this,' he growled. 'They got the island. Needless to say they got the museum, which was why they went to war in the first place, and there's not a damn thing we can do about any of it, short of going to war ourselves. But there's a lot of ways to skin a cat and we're gonna make those little bastards regret the day they decided to fuck around with Uncle Sam.'

'Sorry, darling, lay that on me again, will you?' Kathy O'Brien had ghosted into the study, bearing orange juice and hot croissants with preserves.

The Admiral's eyes were still glued to the screen, but he was hungry, having been there, on and off, all night. He said nothing but reached out absent-mindedly for one of

343

the croissants and he let out a yell because it was so hot. 'Jesus Christ!' he cried, adopting one of his favorite mock-wounded expressions. 'What the hell is that? A pastry grenade?'

Kathy, who looked like Julia Roberts with red hair, was wearing a dark-green silk robe and she laughed, as ever, at the speed with which Arnold Morgan could coin original material.

He turned towards her, smiling in appreciation of the lady he loved. 'I shouldn't think this burn's worse than second degree,' he said pompously, shaking both his head and his right hand. 'I shall require ice, cold water, towels and the home number of my lawyer. You did keep your insurance premiums up? I do hope so.'

'You should, of course, have been on the stage rather than wasting your time trying to eliminate Red China,' said Kathy, expertly cleaving the croissant sideways with a serrated knife and spreading it with butter and strawberry jam. 'Here, take this,' she added, offering the plate.

'Well, why the hell didn't the damn thing burn you?' he demanded.

'Probably because I didn't clamp my hand round the hottest part on top,' she replied. 'Heat tends to rise, you know.'

Arnold then firmly informed her that as the former master of a large nuclear reactor on a US Navy attack submarine, he was acquainted with the rudiments of physics, even if he had temporarily forgotten the heat-retentive properties of the common croissant.

She poured him some cold orange juice and advised him to take the greatest care with the glass since he would probably get frostbite.

But Arnold was no longer listening. 'Jesus, Kathy, will you look at that?'

She turned to the screen where the giant US aircraft

carrier *John F. Kennedy* could be seen listing slightly to starboard and moving slowly through the water.

'The accident on board the *JFK* happened two weeks ago in Japanese waters,' the newscaster reported. 'These dramatic pictures show her making under ten knots, limping towards the US base at Okinawa. They were taken by our associate station in the western Pacific region and according to our sources they caught the *JFK* forty-seven miles south of the American base. The US Navy has denied our request to put a camera team on board for the final miles of the journey and they have denied us all requests for an interview to explain precisely what happened. Last night the Navy was showing no signs of any intention to clear up the mystery of what went on out there west of the Ishigaki Islands on the night of May 22.'

Admiral Morgan ate his croissant thoughtfully. Like the Navy, he was of course keenly aware of what had happened. Two Chinese torpedoes, fired from one single Kilo Class submarine, had crippled the 88,000-tonner, which made her the fifth battle group leader to become unavailable for the protection of Taiwan. Counting the *Ronald Reagan* Group, still in San Diego, *Big John* was actually the sixth.

'Maybe it was for the best,' offered Kathy. 'Maybe Taiwan is ultimately better off as a part of mainland China. Maybe the carrier would have been drawn into a real shooting war if she'd been in her regular patrol area. There might have been God knows how many dead and we could have been sucked right into a long conflict.'

'Wrong,' replied Arnold uncharmingly.

'What do you mean, wrong? You're not always right about absolutely everything.'

'Wrong again,' replied Arnold even more uncharmingly.

Kathy poured them both some more coffee and awaited the short, bludgeoning lecture she knew was on its way.

'Katherine,' he said. 'A mighty navy, nuclear weapons and a strike force of devastating guided missiles has nothing to do with inflicting defeat and destruction upon another nation. It has to do with prevention. An all-powerful nation like ourselves has one useful purpose and that's to frighten the life out of anyone who might step out of line.

'That's why this world is mostly at peace. By that I mean there has been no global conflict for years and years. It's *Pax Americana*, as I have often explained. Peace on our terms. If the *JFK* had been on patrol, with its full air force operational at the north end of the Taiwan Strait, China would not have attacked. Because they would not have dared, because we have the capacity to eliminate their ships, their aircraft, their army, their military bases, their naval bases, their goddamned cities, if you like, any time we feel like it. They attacked Taiwan because we were not there to scare 'em off. As we know, to our cost, they made damn sure we were not there. But it would not have happened if we had been.'

'Well, I suppose so. But I still have never understood why the carrier was so far out of its operational area and how the Chinese were somehow lying in wait. I know that's what you think. But I don't really get it. It was almost as if they *lured* the *JKF* into that bay. That's what the media should be trying to find out.'

'The media are probably going to find out that the carrier was hit. But I agree, it's a real puzzle why the carrier was so far out of its area. I look forward to reading Admiral Holt's preliminary report next week. So do a lot of other people.'

061600JUN07. USS Shark *in the Bay of Bengal.*
15.53N 93.35E. Course zero-eight-four.
Speed 15. Depth 100.
The aging black hull of the 5000-ton Sturgeon Class

submarine moved slowly through the warm blue depths of the eastern Indian Ocean. She was just about at the end of her 2000-mile journey from Diego Garcia and she moved to the north-east, about thirty miles short of the great shelving Juanita shoal, where the ocean floor suddenly rises up from 3000 feet to 120 feet, to form a massive, almost sheer underwater mountain wall of rock, shale and sand. Lieutenant Pearson, watching the chart, in constant communication with sonar officer Lieutenant-Commander Josh Gandy, would order *Shark* well south of that particular hazard, while they made their way east to the rendezvous point at 16.00N 94.01E, twelve miles off the coast of Burma.

Lieutenant-Commander Headley, now in sole control of the insertion of the SEALs, deliberately ordered their speed cut to twelve knots, which would put them on station at the RV point at 1800, approximately two hours before dark. For the past four days they had steamed steadily, submerged all the way through the near bottomless waters which surround the southern shores of the Indian sub-continent. It had been the busiest underwater journey Dan Headley could ever remember, with frequent satellite communications, while Fort Meade and the Pentagon battled for information about the Chinese base on Haing Gyi Island.

Lieutenant Shawn Pearson, like many navigators, was an excellent draughtsman and he provided immeasurable assistance to the SEAL commander, making detailed scale drawings of China's newest naval complex. By the third day they had it pretty well nailed down. They had located a tough-looking chain-link fence, which guarded the southern border of the dockyard. They also had located a guardhouse on the southern perimeter. But as far as they could see, the fence ended abruptly at some dense woodland, which protected the north-western perimeter

347

of the dockyard from the most treacherous-looking marshland area where the Letpan stream splits and forms two wide channels. Each one runs straight through the swamp and out into the unnavigable Haing Gyi shoal, which provides only four feet of water in some places at low tide.

The new satellite pictures being beamed into the submarine were grainy and of very moderate quality, but Lieutenant Pearson's sharp pencil drew hard, accurate lines through the chart of the swamp. *Shark* was just about at her halfway point on her journey from Diego Garcia when Commander Rick Hunter had seen for the first time an excellent way out for his team. 'We bolt through these woods at the back of the dockyard,' he told them. 'Until we reach the swamp, right here. According to Shawn's map, that gives us a run of 1300 yards, at which point we're only 100 yards from this deep tidal stream and that's where the guys are gonna be with the inflatables.'

'Christ, sir,' said Catfish. 'You sure there's enough water in there to get the boats running?'

'Shawn says yes,' replied the Commander. 'According to his chart there's 1.3 meters of water at dead low tide. For the truly ignorant that's about four feet and the boats draw less than a foot when they're running.'

'They draw more than that when they're stationary,' said Catfish. 'Those big engines drop down around two feet, more as she starts to come bow up.'

'Catfish, baby,' said Rick, 'there are guys in this submarine who can make those inflatables talk. They raise the engines, skid 'em along the surface, then slowly drop 'em down and whip 'em up on the stump, no sweat. Don't worry about it. Those boats will get us out. I've just never been sure where to bring 'em in. But I am now.'

'Aye, sir,' said Catfish, 'and I agree it's a damn good spot, right round the back of the island. It's got to be deserted. Shawn says he can't find even a track from the pictures.'

'It's probably full of fucking cobras, and creepy crawlies and Christ knows what else,' said Rattlesnake Davies.

'Well, thank God you're gonna be with us,' said Buster Townsend. 'You can do your jungle thing, blow the heads off a few pythons and stuff.'

'Seriously, guys. We're in good shape for a run through country like that,' said Rick. 'We'll be in our wetsuits and black trainers. We'll have our gloves on, carrying just flippers clipped to our belts. We'll have no heavy baggage, because the explosive will be gone and we'll leave the Draegers behind. They weigh 30lbs and we don't need 'em if we're going back on the surface. Speed's everything. We'll have our knives, machine-guns and ammunition. Soon as we're done, we'll pull up our hoods and get going.'

'You worried about that 100 yards of green marked swamp before the channel, sir?'

'Hell, no. It's tidal there so there'll be thick grass and probably rushes, we'll run straight through it, but the guys in the boats are going to be less than 100 yards away and they'll have ropes to help us if we need 'em. Plus, of course, the spare Draegers we brought in case we have to go over the side. We'll get there, don't worry.'

'When's high tide?' asked Dallas MacPherson.

'Right here on your chart,' said Shawn. 'I've marked it 0330. The water should still be rising when you get to the water's edge. That's if your timing stays the same. You make your shore landing before midnight, after the warship operation. Then you have a three-hour shore mission and a half-hour to reach the embarkation point at 0330. That's correct, isn't it?'

'If there's a real chance of that fucking steam well going up,' said Dallas, 'I'm likely to break the Burmese all-comers record down to that swamp. I'll probably be there at about 0301.'

All the SEAL meetings were like that, informal but completely relevant in every aspect. Each man was free to offer any opinion, or ask any question. Then, when the mission was under way, every man knew not only what he was going to do, he knew precisely what everyone else was going to do as well. Commander Reid had allocated a section of the submarine for the SEAL team to meet and it turned into a kind of locker room, a place where the Leader lectured the guys, pored over the charts, discussed the mission, perfected the split-second timing that would spell success or failure. For the first two days of the journey from Diego Garcia the problems were academic, but as the voyage wore on there was a strange, underlying tension right below the surface. Everyone could feel it, particularly Lieutenant-Commander Dan Headley and his old buddy Commander Rick Hunter.

Everyone knew it all traced back to the night of May 16, out in the Strait of Hormuz when *Shark*'s commanding officer had refused permission for the ship to move in towards the ASDV and evacuate the SEAL team, with their dead leader and dying explosives expert. Then Charlie Mitchell had died before he could receive help and every single member of the big group from Coronado believed that Commander Reid had personally signed the young SEAL's death warrant. Commander Rusty Bennett, mission chief of the team which went into Iran, was extremely angry and felt that the entire tragic incident should be taken to the highest possible authority. He and Commander Hunter had spent much time on it when Assault Team One finally returned to DG, and Lieutenant-Commander Headley was more worried than either of them, because he had made the decision to save the SEALs at all costs and been overruled by his own CO.

350

Dan Headley was unused to being overruled. Indeed, he had been informed that this single appointment as Executive Officer to the Sturgeon Class ship was because of an unspoken concern about the mindset of the Captain.

Both the SEAL Leaders and the XO felt they could not count on the CO to make the right decision if the combat troops came under serious threat. It was always possible that a fast unorthodox rescue might be required and no one believed they would receive the correct degree of support from the Captain. Reid had delegated all details of the insertion to Lieutenant-Commander Headley, cautioning him only about hazarding the submarine. Any deviation from the strict agreed orders of position and timing would almost certainly be met by a rigid adherence to the rules by the CO. The XO had seen it and he was extremely concerned.

Rick Hunter, briefed by Rusty Bennett before he left by air for Coronado, was making a conscious effort not to let it play on his mind. 'Danny,' he said, 'I'm trying to get my mind straight. I'm trying to lead these guys in to accomplish an unbelievably difficult objective. I cannot allow the possible conduct of this nutcase CO to occupy my thoughts. It'll get in the way of the real stuff. I just haven't the time.'

But then, two nights previously, an incident had taken place which had truly unnerved Dan Headley and the only colleague he had confided in was Rick Hunter. It had started a half-hour before the Captain's normal appearance in the control room around 2000. He had asked the XO to come to his office/cabin to confirm their ETA at the rendezvous point off Burma. Entering the room, Dan had been quite startled to find it lit by just a single candle, in a holder on the table. 'Hello, sir,' he had said cheerfully. 'Bit dark in here, isn't it?'

The Captain's reply had been, in Dan's view, pretty weird. 'XO,' he had said, 'sometimes I feel the need for some spiritual guidance and I am usually able to find it in communication with a fellow traveler.'

Dan Headley had looked quizzical. But the CO had not wanted to elaborate and the number two officer in USS *Shark* did not feel like pressing the matter further. He returned to the control room, gathered up his partially completed plans for the insertion and decided to take them down for Commander Reid to peruse for a few minutes before moving up for his watch. But when he arrived outside the CO's room, the door had been slightly open and he could not help but hear the voice of the ship's boss talking inside to someone. But the stilted quality of the language was most unusual. 'Gregory, I am trying to reach you again. I feel you very close but someone stands between us. I think an American officer. Please tell him to go, Gregory. Then we can communicate as we did before. Captain Li Chin, I believe we must talk before I am forced to follow you, wherever that may lead.'

Dan Headley did not know who was in the room with Commander Reid and he was not absolutely certain of the words he had heard. He was pretty sure about Gregory, but there was no Gregory aboard *Shark* as far as he knew and if there was he would have been called Greg. Forget Gregory. Still, maybe he was just on the line to someone. God knows who. But *Captain Li Chin*. What the hell was all that about? *Li Chin*, thought Dan Headley. *That's a fucking Chinaman*! For a brief moment he actually wondered if the CO of *Shark* was some kind of a spy, maybe in touch with an agent. But then he thought, *Steady, Dan, he can't be a spy. He's been a career naval officer for thirty years, commanding nuclear submarines for ten. He's an oddball, no doubt about that. But he can't be a spy*.

At this point he doubted whether he had heard the

conversation correctly. He was dead sure of the Gregory name, but the more he pondered, the more he doubted the part about Captain Li Chin. Nonetheless, he had not felt much like making an embarrassing entry carrying the plans for the SEAL insertion and had tiptoed quietly away, back up to the control room. There he had sat thoughtfully for at least fifteen minutes, running over the conversation he had heard and carefully committing it to his notebook, in the manner of a lifelong naval officer, as if insuring an accurate entry in the ship's log. The notes may have been made calmly, but Dan's thoughts were anything but calm. They were racing: *What about the bit about the American officer standing between them? Commander Reid and frigging Li Chin. What about the bit about the communications? Communications with a Chinese naval captain? Holy Shit! What the hell is going on?*

Lieutenant-Commander Headley doubted his ability to solve the puzzle. But he was determined to take a look around that cabin of Reid's and he waited until the CO came into the control room. After formally handing over the ship to the OOD, he said, 'Oh, sir. Those insertion plans. I just had a couple of details to fill in. You're busy now, but I'll put 'em on the table in your cabin if you like. Then you can take a look when you have a bit of time.'

'Thank you, XO. That will be fine.'

Dan Headley headed once more down to the CO's room and pushed open the door. The desk light was already on and the little portrait of Admiral Pierre de Villeneuve stared out across the small room. Dan put the plans on the desk and kept a ballpoint pen in his hand in case he was disturbed. There was a small bookshelf to the left of the Captain's chair and Dan leaned over to inspect the half-dozen volumes it contained.

There was a travelogue about the South of France, a biography of de Villeneuve and an account of the Battle of the Chesapeake. A book called *The Stress of Battle and Trauma* stood next to the *Oxford Companion to Ships and the Sea*. There was also something called *Edgar Cayce on Reincarnation* by Noel Langley. Dan picked this one up and glanced at the blank sheets inside the jacket. In pencil there were the following words, *Another life, another battle, so many mistakes in* Bucentaure. *I must never repeat them now that I have another chance. June 1980. DKR.*

Dan Headley frowned. He could not risk hanging around for long. Quickly he skipped through the pages of the volume on reincarnation, then pulled out the Oxford companion. On instinct he flicked through alphabetically to page 883, which gave an account of de Villeneuve's highest/lowest moment, Trafalgar. He ran his finger over the French Fleet's line of battle. *Here it is*, Bucentaure, *the flagship . . . struck its colors. Fuck me! This crazy prick I work for thinks he's the reincarnation of de Villeneuve, one of the stupidest battle commanders in naval history.*

Dan Headley put the books back. He still had no clues to the identity of the mysterious Chinese Captain Li Chin. Nor, indeed, to 'Gregory'. He glanced down to the writing pad on Commander Reid's desk and could see only a small sketch of a submarine. Beside it was the name Lieutenant–Commander Schaeffer and through the name were two hard diagonal lines forming a cross, as if to eliminate the name of the late SEAL Team Leader.

Dan shook his head and left, in a hurry. *Do I give a shit who he thinks he is? Does it matter? A lot of people believe in reincarnation, right? I just don't know how seriously people take this stuff. It would be a lot better if he thought he was General MacArthur, or Admiral Nimitz, even Admiral Nelson. But de Villeneuve? Jesus. He's even got his picture on the wall and the guy was a catastrophe. Do we have a real problem here?* The XO made his way up to the wardroom, poured himself some coffee and sat alone in a corner seat, thinking. *What do I really know about the CO? Have I actually seen him make decisions of really momentous bad judgement?*

Dan thought some more and decided that he had twice seen him make decisions that went absolutely by the book. Rigid. Unswerving adherence to the rules and regulations: the kind of adherence submarine commanders consistently ignored. The nature of the underwater beast means you have to be flexible and everyone knew it. Holding hard to the rule book was okay in a peacetime surface ship. But it was often not okay in a combat submarine. *Do we have a problem here? Yes. I think we do. Because Commander Reid twice deliberately made an operation less successful when we plainly needed to make a change in our orders. He caused unnecessary battery-running time in the ASDV for the insertion into Iran. And he may have cost us the life of one of Rusty Bennett's best combat SEALs. He certainly refused to save that life. Two decisions. Two mistakes. Both important. We got a problem.*

Commander Reid was not the only one with a problem on this ship. Lieutenant-Commander Headley had one too, because there was no member of the crew in whom he could confide. It was simply unthinkable for a senior US Navy executive officer to mention to a colleague – who must, by definition, be of a lower rank – that he, the Exec, considered their Commanding Officer had lost his marbles. He also thought it was not anything he could bother Ricky with, since the mighty SEAL Commander was trying to prepare his team for the big push into the Chinese Navy base. *Oh, by the way, the officer in overall command of your only escape route is probably insane.* 'Holy Shit,' breathed Dan Headley.

He contemplated the prospect of dinner. But he wasn't hungry and he walked back to the area of the wardroom aft of the dining-room table, where they kept a small library for officers and, in fact, for anyone of the crew who requested a book on a particular subject. *Shark*, like most US Navy submarines, was a literary democracy.

Dan had no idea what he was looking for. What writings might shed a light on a Commanding Officer who once, certainly in 1980, believed he was the reincarnation of someone else? Anyway, did it matter? Dan himself had once read that General George Patton had believed himself a major-league warrior in another life and wasn't there some story that the General claimed to have known the precise spot where Caesar had pitched his tent when he arrived in Langes, France, to assume his first command? *Maybe it's not that bad*, he thought. *Not that bad at all. However, I wouldn't give a shit if Reid thought he was Alexander the Great, or even Napoleon, but* de Villeneuve*! I mean, Christ, that's beyond belief for a Navy officer. 'I used to be the world's worst battle commander and from now on I'm playing it dead safe, right by the book.' That's what I think we've got here. Except this fucking nutter might be in cahoots with the Chinese.*

The XO scanned along the bookshelves until he reached the section on psychology, a complicated subject for men who command warships and an increasing concern in the modern Navy. He stopped at a volume entitled *Post-Traumatic Stress Disorder. I suppose it's possible that this character has adopted the kind of symptoms he believes de Villeneuve may have developed after Admiral Nelson took out twenty of his fleet at Trafalgar. The most decisive sea battle ever fought. Maybe Commander Reid feels he is supposed to suffer the French Admiral's pain for him. Steady, Headley, you're getting crazier than he is.*

He opened the book, and paused at one of the earliest sections of the textbook formula – 'The Effects of Having Survived a Frightening Traumatic Event'. The subhead read, 'Armed Combat, Shell-Shock, Battle Fatigue'. It was fully twenty seconds before he realized the block of type had been pointed up with a yellow highlighting pen. The next part was not highlighted, but it contained such lines as, 'Reliving the painful memories, images and emotions, i.e. intense fear, horror, helplessness, as if it were happening'. 'Recurring nightmares'. 'Trying to erase the memories'. 'Intense emotional stress in the face of events, present, future, or even imagined, which may resemble any part of the traumatic event'. 'Sudden emotional outbursts', the author wrote, 'anger, fear or panic, may occur, for no apparent reason, as the person tries to avoid thinking or talking about the trauma which haunts him.'

What exactly is this? Some kind of damned conspiracy? Well, you've picked the wrong man to make a fool of, waiting until I'm asleep and then flagrantly disobeying my orders. These were the words of Commander Reid, uttered in temper, without logic, without concern and without reason. Dan Headley pictured that scene in the control room last month, as the SEALs tried to fight their way back from their mission. Was it actually possible that their own CO, as he addressed them, was hearing not just the quiet hum of *Shark*'s turbines as she made her turn in the silence of the dark waters of the Gulf? Was he actually hearing the crash and thunder of British cannon, as Nelson and Collingwood came in quite slowly, in a light quartering wind, hammering both the French and Spanish fleets to a standstill? Two hundred years ago, the morning of October 21, 1805? Was that actually possible?

Lieutenant-Commander Headley shook his head, skimmed the rest of the chapter, but every few moments phrases jumped right out at him – 'avoiding responsibility, isolation, symptoms increasing with age, guilt feelings for the deaths of others'. 'And through it all,' the author write, 'the person may still appear a strong and capable leader. Only those who serve closely with such a man can see the sudden moments of utterly illogical behavior, so often anger, or an obdurate adherence to the rule book, all to camouflage self-doubt.' For good measure, the author added that in his view, real-life trauma was no different from imagined trauma in the mind of such a personality.

Dan Headley liked it less now than he had ten minutes ago. There was a final section on military officers who believed themselves to have been commanders in past centuries. But it was not written in a sinister way. Indeed, the author believed the association with long-past greatness might have given certain men inspiration, even knowledge into the conduct of a battle. But Dan noted that the author did not go into any detail of a commanding officer who thought he had been a catastrophic, world-renowned failure in a past life, had committed suicide and, in his own handwriting, believed he now had a chance to make amends by eliminating mistakes.

One thing he knew for absolute certain. He needed Rick Hunter and he needed him right now. He did not even finish his coffee. Dan stood up and set off down to the SEALs' locker room in search of his oldest friend. He knew the Commander was pretty good with the minds of fractious racehorses and he hoped he could make the species jump, straight into the unbalanced psyche of certain human beings.

He located him at a good time. It was almost 2100 and the SEAL boss had been briefing his team for hours, poring over the new pictures of the Chinese base. When Dan Headley had come wandering into the conference area, aft of the control room, he had stood up and said, 'Okay, guys. That's it. Go get food and rest. Lieutenant-Commander Headley and I are about to solve the problem of the Belmont Stakes. Which horse stays one and a half miles? That's the key. Because most modern racehorses won't last out twelve furlongs in a horsebox, never mind running. We come to any definitive conclusions, I'll let you know who to bet on.'

'No mistakes now, sir. We don't want any screw-ups, right?' called Lieutenant MacPherson.

Commander Hunter and the XO thus returned quietly to the wardroom and asked the steward to bring them some dinner: 'Coupla steaks, green vegetables and salad,' said the SEAL.

'You eating them both?' said Dan. 'Or can I have one?'

'For your information, I no longer have the appetite I had at eighteen,' replied Rick. 'Specially when I'm confined to this ship. No fresh air, no exercise, no physical activity except the communal set of weights we're all using to try to stay more or less ready to hit the Chinese.'

'Okay, Ricky. But I came to find you on a matter of great concern.'

'You did? What?'

'Well, I'm assuming that you know the details of the altercation that took place in the control room of this ship when Rusty Bennett and I tried to take her inshore to save the badly wounded SEAL?'

'Doesn't everyone know the details? Even the staff in Diego Garcia have no other subject to discuss.'

'They're probably correct, too. Because I think we have a major concern here.'

'You mean he might make another foul-up like that?'

'I mean, I think it's inevitable he *will* make another foul-up like that.'

'Why?'

'Because I think that right here we are dealing with a dangerously flawed personality.'

'You do?'

'Yes. I do. That's why I need to talk with you.'

For the next twenty minutes the XO regaled the SEAL Team Leader with the evidence he had found that

359

Commander Reid believed he was the reincarnation of the French Admiral Pierre de Villeneuve, the seagoing doormat of the Battle of Trafalgar.

'Well, everyone in the Navy knows about Trafalgar and the disastrous command of the French fleet, Dan. We all learned it at Annapolis.'

'Right. When you get into it, the performance of de Villeneuve is really shocking.'

'Wasn't he some kind of a coward? I forget the details.'

'Ricky, this guy was terrified of Admiral Nelson. He spent most of 1805 trying to get away from him. Napoleon had him under threat of suspension if he didn't get his act together. Right before the battle he ducked back into the port of Cadiz, trying to hide. When he finally came out, he literally froze with fear. Nelson and Collingwood split the French line right near the Flag, and the French ships took terrible broadsides from the Royal Navy. Admiral Nelson fell at 1315 and never really saw his sensational victory. De Villeneuve was merely taken prisoner after his ship surrendered.'

Commander Rick Hunter nodded quietly. 'You mean our CO actually thinks he is de Villeneuve?'

'Yup. That's what he believes. I just showed you my note of what he wrote in the book. *So many mistakes in* Bucentaure. *I must never repeat them now that I have another chance.*'

'Well, maybe he won't,' mused Rick Hunter.

'Shithead, you're not hearing me. I am saying that in his mind this guy is suffering from the trauma of what happened out there off the coast of Portugal in 1805. He believes he is responsible. The stress of the battle is in his mind and he is exhibiting classic symptoms of that kind of behavior. I've just been reading about it. Trust me, it fits.'

'Okay. It fits. But he doesn't do it all the time, does he?'

''Course not. They never do. Just sometimes, when

events seem to be getting too big, or out of hand, or there is clear and present danger. Or everyone is watching him, willing him to make a major decision. That's when this kind of stress-damaged character can't cope. Because in his mind he hears again the thunder of a past war, and he is consumed with self-pity and it gives him a feeling of superiority because he knows no one else is going through what he's going through. No one else understands the tragedy of a great naval commander, which is why he feels free to shout and lay down the law in that self-righteous way. That's where it all came from, Rick. The words are like cast concrete in my mind: *But, sir, we're just trying to conduct a mission of mercy for our own injured people.* And what did he reply? *What exactly is this? Some kind of damned conspiracy? Well, you've picked the wrong man to make a fool of.*'

'Hm,' said Rick Hunter. 'Where we're going, he may have to make a few more major decisions before we're all a lot older.'

'And that's not all.'

Rick Hunter looked at his old friend questioningly. Dan told him of the conversation he had overheard in Commander Reid's cabin. He read over to him, verbatim, what he had written down about Gregory and Captain Li Chin.

'That makes no sense, does it?' said the SEAL.

'Not to us maybe, but it might do for the CO.'

'What are those names again? Gregory and Captain Li Chin?'

'Yup. That's exactly what I heard, or thought I heard.'

'You don't think there was anyone in there with him?'

'No. I do not. It's just that I never heard of anyone with either of those two names.'

'Well. Let's try and piece them together. Say it all at once. How about Captain Gregory Leechin?'

'That's not right. He said *Ly*chin, same sound as in whopper.'

'Or bullshit.'

They both laughed. But Rick pressed on. 'Okay. But you cannot be called Gregory Li Chin. Because that's a very American name, coupled with a Chinese one, which would be very unusual. Gregory is a long name and it sounds very definite. It's not like Ronnie or Tommy. You sometimes get Chinese people called that. I think you heard Gregory right, but I think you might have Li Chin wrong.'

'I might have. But the CO did call him captain. I'm not wrong about that.'

'Well, maybe he was talking to a guy who had trouble with the truth. Maybe he was Liar-chin?'

'You know, Ricky, that sounds really familiar to me. Liarchin. Do we know someone called Liarchin? Captain Gregory Liarchin. Someone maybe famous. Liarchin. That's got a real ring to it.'

'You're right. Who the hell was Captain Liarchin?'

'Dunno. But it sure does sound familiar. How about Gregory? How about Gri-gory like eastern European? How about Captain Gri-*gory* Liarchin?'

'Tell you what, we need to hit the ship's library, conduct a quick search through recent Navy records. There's a good reference section.'

'Someone down there will do it for us, I guess. I don't want the CO to see us down there.'

'Haven't you got a buddy who'll do it quietly?'

'Yeah. The navigator Shawn Pearson will get it done. I'm outta here, back in five minutes and don't eat my fucking steak.'

The XO was back in a few minutes. 'Shawn's going to have a look himself. I told him to fool with the spelling. Grigory Liarchin, or with a 'y', like Lyachin. Something foreign, right?'

'You got it. There's your steak, which you will doubt-less note I did not eat.'

The two officers settled in to their dinner, trying not to speak too much about the submarine's CO. Occasionally a new officer came through the door, but no one stayed more than a few minutes. There must have been urgent vibes being given off by the XO and the SEAL Chief, because no one seemed interested in engaging them in conversation.

It was twenty-five minutes before Lieutenant Shawn Pearson came in bearing a sheet of paper. He handed it to Lieutenant-Commander Dan Headley who read the following four lines of type: *Captain Grigory Lyachin, Commanding Officer of Russia's 14,000-ton nuclear submarine* Kursk, *which sank with all hands in the Barents Sea, sixty miles north of Severomorsk, on Monday, August 14, 2000.*

Dan Headley whistled softly through his teeth. 'Jesus Christ,' he breathed and he silently handed the sheet of paper to Commander Hunter.

'I knew that name was familiar.'

'Sure was. But do you realize what this means, Rick? Our CO thought he was talking to Captain Grigory Lyachin. He thought he was in communication with a guy who's been dead for almost seven years. I'm telling you, he was chatting away like we are now.'

'If I'm reading this correctly, Danny, it's a lot worse than that.'

'How do you mean?'

'What do Admiral de Villeneuve and Captain Lyachin have in common? They both presided over major naval catastrophes and that's what our CO identifies with. He thinks he *is* de Villeneuve and he thinks he has something in common with the Russian submariner. I imagine he's been trying to talk with him for years.'

'The way he was speaking, they're old buddies.'

'Yeah,' said Rick. 'In his dreams.'

'Well, do you think this has sinister connotations for us and the people who work under his command?'

'Normally, I'd say maybe not. A lot of people are spiritualists, trying to get in touch with people "on the other side". Doesn't necessarily make 'em crazy and certainly not dangerous. I mean, there's institutes of learning for spiritualists all over the place. A lot of very clever people think there can be communication between the living and the dead. Who the hell are we to say there's not?'

'I know. But it's not just any old dead we're dealing with here. We're dealing with a couple of guys who have suffered traumatic catastrophe and my immediate boss, who is about to be charged with the execution of one of the most dangerous Special Forces insert-and-rescue missions ever mounted, *thinks* he's one of them and wants to have a chat with the other. It's like your bank manager thinks he's jumped out of a high-rise window eighty years ago, in the crash of 1929 and now he's desperate to get in touch with another suicidal bankrupt bank president before he invests all your money.'

'Well, Danny, you always did have a way with words. But this time I don't like 'em much. What the hell can we do? We can't just lay it on him. He'd have us both court-martialed for causing riot and unrest in the ship.'

'I'd sure as hell rather that than have *him* court-martialed for causing everyone's death in the face of the enemy.'

'I know. And you think this problem he has manifests itself when there's some form of pressure being exerted on him?'

'No doubt in my mind. I've seen it twice.' Lieutenant-Commander Headley went on very slowly, very deliberately, 'Ricky, this is a guy I could guarantee will fold up completely if something goes wrong, or if we had to throw the rule book overboard and play a very bad situation by ear. You know, if we really had to wing it. Which is always possible in missions like this one coming up.'

Those had been virtually the last words the two men had spoken on the distressing subject, because there really was nothing more for them to say. They were both trained to say nothing about naval operations unless it was absolutely necessary. They finished their dinner in near silence.

That entire private investigation of the CO by the XO and the SEAL boss had taken place two nights previously on Monday, June 4. Since then they had both tried to cast it to the back of their minds.

Now it was Wednesday, June 6 and the guys were going in tonight. They were actually going in less than two hours from right now. USS *Shark* came nosing up to her rendezvous point, with her cargo of SEALS making final preparations for the launch of the ASDV. Commander Hunter had everyone ready. They were sitting in shorts and T-shirts only, but their faces were blackened with waterproof combat cream, and the atmosphere was tight as they checked over their wetsuits and flippers, personal weapons and underwater breathing equipment.

They all listened to the monologue of Lieutenant Dallas MacPherson, as he checked the explosive list against the hardware. He seemed to be wisecracking his way through it, like always. 'One velly big bang right here, blow off many Chinese borrocks.' But Dallas wasn't joking. He was coping; coping with the pressure the best way he could, steadying his nerves, fighting down the icy fear they all felt as they prepared to board the ASDV.

Every now and then, one of the younger SEALs

reached out and just touched the shoulder of the man next to him, maybe ruffled his hair, punched him lightly on the arm. It was a technique Commander Hunter had taught them – *Don't go quiet. Don't let it wash over you, or you'll get overwhelmed before you start. Stay in close communication with each other. Remember, in this outfit we don't* send *anyone anywhere. We all go together.*

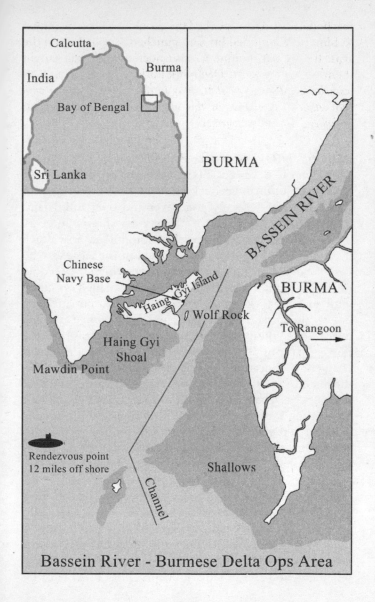

Bassein River - Burmese Delta Ops Area

Eleven

061830JUN07. USS Shark, *Bay of Bengal.*
16.00N 94.01E. Speed 2. Racetrack pattern. PD.
This was Commander Rick Hunter's final briefing of his
team. They had already gone over and over the details,
infinitesimally, back and forth, every measurement, every
millisecond of time, every piece of equipment, how much
it weighed, where it would be stored in the ASDV, who
would carry it in. They knew the point where they would
breach the outer fence, knew it was too high to climb
with their stuff, knew they would have to cut it. They
knew the precise yardage along the fence to the
guardhouse, the precise distance, to the inch, up to the
power station. They knew the timing of the guard
changes; the location of the lights. They knew there was
the likelihood of a bright moon; they knew the terrain, its
firmness, its chances of being muddy. They knew the
doors they must go through and they knew the precise
location of the massive main shaft down to the geothermal
core. They also knew there was a probability of having to
kill to survive.

Now the SEAL Team Leader was painting with a much
broader brush. Each man had a small Navy chart in front
of him and a small, detailed scale map of the Chinese naval
complex. Each man was marking up both sheets, strictly as
they applied to him and the part he would play in the
attack. Each man had already completed his last will and
testament, and a short letter home to either his wife or his

parents, in case he did not survive. The wills were all secured in one of the submarine's safes.

Rick Hunter stood before his team looking much as they did but bigger – face blackened, wearing his wetsuit and black trainers. A larger-scale Navy chart of the area was pinned to a board behind him and he was gesturing with a ruler at the critical points of the mission, talking the SEALs through the timing. 'Okay, we leave here at 1700, proceeding to this point on your chart just off Thamihla Island. That's a distance of fifteen miles and it's going to take us two and a half hours. From there we expect to find the deep-water channel right here and we head on up to this can with the flashing light, okay? We then move up here for four more miles to this buoy with the flasher, right at the start of the natural deep-water channel leading into the base. We'll see it easily. Now that's quite clear, is it?'

The SEALs all nodded affirmative and Rick carried on. 'At this point, a half-mile off the jetties, we exit the ASDV, Catfish, Mike, Buster and myself. We carry in four sticky limpets and place them on the underside of the hulls of the two Chinese warships which are moored alongside – there's a 6000-ton Luhai Class destroyer right here on the photograph. It's 500 feet long and fifty-four feet wide, twin shafts, and a lot of guided missiles and torpedoes. Right next to it is a much smaller ship, a 2000-ton Jiangwei II frigate, only 360 feet long. But it's fast and it carries a lot of anti-submarine mortars. Gentlemen, I assure you it's in our best interests to get rid of it very thoroughly. Both these ships carry helicopters and it would be nice somehow to have them tip into the harbor.'

'Sir, I forgot to clarify. Are you guys getting back in the ASDV to go to our next stop? Or do we just meet up there?'

'No, we're getting back in. The insert wants to be in a

much more lonely place and it's too far back down the channel. We're hitchin' a ride.'

Commander Hunter then confirmed the landing site, a point less than one mile south of the jetties, behind a half-mile-long navigational hazard marked on the chart as Wolf Rock. 'We'll all get out there, about 500 yards offshore, 150 of those yards are marked as a marshy area with a lot of vegetation. We'll walk through there and when we hit the beach we're gonna be only a half-mile from the dockyard fence. It's gonna be dark, desolate and without military guards. The first place we meet people will be the guardhouse and there's only two people in it – one engineer and one Navy patrol guard. That's all. You know what to do.'

From that point on Commander Hunter talked quickly through the well-documented plan. Everyone knew it off by heart. This was just a brief refresher before departure, one final look at the campaign map. One final look, perhaps, into the face of death. They were frightened, as Special Forces must always be a little frightened. But no one flinched.

At 1855 the SEALS began to embark the ASDV, climbing up through *Shark*'s dry hatch, into the mini-submarine itself, which rested in one of the round twin deck shelters up on the casing. For the present it was dry in there and as each SEAL entered the tiny electric underwater craft he checked the precise location of the gear he would personally carry in.

Lieutenant Dave Mills was already at the controls, seated next to his sonar operator/navigator, Lieutenant Matt Longo, whose task it was to locate the secret Chinese channel into the harbour. One by one the SEALs moved into position, the five rookies from Coronado, then the veteran combat SEALs Catfish, Bobby, Rattlesnake, Buster and Chief Petty Officer Mike Hook, followed by

Lieutenant MacPherson, who slipped expertly up through the gap and took his place next to Bobby Allensworth.

Last of all came Commander Rick Hunter who was talking to Dan Headley in the small area below the dry hatch. 'Guess this is it, ole buddy,' said the huge SEAL Leader. 'Don't forget your promise. You're gonna get us out of there no matter what.'

'We'll get you out. The boats are coming in to RV Two one hour before you need them. They'll be transmitting every thirty seconds as from 0245. Two single beeps on your frequency. Good luck, Ricky. It's gonna be fine, but for Christ's sake be careful.'

They shook hands, formally, unsmiling; nodded curtly one to another and parted, Lieutenant-Commander Headley going back to the control room, the SEAL chief climbing into the little submarine.

Immediately the hatches were closed tight and clipped. Rick Hunter's team all heard the sudden rush of water as the departure crew outside flooded down the shelter. They could hear the metallic thuds in the water beyond the hull as the ASDV came free of its steel lines. Six hefty frogmen began to heave it forward on its tracks, away from the mother ship. They waited for ten minutes, riding free in the water, for the deck shelter to close and for the outside crew to rejoin the *Shark*. Then they saw Lieutenant Mills switch on the electric motor and the ASDV swung right, on to its course one-two-zero, creeping now at its maximum speed of six knots towards the tiny Burmese island of Thamihla and the deep-water channel they hoped to God they would find. If they did not find it, they knew they would have to postpone until someone did, because these orders came from on high. Really *high*. Most of the SEALs preferred to get this thing done right now.

Inside the ASDV it was dry, but as they traveled it grew colder. There was no heat in this vehicle, but the SEALs were warm in their superbly insulated Navy wetsuits. They could talk if they wished, but water magnifies all sound and SEALs are trained to say nothing unnecessary on a combat mission. Thus there was hardly a word spoken for the first two hours – not since Lieutenant MacPherson had mentioned, as they flooded down the shelter, that he usually charged a lot of money for his 'world-famous imitation of a fucking goldfish'.

Journeys in an ASDV seem to take for ever. They travel blind, instruments only, and the passengers can see nothing. The submarine is dark, except for the light cast from the orange-colored screens on the control panels. The highly trained assault troops were left with nothing to do except think ahead to their tasks on this night. Sometimes a couple of particular friends, like Bobby and Mike Hook, would catch each other's eye and perhaps smile. But it signified only that each was aware of the other's thoughts, the colossal dangers they were facing and the possibility that one of them, or perhaps even both, might not make it back. SEALs only *think* such private thoughts. They never say them.

The miniature submarine pressed on forward, forty feet below the surface all the way. After two hours and fifteen minutes they slid up to PD and Dave Mills sent up the mast. Seven seconds later they went back down to twenty-five feet and Matt Longo said quietly, 'We're getting into the area, guys. I got us at 15.51N and 94.15E on GPS. Right now I'm searching for the channel.'

The SEALs knew precisely where they were. Hours of study had committed the chart indelibly to their memories. They were in only thirty-six feet of water, but they were headed for a shoal over which there were just fifteen feet in some places, which would put them damn close either to the surface or on the bottom. Everyone involuntarily held his breath as Lieutenant Mills eased the

ASDV along the southern edge of the shoal. They could hear the tiny click of the sounder, testing the seabed.

Lieutenant Longo's monologue never stopped: 'We got twelve feet below the keel. Make that ten, steady at ten. Looks like we got it first time. We need a course of zero-eight-zero.'

Lieutenant Mills: 'Zero-eight-zero it is.'

Longo: 'Sir, this must be the channel. Suggest we speed up a touch. Sounding still steady at ten.'

Five minutes and 300 yards later the ASDV was in fifty feet of water, in the trench north-west of Thamihla. The Chinese had dredged precisely where the engineers in Coronado had said they would. Dave Mills again brought the ASDV to periscope depth. Right in front of him the mast slid upwards and he peered through the viewfinder, ranging right, from dead ahead to zero-four-zero. There it was, about a mile off their starboard bow, the light flashing every two seconds on the red can they had imagined so often on the chart.

'Slight course change at 15.53N 94.16E on the GPS. Come to zero-four-zero through the dredged channel. But we're in patrolled waters. Advise visual every three minutes.'

'That Longo. Clever little prick, right?' Lieutenant MacPherson whispered it just loudly enough for the navigator not to hear.

'Shut up, Dallas,' hissed Rick Hunter. 'I'd like to see you doing what he's doing.'

'Me? Sir, you must be joking. How many times do I need to tell you? I can do it all.'

'As a navigator you'd probably hit it all.'

There was a lot of stifled laugher, which defused some of the tension but not all of it. The ASDV crept forward through the dark narrow channel, its only 'eyes' an occasional look through the periscope. It took them another forty minutes to move all the way to the north end of the dredged channel and at the entrance to the natural deep water they spotted a patrol boat through the periscope. It was coming straight towards them, the unmistakable Hainan Type 037 fast-attack patrol boat, heavily gunned, with a phalanx of ASW mortars. This ship is the coastal warhorse of the Chinese Navy. They have a hundred of them, divided between their three fleets. Lieutenant Longo spotted it way up ahead, with its distinctive low freeboard, making thirty knots through the water, with a big white wake astern, almost as if it had nothing to do with the Chinese naval dockyard off to the west.

Lieutenant Mills whipped down the periscope and took the ASDV as deep as she would go, cutting her speed and steering left towards the edge of the Haing Gyi shoal, trying to put a mile of the Bassein delta between the US SEALs and the oncoming Chinese patrol. She was not transmitting, but Lieutenant Mills was taking no chances. He cut the engines and allowed the submarine to drift down and settle on the sandy bottom. Everyone heard the Hainan go charging past.

'You know what I think?' whispered Matt Longo. 'I think she was Burmese, coming straight down the estuary from their naval base up at the city of Bassein, several miles upstream from here. She looked too settled on her course and she was going too fast to have just exited the dockyard, and she sure as hell didn't look like a patrol boat snooping around the deep waters beyond the Chinese jetties. She was in a real hurry.'

Lieutenant Mills started the engine and engaged the shaft. The ASDV moved immediately forward, bumping off the soft bottom, heading north-east again. Another three miles and they'd be right off the jetties. Thirty minutes from now the SEALs' four hit men would be on their way. They moved on slowly, transmitting on the fathometer occasionally. At 2250 Lieutenant Mills slid quietly up to PD for a visual and there, 500 yards off their port beam, he could see the lights along the jetties. He could also see the shape of one small frigate moored dead astern of a large destroyer.

'Okay, guys,' whispered Longo. 'We're a bit too close. Get out right here. We're still in the fifty-foot channel. Targets are 500 yards to our west. Steer course two-eight-five and you'll come in right against the hulls.'

Rick Hunter came forward to take a visual on the targets and Lieutenant Mills decided they could exit on the surface, since there was not a single sound of any ship, radar or even a remote sonar. The dockyard was silent, unsuspecting, just as everyone had expected it would be. Of course, the little ASDV is dead flat along its upper casing. There is no sail and it's invisible from 500 yards in dark water: a jet-black steel tube in the night.

The Lieutenant, already at periscope depth, lowered the mast and quickly pumped out some more ballast. The ASDV rose another five feet, just breaking the calm harbor surface with about one foot of freeboard, and stopped in the water. Lieutenant Mills opened the deck hatch and Catfish Jones, mask on, flippers on, hood up, Draeger connected, a heavy limpet mine harnessed to his back, attack board under his arm, heaved himself up and over, rolling silently into the water without as much as a ripple. Buster Townsend, similarly equipped minus the attack board, was next. Then Chief Petty Officer Mike Hook and finally Commander Hunter. The SEALs sorted them-selves out, treading water, heads above the surface, waiting for their adrenalin to die down. Adrenalin eats oxygen. The wait was frustrating. They were already running at least twenty minutes late. The detonator clocks would be set for 0345 instead of the planned 0330.

Commander Hunter would lead the way, with Mike

Hook on his left shoulder. Catfish Jones, his attack board set on course two-eight-five, would swim in behind them, with Buster's right hand on his left shoulder. They would not use their arms or hands for the swim, just their legs, kicking the oversized special SEAL flippers every five seconds, covering 120 feet per minute. It would take them around thirteen minutes to reach the Chinese warships.

It was 2307 when Rick Hunter, facing east, finally held his attack board out in front of him with both hands. The big farmboy from central Kentucky drove himself forward, kicking hard and counting for distance. He was a human torpedo, scheduled to inflict about a billion dollars' worth of damage on the People's Liberation Navy. Commander Hunter could kick like one of his dad's stallions. Battleships have left their jetties with less power.

The four SEALs drove forward, the three younger men settling in to their Leader's now easy pace: kick . . . one . . . two . . . three . . . four . . . kick and glide all the way in. After eight minutes the Commander came to the surface for his last look through the mask. Their course was accurate and he paddled quietly back down to their regular depth, fourteen feet below the surface. They were exactly on target, heading for the twin propellers of the destroyer, almost underneath the bow of the frigate.

Five minutes later they were there, right under the shafts in the shadow of the stern, and Rick signaled them to wait while he went deep to check the distance the keel floated above the harbor floor. As he suspected, it was only about three feet. This meant he and Buster could swim from the stern to the halfway point of the 500-foot-long ship, just about two minutes at twelve kicks every sixty seconds. Then Buster would swim under the keel and place his mine exactly opposite Rick's. The subsequent detonation would hopefully break the back of the Chinese destroyer.

Catfish and Mike had only sixty yards to swim, which translated into eighteen kicks, each taking them ten feet, at which point they too would be just about halfway along the hull. Then Mike Hook would swim under the keel and place his charge. Swimming under a hull is a nerve-racking business when it's tight, as this most certainly was. But they were on a rising tide, which was lifting the ship higher, and that's a lot less stressful than a falling one.

Rick Hunter rejoined the other three, about eight feet below the surface. They could hear the hum of the big generators inside the destroyer. Rick and Catfish clipped their attack boards on their belts, then they separated into two pairs, diving down into the dark, kicking their big flippers, driving along the steel hull of one of Zhang Yushu's most prized warships. Hunter counted carefully. On the twenty-fourth kick he stopped, confident now that he was right under the section of the destroyer where all the guided missiles and torpedoes were stored. Here he could see the lights of the ship reflected in the water, but both SEALs knew it would be pitch black when they reached the keel. Rick felt the surface of the hull as he went and it was very rough, covered in barnacles and small sea growth. None of this was good news unless you happened to be a naturalist – the magnetic clamps on the mine were never going to grip this. Buster would realize the same when he reached the other side.

Within a few seconds both SEALs were standing on the sandy bottom in water black as oil. They could feel the rough surface and they unclipped the harnesses which held the limpet-mines on their backs. Rick saw Buster turn and swim underneath the keel, feeling his way in the dark. He himself again ran his hand against the metal of the ship. He uncovered his magnetic clamp and screwed it into the mine with its five pounds of explosive. He tried it on the hull but it would not grip. So he drew his kaybar fighting knife and holding the blade with two hands he scraped a section clean on the hull. Again he tried the clamp and this time he felt it pull, then lightly thud home. He could see the small dial of the timer glowing lightly, showing its twenty-four-hour setting. Rick again checked its timing against that of the clock on his attack board and set it for 0345. Then he ducked under the keel and showed the exact time to Buster who was just finishing scraping with his kaybar knife.

Thus synchronized to the split second, they made the fix to the hull of the ship, took a compass reading and kicked straight back down course one-zero-five to where the ASDV awaited them. Fifty yards in front were Catfish Jones and Mike Hook, whose swim down the hull of the frigate had been much less distance and whose hull had been much cleaner. They picked up the intermittent homing beeps from Matt Longo's fathometer and kicked in towards the hull of the mini-sub. Only when Commander Hunter signaled with four knocks on the hull that all four of them had made it back did Lieutenant Mills return to the deserted surface of the water, and one by one they clambered up and into the dry compartment. They were all breathing heavily as they unhooked their Draegers, pulled off their masks and sat down. Again the hatch was shut and clipped, and Lieutenant Mills took her twenty feet down once more in the now desolate main channel.

'Okay, guys?' asked Rick Hunter.

'No problems for us,' replied Catfish. 'What took you two so long?'

'Much longer swim down the hull and when we got there it was coated with barnacles. You know what little bastards they are to clean off. We couldn't get the magnets to pull until we'd scraped a section. But it's fine. All set for 0345.'

'Same,' said Catfish. 'Damn creepy down there under the hull, though. Wouldn't wanna do it every night, I'll tell you that.'

Lieutenant Mills ran back down the channel, steering course two-zero-zero from the sixteen-degree line of latitude on the GPS. They ran for a little less than twenty minutes at six knots, then they all felt the ASDV make a turn to starboard, slowing down while Lieutenant Longo scanned the water for Wolf Rock. He found it just to their north and guided Lieutenant Mills in until the submarine was 150 yards off its southernmost point. They took a visual and Matt could see its shape jutting out of the water. 'Okay, guys,' he said. 'This is where we say "so long". Your landing place is dead ahead, steer three-two-zero for no more than 350 yards. Right there you'll be in the marshes, north of that river, so you won't have to cross it. You just got a short walk in from there.'

Rick began to distribute big plastic cups of cold water. 'I'm suggesting you drink one of these before we go. Because we're probably going to get hot and we have no time to get our suits off. Just don't want anyone getting dehydrated, because it makes you feel lousy.'

The SEALs drank, pulled up their hoods, loaded up with six satchel bombs, plus medical supplies, radio and one shovel. They took the greatest care loading up two of the rookies with two fifty-foot rolls of det-cord, the hugely volatile detonator link which burns at the rate of *five miles per second* and is beloved by all SEALs. Then they slung their personal weapons on their backs, the Heckler and Koch light sub-machine guns packed in waterproof cases. They lifted out the bigger M-60 machine-gun, which would be used only in a dire emergency, if they had to fight their way out. But their most precious cargo were two heavy armor-piercing bombs, about three feet long in special waterproof carrying cases. These had been especially adapted by naval ordnance in San Diego. They would not explode in contact with other explosive: they would only explode with heavy impact on the point of the nose cone and heavy impact they were going to get.

Inside the ASDV, Draegers were connected and tested, masks pulled down, flippers fitted on, several belts of ammunition in waterproof sheaths were split among the SEALs not using attack boards. The vicious-looking kaybars were adjusted in combat belts, ready for easy access.

At 0016 they began to exit the submarine. One by one they rolled out of the deck hatch and into the still calm waters of the Bassein delta. There was a pale moon rising to the east, casting low ghostly shadows on the water, and there was no sign of life save for the increasing number of black-hooded heads above the surface, each man breathing the fresh night air deeply, treading water waiting for the adrenalin to die down.

It was 0026 when Dallas MacPherson, manhandling the big machine-gun with Bobby Allensworth, slithered down the hull and essentially fell into the water, the heavy gun now made much lighter by the special air pockets inside its waterproof cover. Rick Hunter dived to their swim depth of ten feet, adjusted his attack board and kicked forward on the short swim into the marshes. Ten minutes later all twelve of them grounded into long marsh grass, growing out of firm sand. Rick stood first and listened, pulling back his hood and shoving his mask into a holster on his belt.

They had already decided to hide the Draegers. They were too heavy to carry, and they walked on together to the beach, found a wooded area beyond the sand and dug out a hole to bury them. In an emergency they could run back and find them, if they needed to escape. If not, no one would ever find them. They covered them over with grass, then wet sand, and dumped the shovel under thick undergrowth. The six men with the light attack boards clipped them on to each other's backs; the bombs were similarly carried. The SEALs drew their weapons, Rattles-nake Davies held the wire cutters and Rick Hunter checked the compass. They drew their machine-guns and Commander Hunter decided on a tight group in single file walking carefully through the light grasses 100 yards inshore from the beach.

This part of the landscape, as far as they and the satellite could tell, was uninhabited. The first sign of life they would encounter would be in the guardhouse on the south perimeter wire. So they went forward, moving steadily across the ground, their start point no more than 1200 yards from the fence. As ever, their watchword was stealth. There was no mileage in causing an uproar, nothing to be gained from a gunfight except almost certain death. The SEALs had no back-up, no hope of immediate rescue. The Chinese guards in the dockyard had access to at least three helicopter gunships, plus almost a thousand armed Navy personnel. Not to mention the entire Burmese Navy base upriver with even more access to fast patrol gunboats.

It was imperative that no one should see them, or that anyone who did should live no more than three seconds. The brains back in Coronado believed that the guardhouse would contain a bank of television screens, closed circuit from all over the base. That way one man could watch over the entire complex, positioned down on the main perimeter fence, which guarded the base from the outside world. One guard with access to a panic button, which would summon heavy reinforcements immediately. The only colleague he would require through the night would be an engineer ready to attend to any problems in the electric generation plant, the refueling areas, or anywhere else in the high-tech areas of the naval yards.

The SEALs' plan was almost primitive in its lack of subtlety, but everyone thought it would work. The one thing they must not do was cause a panic in the guardroom which would cause the guard to hit the appropriate button. They walked on, each man certain in his own mind of the sequence of their actions in the next ten minutes. At 0110 they picked up the lights inside the fence and it was plain they were not designed as a security aid, but rather to light up a black-top interior path along which a jeep carried the guardhouse personnel. The lights were dim and focused on the ground, not the fence. The SEALs could see only one light along the fence, not high, about 100 yards from the guardhouse itself. So it was dark as they made their approach, and they had no need to hit the ground and snake their way forward on elbows and knees until they were as close as fifty yards.

They reached the fence in good order and Rattlesnake began to cut a hole in the wire in a dark area forty feet from the little building. It took just a few minutes and Buster Townsend folded it back, away from his buddy's hands as the thick strands were severed. The hole was five feet wide by the time Dallas MacPherson and Bobby Allensworth hauled the big gun through, followed moments later by the entire team with all their equipment. If only they had known it, the Chinese guard and engineer, watching the television inside the brightly lit room, were sitting within shouting distance of one of the most lethal platoons of fighting men in the world.

The only man not through the wire was Chief Petty Officer Mike Hook and no one could see him crouched outside the fence in deep grass carefully aiming a silenced M-14 rifle, the only one they carried, at the light nearest the guardhouse on the wire. At 0130, right on time, the veteran SEAL pulled the trigger and shot the bulb out first time. There was not a sound. But inside the guardhouse a tiny light flickered, confirming a bulb had gone some-where along the south fence. Instinctively the young guard stood up and walked to the screen door, opened it, stepped through and looked along the fence, noticing immediately that the light they could see through the window was no longer there. In Cantonese he called, 'Shit! We have a light blown. We may as well replace it now – the television program is awful.' At which point the engineer also walked out into the night, carrying a white box and a tall stepladder. It was obvious the cheap Korean bulbs blew out on a regular basis, even without Mike Hook's valuable assistance.

Both men were now outside in the dark, the guardhouse unmanned. The SEALs pounced right then. Rick Hunter took the guard from behind, breaking his neck with a tremendous blow from the butt of his machinegun. The man fell dead without a murmur, mainly because the SEAL Leader had a massive hand clamped across his mouth as he died. The engineer never even saw it, because Bobby Allensworth slammed a blow into this throat at the same time as Rattlesnake rammed his kaybar into the man's heart. Two down, the guardhouse in SEAL control. Not a sound as they fell. It was 0136.

Rick and Dallas raced into the guardhouse and stared at the screens. From there it looked as though the place was deserted. There was no sign of a human figure on the top line of three screens. On the second line there was also no sign of life. The trouble was the lettering under the screens was in Chinese and the two SEALs were unable to read which television recorded which area. They stayed watching for a few moments, then suddenly there was life on screen six in the lower line, four men walking across a room, dressed in engineering overalls. In the background there was a tall construction, which seemed to have a large wheel on top, but the quality was not good enough for an accurate assessment. In Rick's opinion it was almost certainly the interior of the electric power station.

No surprises. They had guessed there would be little night security in a remote Chinese base in the middle of a Burmese river, literally hundreds of miles from *any* known enemy, like India, and thousands of miles from *the* known enemy, the USA.

Commander Hunter's one problem so far was the possible discovery of the bodies. There would almost certainly be a watch change at 0400, but by that time he hoped the SEALs would be long gone and the base would be non-operational. Nonetheless, there was a chance that a patrol might call at the little guardhouse some time before 0400. Finding it deserted was one thing. Finding two murdered occupants was quite another. Rick's instinct was to disable the televisions so that no one else could look at them, but he did not dare in case the disconnection triggered an alarm which would send more engineers down to the guardhouse. It was the lesser of two evils, but he elected to leave them operational, counting on no one else seeing the pictures before the 0400 guard change.

Rick watched the bodies being dragged out through the hole in the wire and hidden in the long grasses through which they had just walked, at least fifty yards away from the fence. They clipped the wire back into place. If a patrol did show up, it would be confronted with a mystery, but not with unmistakable evidence of an attack on the base.

It was 0150 when they began their advance on the Chinese dockyard. The twelve black-clad figures walked steadily towards the lights of the main complex, a distance of 200 yards. According to Rick's map there were seven main buildings – the power station, the main control and communications room, a large accommodation block, a long warehouse facing the surface ship jetties and an ordnance store right next to it. Just beyond that was the wide sea inlet where the Chinese had constructed jetties

384

for their patrol boats and, further in, two large dry docks, the type that flood down and sink to allow ships to navigate in, and then wait for the docks to pump out the ballast and rise again to the surface.

Opposite the patrol boat landings were the submarine jetties, but according to Coronado's latest intelligence, there was no underwater boat in residence. Then, even further along the shore, was the fuel farm, housing twelve massive holding tanks, an area 200 yards long by 150, containing a million gallons of diesel. Between the fuel farm and the refueling jetties there was a main fuel control block, a sizeable three-story building 240 feet long. With that out of action and possibly a bad fire among the holding tanks, the base would be totally diminished as a possible operations center. That fuel control block was the farthest building from the SEALs' point of entry. It was also their first target.

Rick Hunter led his men on a 300-yard diagonal route across the rough ground between the outer fence and the accommodation block, deep in the interior of the base. It was all surprisingly badly lit, for which each of the SEALs was grateful, particularly the two rookies bringing up the rear, carrying the big machine-gun and ammunition belts which Lieutenant Allensworth would handle in an emergency. A big weight like that always makes assault troops feel vulnerable, slower and less mobile than everyone else, and the two rookies, carrying the machine-gun between them, preferred the dark to the light.

The Commander led them carefully and they made no sound as they crossed the uncut, uneven grass. They saw no one and even as they passed the rear of the accommodation block there was no discernible light in any window. Rick was trusting his map now, because the base was unknown territory, and the map was telling him that at the end of the accommodation block they would make a right-hand turn and see in front of them a floating pontoon dock, with a gantry crossing the sea inlet, right behind the innermost dry dock. The gantry was better lit than any other area and Rick decided that if they were going to be seen, and caught, it was going to be as a team right in the middle of that illuminated bridge. He thus decided to regroup on the pontoon and send each man over the bridge one at a time, nice and slowly, attracting no attention. He sent Dallas MacPherson over first and the young Lieutenant did as he was ordered, strolling non-chalantly over the metal bridge as if he owned the place.

One by one they made the crossing, until eleven men were over, when Rick Hunter picked up the big machine-gun on his own and walked it over the gantry to join the others. Then the pace stepped up about 200 per cent. There were almost no lights on this side, just a low four-foot steel-railed fence to protect the fuel farm. Rattlesnake and Buster cleared it together, racing through the holding tanks and planting a powerful, high-explosive Mk-138 satchel bomb against the two at the centre. They joined them with det-cord and wired it into the detonator, setting the timer for 0345. Then they jumped the eastern fence and worked on two more bombs, carried in and left in position on the outer back wall of the control center by Rick and Bobby. Each satchel held ten blocks of explosive. There was enough TNT against that wall to knock down the Yankee Stadium and Rattlesnake thought privately, *I just hope to Christ no one finds it before H-Hour, 0345.*

Meanwhile Dallas and Mike Hook were edging round the control block searching for a main electricity inlet or outlet. The other team, Rick Hunter and Bobby Allensworth, were searching for the main fuel lines, which they never found. Dallas and Mike, however, were lucky. They opened up a big manhole in the ground and found a labyrinth of heavy-duty cable, coated in plastic, in brown, red and blue. Dallas said to wind six turns of det–cord round the central point and set the timer on the detonator for 0345. 'Okay, guys, we're done this side of the inlet,' whispered Rick Hunter. 'Let's round up the lookouts and head back over that creepy little bridge.' Twenty minutes later they were once more in the shadow of the accommodation block, their loads lightened considerably.

It was 0225 and there were two targets left: the control and communications block, which represented about five per cent of their problem, and the power station, which was the other ninety-five per cent. The control block was important because without it the Chinese were unable to contact the outside world. But the power plant represented a fighting chance of obliterating the entire naval base.

With incredible stealth the SEAL team moved way back into the rough ground over which they had walked from the guardhouse. They could now see the silhouette of the station and, as Dallas MacPherson observed, 'It looks a whole hell of a lot bigger right here than it did on the photograph.'

He was right. The building loomed high, maybe five stories up. On its southern side it was ninety feet long, and it was plainly bigger than that on the western and eastern walls. The only door they could see was set into the wall on the west side right-hand corner looking in. There was a high outside metal staircase running up the east wall, probably for use as an emergency exit. A tall chimney jutted out of the roof, probably to release surplus steam. To the right of the station, as the SEALs lay watching, was the control and communications block, situated centrally between the station and the dockside warehouse. They would deal with that first, because it was relatively simple, the mere placing of two bombs strategically.

The planners in Coronado had discussed the possibility

of getting a couple of guys on the roof and winding a few coils of det-cord round the entire bloom of rooftop aerials, but decided, in the end, against it: too hard to climb it without specialist gear and the SEALs were already fully loaded; too much chance of being detected, even stranded up there if things went awry below; too little advantage gained, since there was soon to be no electricity whatsoever throughout the base, or whatever was left of it.

This time the bombs would be placed by Buster and Rattlesnake, both experts in such matters. Mike Hook, carrying the big gun for covering fire, accompanied them across the ground, assisted by one of the rookies. They set themselves in position covering the main door of the building and the short southern wall. They could also cover the black-top perimeter road. The two SEALs from Louisiana moved like lightning to the building and their luck held. At the rear of the structure there was a short flight of concrete steps going down to a semi-basement and, remarkably, the door was open. Buster and Rattlesnake crept in and placed their two satchel bombs right by the main boiler. They spliced in the wires, set the detonator for 0345 and moved briskly out of the area, shutting the door carefully behind them. Still no one disturbed their lethal tasks. It was exactly 0245 and they were now running a half-hour late, not twenty minutes.

But no one could deny the fates had been with them. The base, though occupied by a large number of military personnel, was, like all bases, quasi-civilian in character. One of the two duty guards had been an engineer/electrician. All the men on duty in the power station were civilians and there appeared to be no duty guard in there. They had seen no patrols along the docks either, presumably on the basis that no one was expected to attack a Chinese guided-missile warship with several hundred trained Navy staff on board.

Now, late or not, the SEAL team was making its way forward to its main objective, taking no chances, moving on elbows and knees through the rough grass. The plan had been perfectly memorized by each of them. Commander Hunter would enter the station, backed by Lieutenant Allensworth, Catfish Jones, Mike Hook, Dallas MacPherson and two rookies. They would take in with them the two steel armor-piercing bombs and four sizeable hunks of C-4 plastic explosive, plus a couple of hammers, jammed in the rookies' belts. In Commander Hunter's opinion they would have to fight to take control of the power station, probably killing everyone who stood in their way. They knew from the television screens in the guardhouse there were at least four, and possibly more, engineers on duty, but as a civilian installation that would probably be all. The problem with an assault like this was that anyone who got in the way had to die. There was no question of stunning or disabling, or even drugging with chloroform. What if the victim suddenly awakened and sounded an alarm? The stakes were too high for such a risk – any risk, come to that.

Outside the power station, twenty yards into the rough ground, Buster and Rattlesnake would man the big machine-gun, covering the door and the approach road. The rookies would be deployed as lookouts on the near corners of the building. At 0255 the seven-man SEAL assault force set off towards the raised door of the geothermal generating plant. It was pitch dark, the moon having vanished behind low rain cloud, and there was just one dim bare bulb lighting the eight steps up to the doorway. The SEAL Leader opened it carefully, but did not enter. No one moved and certainly no one came to find out who had opened the door. One by one the team slipped into the building, weapons poised to cut down any opposition. If it was just one man or two, they would use knives. Any more and they would simply take them down with sub-machine gun fire: noisy and slightly risky, but the only option. They shut the steel door hard behind them, trying to contain any noise they might make inside the reinforced walls of the building.

They knew what they were looking for. The engineers at Coronado had sketched it for them several times: one massive shaft with a giant cast-iron valve on top, the kind of heavy-duty machinery that might feasibly be holding back a volcano, powered by the core of the earth.

The room they now stood in was pure concrete, with a square exit into another room in which the noise was all-embracing. They could see huge turbines, with ten-foot-high wheels, spinning at a steady speed, plainly generating the electricity. The Coronado guys had said they should immediately look for a kind of mezzanine floor below, because the steam power was upwardly powerful. It would surge up the shaft and then find itself guided by the valve system, just below the turbines. What Rick Hunter sought was steps, downward steps, and the seven men fanned out, walking through the turbine room, hesitating as they came out from behind the giant machines, treating the room as if they were clearing a block in a conquered city. They moved stealthily, their MP-5s held out in front, trying to listen, to catch any additional sound from above the hum of the machines. Up ahead they could see another opening in the thick, cast-concrete walls and right in the center of that gap was a wide flight of stone steps, ten of them, leading down, Rick thought, to the main geothermal shaft.

So far the place seemed deserted. But no one imagined it could be, with millions of dollars of machinery working ceaselessly, apparently unsupervised. There had to be a team of guys in charge somewhere. But where were they, that's what Commander Hunter wanted to find out.

The answer was not long coming. Right at the bottom of the steps leading to the main shaft three Chinese engineers suddenly appeared. In absolute shock, they stared up at the black-faced hooded giants who towered above them on the upper steps, armed with sub-machine guns. No one knew quite what to do, certainly not the engineers. One of them helplessly raised his hands, another called out loudly, a third shouted something in Chinese. Then Bobby Allensworth stepped in front of Commander Hunter and hit the trigger, firing from the hip, four short bursts. No one was as fast as Lieutenant Allensworth. In another life he'd have been at the OK Corral. Bullets from his MP-5 slammed into the three men, each of whom took at least three shots, either to the head, throat or heart. It was whipcrack reaction from a trained professional killer. No sooner had the bodies slumped to the ground when a fourth man came running round the corner, stopped dead in his tracks, then stopped dead in his life as the MP-5 held by Rick Hunter's bodyguard spat a single round to his heart.

Even the SEALs were shaken by the speed at which it had happened. Commander Hunter turned to Bobby, whose prime task it was to protect the SEAL Leader, and just nodded, confident the noise from the turbines had suppressed any possibility of the shots being heard outside. Lieutenant Allensworth said, 'Sorry I had to do that, sir. But I was afraid one of them might have had a button or an emergency bleeper. Just didn't wanna give 'em no time. No time. No, sir.'

'Thanks, Bobby. There was no alternative. I agree. Come on, let's get after that main shaft.'

Still their luck appeared to hold and they located the shaft two minutes later at exactly 0310, at which precise time the telephone was ringing forlornly in the guardhouse out on the fence. Lieutenant Bo Peng, an engineer in the moored destroyer, was trying to call his brother Cheng who was on duty on the perimeter. He usually called him when they were both on the midnight watch and they sometimes shared tea in the ship's wardroom when the watch was over. Lieutenant Bo could not for the life of him understand why Cheng was not replying, or alternatively, why the answer and automatic relay machine was not connected. It was a golden rule among the guards and Bo was baffled by the silence out on the boundary guardhouse. He was a persistent and ambitious young man of twenty-four and he called the duty officer of the base, reporting that there was no reply to the telephone in the guardhouse and why was that? There was not even a way to leave a message and that was disgraceful in a military complex.

The duty officer was not altogether crazy about Bo's tone, but he was also wary that a warship officer with a serious complaint about the shore personnel would be listened to. In a few minutes he could be on the line to the destroyer's CO, a chore he was not prepared to deal with. So he answered crisply, 'I'm sorry about that, Lieutenant. I have no idea what could be wrong, but I'll play it by the book and send a full night guard patrol down there right away.' Three minutes later a complement of six naval guards, armed with Russian Kalashnikovs, was piling out of the accommodation block and boarding a waiting jeep. It was the first time they had ever been summoned to do anything after dark and they almost went the wrong way.

Rattlesnake and Buster watched them leave, burning rubber outside the building and then making a U-turn, heading wrongly for the dry-dock inlet. At the end of the first throughway between the buildings they swung right, down between the power station and the main workshops. They shot through the gap between the warehouses and the ordnance store, and then made a corrective right turn along the jetties. Lieutenant Bo, high above on the upper deck of the warship, watched them go roaring down the black-top towards the guardhouse. Once there, of course, they discovered the place was strangely empty. No duty guard. No duty night engineer. All six men jumped out and began to look around outside, spending several minutes calling out for the missing men. The patrol leader, however, Lieutenant Rufeng Li, went back into the little outpost's control room and took a look at the television screens.

At that precise moment in the power station Rick Hunter, noticing a scanning camera in the corner of the steam entry room, took it out with a volley of bullets at twenty-five-foot range. Lieutenant Rufeng was thus watching the screens when one of them just blanked right out. It did not even fizz, or show interference. It just blacked into nothing. The Lieutenant, however, did not suspect that something drastic was happening. He just thought that the two missing men were working wherever that screen had failed. He took a close look at the wording below, which told him the camera was located on the upper south-west corner of the main shaft room in the power station.

He walked outside and summoned his patrol. He took his time, lit a cigarette and told them laconically that he had solved the mystery: the two missing men had gone to attend to some kind of machine failure in the power station and, while it was irregular to leave the guardhouse unmanned, the problem might have been quite serious. They had obviously gone to deal with it together. After all, no guard had ever been called to deal with a prowler of any kind since the base had opened six months ago. He held his cigarette in his front teeth, an affectation just learned from a tobacco commercial on the Internet. He smiled languidly. It was a smile that said, *don't worry, gentlemen.*

The reason I have achieved a position so superior to your own is my natural penchant for using the little grey cells rather than running around in a frenzy. At that moment, in his own mind, Lieutenant Rufeng was the Hercule Poirot of the Orient.

It was 0325, and Rick and his team were working furiously in the shaft room, trying to shut off the lower valve, the one 3000 feet down, right above the boiling steam lake. They had located a control board and made the switches, three big ones, which Rick and Dallas believed had shut down all three valves. The main one, located on the huge pipe where the steam divides off into the separate turbine feeds, was certainly closed. The turbines were already slowing. Any second now the reserve diesel generators would kick in and it would not be long before the failure of the power plant was noticed.

The massive control valve at the head of the shaft, located at floor level in the lowest room, was also closed. But the SEALs could not reach the most important one of all, constructed in cast concrete, high in the roof of the lake, the first line of defense if for any reason the steam had to be halted. However, the switches were all three in the same position and they could do no more. In any event they now opened up the top two valves and let the remaining steam escape. Lieutenant MacPherson observed that if they were wrong about the switches they'd probably blow up most of east Asia, including themselves. 'And wouldn't that be a blast?' he added. Dallas always found time for irony even when he was working flat-out. It was impossible not to like him. He was sweating like a Burmese panda. He had just blown out two sections of pipe below the center and upper valves, and there was steam leaking, but it was not pressurized.

The bottom valve, over the underground cavern, was plainly shut. The opening of the top two for several minutes had allowed the pressured steam to rise up through the system and then die out. It was hot, but not diabolically so. Dallas and Mike Hook were feverishly trying to fix the first bomb inside the fractured shaft, winding it with det-cord immediately below the center valve.

There were only seventeen minutes left to tie up the second bomb through the hole in the shaft below the higher valve directly above. That, too, had to be secured with det-cord. Then, when the first detonator popped the cord, the lower bomb would scream down the shaft, arrowing through the remaining steam and slamming into the bottom valve with terrific force. It just might split the entire main shaft asunder. Thirty seconds later the second det-cord would pop and a large hunk of white Semtex explosive would blow the cast-iron upper valve to pieces. This would release the second bomb to drop down the shaft, gaining speed for 3000 feet, then exploding somewhere in the rubble at the shaft base, or even in the waters of the underground lake itself; maybe even in the *floor* of the lake, slightly north of hell, presumably. Dallas said that if that happened it might actually cause a brand spanking new volcano to erupt from the core of the earth. 'I always told my daddy I intended to leave a mark on this earth, but I bet he never thought I was gonna change its goddamned shape!'

Even without the wit and imagination of Lieutenant D. MacPherson, this was a drastically complex and dangerous set of linked explosions and no one knew what on earth the result would be. Whatever happened, the colossal forces of the steam, sufficient, it is always said, to blow a four-ton rock 400 feet into the air, would now be unleashed to roar furiously into its only escape route, straight up the remains of the shaft. It would most definitely blast off the roof of the power station and probably rupture the entire foundation of the structure. The milk-white superheated plume of steam, thundering into the sky from the floor of the generating plant, would probably reach 3000 feet. It would take weeks to cap it, especially if the concrete foundation was split, and even this would take special equipment unlikely to be available within 1000 miles. But from the US Navy's point of view, the main issue was that the Chinese base in the eastern waters of the Bay of Bengal should become history.

Meanwhile Dallas MacPherson, assisted by Mike Hook and Catfish Jones, was manhandling the second bomb up to the huge upper valve, the one that had to be obliterated. It was 0330 and they had the bomb well secure on its moorings. They eased it through the gap and made it fast, hanging in the shaft, swinging in the spooky plumes of white steam still drifting up from below. Dallas wound in the last of the det-cord, wrapping it round the spokes of the red wheel on top of the valve. Then they placed the C-4 plastic explosive in three places on the cast-iron casing of the valve itself. Just below them Rick checked his watch; it was 0334. They had to get out of here before the base started to explode. They dare not set the timers in the power plant for anything less than a half-hour from the moment they began to head for the marshes where the boats were waiting.

The Leader's mind raced: *Say forty minutes from now. Gives us ten minutes to get clear of the building, then a half-hour to get clear of the island. Is that enough? Don't wanna get killed by flying masonry. I'm gonna make it forty minutes from now. Just hope to hell it's not too much time for the Chinks to discover the plot.* 'Set that clock for 0415, Dallas,' he said. 'That's thirty minutes after the ships, the fuel and the buildings blow. There's gonna be a lot of chaos. Hopefully the blast from the control and comms building, plus the ships, will blow the ordnance store as well. But we have to get outta here in one piece. We're not committing suicide. My daddy wouldn't like it. No, sir.'

At that exact time, 0334, the night patrol jeep was running back down the black-top from the guardhouse. When it arrived at the point where the road curved right along to the jetties the driver swerved left and headed for the power station, driving across the rough ground. Rattlesnake Davies, lying in the grass with the machine-gun, nudged Buster and they turned round and saw the lights of the jeep coming towards them; not directly, but approximately. 'Jesus Christ, have they seen us?' he whispered.

'No. But I hate the coincidence,' replied Buster. 'What do we do?'

'Nothing. Keep our heads down. I think they'll go by. First sign they ain't goin' by, we take 'em out with the ole MP-5s, all of them, however many.'

By now the Chinese jeep was almost on them, still making a straight line, at a narrow angle towards the southern wall of the power station. If it did not stop, it would pass twenty-five feet in front of them. Buster and Rattlesnake, now gripping their small sub-machine guns, followed the vehicle with their eyes, every sense alert. If it stopped, there were going to be six dead Chinese guards, no question about that, because they would not see the prostrate SEALs until it was much too late. But Buster and Rattlesnake both knew the real problem would come after that; after the base rippled into life at the sound of gunfire. Ten minutes later it would ripple into death at the sound of high explosive. It was 0335.

Events were moving rapidly. Rick Hunter and his team were hurrying back through the power station towards the exit room through which they had arrived and, to their horror, Rattlesnake and Buster were watching the Chinese patrol's jeep pull up outside that door. There was no sense of urgency, but it was obvious that they were going in. The SEALs' rookie lookouts were flying across the grass back to the rendezvous point. They hit the ground together right next to Buster. 'Jesus Christ,' said one of them. 'The bastards are going in. They'll be behind the guys. Oh, shit! Buster, they'll fucking kill 'em.'

By now the guards were climbing out of the jeep and Rattlesnake Davies, without a word, wriggled left to the standard M-60 machine-gun they had set up in the grass. Buster had already laid the 100-round ammunition belt in the clip and it was aimed at the power station door. Lieutenant Rufeng and his deputy were on the steps, the other four immediately behind them. Each man carried his Kalashnikov. Without a word, Rattlesnake Davies, the SEAL from the Louisiana bayous, opened fire with the M-60. The range was only seventy feet and the fatal 7.62-NATO rounds tore a path straight at the steps, killing the man now opening the door and virtually taking Lieutenant Rufeng's head off. The other four guards, stunned at the explosion of blood running down the steel door in the dim light of the bare bulb, wheeled round, trying to see where the gunfire was coming from. They tried to raise their Kalashnikovs, but they were facing Rattlesnake Davies directly now and that was a very poor strategy. He blew all four of them away, the force of those big shells, almost four inches long, slamming into them actually knocked them sideways into the jeep, one of them hurtling backwards over the hood, his uniform riddled with bullet holes.

It was 0336, the darkest time, and the sound of the SEALs' machine-gun, rattling away in the night, had echoed around the base. A light went on in the accommodation block, someone came to the window of the communications room. Up on the foredeck of the Chinese destroyer two seamen on their watch looked up in surprise. It was gunfire, unmistakable machine-gun fire, and it was only 160 yards away. They raced aft towards the near-deserted comms room below the aerials.

At which point, 175 yards away, Commander Hunter opened the door to exit the power station and nearly fell over the blood-soaked bodies of Lieutenant Rufeng and his colleague. The thick, reinforced walls of the turbine room had spared them the anxiety of listening to Rattlesnake take out the entire Chinese night patrol, but Rick was amazed by what he saw. He jumped over the two bodies, followed by Catfish, Bobby and Dallas, grabbed the rail and jumped the steps in two bounds. In front of him was the jeep, three more bodies sprawled around it and one lying on it. 'What in the name of Christ?' he muttered, just as Rattlesnake, Buster and the three rookies came charging in from the rough ground, Buster saying too loudly, 'We had no choice. Let's go-go-go down to the marsh. Do we take the jeep?'

'Hell NO!' said Rick. 'It's too easy to follow. We're better off in the dark, running on our own. Get my fucking attack board off my back, will you? We need the compass. Okay, let's go, that way, make a diagonal back to the fence at the jungle end. GO NOW! ALL OF YOU! FOR FUCK'S SAKE RUN!' With that, the SEAL Leader grabbed the M-60 from Rattlesnake and one of the rookies, and tucked it under his arm, checking the belt to see what was left – about thirty-six rounds. He was the only one of them strong enough to handle it comfortably alone. 'Dallas! Quick. Blow that fucking jeep up, willya? It's faster than us and they may follow. Catfish's got the grenades.'

But Catfish was off and running. Dallas, who had once considered an athletic career at 200 meters – an ambition abandoned only when he failed to make the 1992 US Olympic team at the age of fourteen – could still run like hell and he caught Petty Officer Jones in short order. He ripped the pin out of the grenade and hurled it back at the jeep. Six seconds later, with the SEALs in full flight heading for the woods, it exploded in a fireball.

It attracted the instant attention of all four half-dressed but fully armed guards running out of the accommodation block. The light from the jeep illuminated the eleven black hooded figures pounding across the rough ground making a south-west course towards the trees. Even though they were frightened and disorganized, the Chinese instinctively opened fire. They were shooting almost blindly into the dark, in high but flickering light from the gasoline flames. But a bullet caught Buster to the right of his shoulder blade, paralysing his arm and knocking him flying to the ground. The Chinese saw the SEAL go down, but they did not see Commander Hunter rumbling along thirty yards behind his men with the M-60 poised. Rick stopped, steadied the weapon, then opened fire at the four running Chinese, cutting them down, dead in their tracks in a bloody scream of anger and fear. Then he turned the machine-gun on to the accommodation block itself and blew out all the side windows, in an attempt to discourage anyone else from giving chase.

Meanwhile, Dallas and one of the rookies had the wounded Buster on his feet with both arms round their necks. But the pain in his right side was agonizing and he screamed as they tried to carry him to the trees. Rick Hunter finally caught them up, ordered everyone to stop for twenty seconds and injected a shot of morphine into the stricken SEAL's right shoulder. 'Let's go,' he said. 'Fast as we can. Buster, that shoulder's gonna ease in a few minutes, old buddy. Don't worry about it.'

Buster Townsend, blood pouring down his back, nodded and smiled. 'Thanks, guys,' he said. So they struggled on, plunging into the wood, glad of the dark, glad of the cover.

Behind them they had left abject chaos. The fact was that the Chinese Navy was fully aware the base was under attack. But they had no idea yet of the scale of the operation. Nor, indeed, who was mounting it. They knew only that there appeared to be a gang of madmen running around murdering people. The air was alive with the transmissions of cell phones as the comms rooms in the two warships talked to each other and to the main control center of the base. The Commanding Officer of the Jangwei frigate was fastest into his stride. He hit the buttons to the destroyer suggesting they get helicopters into the air, with lights and pilots with night goggles. It was plainly essential to locate the killers as soon as possible.

The CO of the destroyer reacted equally quickly. Both his helicopters were in a ground-crew service area, way over beyond the fuel farm. It was a workshop complex, with fuel pumps. But the choppers rarely used it and the US satellite trackers had scarcely bothered with it. The Captain knew they were there and he moved fast to alert the air crew. Which was just as well, because it was 0344 when the destroyer's CO was on the phone and his ship was just about twenty-three seconds away from being blown sky-high, as was the frigate directly astern of him.

Twelve

0345 Thursday, June 7.
Haing Gyi Island, Burma.

On an academic level, it was Commander Rick Hunter's limpet mine, expertly clamped flat among the barnacles on the port side of the Luhai destroyer's keel, which exploded first. Buster Townsend's mine exploded two and a half seconds later. The viciously tailored 'shaped' charges magnified the power of the detonation five-fold and the limpets blew two gaping holes, one on either side of the keel, the blast slicing through the steel hull of the 6000-ton warship. Generally speaking, this was all bad news for the People's Liberation Army/Navy, but not quite so severe as it would become four seconds later when the Luhai's torpedo magazine went up with a thunderous explosion, killing half the ship's company.

Any onlooker might have been dumbfounded at the scale of the explosion, stunned by the flames and billowing jet-black smoke. It would nonetheless have been difficult to focus attention strictly to the destroyer, because eight seconds after the torpedoes blew, the 2000-ton Jangwei II frigate, moored dead astern, did a passable imitation of Hiroshima 1945, when the limpet mines fixed by Petty Officer Catfish Jones and Chief Mike Hook detonated with massive force under the guided-missile magazines.

The little Jangwei, only 360 feet long, a ship which punched a lot harder than its size, paid the penalty for that and literally blew itself to pieces. The entire complement of guided missiles, the SSM 6 YJ-1 Eagle Strikes, the CSS-N-4 Sardines, the 1-HQ-7 Crotales, all contributed to the crushing explosion and the docks shuddered, lit up with two towering fires which could be seen ten miles away. Six men would survive the frigate, only fifty out of 250 in the destroyer. Automatic fire alarms began to howl throughout the base, but they were drowned out by the colossal explosion in the fuel farm as one million gallons of diesel and jet fuel detonated into a raging furnace, courtesy of the Louisiana SEAL Rattlesnake Davies and the now wounded Buster Townsend. Their carefully timed Mk-138 satchel bombs had blown apart a total of five holding tanks and within moments the other seven had formed a gasoline inferno.

The roar from the fire almost – but not quite – drowned out the noise of the two other bombs blasting apart the fuel control center. In the middle of all this the coils of detcord, wrapped round the main electricity cables by Dallas MacPherson and Mike Hook, exploded with sufficient force to blow the manhole cover sixty feet into the air and permanently wreck the electronic fuel control system. Way over on the other side of the inlet, too, an unbelievable blast right by the main boiler in the basement of the control and communications center paid further tribute to the smooth black skills of Buster and Rattlesnake. The explosion literally caused the entire building to cave in, crushing all of its five occupants to death.

Residents of the base, at least those not gunned down in their tracks by the marauding US Navy SEALs, believed they were witnessing the end of the world. Any other explanation seemed utterly inadequate. The whole spectacularly awful scenario had erupted in under two minutes; out of nowhere. There was zero evidence of an attack either from the air or the sea. The place just seemed to be blasting itself to pieces.

Meanwhile, struggling through the woods on the north side of the base, the SEALs were still 1200 yards from the edge of the marsh. Buster was losing blood and he was still in pain despite the morphine. Rick Hunter ordered them to stop, while he examined the wound and, to his dismay, discovered the bullet was still lodged in the flesh on the right side of Buster's upper back and he was losing blood fast. He took Dallas MacPherson aside and told him to bring out the rest of the medical kit. Between them they had sticky and plain bandages, plus disinfected swabs for just this kind of wound, plus more disinfectant. But they had no groundsheets and they had to kneel Buster down. He kept losing consciousness, and Rattlesnake held his head and splintered shoulder. Dallas steadied the tiny pinpoint light beam they had brought, and Rick Hunter gritted his teeth and, using a large pair of tweezers designed for this particular task, gripped and pulled the bullet out. Blood cascaded from the wound and Dallas tried to stop it with a strip he tore from his own shirt. Rick used a gauze pad soaked in strong disinfectant to clean it. For the first time Buster Townsend screamed and Rattlesnake Davies, one of the toughest men ever to wear the Trident, broke down and wept at the agony of his lifelong friend.

Rick Hunter kept going. He used another gauze pad and pressed it on the wound. Dallas fixed it tight with a roll of bandage which he wound round Buster's chest, then stuck it down firm with the sticky tape. They stuck another length of this round Buster's upper arm, taping it tight to his side. Then Rick Hunter injected him with more morphine, the SEAL climbed back to his feet and Rattlesnake just said, 'I'm taking him.' He put Buster's good arm over his shoulder and held his wrist, and with his own arm round the wounded man's waist they pushed forward, walking as best they could through the undergrowth of the Burmese forest. 'I'm glad we did that,' said

Rick. 'We've stopped the blood, stopped the infection and it isn't going to get worse before we reach a doctor.'

Moments later Mike Hook's radio, tuned to the frequency, picked up the bleep-bleep-bleep of the homing device in the inflatables, now parked somewhere down by the Letpan stream. 'Got 'em, sir. They're waiting.'

'Good job, Mike, we just gotta stay on this course,' said Rick. 'It's due west and the attack board compass has us headed two-seven-zero. We're right on the money – gonna pop out of these woods on the left-hand fork of the stream, precisely where Shawn drew the spot.'

'You want a couple of us to make a bolt for it?' asked Lieutenant MacPherson. 'Just to let the boat drivers know we're on our way – tell 'em we got a problem?'

'Good call. Why don't you, Mike and one of the rookies take that other little radio and get down there? Bobby'll handle the transmitter. And use your compass – you know they say it's impossible to walk through trees in a straight line?'

'Okay, boss, see you in about fifteen minutes.'

070400JUN07. USS Shark. *Bay of Bengal.*
16.00N 94.01E. Speed 3. Racetrack Course. PD.
The watch changed at 0400 and Lieutenant-Commander Dan Headley still had the ship. No sign yet of Commander Reid, who had remained distant throughout the SEAL operation at Haing Gyi. Dan Headley knew he was not coming, at least not formally, to take over the ship. Although he thought the CO might show up casually a little later. He had seemed extremely relieved when the XO had requested that he handle *Shark* during the Special Forces operation.

At that moment Lieutenant Pearson came into the control room and said the CO wished to see him in his room immediately.

'Any clues why, Shawn?'

'None, sir. He just stuck his head out of the door when I was passing and said to tell you.'

'Okay. Officer of the Deck, you have the ship.'

'I have the ship, sir,' replied Lieutenant Matt Singer.

Dan Headley made his way down to Commander Reid's room, and was surprised to find the CO unshaved and looking fraught, which he considered was several degrees worse than worried. 'Hello, sir,' he said. 'What's up?'

'We have a very serious problem,' replied the boss of USS *Shark*.

'We do?'

'We certainly do and before I elaborate I want you to understand that I am talking about a subject on which I am something of an expert.'

'Of course, sir.'

'Mercury, XO, is just coming into retrograde.'

Dan Headley had rarely, probably never, been quite that bewildered. 'No shit?' he said lamely.

Commander Reid glared at his second-in-command. 'Do you, XO, have any idea how serious that can be? ANY IDEA WHATSOEVER?'

'Who, me?'

'Plainly, Lieutenant-Commander, I am addressing you.'

'Well, sir. I'm not quite sure what you mean.'

'MERCURY, XO! One of the greatest planets of the universe, will be in retrograde by dawn. MOVING BACKWARDS. CAN YOU UNDERSTAND THE SIGNIFICANCE OF THAT, XO?' Commander Reid's voice was rising and so were Lieutenant-Commander Headley's antennae. 'Astrology is what we are discussing, Mr Headley. Astrology. The ancient study of cycles – created originally by the Chaldeans of Babylonia 3000 years before Christ. Babylon, XO, Iraq in the modern world.'

'Oh, Saddam's mob. Guess I hadn't figured them as students of the universe.'

'Maybe not, maybe not. But I am a student of the universe and I must tell you that when the planet Mercury begins to turn in an apparent backward motion things can become extremely difficult. It's one of the ancient laws of the zodiac.'

'Sir, look, I am sure this is all very fascinating, but I've got twelve very brave men trying to get out of a Chinese naval base under the most terrible circumstances. Could we go into retrograde some other time?'

'XO. ARE YOU ACCUSING ME OF IRRELE-VANCE? THERE IS NOTHING MORE RELEVANT THAN MERCURY IN RETROGRADE. I'M TALKING OF MATTERS AS OLD AS TIME, FOR GOD'S SAKE!'

'Sir, I'm talking about high explosive, the destruction of a major Chinese Navy installation. I'm talking about life and death.'

'And what could be more significant to that matter of life and death than the slow reverse motion of a mighty planet, stilled briefly in the heavens? MERCURY IN RETROGRADE, SIR! WE ARE ABOUT TO BE BOMBARDED BY THE TIMELESS, MADDENING EFFECTS OF THE PLANET THAT CONTROLS US!' His voice rose even higher. '*CAN YOU UNDER-STAND THAT, XO?*'

Dan Headley was at a loss. But at that moment the phone rang. The CO grabbed it and handed it over immediately. 'Sir,' Lieutenant Singer's voice was almost as urgent as Commander's Reid's. 'Can you come back? The SEALs have a problem. Buster Townsend has been badly wounded. They're being hunted down by helicopters, sir. It's bad. Please come back up here.'

Dan Headley's heart missed at least two beats, maybe three. 'Sir, excuse me. We have a problem.'

'PROBLEM? PROBLEM? OF COURSE WE HAVE

A PROBLEM. WE'RE IN RETROGRADE. WHICH PLANET IN THE GREAT SCHEME OF THE UNIVERSE DO YOU THINK CONTROLS ALL TRANSPORTATION AND COMMUNICATION ISSUES?'

'Me? I'm not really sure about that, sir. But I gotta go.' With that, Dan Headley charged out of the door and long after he had turned the corner for the companionway he heard the CO shout, 'MERCURY, SIR, MERCURY! WHERE THE HELL DO YOU THINK IT WAS ON AUGUST 14, 2000? ANSWER THAT, DAMN YOU.'

Dan heard that all right. It was the day the *Kursk* hit the bottom of the Barents Sea. *We got a problem okay. But it's not some hunk of fucking rock flying backwards around outer space. It's sitting right back there in that little room – Reid in Retrograde is a lot more like it.*

Inside the control room there was an atmosphere of extreme concern. Lieutenant Singer was on the line to comms. The satellite signal just in from the driver of the lead inflatable was brief and forbidding. It read:

070410JUN07. 16.00N 94.19E – SEAL team delayed in escape from Haing Gyi. Townsend walking wounded. PLAN has helos up searching shoreline to Letpan stream. Nine SF trapped in high woods unable to reach boats. Attempting new RV downstream. Inflatables not located. Chinese base history. Hunter.

Master Chief Drew Fisher had the conn and Lieutenant-Commander Headley read the signal carefully. Lieutenant Singer handed him one of the ten-inch-wide scale maps on which Lieutenant Pearson had drawn in the details of the triangular island and they appreciated the situation.

There was a distance of 1000 yards downstream of the rendezvous point along the edge of the marsh. Right there the map showed a wide inlet of water running into the shore. Shawn's map showed trees almost forty feet high all the way. There was no doubt Rick would make his way along there and make a rush for the boats. Since the helos had plainly not yet located the inflatables there was obviously high grass cover in the marsh. The problem was probably the inlet – everyone would have to break cover in there and then attempt to charge out through the shallows across the Haing Gyi shoal. Three miles.

'Mother of God,' whispered Lieutenant Singer. 'They haven't got a prayer on the open water.'

'You mean the helos?'

'Yes, sir.'

'Actually, they have two chances, Lieutenant. To break cover in secret, unseen by the helos. Or to shoot the fuckers down. They have three standard M-60s, right? One already in each boat, one with the team.'

'You need to be a bit lucky to down a helo with one of those, sir. But I know it's been done plenty of times and they do have six belts of ammunition in each boat.'

'Where would you rather be, Lieutenant? On the ground with the guys holding the ammunition belts, or in a helo being machine-gunned by Commander Hunter?'

'On the ground with the Commander, sir. No question. But what are we going to do?'

'Tell comms to get a signal in. Tell the boat driver to let us know the moment they're under way. We're going in to get 'em.'

'Christ, sir. There's only about thirty-five feet of water this side of the big shoal.'

'I don't actually give a fuck if there's only two feet. We're not leaving them.'

'I'm afraid that decision will be made by me.' All three men in the control room turned to see Commander Reid standing there, very calmly, in marked contrast to his demeanor of just a few moments ago. 'Debrief me, XO. I need to appreciate the precise situation if you are planning to endanger the lives of my entire crew and, indeed, of USS *Shark* itself.'

Lieutenant-Commander Headley walked over to him and his tone was icy. 'This is the map of the island, sir. The X there marks where the boats came in to embark the SEALs. This mark is where we anticipate the team will move in order to embark further downstream. There are PLAN helos up, but they have not yet discovered either the boats or Commander Hunter's team.'

'I assume they will attempt to cross this wide shoal at high speed?'

'I agree, sir, and I'm proposing we come in on the surface and meet them. If we have to, I'll take the helos out with Stingers.'

'Not on my watch, you won't, XO. How dare you decide in my ship virtually to declare war on China? In the open sea, firing publicly on Chinese aircraft quite properly defending their own base. No, sir. For that you will need not only my permission but that of the Flag and probably CINCPACFLT. Do you have any idea of the conse-quences of what you are proposing?'

Dan Headley stared him hard in the eyes. There was total silence in the control room. Commander Reid shook his head and turned away, walking out through the door.

Lieutenant-Commander Headley did not acknowledge what had been said. He just turned back to Lieutenant Singer and stated, 'Please carry out my last order, Matt. Get that signal in to the boat drivers. We must know immediately they leave.'

'But what about the CO, sir? He plainly doesn't think we should go in.'

'No,' replied Dan, 'he doesn't. Now get that signal

away and tell comms to stand by for the reply.'

The Boat Chief, MCPO Drew Fisher, looked at the XO and said quietly, 'We're going in to get 'em, right, sir?'

'Do you want to leave Rick and the guys to die out there, Drew?'

'No, sir. No. I do not.'

0414. Haing Gyi Island.
It was just beginning to rain. Commander Hunter and the other eight SEALs were struggling through the thick tropical forest. They'd made their course adjustment in radio contact with Lieutenant MacPherson, who was now helping to drag the big inflatables along the shore in about two feet of water, too shallow to paddle, under a canopy of insect-ridden grasses. 'Jesus,' he said. 'I'm supposed to be a combat SEAL not Humphrey fucking Bogart.' He was right. It was like a scene from *The African Queen*. All they needed was Katharine Hepburn manning the machine-gun.

However, the deadly nature of this night was brought into all of its terrible reality by the clattering of the helicopters overhead, searching for the killers who had infiltrated their base and destroyed it. Back under the trees, Rick could hear them coming in low, circling the area. Right now, however, all nine SEALs had but one thing on their minds. It was just 0415 and the armor-piercing bomb should be on its way. They would not hear the blast, one mile away and 3000-feet below the surface of the earth. But they should hear something in the next couple of minutes. Rick told them to keep moving and the sense of anticipation grew more intense with every stride they took.

Then they did hear it: a dull, muffled rumble, more like a distant earthquake. Then there was nothing, until suddenly, in the weird silence of the night, an explosion

411

shook the island to its foundations. A colossal crash, erupting out over the forest, as the roof of the power station was blasted a hundred feet into the air, followed by a shattering white light which lit up the area. A giant bright plume of incineratingly hot steam, fifty feet across, gushed skywards, higher and higher above the island, burning into the rain clouds, 1000 feet, 2000 feet, roaring like the oil flame on an old-fashioned boiler – a million old-fashioned boilers. The noise was an unearthly, unnatural, uncontrollable sound, gushing out of the very core of the earth. Up through the trees Rick Hunter and his men could see the dead-straight, ivory-white tower, like an endless skyscraper reaching up into the stratosphere, into the heavens, for all they knew.

Aside from the fact that it most certainly signaled the end of China's naval base in Burma, the howling tower of steam did the SEALs one other colossal favor. It totally distracted the three PLAN helicopters, two Russian-built ASW Helix-As, and a single Helix-B assault craft carrying its full complement of UV-57 rockets. All three were a mere 500 feet away from the power station when it blew and they swerved instinctively away from the white inferno as it slammed the roof into the sky, showering the local air space with bricks, concrete, dust and metal beams. With everything on fire down below it was difficult for them to land. Also, there was no electric power anywhere. There was no one to consult with. The pilots did not even know if there was anyone left alive. They had managed to get airborne as a result of the last-second message from the late CO of the destroyer, but they had done so at huge risk, flying out and away from the fire in the fuel farm, then picking up a new signal from the emergency transmitter in the accommodation block.

The officer had delivered the message under immense stress. He was badly wounded and his signal was more like a MAYDAY than an order. He just had time to tell the lead pilot the direction the killers were headed – down to the marsh – before the radio went dead. As it happened, there were six officers still in the accommodation block and they were trying to transmit to the helos. There was no one else at this stage to transmit to. The big red-and-white Helix choppers were all very capable, two of them had the weapons to destroy a submerged submarine and the other had rockets to outrange the US Stingers. But they were also very exposed and very noisy. With their twin high rotors and four-corner landing wheels they looked like a cruising flight of pterodactyls. The pilots brought them in to land, out on that rough ground 200 yards from the steam, and all nine occupants – pilots, navigators and gunners – ran for the accommodation block to receive whatever orders there might still be.

That left the SEALs, for the moment, unthreatened. Commander Hunter instructed them to keep going. He told them to carry Buster somehow between them, and Rattlesnake and his rookie assistant made a chair with their linked hands. Buster was able to sit in it, and he could lean back into the powerful arms and chest of Catfish Jones. Once they found a regular stride they were able to move fast, with Buster's weight distributed between them. Much faster than if he had to walk himself. They pressed on beneath the trees, struggling forward, dreading the sound of the returning helos. But none came and Rick led them on down to the inlet, watching the compass, trying to keep on course two five-five, more southerly than their previous route. The roaring of the steam provided them with inspiration, a feeling of self-congratulation. They had done what they came to do and to a Navy SEAL that represents the meaning of life.

At 0440 they noticed the reeds and grasses petering out, and there was a new urgency in the bleeper sounding out from the inflatable boats. Rick knew they must be close and then he saw the water, gleaming in a kind of aerial phosphorescence from the snow-white steam towering over the entire island. It was a wide, shallow inlet, probably fifty yards across, and down the inlet, possibly 100 yards away, they could see five black figures trying to drag the boats nearer. Rick Hunter snapped sharply into the radio receiver, 'DALLAS. RIGHT HERE. Over.'

'Okay, sir,' the reply came back. 'It's just too shallow. We can't get the boats nearer, even empty. I'm coming back to the shore now. Hold everything. Over.'

One minute later Lieutenant MacPherson, followed by Mike Hook, came splashing through the shallows. 'Sir,' he said. 'How about that? What about that steam? Way to go, right!'

'Way to go, kid. What now?'

'The bottom of this creek's firm. Let's get Buster inboard. The guys are hiding the boats under that grass. It's a beautiful overhang – choppers never even saw them. C'mon Rattles. Okay, Buster, ole buddy, let's go home.'

The full team stepped into the water and began to move on down to the boats, Rick now carrying the M-60, all the others holding the MP-5s, one rookie with the second belt of ammunition. Their hoods were up, wetsuit trousers folded and clipped over the tight rubber shoes, custom-made to fit the flippers. With no Draegers, bombs, explosives or hardware, it was easy going.

Except that suddenly, out there above the trees, they could hear the sound of the helos returning, the pilots now firmly briefed as to the direction the fleeing murderers had taken: *They have to be down along the shore of that stream. Look for boats and look for men in black combat suits.* The helos all had their square rear doors open and inside each one a gunner crouched behind a machine-gun twice the size of the M-60, aiming it out through the gap. Up front the navigator, wearing night goggles, sat beside the pilot, calling back target instructions.

This was big trouble. The SEALs were close to the boats, but there was no protection in there and walking down the bright water of the inlet they were at their most vulnerable point of the entire mission.

'Get into the shore and hit the deck right now.' Rick Hunter was not joking and he was not in time, either. The lead helicopter came battering in over the treetops. It was heading west out over the water when the rear navigator spotted movement in the shallows. He snapped out an order to the pilot to bank left and hover at 100 feet. Then he told the gunner where he had seen movement and he opened fire, raking the shoreline with a fusillade of bullets, ripping into the grass, making vicious lines in the water. The first burst hit the last man into the reeds, and Catfish Jones took the full volley in his back and head. He fell dead into the shallows, still trying to hold on to Buster Townsend. Rattlesnake Davies, now left carrying Buster all on his own, saw Catfish hit the water, saw the bullets lashing all around him and still went back to try to drag him to safety.

By some miracle the bullets missed Rattlesnake and even though he knew Catfish was surely dead, he would not let go and he dragged the former North Carolina fisherman out of the firing line, and kept saying over and over, 'C'mon, Catfish, buddy, we'll be all right. I know we'll be all right. Just keep comin', buddy. We're gonna be fine.' When at last he was under cover, he turned Petty Officer Jones over so the others could not see the terrible effects of the bullets, especially not the gaping hole in the back of his head.

Rick Hunter knew instantly what had happened. 'We just have to keep still,' he told them all. 'Remember that machine-gunner has no idea whether he hit anyone or not. Heads down, don't move and say a prayer for Catfish. He was a great and brave man. But we have to go forward and save ourselves.'

'Sir, we're not leaving him, are we, sir?' Rattlesnake Davies was beside himself. 'I can't leave him, sir. I can't leave him.'

'Don't be fucking stupid, Rattles. Of course we're not fucking leaving him.' The Commander knew exactly how to talk to people who were on the verge of losing their grip.

'Jesus, sir. How the hell are we going to get outta here?' said Lieutenant MacPherson.

'By using our brains, staying quiet, holding our nerve, hiding when we have to and hitting back hard when we get a chance.'

'What worries me most is the daylight coming,' said Dallas. 'It's headed for 0500 and I'm guessing it's gonna be light by 6.30 – we got ninety minutes max to make the open water.'

'It ain't gonna be all that great when we do, unless we can get some help. I'm counting on my buddy Danny for that.'

They could now hear the three helos making a long circle out over the Haing Gyi shoal and their clatter died out to the east, which signified they were coming right back in roughly six minutes from now. Commander Hunter rallied his team. They got Buster to his feet and walking. Two of the rookies dragged Catfish Jones's body out into the water, face up, and began to pull him through the shallows towards the inflatables only fifty yards away. It was slower than anyone wanted, but the skies seemed clear and the fresh water running down towards the ocean was cleaning the wounds of the dead SEAL who had destroyed the Chinese frigate.

They reached the boats safely, placed Catfish in one and

stretched Buster out comfortably in the other. The two Navy boat drivers, seamen Ward and Franks, helped load the rest of the men inboard. Rattlesnake was in with Buster, plus Rick Hunter and the two rookies who had served with them outside the power plant. Lieutenant MacPherson was in the other boat. Two more rookies went into the second craft, where Mike Hook was already sorting out the gear and organizing the M-60. They were still in the cover of the overhanging trees, but the weight had put the boats on the bottom. Commander Hunter and Lieutenant Allensworth went back in the water and the skies were clear. It was still dark and the Team Leader decided they should at least be floating ready for the moment when they would make a run for it, straight down the widening river and across the shoal. 'The grass is just as good to hide down there another fifty yards as it is up here,' he said, 'and there's probably five feet of water. Bobby and me'll drag us down there. I'll pull, he'll shove. I don't like boats aground in a foot of water.'

Rick Hunter seized the painter of the lead boat and heaved. Astern Bobby Allensworth pushed with all his strength and the boat moved. Rick heaved some more and the boat slid off the mud with water under its keel. 'One at a time. We'll take 'em separately,' he said. 'Use the paddles to stay as far into the grass as you can.' Commander Hunter began to haul the boat along, with Bobby at his side, preventing it from drifting out into the bright stream.

They'd gone twenty-five yards when the helos came back and the sound of the steam roaring out of the power plant deadened the noise of the engines. Bobby Allensworth saw them before he heard them, and yelled at Rick to shove the boat inshore and then hit the water. The SEAL Commander turned, saw the helos about a half-mile off, racing into the inlet where they had opened fire

417

before. The pilot banked right, losing height as he came in over the trees. The navigator thought he spotted something in the water and ordered the gunner to open up along the bank again.

Once more the bullets from the big Russian-made machine-gun ripped into the left bank and he kept firing all the way down its length. The two SEALs dived face down into the water and the helicopter overflew them. But the second one didn't. Rick Hunter and Bobby surfaced without knowing it was there and the second machine-gunner, himself wearing night goggles, spotted them and rained fire down on them. The chopper was so low it could hardly miss and with heart-breaking courage the SEAL from the Los Angeles ghetto flung himself on to his Commander's back and took eleven bullets, which jolted his entire body, obliterating his spine, neck and head. He died instantly, clinging to Rick's back, still the devoted bodyguard.

Rick Hunter forced himself up out of the mud, safe but wet. 'Shit, Bobby,' he said. 'You trying to drown us both?' Then he saw Bobby Allensworth, lying in the water, face up, blood streaming down his face where two bullets had almost gone right through. Rick just had time to lift him up and into the boat, before he broke away, momentarily burying his head in the blank rubber side of the hull. No one had ever seen Rick Hunter that close to breaking before.

Lieutenant MacPherson saw what happened and now he, too, went over the side, manhandling the craft into the deeper water. 'Those fucking little creeps,' he said. 'But at least we know where we stand. We gotta float and we gottta fight. Get those fucking M-60s ready right now and start the engine.' They drove along to Commander Hunter, while Chief Mike Hook laid out the ammunition belts for the M-60s, none too soon. The Chinese helicopters were making a long turn, clearing intending to return to the inlet.

'Sir, I'm sorry,' said Dallas. 'Really sorry. But I got the machine-gun ready in our boat. You all set here? Get under the grass again. We'll let 'em have it as they come in, sustained fire on the leader, right? Everything we got, to down one of 'em. Discourage the others, right?'

'Right, Dallas. Let's go.'

But the Chinese pilots were not certain they had done any damage at all so far. So they fanned out, with just the leader flying back down the bloodstained little waterway. He came in low and as he did so, the SEALs opened fire with everything they had from the little boats behind the grasses. Dallas blew thirty rounds straight into the rear door of the chopper, killing the gunner and, somehow, the navigator. Mike Hook blasted away at the engines, set topside left and right below the rotors, and Commander Hunter, firing with a venom he had never experienced before, emptied an entire belt of 100 rounds into the cockpit area of the rocket-firing Helix-B. It might have been the engine, it might have been the bullets smashing through the side windows, it might have been anything. Whatever it was, the helicopter was suddenly belching flames and it spun over and slammed into the water at 130 mph. 'Fuck me,' said one of the rookies graphically.

At which point they could all see the lights of the two remaining Helix choppers wheeling round to the north, running up the narrow island where the downstream channel parts, before slowly turning east, back towards the blazing naval base.

The two surviving pilots were confused. They had just seen thirty-three per cent of their attack force destroyed. The ships upon which they normally served were gone. There was no fuel. No electricity. Hundreds were dead. The entire base was engulfed in fire. In the epicenter of the inferno was a roaring white phenomenon, direct from hell. They had no one, formally, to whom they must report and they had just seen, first hand, the firepower of their adversaries. No two Chinese warriors had ever had so little stomach for the fight. They headed again for the rough ground opposite the power station, to land once more and inform the remaining group of officers what had befallen them.

The SEALs, of course, did not know all this. But Commander Hunter again rallied his battered team. 'Guys, we have to break out of here some time and it might as well be now. How many ammunition belts do we have?'

Seaman Ward, a tough-looking Irishman from Cleveland, said, 'We brought six. You guys had one left, which you used, sir. So we got four unused and half of two others.'

'Okay, divide 'em up. We'll take one gun in the lead boat, which I'll handle. Lieutenant MacPherson and Chief Mike Hook will operate the other two. Get the paddles and shove out. Soon as the water's deep enough, drop the engines and go. Someone fire up the radio and I'll get the signal in to the satellite.'

The two boats paddled out through the shallows and into the wide channel. It was definitely getting light now; not sufficiently to see Shawn Pearson's map clearly, but the tiny point of the flashlight showed three feet of water. They dropped their engines at 0520 and under deserted skies, still lit up to the east by the burning naval base, they accelerated the engines mildly, making course two-six-zero, eight-knots, straight for the uncertain waters of the Haing Gyi shoal.

0528 USS Shark. *16.00N 94.01E.*
Speed 3. Racetrack Course. PD.
Lieutenant-Commander Headley read the new signal with absolute horror:

070520JUN07. 16.00N 94.18E. Under heavy fire from pursuing helos. Lieutenant Allensworth, Petty Officer Jones both killed. Inflatables undamaged. Headed for Haing Gyi shoal course two-three-zero flank speed. Downed one Helix. We have ammo and still three M-60s. Request *Shark* assistance. Difficult for us in open waters. Hunter.

The CO was again not in the control room. Dan Headley summoned the senior executives in the submarine. Master Chief Drew Fisher was already in there and the Officer of the Deck, Lieutenant Matt Singer, had the conn. Lieutenant Pearson came in, accompanied by the Combat Systems Officer, Lieutenant-Commander Jack Cressend. The Sonar Officer, Lieutenant-Commander Josh Gandy, came in last. 'Gentlemen, I am going to read out to you two signals we have received in the last two hours from the SEAL team we inserted last night into Burma.'

From their faces it was not difficult to discern the pain each man felt from the death of the two SEALs and the wounding of another.

'As you can see from the signal, they are essentially making a run for it,' said the XO. 'A high-speed run back to this ship. They have about eighteen miles to travel, which puts them in open waters for around forty-five to fifty minutes. The Helix will make 130 knots, no sweat. He could get here in about eight minutes. Which makes the SEAL team sitting ducks. Those damn Russian choppers carry a lot of hardware and they plainly have heavy machine-guns. The guys might shoot one of 'em down, but they might not. The odds have to favor the helos. Which means that Rick and the rest of the guys will all be dead some time in the next hour.'

Dan Headley paused and he could see the unease written on their faces. 'It is my view', he said, 'that we comply with their request and head on in to save them. As you know, we're just about on the fifty-meter line and we have about eighty feet below the keel. We can probably move in at fifteen knots PD for four miles, but we can make twenty-plus on the surface, so I'm proposing we surface right now and go straight for it. There is no serious Chinese naval presence left in the area, thanks to them. But we may have to take the Helix out with the Stingers. The sooner we get the inflatables under Stinger cover the better chance they'll have. Gentlemen, I am proposing we make all speed inshore to rescue them. Is anyone not in favour of that action?'

Lieutenant Pearson, Lieutenant-Commanders Cressend and Gandy said, almost in unison, 'In favor, sir.'

Chief Fisher said, 'You don't even have to ask, sir. Sure we're in favor. We have the gear to save 'em. Jesus Christ, let's *go*.'

'Officer of the Deck, steer course one-one-zero, stand by to surface.' There was no mistaking the firm edge to his voice.

'Aye, sir,' said Lieutenant Singer with equal emphasis. Like the XO and Chief Fisher, he understood this was tantamount to a total confrontation. He had, after all, heard their Commanding Officer insist that such a decision was going to be made only by him. Commander Reid had also left little doubt that his decision was likely to be negative. His words had betrayed his own worst fears: *Do you have any idea of the consequences of what you are proposing*?

USS *Shark* nonetheless surged forward, shoving her blunt nose through the water at twenty-two knots on the surface of the Bay of Bengal.

'Depth twenty fathoms, still fifty feet below the keel, course steady one-one-zero, making twenty-two knots.'

The submarine had been virtually stationary for twelve hours and the sudden dramatic change in speed was obvious to everyone. But to the XO, Lieutenant Singer and Chief Fisher there was something far more dramatic waiting in the wings, and there was not long to wait. Commander Reid came through the door with a face like an ocean storm. But he spoke quietly. 'Lieutenant-Commander Headley,' he said. 'Where precisely do you think you are taking my ship entirely without my permission and, I suspect, entirely contrary to opinions I have already expressed?'

'Sir, I am taking the ship inshore on a rescue mission to save a team of United States Navy SEALs from what I consider to be imminent death. I am certain this course of action is approved by every man serving on this ship including, I hope, yourself.'

'Well, your certainty is misplaced. I wonder if you would be kind enough to inform me why you believe death to be imminent?'

'Because they are being pursued, sir, by two Russian-built Helix helicopters and they are in open boats, inflatables, on the open sea, protected only by three M-60 light machine-guns, which will probably be no match for the weapons against them.'

'Are the Helix aircraft ASWs?'

'I believe one of them must be, sir. They came from the two warships moored in the base. So I doubt there would be more than one Type B assault craft. There were almost certainly two Type A ASWs, which means there's at least one left. The guys downed one of the three.'

'I see. And how do you propose to continue this mission of mercy. On the surface?'

'Yes, sir.'

'I see.' Commander Reid's tone was cold. 'Now I want to get this straight. You are proposing to take *my ship, on the surface* into the direct path of an oncoming Russian-built helicopter, which may be carrying rockets which outrange us? IS THAT CORRECT, LIEUTENANT-COMMANDER?'

'Yes, sir.'

'Have you gone mad, XO?'

'I do not believe so, sir.'

'Then explain yourself, sir, and while you are about it, consider, if you will, the conversation you and I had less than two hours ago.' Commander Reid's eyes were moving back and forth across the control room. His head was turning only slightly and his stare was upon all three of those present. 'RETROGRADE! RETROGRADE, XO! The great planet Mercury is in retreat. I have tried to explain this to you and I trust you have relayed my concerns to the crew. WELL, HAVE YOU?'

'No, sir.'

'WHY NOT, DAMN YOU! DO YOU THINK THERE IS SOMETHING MORE IMPORTANT?'

'I am not really qualified to offer an opinion on that, sir.'

'NO, XO. NO, YOU ARE NOT. Because you are an ignorant man. Like all these others. You know nothing of the cycles of the Universe. You know only minor details. Details of your own insignificant life and those immediately around you. You know nothing, XO. Nothing.'

'As you wish, sir.'

'I have tried to be patient with the terrible depths of your ignorance, Lieutenant-Commander. I have attempted to explain that Mercury rules so much of our lives, particularly those of serving naval officers, because of the planet's supreme involvement with transportation and communications. It is apparent to me, as it must be apparent to you, that the forces of the planet are already at work. If you happen to have been Chinese, working at the naval base, you have faced catastrophe probably unprecedented in your lifetime. And what has been destroyed?

424

Ships, fueling facilities and communications. The essence of any naval base. The targets of the great planet.

'As for our own operation. Plainly the SEAL mission has gone drastically wrong. The journey they are now on may be their last. AND YOU, XO, ARE TRYING TO TAKE MY SHIP INTO THE PATH OF A HELICOPTER ARMED WITH ROCKETS WHICH CAN PIERCE OUR PRESSURE HULL? RIGHT NOW, WITH MERCURY RETROGRADE? NO, SIR. NO, YOU WILL NOT.'

'Not everyone believes in astrology, sir.'

'No, of course not. But many great men believe in it. Who was the greatest US President in recent years, the man who rebuilt the Navy?'

'President Reagan, sir.'

'Exactly so. He and his wife believed. They understood the cycles of the Universe. They took expert consultation, as many great men before them have done. And now, XO, turn this ship round and return to our official rendezvous point, 16.00N 94.01E. AND WHILE YOU ARE CARRYING OUT MY ORDERS, REMEMBER THE OLDEST RULE OF THE NUCLEAR SUBMARINE COMMANDER: NEVER, NEVER, EVER, TAKE YOUR SHIP TO THE SURFACE IN THE FACE OF THE ENEMY. TURN IT ROUND, LIEUTENANT-COMMANDER.'

Dan Headley replied slowly and carefully. 'I am afraid I cannot do that, sir,' he said.

'Lieutenant-Commander, I am going to pretend, for the moment, I never heard that. I say again, turn this ship round, RIGHT NOW!'

'I think you heard me, sir. I am afraid I cannot do that. Under any circumstances whatsoever . . . Conn-XO, continue course one-one-zero at flank, same course, same speed.'

'Lieutenant-Commander Headley, you are forcing me to conclude that you are conducting a one-man mutiny on this ship. Hence I now formally place you under ship's arrest and I command you to leave the control room.'

'I am afraid that will not be happening, sir.' With that, Dan Headley summoned the senior executives of the ship back to the control room. One by one they entered, the Lieutenant-Commanders Jack Cressend and Josh Gandy, the Navigation Officer, Lieutenant Shawn Pearson. Master Chief Fisher and the Officer of the Deck, Lieutenant Matt Singer, were already there. 'I have consulted with the ship's senior execs already, sir,' said Dan Headley. 'It is the opinion of each man that it is our duty to save the platoon of SEALs if that is possible. We are a warship and we're certainly equipped to deal with a couple of aging Chinese Navy helos. The SEALs have just acted with the utmost bravery, successfully carrying out the orders of, I understand, the President of the United States, the National Security Adviser and the Chief of Naval Operations. Only if I receive direct orders from one or all of those three men will I cease and desist in my efforts to save our colleagues.'

Commander Reid swelled into what looked like the opening moments of a towering rage. 'XO!' he bellowed. 'Do you have any idea what it would be like if one of those helicopters hit and sank us – could you imagine us being like the Russians in the *Kursk*, trapped on the floor of the ocean, suffocating to death? CAN YOU IMAGINE THAT, XO?'

'Perhaps not so well as you can, sir.'

'If you only knew, Lieutenant-Commander. If you only knew, as I know, the terror of such moments.'

Surrounded by his fellow officers, Dan Headley stared straight back at the Commanding Officer and he spoke kindly. 'Sir, it is my opinion that you have not been feeling terribly well recently. You have been under strain and I think everyone would prefer you to grab some sleep, while we take care of this rescue. As you know, we are moving towards the SEALs as fast as we can go and I am afraid nothing is going to stop that. The crew will not leave the SEALs to die and that is an end to it.'

Commander Reid once more bristled with fury. 'THE ONLY THING AT AN END RIGHT NOW IS YOUR CAREER, XO, AND THE CAREERS OF ANYONE WHO WISHES TO SUPPORT YOU IN THIS LUNATIC ADVENTURE.'

'I don't think so, sir. But perhaps you would now leave the area, because we are about to become very busy. Lieutenant Pearson, if the guys were in the shoal waters at 0535, making twenty-five knots, where are they now? How far from us?'

But before Shawn Pearson could run those calculations, Commander Reid exploded. 'I WILL NOT HAVE THIS DEFIANCE. I AM THE COMMANDING OFFICER OF THIS SHIP AND I WILL NOT HAVE HER TAKEN DELIBERATELY INTO A FATAL CON-FRONTATION. NOW STEP ASIDE, OFFICER OF THE DECK. I'M TAKING THE CONN. XO, YOU WILL ALSO STEP ASIDE WHILE I ISSUE NEW, CORRECT ORDERS TO THE PLANESMAN. I WANT THIS SHIP TURNED AND RUNNING BELOW THE SURFACE IMMEDIATELY.'

No one spoke. No one moved. *Shark* kept running forward, fast, on the surface, towards the SEALs.

Lieutenant Pearson broke the ice. 'Sir, I don't think they could have reached the shoal before 0540. The approach from the channel through the marshes is very shallow, medium speed at best. But they could have rushed across the shoal. There's always three or four feet there, even at low tide in the worst parts. Four miles would have taken them probably twelve minutes, so they would be right off Mawdin Point, running fast, west, at 0552. Right now I have 0550, two minutes from now there should be eight miles between us, closing at forty-seven knots. Probably see 'em from the bridge in around ten minutes.' Lieutenant Pearson had spoken as if the CO were not even in the control room, never mind in control of the ship.

The XO turned once more to Commander Reid and said quietly, 'I'm putting you on the sick list, sir. I think that would be best for everyone.'

'XO, you are doing no such thing. I am taking command of this ship, and I am turning round and going below the surface, where I intend to remain. If the SEAL team arrives being pursued by the Helix helicopters, I will remain below the surface. Because, XO, unlike yourself and others in this room, I am governed by Navy Regulations. Nuclear submarines do not travel on the surface in the face of the enemy. NOW STEP ASIDE.'

Lieutenant-Commander Headley did not move. He simply said, 'Under Section 1088 of United States Navy Regulations I am relieving you of further duty. Since you have refused my offer of placement on the sick list, I am placing you under arrest. I am next in the succession to command. I am plainly unable to refer the matter to a common superior and I am confident that your prejudicial actions are not caused by instructions unknown to me . . .'

Commander Reid raised his arms in exasperation, holding them high and slightly to the front, like a Catholic priest before communion. 'MY PREJUDICIAL ACTIONS! How dare you, XO. This entire episode has been caused by your childhood friendship with Commander Hunter. We all know you and the SEALs have been buddy-buddy ever since we arrived in Diego Garcia. This has come down to loyalty. Your loyalty to those damn brutes in the rubber inflatables, against my

428

loyalty to the 107 officers and men in this nuclear submarine. YOU ARE A DAMNED CHARLATAN, Lieutenant-Commander. You may have fooled some of the crew, but you have not damned-well fooled me. SO STEP ASIDE.'

'COMMANDER REID. YOU ARE UNDER ARREST.' Dan Headley was not speaking kindly any more. 'Chief Fisher, go and round up six seamen and escort the former Commanding Officer to his room, where he will be confined until further notice.

'Now, Officer of the Deck, continue at the conn and continue this course with all speed. Lieutenant-Commander Gandy, have comms try to contact the little boats. Lieutenant-Commander Cressend, have Stinger missiles brought up, ready to be fired from the sail. Lieutenant Pearson, report to the bridge. I'll be there in a few minutes. That's all.'

Every man so addressed replied with a sharp, 'Aye, sir.' Then Lieutenant-Commander Headley turned back to Commander Reid. 'I should very much like to think you are just undergoing psychological problems, which may have been with you for a long time. However, the only alternative view available to me is that you are nothing short of a damned coward.'

'Those are the remarks of an insolent and very misguided officer,' replied the ex-CO. 'I have the lives of the 107 officers and men in this ship very much on my mind and I am aware that, in order to save your friend Hunter, you are quite prepared to sacrifice the lives of every one of us.'

'I suppose it would never occur to a man like you that we can fight and win this thing, down the Chinese helicopters flying out of their burned-out base and save the lives of perhaps ten of the bravest men ever to have operated on behalf of our country. I don't suppose it would have occurred either to that French creep you so admire, or think you once were, or whatever crackpot thoughts go on in your mind.'

'You'll damned well pay for this, Headley. I'll have you court-martialed the moment we return to an American port.'

'You may try, of course. That's your prerogative. I shouldn't wonder if you did not have a few questions to answer yourself, about the death of yet another SEAL you flatly refused to help. Charlie Mitchell was his name and I can tell you now, Commander Bennett is unpleased.'

At that point, Master Chief Fisher arrived with a group of seamen. 'Take him below, Drew,' ordered the XO. 'Lock him in his quarters until further notice. If he resists, carry him. Just get him out of my sight.'

'And what am I supposed to do shut up in there until you feel inclined to release me?'

'I neither know nor care. Why don't you ask your dear friend Captain Grigory Lyachin. He'd probably help. I shouldn't bother to contact Villeneuve. He'd probably tell you to commit suicide, as he did.'

Commander Reid departed under escort, hissing venomously, 'You out-and-out bastard, Headley.'

0554. Bay of Bengal.
Off Mawdin Point, west coast of Burma.
The two fast inflatables, throttles wide open, raced across the flat sea. Out to the east the skies were colored rose-pink, but the sun had not yet risen out of the endless rice fields of the delta. No sun, no sign of the helicopters returning. They made a course change, heading, now, roughly west-nor'west, two-nine-zero, directly towards USS *Shark*. If the submarine remained at the rendezvous point they had a run of fifteen miles – perhaps forty minutes. But everyone hoped against all hope that *Shark*

was on her way in to try to save them. One of the rookies was balancing, standing up in the inflatable, holding an aerial way above his head, while Lieutenant MacPherson attempted to raise the submarine's comms room on the VHF radio. So far they were receiving nothing.

They raced on for another mile, then the lookout in the rear boat spotted them — the two Chinese Helix-A choppers battering their way across Burma's western headland, slowly, making a search along the shore, under strict instructions from the gathering of surviving officers at Haing Gyi to hunt down and destroy the criminals who had blown up the base.

Instantly, Commander Rick Hunter shouted, 'Man both the M-60s, don't waste your ammunition by firing too soon, they'll probably come in right on our six o'clock and then bank away. All three of us go for the cockpits first, then, Dallas, go for the rear doors. Try to take out the gunners. Mike you again go for the engines. I'll keep banging away at the pilots. Fire on my command.'

Moments later the Chinese pilots spotted the little boats, almost two miles away, holding a steady course, separated by a distance of only thirty yards.

Commander Hunter then ordered the boats to split up. 'Just make sure neither helo can fire at both boats at the same time.'

In thirty seconds the Helix-As were on them, coming in low, dead astern. 'Fire!' yelled Rick Hunter and the SEALs opened up, but it was very difficult in the bucking inflatables. They drove them away, neither helicopter managing to get a clean burst of fire at the boats. But they came round again. The leader banked right, giving his gunner a clear shot, and he raked the water and then the inflatables with bullets, ripping four large tears in the rubberized hull and hitting Commander Hunter in his upper thigh, and one of the rookies in the chest. A blistering fusillade of bullets from Dallas and Mike Hook drove the other one away, but neither chopper was damaged and, with blood pouring from his wound, Rick Hunter swung his machine-gun round and turned to face them again.

The two pilots, however, flew back to the east. One of their machine-gunners was badly wounded and they needed to caucus. That gave the SEALs three more minutes to restore order. Buster Townsend, using his good arm, tried to get a tourniquet round Commander Hunter's thigh, but it was not very successful and the blood kept flowing.

Then they saw it: the black hull of USS *Shark* barreling in over the horizon, a huge bow wave flooding blue water aft down the hull, splitting at the sail, and cascading off port and starboard. Commander Hunter, gritting his teeth, shouted, 'Steer straight for the submarine. GO-GO-GO!' There was about a mile between them, now, and they were closing at forty-seven knots. That represented only a little over a minute's running time.

Too long. The Helix-As were heading back towards them and they had the hang of it now. They came in low at an angle, the machine-gunners firing at will. Rick and Dallas both went for the rear door and again they hit one of the gunners, but the Chinese fired four lethal bursts and hit the lead boat, which was now shipping water. A vicious line of bullets ripped through the little craft, hitting Buster Townsend three times in the chest and killing him instantly as he tried to bandage the Commander. One of the rookies was also killed and Rattlesnake Davies took a bullet in his right upper arm.

The SEALs could not possibly survive another such onslaught, and both helos were on their way back again. Dallas and Mike Hook were still trying to clip in a new ammunition belt, and Rick Hunter, his hands sticky with blood, tackled them alone, blasting away at the cockpits. But this time the lead helo changed tactics, kept going forward and then swung hard to port, right across the bow of the sinking inflatable. Big mistake, because it flew right into the range of one of *Shark*'s missile men, waiting patiently on the deck behind the twin dry-dock shelters, the only one not up on the sail.

He aimed the five-foot tube straight at the helo, hit the buttons the infra-red-homing, heat-seeking Stinger needed and fired it dead straight at 600 yards' range. It blasted out of the tube, almost knocking the operator flat, adjusted its flight and streaked in at Mach-2, straight at the Helix. It slammed into the starboard engine and blew the entire aircraft to shreds. The second Helix banked round, determined to loose off a depth bomb against the hull of the submarine. But he was not in time. The missile men up on the sail had two more Stingers in the air before he could adjust height and course, and the astounded SEALs watched both engines explode in one single raging fireball, right below the rotors, before it joined its cohort, crashing into the waves off *Shark*'s port-side bow.

More boats were being launched off the deck to pick up the SEALs who were in the water and the crew of the second inflatable which, miraculously, was still floating, even though its entire starboard side had been split open by the bullets. Rick Hunter and Rattlesnake were hauled out first, and assisted up on deck. Stretchers were produced immediately for both the wounded SEALs. Body bags were brought up for Catfish, Bobby, Buster and the young SEAL Sam Liefer. They hauled Mike Hook, Dallas MacPherson, the two drivers and the four rookies aboard. Commander Hunter was drifting in and out of consciousness and they strapped him into the stretcher while they lowered it through the hatch on its way to the medical room, where the Navy doctor and his assistants awaited him.

Lieutenant-Commander Dan Headley was also down there to meet his old buddy, but Rick was very weak and needed a blood transfusion. Buster's tourniquet had probably saved his life, because a bullet had hit within millimeters of the femoral artery. He was awake for just a few seconds under the lights of the medical center when he saw Dan standing next to him. 'I can't believe this. I thought the game was up,' said Rick.

'You didn't think I'd leave you to die, did you? You didn't leave me.'

'Hey, thanks, shithead,' muttered the SEAL Commander, as they wheeled him into the emergency area.

Lieutenant-Commander Headley was now left alone with the consequences of his actions. He returned to the control room and ordered *Shark* back into deep water. Then he found a quiet corner to draft a signal back to San Diego and it took him longer than he had spent saving the SEALs. In the end it read:

To: COMSUBPACFLT. 070700JUN. Am 16.00N 94.01E. At 0540 this morning under Section 1088 Navy Regulations, I took command of the ship and placed Commander Reid under arrest on grounds of psychological instability. Commander Reid refused request for assistance from US Navy SEAL assault team operational in Bassein delta. All senior executives in agreement with my actions. USS *Shark* subsequently carried out rescue. Four SEALs killed in action before we arrived to save remaining eight men, including badly wounded Commander Hunter. Two Chinese Helix helicopters destroyed with missiles. Submarine undamaged. Request immediate orders to return either Diego Garcia or San Diego. Signed Lieutenant-Commander D. Headley, CO, USS *Shark*.

Dan put the signal on the satellite a little after 0700. He then appointed an official second-in-command, the Combat Systems Officer, Lieutenant-Commander Jack Cressend. Then he retired to sleep until 0900, having been awake for almost twenty-four hours. To sleep, perhaps to come to terms with the word 'mutiny' and to await his fate.

It was 1430 in Pearl Harbor when the communication from Lieutenant-Commander Dan Headley landed on the desk of Rear-Admiral Freddie Curran, Commander Submarines Pacific Fleet. In fact, it did not actually land, it just fell right out of the sky with a resounding thud, like a time bomb. Not in living memory had there been a mutiny in a United States warship on the high seas. Rear-Admiral Curran just stared at it for a few moments and tried to decide whether to have *Shark* routed back to Diego Garcia to rejoin the *Harry S. Truman* carrier battle group. Or to order the submarine to make all speed home to its base in San Diego, a distance of more than 12,000 miles – three weeks' running time. So far as Admiral Curran was concerned, most of the US Navy was already in the area of the Indian Ocean and the Arabian Sea, so it was scarcely imperative to get USS *Shark* back on station. Right now he was holding not so much a hot potato as an incandescent potato and that three-week cushion would give everyone time to decide a reasonable course of action.

It was clear from the signal that *Shark*'s XO had acted with the highest possible motives and there was no doubt that the veteran Commander Reid was something of an oddball. *But Christ*! thought Admiral Curran, *mutiny is mutiny, and it took place in a United States warship on the high seas*. He hit the secure direct line to the Pearl Harbor office of CINCPACFLT, Admiral Dick Greening, and read him the signal.

The Commander-in-Chief of the Pacific Fleet gulped. Twice. 'Mother of God,' he said. 'Mutiny?'

'Well observed, sir. I'd come to a similar conclusion myself.'

'I assume you've ordered the submarine back to San Diego.'

'I was about to do so and I will have done it in, say, fifteen minutes.'

'Okay.'

Admiral Curran's signal was carefully worded: 'Lieutenant-Commander Headley. Received your signal 1430. Return USS *Shark* San Diego immediately. Admiral Curran. COMSUBPAC.'

Dan Headley read it minutes later. 'Wonder if they'll give me a job at Hunter Valley?' he pondered. 'Because if the Navy court-martials me for mutiny, it's all over in dark blue. This is probably my first and last command. Kinda unusual end to an otherwise exemplary career.'

Meanwhile the surgeon operated on Rick Hunter's ripped thigh. The bullet had mercifully not damaged the femoral, but it had caused havoc with all the other blood vessels. The doctor stitched carefully for three hours, after a major blood transfusion for the mighty SEAL Leader. It was several hours before Rick could sit up in his bed and make any sense. All through the late afternoon he listened to Dan Headley's account of the mutiny in the privacy of the sick bay. At 1800 he decided to send in his own short satellite signal to Coronado. It read:

SEAL mission on Haing Gyi Island accomplished. Naval base, plus two PLAN warships destroyed. Four of our platoon killed including Lieutenant Allensworth, Petty Officer Jones and Buster Townsend. We also lost combat SEAL Sam Liefer. Both Riff Davies and myself were wounded. We would all have died but for the

436

actions of Lieutenant-Commander Dan Headley. Signed Commander Rick Hunter, on board USS *Shark*.

That signal went straight in to SPECWARCOM and arrived on the desk of Admiral John Bergstrom in the small hours of the morning. Its result was to put the Navy of the United States of America into one of the biggest quandaries it had ever experienced: whether to court-martial for mutiny a man who was not only an outstanding commander but also a plain and obvious hero.

Thirteen

Lieutenant-Commander Headley had offered Commander Reid every courtesy, including the freedom to send in his own signal to CINCPACFLT in Pearl. It went, of course, direct to Admiral Dick Greening and portrayed the actions taken by Shark's XO as nothing short of 'making a mutiny':

> My command was removed by my own Executive Officer in the most shocking and totally unjustifiable manner. The XO was tacitly supported by other senior officers in the crew, but not verbally. They merely failed to object to this plain and dangerous breach of Navy Regulations. I am thus drawn to the opinion that Lieutenant-Commander Headley stands guilty of making a mutiny and ought, by rights, to be court-martialed forthwith. signed Commander D. K. Reid, Commanding Officer, USS *Shark*.

'That', pondered the Commander-in-Chief, 'is not the message of a man looking for peace.' In that moment he understood that battle lines were about to be drawn, despite the obvious danger that press and public opinion might consolidate behind the hero who saved the embattled SEALs, and against the right and proper Commanding Officer of the nuclear submarine. So, as USS *Shark* made her way home across the wide Pacific Ocean, the High Command of the United States Navy was forced to acknowledge the probability of a court martial: a court martial which could very well split opinion in half, both in the Service and in the entire nation, if the press managed to grasp its significance.

Admiral Greening viewed the situation with such seriousness that he consulted immediately with the Pacific Submarine Chief, Admiral Freddie Curran. The two men left Hawaii that evening for Washington, to consult with the CNO, then with the Chairman of the Joint Chiefs, before taking the matter inevitably to the White House.

There was nothing on record in the annals of the US Navy which showed a court martial for mutiny and the CNO, Admiral Alan Dickson, was especially anxious for that situation not to change, certainly not on his watch, because mutinies, although rare, possess a special glory of their own. The leader inevitably presents himself as a Samaritan, saving his ship from disaster. Worse yet, he is frequently believed. Even in fiction, the most famous case being *The Caine Mutiny*, Captain Queeg was widely accepted as some kind of an obvious nutter.

Admiral Dickson greeted Admiral Greening with grave concern. Essentially, this should have been the province of the submarine fleet commander, Admiral Curran, but this was likely to be bigger than all three of them. An hour later only one fact was obvious: to get rid of the spectacle of putting a Navy hero on trial for his life and career it would be necessary to stop Commander Reid from pressing charges. Even then, a Navy Board of Inquiry might still recommend a court martial. In fact, they would almost certainly recommend that in any instance of mutiny on the high seas the offending officer must, by the very nature of his crime, face the most searching examination by his peers. That, of course, was all very fine, since Navy Boards of Inquiry can be carried out in the strict privacy of the Service. But there are certain crimes, transgressions and errors which, if committed by a senior officer, must be examined and certain findings must, by their very seriousness, be continued into a court martial.

Admiral Alan Dickson was extremely worried. They must, he knew, convene a Board of Inquiry, just as soon as *Shark* reached San Diego and, although it might be possible to lean on its members not to recommend court martial, that was a risky course of action. Members of official Navy Boards are apt to consider themselves sacrosanct in all their deliberations, and they would be well capable of recommending a court martial and making their decision public. Meanwhile, he and the two Admirals from Pearl Harbor were obliged to inform the Chairman of the Joint Chiefs that they stood on the verge of a public-relations nightmare and that they faced a terrible quandary: do we charge and court-martial Lieutenant-Commander Dan Headley for 'mutiny in a US warship on the high seas'? More important, what the hell can we do to stop it?

At 0900 the following morning they all stood in the office of the CJC, General Tim Scannell, and deliberated the issue: to court-martial the hero of the Bay of Bengal, the fearless naval Lieutenant-Commander who drove into the face of the enemy, destroyed that enemy and rescued one of the finest US Navy SEALs assault teams ever to serve the American people. 'Jesus Christ,' said General Scannell. 'The Big Man, over yonder, is not going to love this.'

Nor did he. The three Admirals and the General carefully explained the ramifications to Arnold Morgan and the President's National Security Adviser told them the whole scenario was a 'complete goddamned horror story'. His reason was, characteristically, one which they themselves had not considered. 'Gentlemen,' he said, 'I may not yet be ready to inform the People's Republic of China about our actions, neither in the Strait of Hormuz nor in the Bassein river delta. I intend to let them know when I'm good and ready, but that may not be quite yet. Now the trouble with a court martial, such as the one you are considering, is that it will promote, for one reason or another, *outrage*. Outrage on the one hand, in support of the case of a towering American hero, recognized by the SEALs as the savior of their mission. Then there will be another kind of outrage by the traditionalists, on behalf of the Commanding Officer, *outrage* that any half-assed little two-and-a-half can suddenly seize command and control of a US Navy nuclear submarine just because he doesn't damned well agree with something.

'Either way, whichever way a court martial jumps, you're gonna get outrage and you know what outrage does? It makes people talk. Animatedly and indiscreetly. In short, gentlemen, it blows gaffs, hard and fast. It causes people to vent their outrage to media assholes and other third-class citizens, and it causes that which we want to remain secret, for the greater good, suddenly to become very public. Media assholes, who know close to nothing in any depth about any subject, cannot tell the difference between what they believe is an exciting and dramatic story and blowing a major secret straight to the pain-in-the-ass Chinese, in flagrant disregard for the stability of world peace and world markets. That's what being a media asshole is. They have to take an examination in advanced ignorance and intermediate crassness before they're allowed to join. But – and you can mark my words on this – not one of them will put in a check call to the military: *Is this okay to use? Or might it put us in a compromising position with the Chinese?*

'No, gentlemen, that is not what they will do. They will instead seize upon the outrage of someone involved in this court martial and blab it all over the earth, to the possible damage of the USA. Not one of them will give a damn about the consequences. Children, gentlemen, always remember, they are essentially children. Which is why we gotta try to head off this court martial.'

Admiral Morgan's military visitors nodded in agreement. Alan Dickson was extremely worried. 'It's just the procedures, Arnie,' he said. 'You know them better than I do. Right here, we have a wounded, hurt and dangerous Commanding Officer. He's been humiliated in front of his friends, in front of his peers and in front of his family. There is nothing else in his mind except clearing his name. On the other hand we have a plainly gallant and probably brilliant XO who, for whatever reason, believed his own CO was prepared to let the SEAL team die. So he seized the ship, arrested the CO and carried out his own program perfectly, destroyed the enemy and saved the SEALs.'

'Well said, CNO,' replied the NSA. 'That states it just like it is. I realize there is no way we can avoid a formal Navy Board of Inquiry, just to establish the facts. It's the events after that which may burn out of control. Because to exonerate Headley they gotta write the CO off as some kind of nut and they will not do that unless they are certain, to a man, that the guy is deranged.'

'That's not going to happen,' said Admiral Freddie Curran. 'Commander Reid is going to show up at the Inquiry, all scrubbed up in his number ones, and give his evidence in tones of calm, but surprised, incredulity. They might make him look a bit eccentric, but no group of veteran officers serving on a Navy Board is going to write off a fellow officer of thirty years' standing, ten of them commanding a nuclear submarine. "There, but for the Grace of God, go I."'

'Then our only chance', said Admiral Morgan, 'is to get with Commander Reid as soon as he arrives back in the USA and try to persuade him to admit he was not feeling well, and that he handed over command of the *Shark* voluntarily to his XO, who performed heroically.'

'That is correct, Admiral,' replied the CNO. 'But there's not a snowball's chance in hell of him agreeing to that. I could nearly guarantee we'll find a man bent on revenge, determined to punish the men who overthrew him in his own ship.'

'Yes. I am afraid you are right,' the Admiral replied. 'But we have to try. Because in the end, if Commander Reid wants that XO court-martialed, the Navy will have absolutely no option but to court-martial him.'

'And at that moment', said Admiral Dickson, 'we will be holding the flimsiest of redoubts against a massively hostile press and public, and I, for one, am not looking forward to it.'

'Do you think we could try the national security tack, the highly classified nature of the entire mission?' Arnold Morgan asked.

'That's probably our best shot, sir,' replied Admiral Dickson, 'certainly the one we should try first – and, of course, we do have the argument that events proved Lieutenant-Commander Headley correct. He achieved his objectives.'

'It's a powerful, but not necessarily winning, argument,' Admiral Morgan said thoughtfully. 'Though an old friend of mine, Iain MacLean – he's an ex-Royal Navy Flag officer submarines – once told me it was the best way to convince everyone of the merits of the case.'

'They'd never had a tougher one than this, though?' asked Admiral Curran.

'Tougher,' replied the National Security Adviser. 'They went to war over such a quandary.'

'They did?'

'Sure they did. The Falklands War. Iain MacLean was there.'

'I don't quite follow, sir?'

'Well, when the Argentinians invaded in the spring of 1982, they put a force of about 15,000 on the islands, which put the old Brits in a bit of a spot. They had this group of goddamned rocks, containing about 1800 of their citizens, in the middle of the South Atlantic, 8000 miles from home. They'd sold their carriers, there was no air cover for any assault force to land, the Falklands were now fortified by a well-equipped army, protected by a land-based air force. Unsurprisingly, the military advice was absolutely negative. The Royal Air Force said forget it, the Army said no air cover, no go. The United States wrote the whole thing off as impossible. In fact, everyone said it was impossible for the Brits to travel that far and win the islands back.

'Except for one man and he happened to be the First Sea Lord, Admiral Sir Henry Leach, another old friend of mine. He said it could be done. He knew the carriers were sold, but not yet gone, and he convinced Margaret Thatcher the Navy could do it. As most of you know, it was a goddamned shaky exercise. The Brits lost seven warships, more than 250 men and they fought like fucking tigers to pull it off. But they damn near lost it and, if they had lost it, one man would have taken the blame for probably Britain's most humiliating defeat: Henry Leach. However, they did not lose it. They won it, thanks almost exclusively to Admiral Sandy Woodward and the Parachute Regiment. Without them, they *would* have lost it. Trust me. But the notion of taking an unforgivable risk, which you could say Henry Leach did, is never mentioned. Why? Because he was proved *right*.'

'Guess we could do with a few more like him around here,' said Admiral Greening. 'Guys with the courage of their convictions, guys prepared to operate with no thoughts whatsoever for their own self-interest.'

'Guys like Dan Headley,' said Arnold Morgan softly.

Two weeks later, Friday, June 24.
San Diego.

Admiral John Bergstrom paced the inner sanctum of the offices of SPECWARCOM. Before him sat the silent figures of the professional heads of America's Pacific Strike Force, Admirals Freddie Curran and Dick Greening. 'You realize that my ultimate successor in this chair, Commander Rick Hunter, is quite prepared to put his entire career on the line and resign his commission over this, do you not?'

'Of course we do, John,' Dick Greening replied. 'I am simply trying to ask you if you feel just as strongly. Will you also resign if Dan Headley is court-martialed and found guilty?'

'Right now it is not necessary for the United States Navy to know whether I will resign. However, you should bear in mind that I have not yet decided not to.'

'John, I know how badly you all feel about this,' said Admiral Greening. 'But I am afraid you have to inform the appropriate authorities if you intend to announce your retirement if the Navy Board recommends the court martial of Lieutenant-Commander Headley.'

'Listen, you guys,' said Admiral Bergstrom, slipping into the easy informality this particular high command had always enjoyed. 'We've all known each other for a lot of years, and I think we all know the pros and cons of this case. But I am here to tell you I have never known such intense feelings of betrayal by the SEALs. It is common knowledge that this nutcase captain of yours refused to help the guys coming out of Iran. Indeed, he left one of my men to die and he would have left the whole lot of my men to die coming out of the Bassein delta. You guys have somehow appointed a fucking psychopath to take my SEALs in and out of an area of operations. Twice. There's no way we're gonna sit still for that.

'Anyway, my position here would be untenable if you decide to jail Lieutenant-Commander Headley for making a mutiny. I'd never be taken seriously again. Not by the Special Forces. I would *have* to resign because I'd be a standing joke — the SEAL chief who sent the guys in, put 'em in the hands of a rule-book shit who everyone knew was fucking crazy. Do you have any idea what that would do to the morale of this place? Guys, you have somehow to stop this bullshit, you have to award Dan Headley a high decoration and somehow get this fuckwit Reid the hell out of the United States Navy. Quietly, if possible.'

Admiral Greening nodded in agreement. 'If it were that damned simple we wouldn't be sitting in this room, John,' he said. 'But it isn't. These things develop a life of their own. We have, right here, a ten-year veteran of nuclear submarine command who was arrested on the high seas by his own XO and fellow officers, relieved of command of his own ship, locked up and told to shut up, while his orders were flagrantly contravened. Those actions plainly give him the right to be heard at least. The right to request a full Navy Board of Inquiry. The right to defend himself in front of his peers.'

'Okay, okay, I have it,' replied the SEAL boss. 'But let me ask one question. In this specific case, who was right, Headley or Reid? I mean both morally and in terms of war-fighting expertise, and even gallantry, concern for others. Headley or Reid?'

'Headley. Plainly. Headley was right,' replied Admiral Greening. 'But I'm afraid that's irrelevant. Being right gets you off the hook, so long as no one cares to push the case. But here we have an antagonist who has been wronged in his own eyes and does not give a flying fuck whether Headley was right or not. We have a CO who is brandishing the goddamned official book of rules and saying loudly, "I'm the injured party, and it says so, right

here between these sacred covers." Well, Admiral
Bergstrom, we got a problem, a real, live problem, and we
gotta deal with it. If you don't like it, Johnny, baby, I'm
afraid that's show business.'

Admiral Bergstrom chuckled. 'You want me to get a
couple of guys to take him out, nice and quiet?'

It was, of course, only a joke, a black, macabre joke. But
the iron-sweet simplicity of the solution was not lost on
the two visiting Admirals and neither of them laughed.
Admiral Freddie Curran just said, 'Precisely the kind of
solution one would expect from the SEALs. What's that
motto of theirs? Oh, yes: *There are very few of the world's
problems which cannot be solved with high explosive.* Isn't that
it?'

'Guess so. And it's mostly right.' The SEAL Chief
looked grim now, because the consequences of this
impending Board of Inquiry were beginning to look so
far-reaching that they were way out there beyond the
horizon. 'When do you want to initiate the Inquiry?'

'Oh, right away, John. Here in San Diego as soon as
Shark arrives back. She's due Tuesday night. We'll aim for
Thursday. Most of the men are entitled to leave, so we'll
get under way while they are all right here in the base.'

'Will it take long?'

'I'm not sure of that. If the Board is in any way
compliant they'll agree to make a firm decision, one way
or another, as soon as they have ascertained the facts. They
are not sitting in judgement on the case. They are just
being asked to establish the simple truth and most of that's
not in dispute:

'One: Was there a mutiny on board the submarine?
'Two: Was Commander Reid relieved of his command
and placed under arrest?
'Three: Who was responsible?

'Four: Did that officer have the support of the senior officers?

'Five: Why? What had the CO done wrong?'

'Dick, we're talking real basics then, at this stage?'

'Absolutely and those basics should be established very quickly. Which will allow the Board to arrive at one of two conclusions: (a) there was a mutiny, and the ringleader *must* be court-martialed under Navy Regulations; (b) there was no mutiny, the CO was under psychological stress and Lieutenant-Commander Headley was well within his rights to assume command of the ship under Navy Regulation 1088.'

'Yeah,' said Admiral Bergstrom, 'but (b) requires the CO to *agree* he was under stress and that Headley was correct to take over.'

'Afraid so,' Admiral Greening confirmed, 'and my forecast is that he will do no such thing. We will talk to Commander Reid at the highest level. Admiral Dickson will have him in to the Pentagon, maybe even to Admiral Morgan's office in the White House. They'll pressure him, but I cannot see him agreeing to accept the most complete humiliation any CO can suffer. Just can't see it.'

'Well, I've got another curve for you,' replied Admiral Bergstrom. 'Tonight, at approximately 2100, Commander Rusty Bennett is arriving back here from Diego Garcia and he has a major problem with your Captain Reid leaving that young combat SEAL to die out there in the Gulf. To my certain knowledge he is filing a formal complaint about the conduct of *Shark*'s CO during the time the guys were trying to get out of Iran. He's alleging that the seas were clear of any potential foreign warships and the skies were clear of foreign fighter aircraft. He's alleging cowardice of the very worst kind against your Captain Reid. I've seen the preliminary and it ain't pretty reading. Rusty, you know, was in the submarine at the time.'

'I think that may be rather helpful,' said Admiral Curran. 'Even Captain Reid may not relish the idea of appearing at a court martial and having to listen to two counts of cowardice against him by two different officers from two different but connected areas of operations.'

'The problem there is Commander Reid's degree of whackiness,' replied Admiral Greening. 'Let's face it, not to go beyond this room at this moment, he must be a whacko. You don't get guys like this hitherto outstanding XO Dan Headley and two proven SEAL combat Commanders, Hunter and Bennett, *all* thinking he's a complete jerk, along with a lot of other senior submarine officers, unless there's something the matter with him. And it's been my experience that the more of a whacko a guy is, the more he's likely to adopt a firm, unyielding defensive position. If he were normal he might say, "Okay, I'll back down, you guys save my career. I'll go for a little psychological help, and I'll leave the Navy with honor and a full pension. No court martials, no trouble." Unhappily, that is not the way of the greater-crested common whacko. He is apt to see the world from a very narrow perspective: his own. The psychologists call it loss of insight. It means that you can no longer grasp the views of anyone else.

'How many major murderers appear sorry? Full of regret? Very few. They try to justify their actions. Remember Son of Sam, in New York? Wasn't his fault, was it? There was a voice telling him to get out there and start killing. And what about that fucking dingbat they had in England, the Yorkshire Ripper, who murdered all those women? He was just cleaning up the streets, right? He wasn't sorry, despite battering innocent women, students, to death. He went to jail, mystified that society had turned against him. Pleaded not guilty, didn't he? Plainly, I'm not saying Commander Reid is a criminal. But I'd bet he's a whacko and whackos never make life easy. They defend. To the death.'

The journey back from the Indian Ocean had been fraught with tension. *Shark*'s original CO being confined to his cabin was a constant reminder to the entire crew that they were steaming back into big trouble. In the beginning a lot of the younger crew, anxious to see wives and girlfriends, wished to hell that Commander Reid could be reinstated in order to free them up to go home as soon as they docked. They anticipated a very formal welcome, which might even see certain popular and trusted members of the crew placed under arrest. Everyone knew he had been to some degree a party to mutiny. However, the presence of the wounded SEALs on board was a vivid reminder of the supreme heroism of the *Shark*'s XO and his fellow officers.

Everyone was in awe of Commander Hunter and 'his guys', and rumors of their success and bravery swept through the submarine. The four body bags stored in the torpedo room were also a chilling reminder of the SEALs' desperate battle for the Chinese base and, by the time the submarine approached California's coastal waters, opinion was hardening. Opinion that they, the *Shark*s were a part of this great and selfless campaign, and more and more of them began to stand four-square behind the Exec who had saved the Special Forces.

It was 2030 when USS *Shark* came in sight of the coast. She was making twenty knots through a warm evening, on a calm surface, which rose with the long Pacific swells but offered no discernible chop. Lieutenant-Commander Dan Headley stood on the bridge, along with the Navigation

Officer, Lieutenant Shawn Pearson and the Officer of the Deck, Lieutenant Matt Singer. Directly below them in the control room, Lieutenant-Commander Jack Cressend had the ship, with Master Chief Drew Fisher at the conn. They rounded Point Loma, heading up into the narrow channel which leads both to the US naval stronghold of San Diego and also to the headquarters of SPECWARCOM. Above them, to their port side on the heights, was the Fort Rosecrans National Cemetery, where Buster Townsend and Bobby Allensworth would both be laid to rest this week. The bodies of Catfish Jones and his colleague were being flown to their home states.

Shark slowed as she reached the narrows. She stood fair up the channel leaving the North Island Naval Air Station to starboard. Then she made her hard right turn towards the towering stilts of the Coronado Bridge and into the sheltered waters of San Diego Bay. Lieutenant-Commander Headley brought her alongside at 2120 and the mooring lines were attached. On the dock stood the resolute figure of Commander Rusty Bennett, in company with Admiral Bergstrom. The Pacific submarine boss, Admiral Freddie Curran, was also there. There were eight naval guards on duty too, along with a throng of wives, girlfriends and colleagues from the base.

As *Shark* was made fast and the men began to file out on to the deck there was a spontaneous burst of cheering from the crowd. The figure of Lieutenant-Commander Dan Headley stood motionless, unsmiling, on the bridge, watching the scene below as families looked forward to being reunited after months and months apart. It did not seem that much different from any other submarine home-coming in San Diego. But it *was* different. No ship had ever returned here after a mutiny on the high seas and there were certain protocols which had to be observed. Plainly, Commander Reid would be escorted immediately to the offices of the Submarine Fleet HQ in San Diego and, probably separately, Lieutenant-Commander Headley would also be required to attend a debriefing.

Admiral Curran had made it quite clear that no one was to be arrested. There was not to be a semblance of authoritarian action, just a formal welcome and a routine conference among senior officers. The less anyone knew about the events in the Bay of Bengal the better. Meanwhile, the two conflicting signals, sent from a distant ocean by *Shark*'s Captain and XO, were not much short of nuclear meltdown in Admiral Greening's private filing system.

Commander Reid was the first officer to leave the ship and he was greeted by Admiral Curran. The two men left immediately in a staff car for the central office complex. Thirty minutes later Lieutenant-Commander Headley, in company with the limping Commander Rick Hunter, crossed from the submarine to the shore where Commander Rusty Bennett and Admiral Bergstrom awaited them. They shook hands and separated, the two SEALs boarding a staff car with the Admiral, Dan Headley boarding another car alone with a staff driver. Curiously, there was little for the XO to say. His defense of his actions would be unwavering, scarcely varying from the short signal he had already sent.

The problem was Commander Reid. Could he be persuaded to agree that he was not in a proper frame of mind to conduct the SEAL rescue and that he had willingly handed over command of the ship to his number two? Within a half-hour the answer to that was obvious. No. With Admirals Greening and Curran *Shark*'s former CO boarded a military jet for Washington at first light on Monday morning, June 27.

They arrived at the Pentagon from Andrews Air Base at 1500 and were escorted immediately to the office of the

CNO, Admiral Alan Dickson. There, for the next four hours, the Head of the United States Navy, the Head of the Pacific Fleet and the Head of the Pacific Submarine Fleet attempted to persuade Commander Donald Reid that there was nothing to be gained from the court martial of his XO, save for the worst publicity the Navy had ever suffered.

The Commander did not agree. He felt there was something else to be gained: the salvaging of his own personal reputation. He was damned if he was going to condone in any way the actions of a group of mutineers, who had seized his ship and contravened his perfectly reasonable orders not to put a nuclear submarine in the path of anti-submarine-warfare Chinese helicopters with long-range capacity. Nothing that any of the Admirals said made even the slightest impression on him. Commander Reid knew his rights, he knew the Regulations of the United States Navy and he was going to play those rights by the book, the way he had always conducted his career. 'I intend, CNO,' he said, 'to stand before the Navy Board of Inquiry and to tell the absolute truth about the events that took place in the Bay of Bengal. I shall demand the court martial of the ringleader of the mutineers. With respect, sir, you must know I am entitled to that.'

'You may be so entitled,' said Admiral Dickson wearily. 'We are asking you to reconsider, in the interests of the greater good of the United States Navy and its image before the public.'

'Your request, with the greatest respect, is declined,' he replied firmly. Then Commander Reid shook his head and said almost in a mutter, as if speaking only to himself: 'This is not my fault, not my fault at all. I told him over and over the planet was in retrograde. If he had just had the sense to listen to me . . .'

453

'I'm sorry, Commander,' said the CNO. 'I didn't quite catch that?'

'Oh, nothing, sir. Nothing at all. I was just thinking and wishing things could be different. But I'm afraid they cannot.'

All three Admirals realized there was no point in pursuing this. Reid's mind was made up, and nobody was going to change it for him. He saw the situation with the obdurate vision of the unjustly accused. He not only wanted to preserve his own reputation, he also wanted to end the career of his XO. Commander Reid had no grasp whatsoever of the evidence which would be given on behalf of Lieutenant-Commander Headley and he had no interest in it. He knew only one thing: he had wished to play it safe, to keep his submarine out of harm's way, and he had been thwarted by the reckless actions of some damned two-and-a-half, who had never commanded a warship in his life.

On the flight back to San Diego Donald Reid sat separately and silently all the way, several seats behind the two Admirals. In contrast, they had much to talk about, because they were both struggling to find a way out of this particular mess. But there wasn't one, unless Reid reconsidered his position and, judging by his demeanor in the office of the CNO, *Shark*'s former CO had a very private agenda of his own, an agenda which would not easily be intruded upon.

'He's a strange kind of a guy, don't you think?' Admiral Curran said quietly. 'He has that confidence some people have. As if they could never be wrong. By the way, what did you make of that last stuff he was muttering? I couldn't really hear it.'

'No. I couldn't either,' replied Dick Greening. 'But I seemed to catch the word "retrograde". Tell the truth, I'm not real sure what it means.'

'It means going backwards, doesn't it?'

'Beats the hell outta me. But if it does mean that he must have been referring to our conversation. That sure as hell was going backwards.'

Eight days later, 0900 Wednesday, July 4.
San Diego Naval Base.
America's national summer holiday was still in beach–bound progress on this bright, sunlit California morning. The temperature was a near-perfect seventy-eight degrees and a light south-wester off the Pacific promised to keep the sun worshippers relatively cool before the fireworks in the evening.

In the shaded gloom of the big office he always used in San Diego, Admiral Dick Greening felt almost sick with worry. He had before him a memorandum, signed by Captain Stewart Goldwin, who was presiding over the Board of Inquiry. It read:

After three days hearing evidence in the USS *Shark* case, it is clear there was indeed a mutiny on board the submarine while on patrol in the Bay of Bengal. The facts are not in dispute. There was great sympathy for Lieutenant-Commander Headley, whose actions were courageous in the extreme. However, Commander Reid is demanding the court martial of his Executive Officer for making a mutiny on the high seas. And Navy Regulations permit a commanding officer to make such a demand.

With reluctance, I and my fellow members of the Board believe there is a prima facie case for a court martial and we are sending our findings to the Trial Service Office. The Judge Advocate General will then decide where Lieutenant-Commander Headley should indeed stand trial.

455

Admiral Greening stood up and walked across the office to a wide computer screen on the wall. He punched up the numbers 16.00N 94.01E. There before him was the exact stretch of ocean where this terrible drama had been played out. He could see the island of Haing Gyi, the swamp, the little creek running through it. He could see the Haing Gyi shoal marked clearly, the shallow water across which the fleeing SEALs had raced in their fast but tiny outboards. He could see the low, marshy headland of Mawdin Point and in his mind he pictured the scene: the Chinese helicopters mercilessly machine-gunning the Americans as they tried to get away; Catfish Jones dead, Bobby Allensworth dead, Buster Townsend dead, Rick Hunter pouring blood, still firing; all of them helpless sitting targets in the open boats. He imagined the terror, the courage. Then he imagined the sudden appearance of *Shark*, lambasting the choppers with their Stingers, saving the eight survivors of this awesome SEAL mission.

And now they want me to approve the court martial of the man who commanded the submarine? 'Jesus Christ,' said the Pacific Fleet Commander. It was as well there was no one in the room to see him so upset, as he stared at the screen, hearing again in his mind the staccato rattle of the murderous Chinese guns.

1500 (local) Same day.
Office of the National Security Adviser
The White House, Washington DC.
Admiral Morgan was displeased in the extreme. 'Alan,' he said, 'there's gotta be some way we can stop this. You want me to get the President to intervene?'

'I don't know,' replied Admiral Dickson. 'The trouble with the damned Navy is that certain things are just like presidential elections – ain't nothing anyone can do to stop 'em. They just happen.'

'Tell me about it. How about a presidential pardon for Lieutenant-Commander Headley? The man in the Oval Office, as Commander-in-Chief, has to be able to do at least that.'

'Well, I guess he could. Somehow. But that's not really the issue, is it, Arnie, old buddy? The press will want to know if the Navy has gone off its trolley, court-martialing such a man as Dan Headley. As you pointed out, it's the very act of court martial that is going to bring this whole thing right out into the open, where we don't want it to be.'

'Who's the Judge Advocate General in this case?'

'Veteran surface ship Commander, former lawyer, Sam Scott from Oregon. About as rigid a man as you could find. He'll play this case by the book. He'll look at the recommendations of the Board, check his goddamned law books and then decide that Lieutenant-Commander Headley should stand trial as charged.'

'Could we reason with him?'

'No chance. He'll just say what happens if the CO resigns and goes public, in a book, which will inevitably detail what he thinks is a cover-up.'

'Well, I guess it would be.'

'Sure would.'

'Well, what can we do?'

'We can put in a massive effort to help Dan Headley beat the rap.'

'But that'll mean we have to prove Reid is insane.'

'Correct. Then the media will jump all over us for putting in charge of submarines men who ought rightly to be in an institution for the seriously nerve-racked.'

'Damned if we do. Damned if we don't.'

'This case was always thus, Arnie. Either we talked Reid into a complete capitulation, which we couldn't, or we were going to find ourselves in the deepest possible shit. Where we now are.'

'Yeah. But it's not quite over.'

'Enlighten me, NSA.'

'We owe it to this Lieutenant-Commander Headley to help him prove his boss was both nuts and a fucking coward. And the press can go fuck 'emselves.'

'Yes, sir.'

0900 Wednesday, July 18.
Office of CINCPACFLT
Pearl Harbor.

The Judge Advocate General's decision took two more weeks to arrive. Now it lay smoldering on the sunlit desk of Admiral Dick Greening, just as it lay smoldering on the desk of Admiral Alan Dickson in faraway Washington DC.

After careful consideration of the evidence and obser-vations of the Navy Board of Inquiry which examined the events on board USS *Shark* in the Bay of Bengal, I have decided there is a prima facie case for the court martial of the Executive Officer Lieutenant-Commander D. Headley. He will thus stand trial for making a mutiny on the high seas on the morning of June 7, 2007, on which date he did relieve his Commanding Officer, Commander D. K. Reid, of his duties under Section 1088 of Navy Regulations.

On the basis of the depositions before me I have recommended that Commander Reid undergoes psychological examination by three doctors, including but not limited to one civilian practitioner.

My findings have been referred to the Trial Service Office for selection of trial counsel and defense counsel. I have recommended a senior judge advocate shall attend the proceedings, which will be heard in the Trial Service courtroom at the San Diego Navy base on a date to be arranged. Signed Captain Sam Scott, Judge Advocate General.

It was not unexpected, but the reality of the situation suddenly loomed before the Pacific Fleet Commander. This was it, the court martial of a US Navy hero, whose actions were witnessed not only by a crew of over a hundred completely supportive, very talkative seamen on board a fighting nuclear submarine, but also by eight highly regarded members of the US Navy's Special Forces, all of whom owed their lives to the actions of Lieutenant-Commander Headley. Their story was already well on its way around the SEAL bastions of neighboring Coronado and Little Creek in Virginia. Offhand, it was difficult for Admiral Greening to think of any member of the Service who would not know at least a vague version of this melodrama by nightfall.

As Commander of the Pacific Fleet he was required to 'sign off' on the court martial, as indeed was the CNO in the Pentagon. Dick Greening was going to hate doing that, but he had no choice. Dan Headley was going to trial, *against* the express wishes of everyone involved in any way in the events of that morning in the Bay of Bengal. Except for those of Commander Reid and his were the only ones which counted.

Admiral Greening picked up the phone to Admiral Dickson, who was already on the line to Arnold Morgan. It was merely a matter of waiting for the press to get hold of the details, from any one of the hundreds of Navy men, and women, who now knew all about it. But the media would not be looking and it might take them a while. Though they'd sure as hell make up for their lateness when they did find out.

Admiral Morgan's wishes were very clear: Lieutenant-Commander Headley and his lawyer were to be given every assistance in their case to prove that Commander Reid was in no fit state to run the SEAL escape and rescue from the Burmese island. It was the only way out of a scandal which would surely engulf not only the Senior Service but also, possibly, the Administration itself.

In fact, it took five days and even then only half the story was published. On its front page, the *San Diego Telegraph* ran a double-column item, towards the top of columns four and five, under the two-deck headline MYSTERY OF NAVAL SEAL RESCUE OFF BURMA. To the connoisseur of such matters it was plain that the writer knew more than he dared print. But the newspaper printed enough:

The United States Navy last night refused to comment on a report that a US Navy SEAL assault team, out of Coronado, came under direct attack from Chinese helicopters while escaping from a mission on a Burmese island.

It is believed that at least two of the SEALs were killed and that others may have been wounded. There were no details available as to the nature of the mission and a Navy spokesman would only say, 'All Special Forces operations are highly classified and this one is no different.'

Five weeks ago reports from Rangoon stated that a new Chinese naval base on the island of Haing Gyi in the delta of the Bassein river, western Burma, had been badly damaged by a massive explosion inside a geothermal electricity generation plant.

The Navy spokesman would neither confirm nor deny that the SEAL team had been involved in this destruction.

Further reports suggest there was an American nuclear submarine in the area of the Bassein delta on or around June 7. There was no information available as to the identify of the ship, but an insider told the *Telegraph* last night that the Sturgeon Class nuclear boat USS *Shark*, under the command of Commander Donald K. Reid, was operational in the Bay of Bengal at the time.

Last night Commander Reid could not be reached. His Executive Officer, Lieutenant-Commander Dan Headley, would not comment on any part he may have played in the rescue of the surviving SEALs.

He would only say, 'Throughout *Shark*'s recent Middle East patrol, I carried out my duties as a US naval officer to the best of my abilities.'

Accompanying the story was a single-column picture of Commander Reid, under which was the caption 'Unreachable'. There was also a picture of Lieutenant-Commander Dan Headley, beneath which was the distortion of a caption, 'I carried out my duties'. The story was signed, 'Geoff Levy, Staff Writer'. But he had plainly been briefed about the entire scenario, either by a member of the submarine's crew or by a San Diego resident SEAL. However, young Geoff had been unable to obtain any official confirmation and he wrote only what he thought was more or less safe, given that he was trespassing in a top-secret military area.

The Navy's high command in Pearl Harbor, San Diego and Washington glowered at the report as the e-mails were downloaded from computers all over the fleet and its executive offices. The media's high command, almost shrieking with glee, set about running the story to ground. But they made little headway, because essentially reporters needed to be in San Diego where most of the crew and SEALs were stationed.

Once more Geoff Levy's man came up trumps and on Wednesday night, July 25, the *San Diego Telegraph* went to bed with end-of-the-world type stacked in two decks, clean across the top of its front page: NAVY COURT-MARTIALS SUBMARINE EXECUTIVE OFFICER FOR MUTINY ON THE HIGH SEAS. Beneath the headline was the sub-head 'Heroic US officer who saved the SEALS is accused'. Someone had not only blabbed. Someone had blabbed in spades – leaked the court-martial recommendation from Captain Sam Scott – and suddenly Geoff Levy was a media star.

Admiral Arnold Morgan held his head in his hands as the young San Diego journalist said on national television, 'I've been on the Navy beat for my newspaper for three years now and I have never known such outrage. I don't know what the hell is going on, save for my sources, but I'm telling you, there are a lot of very furious guys in the US Navy right now. Most of 'em think Dan Headley should be given the Medal of Honor.' 'Holy shit,' groaned the NSA.

By midday on July 26, the fertilizer was clogging the bilge pumps. The Navy Department in Washington was under siege from the media. The San Diego base switchboard was jammed by phone calls from newspapers and television. All lines to the command office of the SEALs in both Coronado and Virginia were occupied by journalists, researchers and columnists. The questions were all the same: What really happened out there in the Bay of Bengal? Why is the hero of the operation being court-martialed by his own Navy? Where is Lieutenant-Commander Headley? Can we speak with him? If not, why not? Do the SEALs agree Lieutenant-Commander Headley should be court-martialed? What has he actually done to deserve this?

Photographers were camped in groups at the main gates to the base. They were massed outside the Pentagon, outside the base at Coronado and at Little

Creek, Virginia. By late afternoon, infuriated by the lack of co-operation of the US Navy, they swung their attention to the White House, demanding a statement either from the National Security Adviser, the Defense Secretary or the Commander-in-Chief himself, the President of the United States.

In the opinion of both Arnold Morgan and Admiral Alan Dickson there was absolutely nothing to be gained by saying one word to any of them. 'No comment' would send them into a frenzy. 'We are unable to confirm anything at this time' would drive them mad. 'All matters such as these are highly classified and in the interests of national security we will say nothing' would have been a red cloak to a fighting bull. What national security? Are you saying the SEALs attacked that Burmese island? How many of them died? Why are members of the crew saying Lieutenant-Commander Headley rescued the survivors? What's he done wrong? If he mutinied, why did he mutiny? Did the CO funk it or something? To hold a press conference, or even to issue a press statement, would be to open the floodgates. Better to let them get on with it, block all calls at the switchboard, or the automatic answer machines and let the cards fall where they might.

Where they fell was all over the place. In the following three days, right up until the last editions of the Sunday tabloids were on the presses, it was as if no other story in the entire country mattered. The inaccessibility of the Navy bases and the personnel involved seemed only to fan the forest fire of leaked knowledge. There was even a posse of photographers outside the locked wrought-iron gates of Bart Hunter's farm in Lexington, Kentucky, trying to catch a glimpse of the SEAL Leader's father. Local journalists even managed to interview Bobby Headley, Dan's father, when he mistakenly answered the telephone late one evening.

But the Navy said nothing. The media slowly pieced it all together in various forms. The general drift was that the SEALs had attacked the Chinese base in some kind of retribution for China's capture of the island of Taiwan. They had been caught and attacked on the way out, and there had been an altercation between the Commanding Officer of USS *Shark* and his Executive Officer. The CO had been overruled by the XO, supported by the majority of the officers on board, and *Shark* went in to save the SEALs. This mission was accomplished and now the Navy was charging the Lieutenant-Commander who master-minded the rescue with mutiny. It was obvious to everyone that almost every officer and enlisted man in the US Navy was up in arms about this, and almost every commentator in the entire country – newspaper, radio or television – was of the opinion that the Navy, the Government and presumably the President, the C-in-C of all the Armed Forces, had collectively gone mad.

The *New York Times*, with a searing inside 'exclusive', revealed that the entire high command of America's most elite troops, the Navy SEALs, had threatened to resign *en masse* if the court-martial proceedings were not called off. All this was achieved without one single identified source inside the US military. It was as Admiral Morgan had forecast, the *outrage*. That's what binds people together, a shared grievance, a communal anger, and there sure was profound anger at this ensuing court martial of Lieutenant-Commander Dan Headley.

Nonetheless, media or no media, the legal wheels turned relentlessly inside the Navy's Trial Service Office. The trial counselor was duly appointed, Lieutenant-Commander David 'Locker' Jones, a forty-six-year-old lawyer from Vermont, who had attended the Naval Academy but left the Service for the law during his first three years in a surface ship. Ten years later he returned after a messy divorce involving a client's wife. For the past four years he had been an extremely able naval lawyer, much admired throughout the legal department both on the west coast and in Washington.

David Jones was a broad-shouldered ex-athlete of medium height and thinning fair hair. He wore his nickname 'Locker' with good humor. 'Davy Jones's Locker' being, of course, seamen's slang for the bottom of the ocean, the final resting place for sunken ships, articles thrown overboard, or burials at sea. And Locker Jones was renowned not so much for his thoroughness as for his grasp of the very finest points of law, an ability to cut through a swathe of fascinating evidence and make it irrelevant, a knack of nailing the one salient fact which could make a case swing one way or the other. Lieutenant-Commander Headley could scarcely have been dealt a more deadly opponent.

The Judge Advocate, who would sit in on the case, insuring the significant points of law were followed, was the veteran Atlantic destroyer Commander Captain Art Brennan. He was a tall, gray-haired former lawyer from Rhode Island, again a man who had joined, left and then rejoined the Navy. He was a traditionalist with a wry sense of humor and a surprisingly irreverent way of looking at the world. On the face of it you would put the fifty-four-year-old Captain Brennan in the corner of the wronged CO. But those who knew him better suspected he would keep a careful watch on the rights of Lieutenant-Commander Dan Headley.

The defense counsel was a matter for agreement between the Trial Service Office and the accused officer and they chose easily the best man available to them – the sardonic, dark-haired Lieutenant-Commander Al Surprenant, whose career, thanks to a wealthy father, had gone: Choate School, Harvard Law School, excellent degree, boredom with Law,

United States Navy, commission, rapid promotion, missile director battle cruiser Gulf War, US Navy lawyer, Norfolk, then San Diego after he married a Hollywood actress. Lieutenant-Commander Surprenant was generally regarded as the one man in the US Navy who could nail Commander Reid and bring in a 'not guilty' verdict for Dan Headley. He would prove thorough in his preparation, single-minded about the innocence of his client and brutal in his treatment of the CO, who he knew beyond any doubt had left one man to die and had been about to leave eight more to the same fate.

The date of the court martial, the first such trial for mutiny in a US Navy warship, was set for Monday, August 13. It would take place deep inside the San Diego base, in the Trial Service courtroom, which was much like a civilian courtroom, save for the fact that it was all on one level, no raised dais for the men who would sit in judgement on the submarine's XO. The panel would consist of five men, three Lieutenant-Commanders and one Lieutenant, all serving under the President, an ex-submarine CO, Captain Cale 'Boomer' Dunning. This particular officer would bring strong combat experience to the deliberations of his team and, to those who knew him, a genuine appreciation of the split-second flexibility required in the command of a nuclear boat on a classified mission. By anyone's standards the US Navy was giving Lieutenant-Commander Headley every possible chance of a sympathetic hearing; perhaps more in their own interests than in those of the hero of the Bay of Bengal.

Meanwhile, the media continued to worry the life out of the story. They had no official information, but they were getting a ton of unofficial leaks. It seemed that with each new breakthrough, each new snippet of possible truth, there was a counter-attack. One television network came up with an entire career study of Commander Reid, citing his exemplary record. No sooner had this aired than a newspaper came blasting out on to the streets with the story that he had allegedly left a combat SEAL to die. It went on day after day: Was the horseman from Kentucky a reckless gambler? Did the Lieutenant-Commander owe the SEAL Chief money? Had Commander Reid lost his nerve? Was there a fist fight in *Shark*'s control room? Is the US Navy out of control? Day after day the media bore into the events that surrounded the mutiny. But still the Navy would reveal nothing. Not even the date of the court martial. The press seethed with indignation, not because of a potential miscarriage of justice, but because this story about the wronged hero had captured the imagination of the American public and they were unable to get a serious grip on the facts. Nor would they ever do so.

The day of the court martial dawned bright and warm. Shades in the white-painted courtroom were down and the air-conditioning was humming. The long, curved mahogany table at which the panel would sit formed a shallow well in the room and the deadly serious nature of the case was highlighted by twin flags of the United States of America, set immediately behind the five oak captain's armchairs. Between the flags, hung at an angle, was a ceremonial naval sword, which would be used especially at this court martial, reviving an old tradition. Its gold-plated brass hilt was set around a white fishskin-covered grip. The back piece was surmounted with an eagle-head pommel. The thirty-one-and-a-half-inch steel blade was encased in a hand-stitched black rawhide scabbard with brass fittings. Before the verdict was announced, it would be removed from the wall, unsheathed from its scabbard and placed upon the table. If the verdict was to be guilty, the sharp end would point directly at the accused officer. If he was to be judged innocent it would be pointed away from him, towards the wall.

Aside from the five-man panel which would sit in judgement, there would be the two opposing lawyers, plus the observing Judge Advocate. Also permitted to sit in on the trial was the SEAL Commander-in-Chief, Admiral John Bergstrom, plus the Pacific Submarine Fleet Commander, Admiral Freddie Curran. There would be two regular court stenographers officially recording the proceedings. Two armed Navy guards would be on duty at all times, with two more outside the door. Witnesses would be called into the courtroom but would not be permitted to remain after their evidence was presented. No outsiders, public or media, would be permitted within a mile of the place.

At 0900 sharp, Lieutenant-Commander Headley arrived with his defense counsel. They took their seats at the table set up for the accused man and began poring over the trial papers. In the following thirty minutes the witnesses arrived and were seated in a large ante-room along the corridor. Two naval lawyers plus two guards were detailed to insure there was no discussion about the case, no possibility of corroboration between interested parties.

At 0930 the three Lieutenant-Commanders, plus the much younger Lieutenant, walked into the courtroom from a private door behind the long table and took their seats. Captain Dunning, like his colleagues in full uniform, arrived three minutes later, carrying a large leather binder, and sat in the center chair. He wished everyone a formal 'good morning' but wasted no further time. 'Gentlemen,' he said, 'please proceed with the case against Lieutenant-Commander Headley, charged this thirteenth day of August with making a mutiny on the high seas, while serving in the nuclear submarine USS *Shark* on the morning of June 7, in the Bay of Bengal. Lieutenant-Commander Jones, perhaps you would outline the case for the benefit of the court?'

The prosecuting counselor rose from his seat, a look of obvious concern upon his normal, wide, frank face. He hesitated for a few moments, then said firmly, 'Sir, it gives me no great pleasure to prosecute this charge, because I do not believe any of the parties acted in any way through self-interest. On the one hand we have a dedicated, experienced commanding officer concerned with the safety of both his ship and his men. On the other we have an equally dedicated Lieutenant-Commander desperate to save a team of US Special Forces which was under attack.

'The facts are not in dispute. The Navy SEALs transmitted a cry for help, citing their Chinese attackers in hot pursuit with helicopters and heavy machine-guns. Commander Reid's view was that the helicopters were almost certainly ASW aircraft and at least one of them would be armed with rockets, and that to bring USS *Shark* to the surface was tantamount to suicide, because of the threat both to the submarine and the crew. It was, in a sense, one of the oldest quandaries any CO can face: will I sacrifice a very small number of men – in this case eight – in order to protect some 110 men, plus a very expensive nuclear ship?

'Gentlemen, Lieutenant-Commander Headley thought not. He thought he could save the SEALs and he rallied the senior officers to his cause. Despite the protests, indeed the orders, of his Commanding Officer, he seized control of the ship. He arrested the CO under Section 1088 of Navy Regulations and had him marched off under escort to his cabin, where he was incarcerated. Then the XO went in and successfully saved the SEALs under the most gallant circumstances.

'But I submit we are not here to assess gallantry, we are here to assess right and wrong, and I quote now the Regulation which governs the actions of Lieutenant-Commander Headley on that most fateful morning.

469

'Navy Regulation 1088. The relief of a commanding officer by a subordinate:

'1 It is conceivable that the most unusual and extra-ordinary circumstances may arise in which the relief from duty of a commanding officer by a subordinate becomes necessary, either by placing the CO under arrest, or on the sick list. Such action shall never be taken without the approval of the Commandant of the Marine Corps or the Chief of Naval Personnel, as appropriate. Or the senior officer present, except when reference to such higher authority is undoubtedly impracticable, because of the delay involved, or for other clearly obvious reasons.

2 In order that a subordinate officer acting upon his or her own initiative may be vindicated for relieving a commanding officer from duty, the situation must be obvious and clear, and must admit of the single con-clusion that the retention of command by such commanding officer will seriously and irretrievably prejudice the public interests.'

Lieutenant-Commander Jones paused, then continued, 'The Section is quite detailed but I mention the salient points, that the subordinate officer so acting must obviously be unable to refer the matter to a common superior and must be certain that the prejudicial actions of the CO are not caused by instructions unknown to him. He plainly must have given the matter much careful consideration and, this is important, *have made such exhaustive investigation of all the circumstances as may be practicable.*

'The final paragraph in this area is one upon which I take the gravest issue: *that the officer must be thoroughly convinced that the conclusion to relieve the CO is one which a reasonable, prudent and experienced officer would regard as a necessary consequence from the facts thus determined to exist.* I intend to convict Lieutenant–Commander Headley on the words of that last paragraph and I call Commander Reid as the first witness for the prosecution.'

The doors to the court were opened and the former CO of USS *Shark* walked into the room. He was immaculately dressed in uniform and made his way to the witness chair which had been placed on the left-hand side, in order that the witness could address both the panel and the examining lawyers. The Judge Advocate rose and walked across to insure the oath was taken correctly. With his hand on the Bible, Commander Donald Reid calmly swore to tell the truth.

After the briefest of identification procedures Locker Jones went straight to work. 'On the morning of June 7 were you startled to find your ship was moving fast at periscope depth in flagrant defiance of your most recent orders?'

'I was.'

'Where were you at that time?'

'I was in my cabin. The XO had the ship.'

'What action did you take?'

'I returned to the control room immediately and I ordered Lieutenant–Commander Headley to turn the submarine round and to return to our rendezvous point, the place defined in our orders, 16 degrees north, 94.01 east.'

'Did he carry out your orders?'

'No. He did not. He refused.'

'For what reason?'

'He said he was on a mission of mercy to save the very small team of Navy SEALs, only eight of them I believe.'

'How did he propose to do this?'

'He said he was taking the submarine on the surface at flank speed in order to effect a rescue.'

'Were you able to approve this?'

'Certainly not. No commander of a nuclear submarine takes his ship to the surface in the face of the enemy. It's one of the oldest rules in the book. No one does it.'

'Were you aware of the enemy?'

'Well, I knew they were Chinese and I knew they were helicopters. Two, we were told.'

'What did you deduce from this?'

'I assessed that they would be helicopters from the two ships we knew were in the Haing Gyi dockyard, a frigate and a destroyer. The chances were very high that at least one of them, probably both, would have an ASW capability, plus, probably, rockets which would both outrange us and pierce our pressure hull. We are not really built to fight on the surface, you know.' The court was listening to the refined voice of reason.

'No, of course not, Commander,' replied the prosecuter. 'Absolutely not. I am sure everyone in the room appreciates that. But I continue. Did you communicate your assessment of the situation to your Executive Officer?'

'I sure did. I pointed out to him that there were almost 110 officers and men on board my ship. We had a brave and experienced crew, a first-class crew. I pointed out that to take the ship straight into the range of air-to-surface missiles on the surface, on the open ocean, was contrary to everything I had ever known, been taught, or believed in the US Navy. Quite frankly, it was a risk I could not possibly take. Nor, I suspect, would anyone else in my shoes. Also, I did not believe the US Navy would be greatly thanked for putting a smashed nuclear reactor in the middle of the Bay of Bengal to pollute for the next forty years. I had much to consider and I did not believe the lives of the SEALs, just eight of them, warranted the potential destruction of USS *Shark* and her crew.'

'Thank you, Commander. No more questions.'

The court was amazed at the brevity of Locker Jones's examination; amazed that he had not extracted, chapter and verse, the circumstances of the arrest of the CO. Instead he had concentrated on one precious factor – the course of action the Captain of the submarine had proposed, and was it sufficiently crazy to have him placed under arrest and relieved of command? It was a vintage ploy by the prosecuting counsel, a method of avoiding endless testimony and confusing contradictions. He had presented his star witness in a lean, pared-down light: the order he had given and the reasons for it. Was it the order of a madman? Not so far, of that everyone in the room was very certain.

The frowning figure of the defense counsel, Lieutenant-Commander Surprenant, climbed to his feet to begin his cross-examination. He was perhaps more aware than anyone of the brilliance of the strategy of Locker Jones. 'Commander Reid,' he began. 'I want to ask your indulgence right here, because the reasons for Lieutenant-Commander Headley's actions date back for several weeks and I am sure you will not object to answering my questions while we establish them in this courtroom.'

Commander Reid shook his head as if to say 'No problem', but his counsel was instantly on his feet, snapping, 'Objection.'

Captain Dunning stared quizzically at the prosecuter, who said, 'Sir. The CO is not on trial. He is here to give his reasons for his orders on that particular morning, in those particular circumstances. I am at a loss to understand why defense counsel wants to delve into the past. Lieutenant-Commander Headley, under Section 1088 of Navy Regulations, must demonstrate that his CO issued an order that could not possibly be obeyed without being prejudicial to the public interest.'

Captain Dunning looked doubtfully at Al Surprenant, who responded quietly, 'Sir, it is possible that a pattern of behavior by a single individual may become so unnerving for those who serve under him that an action to relieve command becomes necessary. Not just from the immediate orders, but from that pattern of unreliability. With respect, I intend to proceed along those lines.'

'Overruled.'

Lieutenant-Commander Surprenant now took his time. He shuffled his file papers, then looked up and inquired, 'Commander Reid, may I ask if you recall the events of May 16 in the early morning, just before first light?'

'Well, I certainly know we were waiting at our rendezvous point for the Special Forces team to return from a mission.'

'Who had the ship?'

'Lieutenant-Commander Headley. Our orders were clear. It was a highly classified operation and we were detailed to remain at our RV in the Gulf of Iran while the ASDV returned with the team on board.'

'And were you ever informed of a problem during their escape from plainly hostile shores?'

'No, I was not.'

'I believe you were not in the control room?'

'That is correct. My XO had overall responsibility for the return of the SEAL team.'

'What caused you to return to the control room?'

'The submarine began to move forward in complete contradiction to our orders, which had been issued by the Flag. Our RV point was in hard copy.'

'When you did return, what did you learn?'

'Well, there had been some kind of an attack on the team, inshore, and they were on their way back, bringing with them an apparently wounded man.'

'They were also bringing back the body of their Leader, Lieutenant-Commander Ray Schaeffer, I believe?'

'So I was informed.'

'So. The Leader had been killed and another SEAL was badly wounded, and they were desperately trying to get away, trying to get back to safety after achieving their objective?'

'So I believe.'

'Did Lieutenant-Commander Headley inform you that it was perfectly safe under clear skies, and on empty seas, to go in six miles, fast, towards the ASDV and get them back on board with all speed?'

'He was already headed inshore when I reached the control room.'

'When you learned they had a top combat SEAL on board, dying, next to his already dead Leader, I believe you issued an order for USS *Shark* to turn round and return to the rendezvous point, leaving this heroic blood-soaked American Special Force essentially to get on with it as best they could?'

'Well, I was certain about my orders: to remain on station until they arrived back.'

'When Lieutenant-Commander Headley informed you of the seriousness of the situation, that a man was dying, I believe you uttered the phrase, "You can't run a navy for a guy who's probably cut his goddamned finger"?'

'I do not recall that.'

'So you turned round and went back to the RV?'

'Yes.'

'Do you recall a strong protest from the SEAL mission controller, Commander Rusty Bennett, almost begging you to go inshore and save his man?'

'No. I do not recall that.'

'Do you recall the condition of the wounded SEAL when they finally arrived back?'

'You know perfectly well that I do.'

'What was the condition?'

'Do you really have to persist in this unhelpful manner?'

'*What was that condition, Commander?*'

'The SEAL was dead.'

'Thank you. Is it your opinion that he might have been saved if you'd got him aboard a half-hour earlier?'

'I have no idea. I'm not a doctor.'

'How long had he been dead before your crew got him back aboard?'

'I believe fifteen minutes.'

'Thank you. Would it surprise you to learn that from that moment on, both your crew and the SEAL assault teams regarded you as a heartless, somewhat remote figure who cared nothing about any of them?'

'OBJECTION! Counsel is harassing the witness, asking a question to which he could not possibly know the answer.'

'Sustained. Strike that last question from the record.'

But Al Surprenant smiled the quiet smile of a man who had said precisely what he wanted, and rephrased it good-naturedly: 'Commander, would it surprise you to know that a lot of your crew did not agree in any way with your decision to let the man die?'

'OBJECTION! Commander Reid did not decide to let the man die. He simply followed the orders of the Flag. Counsel continues to harass the witness.'

'Sustained. Strike the question.'

'Very well,' Al Surprenant went on. 'In the light of everything, let me ask you this, thirty-six hours previously, do you recall refusing to go inshore for a few extra miles, thus saving the battery of the ASDV when the navigator had informed you there was plenty of water depth?'

'No. I do not recall that.'

'Would you feel happier if I read it to you directly from the ship's log?'

'OBJECTION. Counsel is treating the witness as if he is on trial, attempting to humiliate him before the court, and now he wants to produce evidence against him we have not even seen.'

'Sustained. But leave the record.' Boomer Dunning was a picture of calmness in increasingly stormy waters.

'Commander Reid,' continued the defense counsel, 'would you say you were a man who followed orders to the letter, allowing no leeway and no room for flexibility?'

'No, I would not. I'm as flexible as the next man. But not when it comes to the safety of my ship.'

'Would you say you were as flexible as, say, Admiral Pierre de Villeneuve?'

Locker Jones shook his head and held his hands apart in mock outrage. Captain Dunning stared at the former CO, awaiting an answer.

When it came, there was a frisson of unease in the room. 'Damn you, Headley,' he hissed, almost under his breath.

Now Lieutenant-Commander Surprenant was on him. 'Damn whom, sir? Damn whom? I did not quite catch that.'

Commander Reid's face was beginning to redden and he started to look angry. He made no reply.

Again Al Surprenant came in: 'I asked if you were as flexible as Admiral de Villeneuve. Please answer me. I know you are well acquainted with each other.'

Locker Jones had never even heard of the French Admiral, or if he had, he'd clean forgotten it. But it was hard to object because he could not tell if there was venom behind the innocence of the question.

Still Commander Reid said nothing and the President stepped in, requesting defense counsel to clarify the question for the benefit of the panel and, indeed, the prosecutor.

'Sir,' said Al Surprenant, 'Admiral de Villeneuve was the commander of the French fleet at the Battle of Trafalgar. He presided over probably the biggest disaster in a sea battle in history. He lost twenty ships, was captured by the British and soon afterwards committed suicide. There is a picture of him on the wall of Commander Reid's cabin, which is unorthodox for a US Navy commanding officer at best.'

'I see,' said Captain Dunning. 'Well, I suppose it may be relevant. Please proceed.'

'Thank you,' said the defense counsel and, turning back to Commander Reid, said flatly, 'Is it not a fact that you believe you *were* Admiral de Villeneuve in a previous life?'

'Millions of people believe in reincarnation,' replied the Commander.

'And so they may,' said Lieutenant-Commander Surprenant. 'But that scarcely answers my question, does it? Shall we try again? Do you believe you *were* Admiral de Villeneuve in a previous life?'

'Well, even General Patton believed he had been a great warrior in a previous incarnation.'

'So he may have. But would you be willing to give my question yet another try? Do you believe, Commander Reid, that you actually *were* Admiral de Villeneuve in a previous life? That's a yes or a no.'

'Well, we do share some deep French roots.'

Captain Dunning interrupted. 'Commander Reid, please answer the question. Yes or no.'

'No,' replied *Shark*'s former CO. 'I do not believe I actually *was* Admiral de Villeneuve.'

'Thank you, Commander,' said the defense counsel. 'And now, if I may, I should like to read something to you — *Another life, another battle, so many mistakes in* Bucentaure.

478

I must never repeat them now that I have another chance. June 1980 DKR. Do you recognize those words, Commander?'

'Well, vaguely, yes I do.'

'Who wrote them?'

'I did.'

'Where did you write them?'

'In a book, I believe.'

'A book about reincarnation, wasn't it?'

'Maybe.'

'Commander, perhaps you would care to tell the panel whose ship was the *Bucentaure*?'

'It was Admiral de Villeneuve's flagship.'

'In your own words, Commander. *I must not repeat the mistakes in* Bucentaure, *now that I have another chance.* Sir, you believe you are the reincarnation of one of the worst naval commanders in history, correct?'

Locker Jones had had enough. He leapt to his feet and almost shouted, 'OBJECTION! This quotation, written more than twenty-five years ago, was plainly pilfered from the private quarters of the Commanding Officer of USS *Shark*, unlawfully and disgracefully. It cannot be admissible evidence in any court of law in the free world.'

Captain Dunning nodded. But he said, 'This is not a civilian court of law, where lawyers are trained to find loopholes to free guilty people. This is a United States Navy court martial and we have no other objective except to find the truth. We are not some kangaroo court trying to trick people – we are assessing the guilt or innocence of men who are trained to take charge of ships worth $400 million. Everything is relevant in this regard.'

'But my client is not on trial, sir,' protested Lieutenant-Commander Jones.

'I know he's not,' replied Boomer. 'Objection overruled.'

Al Surprenant continued, 'Commander, do you think it might be unnerving for a crew to discover their leader believes he was a Navy disaster area in a previous life?'

'I cannot say what they might feel.'

'But do you think they *might* quite properly be concerned?'

'OBJECTION. The question's been asked and answered.'

'Sustained.'

'Commander,' said the defense counsel. 'Are you a spiritualist?'

'In some ways.'

'Does that mean you have merely inherited the spirit of Pierre de Villeneuve, or do you believe you have been in contact with people from . . . er . . . the other side, I believe is the phrase?'

'Like many millions of others, I may have.'

'Commander, have you spoken lately with Captain Grigory Lyachin?'

Donald Reid remained silent.

'Someone enlighten me,' interjected Boomer Dunning. 'Who's Grigory Lyachin?'

'He's the Russian submarine Commanding Officer who died with his crew in the *Kursk* in the Barents Sea seven years ago,' said Al Surprenant. 'Commander Reid, would it surprise you to know certain senior members of your crew heard you talking to him by candlelight in your cabin?'

'DAMN THIS. DAMN YOU ALL! I'M NOT ON TRIAL HERE.' The ex-CO of *Shark* was standing now, shouting back at the defense lawyer, all semblance of self-control slipping away.

Lieutenant–Commander Jones was also on his feet. 'Sir, I really must object most strenuously to this line of questioning. Defense is attempting to paint this veteran

Commander of many years' standing as some kind of weirdo, which is patently unfair.'

'Your word, not mine,' interrupted Al Surprenant. 'Thoughtful of you.'

'SILENCE,' snapped Captain Dunning. 'Please be seated and listen carefully. If I consider the questioning of a witness to be irrelevant or unfair, I shall make my views known. If you object to anything, please say so, and I will make a judgement. But I will not tolerate banter. For the record, I do think it is extremely important to know that Commander Reid has some unusual views. I was once in a ship where the Captain was known to pray extensively on a nightly basis and it damned nearly caused a mutiny. Ships are like that. Little things can mean a great deal, especially concerning a CO. This evidence about Commander Reid matters and I am afraid he is going to have to put up with it. He was, after all, instrumental in bringing this court martial and my sympathies are not with him in these instances. Please proceed, Lieutenant-Commander.'

'Thank you, sir,' said Al Surprenant humbly. 'Commander Reid, have you ever tried to contact Grigory Lyachin in a spiritual way? Perhaps to seek counsel or guidance from a man who has paid the ultimate price for carelessness?'

'It was never his fault. Any more than it was de Villeneuve's. They were both let down by others.'

'Then you have been in contact?'

'In a sense.'

'Thank you. Now I should like to return to more immediate concerns. As you know, Lieutenant-Commander Headley, by the morning of June 7, had much on his mind. His CO, a spiritualist who associated himself closely with two massive naval disasters, had twice made decisions apparently detrimental to a SEAL

481

operation – we have established that. He was dealing with a man who played rigidly by the book, presumably to avoid making the same foul-ups he committed at Trafalgar.'

This was too much for Captain Dunning. 'Counselor,' he snapped, 'kindly desist from this soliloquy. You are not asking questions. You are merely ridiculing the witness. Ask, or sit down.'

'Of course, sir,' said Lieutenant-Commander Surprenant courteously. 'Commander, would you be surprised to learn that Lieutenant-Commander Headley *knew* you would refuse flatly to help the SEALs? Because of your beliefs and your record?'

'Yes, I would.'

'You will later hear that he did indeed know. It was the predictability which caused the mutiny. That they all knew you would leave the SEALs to die. I have no more questions.'

'Commander Reid, you are excused. But please do not leave the building.' Captain Dunning wrote carefully in his book.

Then Lieutenant-Commander Jones called his second witness, *Shark*'s Combat Systems Officer, Lieutenant-Commander Jack Cressend, who testified very briefly that he had indeed been asked by Lieutenant-Commander Headley to take part in an act of defiance towards the Commanding Officer, in order to save the SEALs.

At the conclusion of his evidence, a short account of how they did not turn the ship round but proceeded inshore to meet Commander Hunter and his men, Al Surprenant had just one question. 'Lieutenant-Commander,' he said, 'if you could live June 7 over, would you still support the XO in his determination to save the SEALs?'

'Absolutely, sir. I would. No doubt in my mind.'

At this point Lieutenant-Commander Jones announced he had no more witnesses but would confine his cross-examination to those appearing on behalf of the accused.

Immediately, Al Surprenant called Commander Rick Hunter, who walked into the courtroom and swore to tell the truth, before being seated. After identification, the SEAL Commander admitted under oath that he had the gravest worries about the possible conduct of Commander Reid under pressure. He and Lieutenant-Commander Headley knew each other well and had discussed the 'unreliable' nature of the CO, even before the mission began.

'When you first transmitted your distress call to *Shark*, while your men were fighting and dying in the open boats, did you think help would come?'

'Not if Commander Reid had his way. I knew it would not come.'

'Did you think you had a chance to survive?'

'Only if Dan Headley took over the ship, in a big hurry.'

'But for Lieutenant-Commander Headley's actions, would you and your men have been killed?'

'Yes, sir.'

'Do you think he deserves to be court-martialed?'

'No, sir.'

'Why not?'

'Because he's just about the best officer I ever met and he saved all our lives.'

'Do you intend to make any protest whatsoever if Lieutenant-Commander Headley is found guilty of mutiny?'

'No, sir. But I shall resign my commission immediately.'

'After a working lifetime in the Navy and the very real prospect of becoming C–in–C of SPECWARCOM?'

'Yes, sir. I could never feel the same about the Service if they convicted Dan Headley.'

'Thank you, Commander.'

Locker Jones rose. 'You stated that you and Lieutenant-Commander Headley knew each other well. That was not quite the whole truth, was it?'

'Sir?'

'You and Dan Headley are boyhood friends, correct? Best friends, correct? You went to school together, correct? Your father employs his father, correct?'

'All correct, sir. I am privileged to have him and his father for my friends.'

'Is it not probable that you would never hear a word against Dan Headley from anyone?'

'Very probable. Because he does not do things to cause people to utter words against him.'

'He has now, Commander.'

'But not by people who really know him, sir.'

'You think you know him well enough to say he could not be guilty of the crime with which he is charged?'

'I know him a lot better than you do.'

Locker Jones had had enough sparring with the towering wounded hero of the Burma operation. 'No more questions,' he said.

Al Surprenant next called the SEAL Commander, Rusty Bennett, who confirmed the counselor's earlier contention that he had tried to remonstrate with Commander Reid about his decision not to move the ship forward in the Gulf of Iran mission to assist the wounded SEAL.

'Do you recall his precise words, Commander Bennett?'

'Some of them. I told him the rescue was at my request to go in and save the life of one of my most valued men. He then reminded me that I had no rights whatsoever on his ship. Told me he would not have this interference. Then he said, "What exactly is this? Some kind of damned conspiracy? Well you've picked the wrong man to make a fool of." He also said we had waited until he was asleep and then flagrantly disobeyed his orders.'

'What did you think of this outburst?'

'Seemed very strange. You know, like paranoia.'

'OBJECTION! The witness has no idea about the meaning of such a medical term.'

'Sustained.'

'How about nuts?' offered the SEAL from the coast of Maine.

'Better,' said Captain Dunning.

'OBJECTION! The Commander has no right to be making wild statements about insanity.'

'I'll take the word of an experienced Navy SEAL commanding officer that in his opinion someone seemed nuts,' replied Captain Dunning. 'Overruled.'

'Now, Commander,' said Al Surprenant, 'let me ask you the same question I asked Commander Hunter. Do you hold a strong view about the possible conviction of Lieutenant-Commander Headley?'

'Yes, sir. I shall resign my commission if they find him guilty of mutiny.'

'Reason?'

'Same as Commander Hunter's. Dan Headley saved the SEALs' lives.'

'No more questions.'

Locker Jones had none either and the SEAL Team Leader left the room, clearing the way for Al Surprenant to bring in a succession of minor witnesses, Lieutenant-Commander Josh Gandy, Master Chief Drew Fisher, Lieutenant Matt Singer, all offering unerring support for the XO. He brought in two more SEALs, the wounded Rattlesnake Davies and Lieutenant Dallas MacPherson who both offered the opinion that they would have been killed but for the appearance on the scene of USS *Shark*.

He then called, in fairly quick succession, the three psychiatrists who had independently examined Commander Reid. One of them was definite. There was nothing wrong with Commander Reid and on that he could not be shaken. The other two were not sure. Neither would say he was crazy, but they both agreed he held some very strange views for a US Navy Commander.

Al Surprenant questioned, badgered, overstepped the bounds of polite interrogation and then dived back behind them against a barrage of 'OBJECTIONS' from the prosecutor. Once he nearly had an admission that Commander Reid was just too strange, too bound up in his perceived French antecedents, to be trusted with a modern nuclear submarine. But a belief in reincarnation and, indeed, spiritualism, did not constitute 'crazy'. Al proved eccentricity and he proved a profound instability. He *almost* proved a long-held emotional cowardice on the part of the CO. But he did not obtain an admission that Commander Reid was so unbalanced as to be relieved of command on that particular morning.

It was immediately after the lunch break that the defense finally called the accused Executive Officer to the witness chair to testify under oath in his own defense. Before he did so, counsel requested permission to 'read just two or three lines from Section Three of Navy Regulation 1088, which the prosecution apparently deemed irrelevant'. He then stated very simply, ' "Intelligent, fearless initiative is an important trait of military character. It is not the purpose of these regulations to discourage its employment in cases of this nature." '

Lieutenant-Commander Headley sat motionless in the witness chair as the short but powerful words were read out to the court. He saw Captain Dunning nod and he continued to sit bolt upright, immaculate in his uniform, as he began to answer his counsel's questions, firmly and without hesitation.

'When it came right down to it, why do you think Commander Reid refused to help the SEALs?'

'Two reasons, sir. One, he did not want to be associated with another disaster, like he had in another life. Two, he kept yelling that the planet Mercury was in retrograde.'

'He what?'

'He told me that the mighty planet which controls us was stilled in the heavens and that by dawn it would be in retrograde – going backwards, that is.'

'Did you have any comment?'

'I believe I just said, "No shit?" I found it a bit bewildering, given the urgency of our situation.'

'Did this conversation take place in front of anyone?'

'No, sir. This started in his cabin. But then it continued back in the control room in front of everyone after the SEALs had transmitted their call for help.'

'Did you go back to the control room leaving the CO in his cabin?'

'Yes, sir. I was in charge of the rescue operation and I immediately ordered the submarine inshore to get the guys out.'

'You knew they were under attack from Chinese helicopters?'

'Yes, sir.'

'And how did you assess the danger?'

'I planned to down the helos with our Stinger missiles from range 800 yards, hand-held right off the bridge. They're very accurate.'

'What about the danger to your own ship?'

'Negligible in my view. I thought the Chinese might have a couple of missiles. But there was a morning mist and I thought they'd be preoccupied with the guys who were battering them with the M-60 machine-guns. If they carried ASW mortars or depth bombs I knew they'd be largely useless if we were on the surface with Stingers. I thought we were in there with a good shot at success.'

'You were not afraid the *Shark* might be sunk?'

'Sir, *Shark* is a US Navy fighting ship. We had eight valued colleagues being wiped out by Chinese gunships. Of course we went in to save them. That's what we're for. This is the Navy, not the Cub Scouts. Yes, I was afraid. But not too afraid to try.'

'What happened when the CO arrived in the control room?'

'I told him precisely what we were doing and he objected, as I knew he would.'

'How did you know?'

'Because Commander Reid is nothing short of a goddamned coward. And he's plainly crazy.'

Finally uttered, the words hung like the sword of Damocles over the courtroom. 'OBJECTION!' shouted Locker Jones, springing to his feet.

'Overruled,' snapped back Captain Dunning. 'That is the heart of this case. The accused XO has been asked his opinion and he has given it.'

'Was he afraid the ship might be hit and everyone killed?' asked Al Surprenant.

'Of course. He thought because Mercury was in retrograde that might happen.'

'Did he say so?'

'He shouted out, sir, "RETROGRADE! RETRO-GRADE! The great planet Mercury is in retreat." He called me an ignorant man for not knowing what was happening in the zodiac, in front of everyone. He said my life was insignificant, that I knew nothing. That all of our lives, particularly in the areas of transportation and communication, were ruled by Mercury and now the darn thing was kinda spinning backwards.'

'And then?'

'He told me there was no way he was going to allow his submarine to continue on the surface, in the path of an ASW helicopter, not while the planet was in retrograde.'

'Lieutenant-Commander, is the direction in which the distant planet Mercury spins a normal consideration in the United States Navy when making combat decisions?'

'No, sir.'

'Ever?'

'Not in my experience, sir. It was a new one on me.'

'Then what happened?'

'He ordered me to turn the ship round and to proceed in a direction away from the SEALs.'

'Did you do so?'

'No, sir. I told him I could not do that. Would not do that. He told me I was making a one-man mutiny.'

'Did you change your mind and retreat, like Mercury?'

'No, sir. I did not.'

'You proceeded with the rescue?'

'I did. I told the CO I had the support of the entire command of the ship. That I would not leave the guys to be killed. I offered him the sick-list option as laid down in the Regulations. But he declined.'

'And then?'

'I ordered the conn to hold our course on the surface and the missiles to be brought up from below.'

'And you and the crew carried out the rescue. Were you on the bridge, in the line of fire, as it were?'

'Yes, sir. I was.'

'Did you direct the firing of the missiles?'

'Yes, sir. I fired one myself, hit and blew up the second Chinese helicopter.'

Lieutenant-Commander Al Surprenant just shook his

head and blurted out, '*My God! And now they want to court-martial you?*'

'Yes, sir.'

'No further questions.'

The silence in the courtroom was devastating as defense counsel finally sat down and there was a slight air of resignation in the body language of Locker Jones as he stood up to cross-examine. 'Lieutenant-Commander, the court has heard of your lifelong friendship with Commander Hunter. Would it be true to say you would have done anything to save him, including the making of a mutiny aboard your ship?'

'Yes, sir, it would. I would also have done anything to save any of the others . . . and, if I may, sir?'

'Please continue.'

'Sir, you may question me for a thousand years. But I'm going to save you a lot of trouble. I did not hesitate to remove the CO and to proceed with the rescue myself and, if I could live it over again, a thousand times, I'd still do it. I hope I make myself clear, Counselor.'

'Perfectly clear. In fact, you are the perfect mutineer. No further questions. I rest the case for the prosecution.'

There was no summing up by either the court President or the lawyers, as there would have been in a civilian case. Captain Dunning rose and led his panel out. Lieutenant-Commander Headley and his attorney also left the room, in company with Admiral Bergstrom and Admiral Curran. Their wait would not be long.

In the room behind the main court Boomer Dunning called his team swiftly to order. 'I'll take the view of the Lieutenant first, since I do not wish him to be influenced by the opinions of those who outrank him. Lieutenant?'

'Not guilty, sir. Reid is plainly crazy. In my view *he* should be court-martialed, for cowardice in the face of the enemy.'

Boomer nodded. 'Lieutenant-Commander?'

'Guilty. If the CO says no, the risk is too great, that's an end to it. The CO stands or falls by that decision and no one's charged him with anything.'

Captain Dunning turned to the second Lieutenant-Commander. 'Your verdict?'

'Guilty. Headley, for all his good intentions, had no right to seize the ship. Certainly no right to have his CO arrested.'

'And you?' asked the Captain, turning to the last of his four assistants.

'Not guilty. I think the XO was right to assume command. There were grave doubts about the suitability of Commander Reid to make sound judgements.'

'Excellent. But may I just clarify that none of you is interested in a possible change of mind? Anyone want to go over the issue? Or discuss it further?'

No one did. Minds were made up at 2–2. Captain Dunning would decide Lieutenant-Commander Headley's fate. 'Very well, gentlemen. In a few minutes we will return to the courtroom and I will make my casting vote, plus a short summation for the court in order that they understand our verdict.' He sat at a table and wrote carefully on the pages of the large writing tablet inside the leather folder. Then he stood up and beckoned his four colleagues to follow him. They walked through the door and Captain Dunning removed the sword from the wall and placed it upon the table. 'Ask them to come in,' he ordered.

Lieutenant-Commander Headley entered last and stared at the sword almost in disbelief as he took his seat at the defense counsel table.

'I should tell you the votes are divided 2–2 in this case and I now have the duty to pass the casting vote and with it the judgement of the court,' said the ex-submarine Captain. 'I should begin by stating that Lieutenant-

Commander Headley's opinions about Mercury in retrograde or any of the other foibles displayed by Commander Reid are not the bedrocks of the case and we are not here to stand in judgement on them either. We are here, very simply to decide whether Commander Reid issued an order in the early hours of that June morning which was so wrong, indeed so crazy, that he had to be arrested and relieved of the command of his ship under section 1088.

'What was that order? He said he would not leave his nuclear boat on the surface and risk the lives of his 107 crew, and the ship, in order to save eight men. Was that wrong? Possibly, in the light of events. Was it crazy? No. It wasn't crazy. Was there a suggestion of cowardice? Again, possibly. No more. But was it sufficiently outlandish for him to be relieved of command of his ship, arrested and incarcerated in his cabin while his number two took over? The answer is plain. NO. ABSOLUTELY NOT.

'The defendant is guilty as charged. Guilty of making a mutiny on the high seas. But the court does not recommend he be jailed, as would be expected in such a case. But rather that he be dismissed from the Service immediately, under the severest censure. The court further recommends that Commander Reid never again holds the position of Commanding Officer in a US Navy submarine involving Special Forces. That's all, save to remind everyone in this room of the following: If you permitted every lieutenant-commander to seize control of a warship because he does not agree with his CO you no longer have a Navy. You have a rabble in a very dangerous ship. My verdict was reached strictly for the greater good of the United States Navy. It was the only verdict to reach and it always has been, ever since the morning of June 7.'

Long after the principals of the Navy's first court martial

for mutiny had departed Dan Headley still stood helplessly at the defense counsel's desk, staring at the long mahogany table. Still staring at the cruel steel blade of the gilded sword, which was pointed at him alone.

Epilogue

Rick Hunter and Dan Headley returned home to the Blue Grass together. Old Bart Hunter said it was about time and promptly retired, leaving the entire operation of the sprawling Hunter Valley Thoroughbred Farms to his son. Rick thus moved from US Navy SEAL Commander to President of a multimillion–dollar Kentucky corporation in the space of a week. His first reaction was to make over a ten per cent shareholding of the land, mares and stallions to the ownership of Dan Headley. Within one more week the headed writing paper of the Hunter Valley contained the words, *Directors, Richard Hunter (President), Dan Headley (Vice-President Thoroughbred Operations), Bart Hunter (Consultant), Robert Headley (Stallions).*

Bart was surprised, but agreeable. 'Took me and my daddy fifty years to build this place,' he said. 'Took you about ten minutes to start dismantling it, giving it away to our good neighbors.'

'It only took Danny ten minutes to save my life,' replied Rick. 'Guess it's called quality time, right?'

'Well, I'm glad he did. Whatever you think's fair, boy. That's the way to run a business.'

'And a life,' said his son.

Rusty Bennett also resigned from the Navy and returned to the coast of Maine, where he took over the operations of his father's two lobster boats, working out of the little island of Frenchborough, home of his mother's ancestors for 150 years. Six months later he married the prettiest girl on the island, twelve years his junior.

Commander Donald Reid was never heard from again, resigning his commission and moving his wife and family to France, to a small town house in Grasse.

Admiral John Bergstrom was seething at the loss of two of his top commanders and it took Admiral Morgan five weeks to persuade him not to resign. Admiral George Morris recovered and returned to Fort Meade. His newly promoted personal assistant was Lieutenant-Commander James Ramshawe.

The Chinese ambassador to Washington, His Excellency Ling Guofeng, ran into the most thunderous hard time from Arnold Morgan. The US National Security Chief, forced to admit US involvement in the destruction of the naval base at Haing Gyi, made it crystal clear that the United States would tolerate no further Chinese expansion into the Indian Ocean and its confines.

He told him the US could, and would, make its actions on the Burmese coast look like kid's stuff if the Beijing government ever again elected to tamper with the free passage of the industrial world's oil supply. The Admiral actually stood up and lectured him. He told him that Beijing now understood what happened when the American superpower was riled. 'Just you remember, Ling, behave yourselves. No more adventuring in foreign waters. Because if you do, we'll hammer you again. Okay. Okay. I guess you don't care. You got Taiwan, which is what it was all about in the first case. The price you pay is to know that's as far offshore as you guys are going. At least, it is so long as I sit in this chair. As for your most-favored-nation status, you can forget all about that.'

The ambassador stood up to leave. He nodded curtly and headed for the door. As he opened it Arnold Morgan said quietly, '*Pax Americana*, Ling, and don't forget it.'

'I'm sorry,' the ambassador said. 'I don't quite understand?'

'Go figure,' grunted the Admiral rudely.

Also by Patrick Robinson

HMS UNSEEN

Patrick Robinson

'[A] rising master of the naval techno-thriller . . . Far more smoothly written than Tom Clancy' *Kirkus Reviews*

IN IRAQ the President awards his country's highest honour to the man known as Eilat One. Hours later, in the dead of night, he tries to have him killed.

IN IRAN one of the world's deadliest terrorists offers his services to the regime and promises to continue the fight against the United States and bring down America's anger and military might against their common enemy, Iraq . . .

IN ENGLAND, just off Portsmouth Sound, the Upholder-class submarine *HMS Unseen* is undergoing its final sea trials before being handed over to Brazil. Unbelievably, mysteriously, *HMS Unseen* disappears.

IN WASHINGTON Admiral Arnold Morgan begins to suspect that one of his deadliest and most skillful enemies is behind the disappearance of the submarine, the same enemy who is beginning a series of spectacular strikes against the West. Morgan knows of only one man who could possibly be capable of all this. And Morgan knows he must be captured, or stopped, at all costs.

'Patrick Robinson's best book yet. *HMS Unseen*, the third volume of his brilliant naval series set in the near future, is a dazzling, page-turning yarn . . . Be warned, however, once begun, *HMS Unseen* is impossible to put down before its dramatic conclusion. Highly recommended' Carlo D'Este, author of *Patton: A Genius for War*

NIMITZ CLASS

Patrick Robinson

'An absolutely marvellous thriller, one of the best things of its kind I have read in years'
Jack Higgins

INCONCEIVABLE: The nuclear-powered Nimitz-Class Aircraft Carrier USS *Thomas Jefferson*, the most powerful warship in the world, a seemingly unconquerable floating fortress, has disappeared at sea, with massive loss of life, vaporized in what appears to be a tragic nuclear accident.

UNRELENTING: As the shock waves reverberate around the world, reports suggest that something far more sinister lurks beneath the surface of this tragedy. A rogue submarine armed with nuclear warheads is on the loose. No-one knows who is on board, nor where it came from, or how it could have got within striking distance of the *Thomas Jefferson*. Worse yet, no-one knows where it is now, or if it might strike again. As political tensions mount, a deadly chase begins . . .

THE MOST EXPLOSIVE STORY OF THE YEAR: Chilling, compelling, controversial, *Nimitz Class* is the most riveting tale of submarine warfare since *The Hunt for Red October*.

'A stunner that irresistably hurtles the reader to the exciting climax'
Clive Cussler

KILO CLASS

Patrick Robinson

The Russian-built Kilo-Class submarine: diesel-electric, with nuclear capability, silent and undetectable under 5 knots. The only true enemy of the American Carrier Battle Groups – the stealthy, underwater marauder that can chill the hearts of US Navy commanding officers. The Kilo is now available, at a price, to aspiring nations around the world. China has ordered ten. Russia, desperate for foreign currency, has agreed to sell them. The first three are already on their way.

The American Government cannot allow this order to be completed: with the submarines in Chinese hands, Beijing would gain immediate control of the Taiwan Strait, and America's ally on China's doorstep would fall. Word comes down from the White House – stop the delivery, at all costs.

This is to be a 'black' operation, controlled personally by Admiral Arnold Morgan, the President's National Security Advisor. Morgan rallies his forces and begins the deadly game that will be fought out in the icy depths of the world's oceans and in the vast hinterland of Russia's rivers and lakes.

The secret war played out by the superpowers brings the world to the brink of destruction, with China determined to have its submarines, Russia desperate to earn its currency, and America resolved not to allow the delicate balance of world peace to be threatened. And in this war, there can only be one victor . . .

USS SEAWOLF

Patrick Robinson

Silent and lethal, *USS Seawolf*, the US Navy's state-of-the-art stealth submarine, is on an ultra secret mission – to spy on China's brand new ICBM *Xia*-Class submarine.

The *Xia* is the menacing flagship of China's burgeoning Navy build-up. With American security under greater threat than ever before, *Seawolf*'s mission is urgent. So urgent, the submarine is forced into hugely dangerous waters, where disaster is permanently moments away. Slowly they creep through the murky depths of the forbidden South China Sea until, late one night, the executive officer Lieutenant Commander Linus Clarke makes a shocking mistake and collides with a Chinese warship. *Seawolf*'s entire crew is taken captive. Zhang Yushu, Comander-in-Chief of the Chinese Navy, all too aware that the American government will try to rescue their sailors, has them moved to a top security prison.

With the SEAL team on its way in, Admiral Zhang is unaware that among his captives he may have is a prize greater than all the rest put together: *Seawolf*'s mysterious Lieutenant Commander Linus Clarke, an officer whose real identity has been carefully hidden from everyone, even his fellow crew members. But, in the White House, Admiral Morgan knows how desperate the situation really is and he must get *Seawolf*'s crew out whatever the cost. It's a race against the clock, a race in which the stakes are almost too high to bear. A hair-raising struggle between the American Eagle and the Chinese Dragon.

Also available in Arrow

THE ONE THAT GOT AWAY
by Chris Ryan

**The number one bestseller that has now become a
classic from the true hero of the
Bravo Two Zero mission**

The SAS mission conducted behind Iraqi lines is one of
the most famous stories of courage and survival in modern
warfare. Of the eight members of the SAS regiment who
set off, only one escaped capture. This is his story.

The One That Got Away is a breathtaking story of extra-
ordinary courage under fire, of hairsbreadth escapes, of
the best trained soldiers in the world fighting against the
most adverse conditions, and, above all, of one man's
courageous refusal to lie down and die.

'You have personally made SAS history'
General Sir Peter de la Billière

'It's a thrill-a-minute story of terror, hardship, heroism,
bravery and sheer guts.' *Sun*

'Raw and brutal.' *Daily Express*

ZERO OPTION

by Chris Ryan

SAS Sergeant Geordie Sharp, locked in a desperate private battle with the IRA, is required to undertake two top-secret missions, in the full knowledge that, if they go wrong, the authorities will deny all involvement.

In the first operation he serves as commander of a hit team on a Black or 100 per cent non-attibutable task assigned to the SAW, the Regiment's ultra-secret Subversive Action Wing. The target is an Iraqi who defected to Libya after the Gulf War. The aim is to kill him and leave no clue as to the identity or origin of the asssassins. The hit team will have to be absolutely clean – wear Arab clothes, use soviet weapons and ammunition, and bear no trace of any Western organization. If anyone is killed, the body will have to be recovered or vaporised with explosives . . .

Returning to base, Sharp finds he must also carry out a high-level political assassination in mainland Britain. If he fails, his four-year-old son will die at the hands of the IRA. Trapped between opposing forces in a fight to the death, he twists and turns through a nightmare maze, desperately seeking some way of averting tragedy. Who will be hit hardest – Geordie Sharp or the British government?